Praise for *Plague*

WINNER OF THE ARTHUR ELLIS AWARD FOR
BEST CRIME NOVEL

"A swashbuckling highwayman, a beautiful a
King Charles II and a psychopathic stalker. Wha
ask for? Humphreys has a marvellous turn of phrase and a cleverness
which is delightful throughout."

> —Roberta Rich, internationally bestselling author of
> *The Midwife of Venice* and *The Harem Midwife*

"C.C. Humphreys has excelled himself in this richly glorious
white-knuckle ride through a London torn apart by recent civil
war and caught on the edge of plague. The language is lyrical and
lovely and feels utterly grounded in the time. The plot is a perfect crime thriller with something new around each corner: always
unexpected, always satisfying. . . . A vibrant, utterly immersive
wonder of a novel."

> —Manda Scott, internationally bestselling
> author of the Boudica series

"A blend of adventure and historical fiction; ingenious in [its]
plotting, and more pleasurable than pensive. . . . The book features
more twists and turns than a labyrinth."

> —*National Post*

"C.C. Humphreys has managed quite a feat: a book about bubonic
plague and a serial killer in 17th century London written with a
great sense of fun. . . . For a reader whose taste in crime fiction
runs more to dark, contemporary Scandinavians, Humphreys was
a delightful treat."

> —*Toronto Star*

"If you're a history buff who likes adventure and a story that rips right
along, hunker down with C.C. Humphreys' *Plague*. It's got all of the
above and, bonus, much of it is set in the theatre."

> —*NOW* (Toronto)

"*Plague* is thrilling, yes, but it is also harrowing, with scenes of such force and power that some readers might be tempted to close the book and walk away. They won't, though: Humphreys is far too good a storyteller for that to happen. *Plague* is the sort of book you open when you have a spare couple of minutes, and look up from hours later, only after the last paragraph is read."

—*The Vancouver Sun*

"[Humphreys'] books are always a treat to read, immersive and thrilling, but with a depth and skill that elevates them well above pulp. . . . *Plague* is almost an embarrassment of riches."

—*Ottawa Citizen*

"Humphreys does a great job evoking the sights, sounds, and smells of the labyrinthine city, and makes good practical use of history throughout. That is to say, the novel does not feel thick with research, but wears its reading lightly, employing history for dramatic effect. . . . The mix of plague and puritans with popcorn storytelling makes for an entertaining treat."

—*Quill & Quire*

"Humphreys . . . brings to life the Restoration period, persuasively capturing the festive atmosphere inspired by the Stuarts' return to the throne after Oliver Cromwell's puritanical 'reign'. . . . Humphreys' expressive writing style and ability to weave a tale . . . makes for a rich and addictive read, ideal for fans of historical fiction."

—*Publishers Weekly*

"A page-turning portrait of the battles and intrigues of 17th century London."

—*Zoomer Magazine*

"Humphreys brings to bear all his dramatic skills on this compelling tale of mayhem and murder. . . . *Plague* may be his best work yet—a triumphant tour de force that is part adventure, part drama, and full of unexpected thrills."

—*Historical Novel Society*

PLAGUE

ALSO BY C.C. HUMPHREYS

The French Executioner
Blood Ties
Vlad: The Last Confession
Absolute Honour
The Hunt of the Unicorn
Jack Absolute: A Novel
A Place Called Armageddon
The Blooding of Jack Absolute
Shakespeare's Rebel
Fire

AS CHRIS HUMPHREYS

The Fetch
Vendetta
Possession

PLAGUE

Murder
has a
new Friend

C. C. HUMPHREYS

ANCHOR CANADA

Copyright © 2014 C.C. Humphreys
Anchor Canada edition published 2016

All rights reserved. The use of any part of this publication, reproduced,
transmitted in any form or by any means electronic, mechanical, photocopying,
recording or otherwise, or stored in a retrieval system without the prior written
consent of the publisher—or in the case of photocopying or other reprographic
copying, license from the Canadian Copyright Licensing Agency—is an
infringement of the copyright law.

Anchor Canada is a registered trademark.

Library and Archives Canada Cataloguing in Publication data is
available upon request.

ISBN 978-0-385-67994-7
eBook ISBN 978-0-385-67993-0

Cover images: Figures from Hans Holbein's Danse Macabre;
cross © Henry Steadman, Getty Images

Text design: Terri Nimmo

Map on pages viii-ix © Darren Bennett
Image on page xvi © Getty Images/NYPL Science Source;
on page 353 © Getty Images/Culture Club

Printed and bound in the United States of America

Published in Canada by Anchor Canada,
a division of Random House of Canada Limited,
a Penguin Random House Company

www.penguinrandomhouse.ca

10 9 8 7 6 5 4 3 2 1

Penguin
Random House
ANCHOR CANADA

To Ingegerd Humphreys.
Miss Oslo. Spy. Mother. Friend. Much missed.

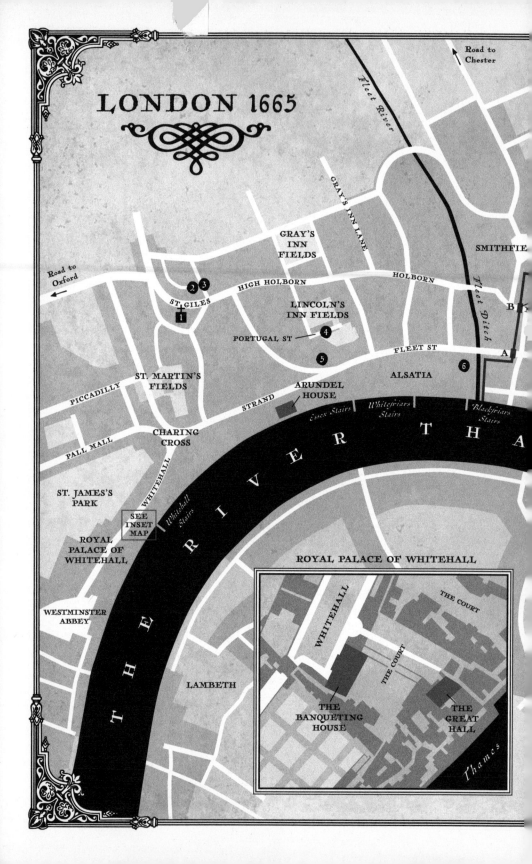

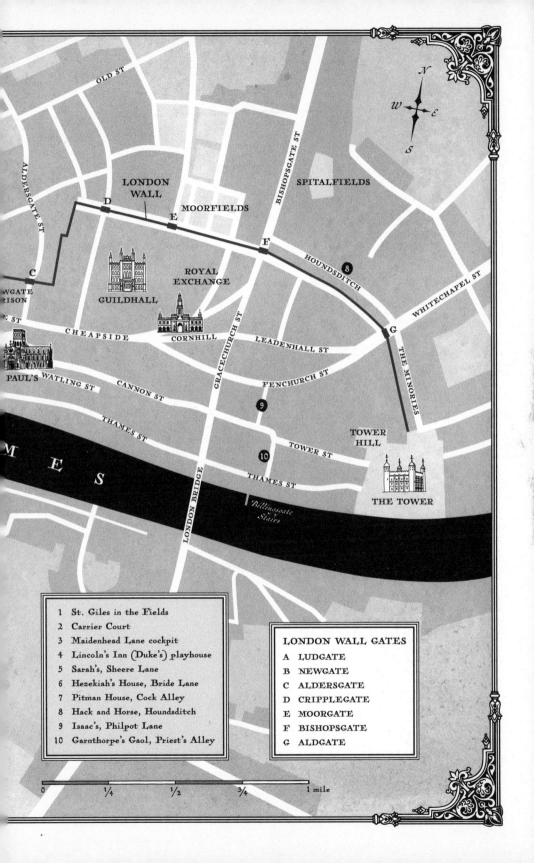

N
W · E
S

OLD ST

ALDERSGATE ST

LONDON
WALL

D

MOORFIELDS

E

BISHOPSGATE ST

SPITALFIELDS

F

HOUNDSDITCH

8

WHITECHAPEL ST

C

ROYAL
EXCHANGE

GUILDHALL

WGATE
RISON

E ST

CHEAPSIDE

CORNHILL

GRACECHURCH ST

LEADENHALL ST

G

THE MINORIES

PAUL'S

WATLING ST

CANNON ST

FENCHURCH ST

THAMES ST

9

TOWER
HILL

M   E   S

LONDON BRIDGE

TOWER ST

10

THAMES ST

Billingsgate
Stairs

THE TOWER

1 St. Giles in the Fields
2 Carrier Court
3 Maidenhead Lane cockpit
4 Lincoln's Inn (Duke's) playhouse
5 Sarah's, Sheere Lane
6 Hezekiah's House, Bride Lane
7 Pitman House, Cock Alley
8 Hack and Horse, Houndsditch
9 Isaac's, Philpot Lane
10 Garnthorpe's Gaol, Priest's Alley

LONDON WALL GATES

A LUDGATE
B NEWGATE
C ALDERSGATE
D CRIPPLEGATE
E MOORGATE
F BISHOPSGATE
G ALDGATE

0   ¼   ½   ¾   1 mile

London 1665

Five years after his restoration to the throne, after a decade of glum Puritanism, Charles II leads his citizens by example, enjoying every excess. Many Londoners flock to the reopened places of entertainment: the cockpits, the brothels, the theatres—where for the first time women may perform onstage alongside the men.

For some citizens, though, the wounds of the Civil Wars, which ended with the execution of Charles I in 1649 and the triumph of Oliver Cromwell and Parliament, have never healed. Especially bitter are radical Christians, those dissenters who enjoyed a brief tolerance under Cromwell and who are again persecuted. For them this liberated age has turned London into Babylon and many dream of an Apocalypse to purge the realm of sin.

Some do more than dream.

With its rambling streets, its great mansions, its fetid tenements, London is a city of contrasts. There is not enough clean water; there is too much garbage, there are too many rats. Refugees from Holland and France live ten to a room beside the English, who resent them.

The city is a labyrinth. At its centre sleeps a monster. When the time is right, that monster will wake. And it will want to feed.

The monster is the Great Plague.

Dramatis Personae

THE HIGHWAYMEN
Captain William Coke
Dickon, his adopted boy
Swift Jack
Maclean
O'Toole

THE THIEF-TAKER AND FAMILY
Pitman
Bettina, his wife
Josiah, their son
Grace, Faith, Imogen, their daughters

RESIDENTS OF ST. GILES IN THE FIELDS
Abel Strong, butcher
Little Dot
Mrs. Queek
Clancy, parish friend of John Chalker
Gentle George, pimp
"Lizzie," whore

THE PLAYERS
Sarah Chalker
John Chalker, her husband
Lucy Absolute
Thomas Betterton

THE COURT AND THE NOBLES
King Charles II
James, Duke of York
Edward Hyde, Earl of Clarendon
John Wilmot, Earl of Rochester
Sir Charles Sedley
Roland, Lord Garnthorpe
Frances Stuart
Barbara Castlemaine
Winifred Wells

THE FIFTH MONARCHY MEN
Simeon Critchollow—Brother S.
Hezekiah Chambers

OTHERS
Colonel Wingate, magistrate, Finchley
Sir Griffith Rich, member of Parliament
Lady Rich
Aitcheson, attendant at the playhouse
Isaac ben Judah, goldsmith
Maggs, servant to Lord Garnthorpe
Mrs. Philips
The Coachman
Mrs. Chambers
The Doctor
Eye Patch, gambler
Tobias Sym, informer
Mistress Proctor, the searcher
Macready
Tombes, the ironmonger
James Morrow, headborough of the parish
Turvey, royal cook

Various Saints, jailers, guards, link boys, servants, searchers, boatmen, playwrights.

PLAGUE

Part One

———❖———

AND I LOOKED, AND BEHOLD A PALE HORSE;

AND HIS NAME THAT SAT ON HIM WAS DEATH.

The Revelation of St. John the Divine 6.8

THE HIGHWAYMAN

April 29, 1665
Tally Ho Inn, Great North Road, near London

Just before he rode away, the captain said, "Good night, then," and touched one blackened toe, setting Swift Jack gently swinging. It was a touch for luck, for sympathy, for memory. Not two weeks earlier he and Jack had been drinking together at this same inn, and he'd been boasting, had Jack, about the special ineptitude of the parish constables in failing to catch his scent.

"Which is astounding," he'd declared, "seeing as how I've not bathed since the coronation."

Captain Coke had laughed but cautioned, "Be wary, man. 'Tis a dead fox that steals too often from the same coop."

But Jack had scoffed—and now he swung from a gallows in Finchley, smelling even worse than he had in life.

Heeling his mount to the trot, Coke thrust his nose deep into his scarf, seeking a hint of sandalwood. The fragrance, though, had long faded and the stench of death accompanied him for some distance. If this night's work goes well, he thought, one of my first calls tomorrow will be on my *parfumier*.

And why should it not go well? Everything pointed to success. Swift Jack had lived by his nickname, always preferring a sudden action on whoever happened across Finchley Common, content whether he stole a shilling or twenty crowns. Whereas Coke planned—selecting a mark, not stumbling upon one; varying the ground across six counties. A highwayman rotting at a crossroads was a blessing too, for like a scarecrow in a field, it warned other road knights to keep away. They did, so Coke did not; while seeing one villain swing made travellers a little less watchful for others. And since the coach that was his mark had a driver in front, a footman behind and the two men within, the less wary they were the better.

Two men within and one woman. Tut, but she was lovely, the lady he'd studied earlier that evening while feigning a doze by the Tally Ho's fire. She'd reminded him of Lavinia, his sister, dead these many years: the same graceful swan's neck, same sharp sweep of nose, the same disdainful manner of looking down it at the antics of her two companions. He'd felt sorry for the woman, the boorish way the men had denied her request to press on while the light was yet strong, mocking her again when they'd at last called for their coach in the twilight and she'd pleaded that now they stay. The older man, her husband by how impertinently he'd pawed her, had demanded she show the other—his younger brother, perhaps, equally drunk— the necklace he'd recently purchased for her, had pulled it roughly from concealment when she'd demurred. Even in the dim light of the inn's fire, the jewels had sparkled, and all the captain's hunches about these travellers he'd followed from their marbled doorstep in St. James's had been confirmed.

He would take the necklace, of course. Its price would not only buy him perfume from Maurice of the Strand Arcade, it would also clear several of his debts and fend off some others. And yet perhaps he would find a way to convey to her, in their coming exchange, that he robbed her with the deepest regret. Their *second* exchange, he reminded himself. For their eyes had met as she'd followed her husband to the tavern door, while the captain had made a show of settling in, loudly ordering another tankard with a jest. She had glanced at him then, and he had smiled. She'd looked away, as modesty dictated, yet not before he'd seen a touch of interest quicken her almond eyes.

At the thought of those eyes, he smoothed down his thick black moustache. She would not see it clearly, under silk as it would be. Still, he would know that he had looked his best.

He flicked the reins and tapped Dapple's left flank, directing the mare down the side path he'd discovered when he'd scouted the route earlier. It took him swiftly to the place he'd selected, the secluded vale where the coach would cross the Dollis Brook.

As Dapple's hooves splashed through water, Coke whistled the usual five notes. The same trill sounded in reply; all was well. The next moment the whistler spun onto the roadway like a whirligig. "The-the-they . . . ? They . . . ?" the boy called, his arms flailing.

The captain smiled. The urchin he'd discovered the previous winter under a layer of snow, blocking his doorway, ribs poking through rags and his body one welt of sores, was rarely calm; but warmth, clothing and food had stilled some of the whirlwind in him. Dickon—a hard name to stutter out—was the best of partners, for he demanded no share of the profit; nothing more, indeed, than a place to curl up at the end of Coke's mattress, the scraps from his table, the heat from his grate.

"They come," Coke reassured the boy, passing down the crust and cold chop he'd saved for his ward from his supper at the Tally Ho Inn. The boy started to cram them between teeth as ramshackle as an ancient cemetery's stones, his eyes moving their opposite ways under a thatch of wheat-blond hair. "So to your place, Dickon."

The falling, the spit, the darting eyes all halted. "Cap'n," the lad said, briskly pulling up his mask, continuing to eat under it, moving away to the appointed tree, the one before which, if all went well, the coach would halt.

As the two of them settled into the gloom at the forest's edge, minutes passed with nothing but birds in the trees and the flick of Dapple's grey ears. Then sound arrived on the night-still air: the squeak of iron-shod wheels in road ruts, the snort of a horse. Closer the carriage came, closer, and then he heard something else. A cry? A woman's, sure. Were those two bullies teasing her as they had in the tavern? Well, I will pay them a little for that, he thought, pulling up his mask till only his eyes showed under his hat's wide brim. No lady as pretty as she should be made to cry. He'd not been able to stop his sister's tears, when all was taken from them. But perhaps he could halt this lady's for a time.

With a cluck of his tongue, the slightest tap of heel, he moved Dapple to the highway's edge. The mare stood as quiet as ever, a grey wraith in the near darkness. The coach ground nearer. There was a splash as wheels spun through the brook. A horse neighed and then the vehicle rounded the corner.

The captain licked his lips. This was the moment. From the saddle holsters, he drew both his pistols and half cocked each. Then, as the coach arrived level, he pulled the hammers full back. "Stand and deliver!" he shouted. "I am Captain Cock! So you know not to fool with me."

But the coach did not stand. The driver did not whip it on, nor did the horses bolt; they just turned wide eyes to him as the front of the vehicle passed by.

Now that, thought the captain, is a first.

In his three years of robberies, many things had happened to him. He had been whipped, foully cursed, had shit thrown at him and, on three occasions, ball discharged. But he had never till this moment been completely ignored.

He kept his pistols levelled as the vehicle slowly rolled on. But no shutter rose from the windows, and the rear was unoccupied. The footman who had clung to it when the carriage departed the inn was no longer there. Perhaps he was within, readying a blunderbuss.

Coke could now see across the roadway to Dickon, his eyebrows high in puzzlement above his mask.

"Stand, curse you!" Coke cried. "No one move. The first who does takes a bullet." He thought of the pretty lady inside, did not like to fright her so. She wouldn't take one, of course, none of them would—for Captain Cock did not load his guns with more than powder, something only he and Dickon knew. He might yet dance the hempen jig as a thief the way Swift Jack now did—but William Coke would never be hanged for a murderer. He had killed enough in the late, deplored wars and wanted no more phantoms stalking his dreams.

But those in the carriage did not know his secret. And they were still ignoring him, the carriage continuing on. "Stand!" he shouted once again, spurring Dapple to the front of the coach. "I mean it, fellow!" he yelled, aiming his pistols at the driver. The man did not react, did not start at all. Even in the gloom, Coke could see the man's eyes were open, though they did not move, nor did he lift his chin from his chest. Then, the horses, at no one's bidding, halted, and in a moment Dickon was at their heads, taking their bits, crooning.

It was the only sound in the vale. Shaking himself, Coke uncocked and holstered one pistol, slipped from the saddle, put one foot and hand onto the carriage. "Rest easy," he growled, though the driver still showed no will to resist him. Indeed, as Coke swung himself up to the bench, the man did not acknowledge him in any way. He had seen men thus frozen with terror when he'd been a real captain. This was nothing like that, and for the first time that night, he felt the chill on his skin.

And then he saw why the driver did not move, why the coach had advanced so slowly. For the reins were wound tight about the man's chest, passing through a bar beside him. Coke tugged the knot—and the whole came apart, the reins slipping, the man sliding toward him. Coke put out a hand to steady him, met wetness, could not help the shove away. As the coachman fell off the bench, his head lolled back, and for just a moment Coke saw the wound, like a screaming extra mouth, under the chin.

The body tumbled off, and struck a carriage stanchion before crumpling onto the ground. The horses jerked at the distinct snapping of bones.

"Ca-Cap'n, what?" Dickon cried.

"Keep their heads!" commanded Coke.

The horses calmed to weight and whispers. And in the near silence that ensued Coke heard a bugle, a hunting call, followed by the yelp of a dog. The animal was still far enough away if it was coming for them, which the next moment he believed it was. He had been discovered, should flee straight. But he could not. Not yet.

He swung himself off the coach. With one foot on the running board, a hand on the door handle, he pressed an ear to the window—glass, the latest in fashion. The man within spent near as much adorning his transport as he did his wife. There were leather curtains beyond and not a sound emerged through them. "Do not," he began, then had to cough to clear his throat. "Do not move if you value your lives," he continued. Thrusting the pistol ahead of him, he jerked open the door.

The interior was dark. Thus, before sight it was scent that took him. It wasn't the first time he'd smelled this odour. He had hoped never to smell it again and hadn't for so long he thought he might have forgotten. But he had not—the stench of guts, freshly pierced, was such a distinct one. As ever, as here, it was overlain with the iron tang of blood.

It took him back, that special savour. He was on a battlefield, which one he did not know. They were all different and they were all the same, blended now by near two decades. Men had died swiftly and in silence, slowly and with great noise.

Then he came, the one who always did when something carried Coke back, some sight, some sound, some . . . scent.

Quentin.

They had served together as officers in Sir Bevil Grenville's regiment for over a year, had laughed, got drunk, saved each other's lives. Were as close as comrades could be. Yet the shot that had erased Quentin's features had erased the memory of them too. Mouth, eyebrows, ears, chin, all wiped away, as if Quentin had become a fresh canvas awaiting an artist's brush. Quentin had moved one hand before the ruin, seeking what? The other hand had held in his own guts, the source of the unforgettable, ineradicable smell.

Sinking against the door frame, the captain closed his eyes, until he remembered that nothing was as terrible as what went on behind them. So he opened them again.

At least the three figures before him had faces. With eyes accustoming to the gloom, he could see those now. And seeing, he lowered his pistol, uncocked it, for even if it had had ball in it, you could only kill someone once.

The walls of the carriage he'd glimpsed in the tavern yard had been primrose but now were mainly red, the colour splashed like a painter's carelessness. The open door had let some blood flow out, but still more pooled among the limbs and entrails of the men, the two of them lying together upon the floor as if embracing.

At least the dead lady was whole, and upright upon the bench. Her cream gown was pinkened now, as if it had been washed with a courtesan's scarlet dress. The source of the stain was a deeper patch of crimson above her heart. Of the three in the coach, she was the only one with her eyes shut. For that, Coke was grateful.

Noise startled him. He turned fast—to Dickon's eyes focused on the horror. "Do not," began Coke, too late.

"No, no, no, no, no!"

"Out, Dickon," Coke ordered, and the boy collapsed, sobbing, onto the roadway.

When Coke turned back, something struck him. This slaughter was not as random as he'd first thought. He'd seen men—aye, women too—torn apart by cannon, hacked by sword, split by pike thrust. This was different. This was more like the killing shed on his father's estate. Within it, there was a place for every part of a pig, for every part would be used. And in this carriage, parts had been . . . placed. Even the blood looked like it had been channelled.

These people had been butchered.

He thought the wars and all he'd seen in them had long since hardened his guts. He was wrong. He lifted his scarf just enough to vomit down the inside of the carriage door.

The horn sounded again, more than one dog this time. Nearer. They had to get away. But first, something had to come from this carnage. Setting the gun upon one bench, he reached both his hands around the lady's neck, feeling under her dress for the clasp of her necklace. It was hard to undo, and he had to lean close. As he did, he glanced up.

The lady's eyes were now open.

He tried to jerk back, but his fingers became entangled in the chain and this delayed him just long enough for the woman to wrap her hands around his wrists. Her cold touch froze him, though the fierceness of her grip would have held him anyway. "Lady, I—I will help you."

He couldn't tell if she heard him. Nothing showed in her eyes, bright with the last of life. Her blue lips moved, soundless. "What is it, lady? What?"

"Pale horse," she whispered, "Pale horse."

The light in her eyes died with her. Her grip slackened; her fingers released him. But his hands were still on the chain, and as the bugle sounded a third time, too close now, he said, "Forgive me," and tore the necklace from her neck.

Then he was out of the coach, pulling the whimpering Dickon to his feet, shoving him toward his tethered horse. Coke turned back to the carriage, grabbed the driver's whip. "Yah," he cried, flicking the tip of the leather between the lead horses' ears. The beasts, reacting to voice and crack, took off at once, and a few moments later Coke was astride Dapple. Pausing only to cram the necklace deep into his coat pocket, he heeled his horse into a gallop, taking the same faint deer path through the woods that Dickon had, just as the horn sounded again, close now, very close.

They were halfway across Finchley Common, still travelling at speed by the light of a rising and gibbous moon, when Coke glanced down and saw just one of his holsters filled. He'd left one of his matched pistols in the coach.

But there was no going back.

2

THE THIEF-TAKER

A few minutes earlier

What was strange about the footman's corpse was that it appeared to have been arranged *after* death.

Pitman did not think the man had moved himself: that in the act of dying, he would so spread out his arms and cross his ankles in imitation of the Crucifixion. He himself was a devout man, but he doubted even he'd have the will to assume such a pose with life fleeing so fast. In his brief examination before he remounted and heeled his horse again in pursuit of the coach, he saw that the footman's head had been near severed. One stroke, he'd wager. By an axe or perhaps a cleaver.

Behind him, the bugle man sounded. Brass brayed, the hounds gave tongue and Pitman flinched. The rule of silence he'd imposed on these men who'd insisted on accompanying him from the Tally Ho Inn on this pursuit had now been violated. A warning for those ahead justified it. Perhaps they were right. A man who killed once like that might kill again.

A man like Captain Cock?

He looked to the mount beside him. "All right, lad?" he asked, leaning down to touch his son's arm.

Josiah jerked up. "Did you see him, Father?"

"I saw him."

"His eyes were . . . his eyes." The boy closed his own, too late to trap the tears. "I wish I had not come."

I wish so too, thought Pitman, squeezing his son's arm. But Bettina had insisted. With three daughters pulling her skirts and two more, by the feel, on the way, she had enough on her plate. "Get him out from under my feet, Pitman," she'd said. "There's never any danger. You say the thieves always come as meek as lambs."

I say it because it is usually true, Pitman had thought. And from all reports, Captain Cock would be especially gentle. His politeness to women; just one driver injured in a dozen robberies, and that because he'd gone for a gun he'd laid down. The captain hadn't even shot him, just cracked him atop the skull with his own pistol.

But now—this body, the head near off? What's happened, Captain? Have you gone mad at last? Like so many who fought in the Troubles, then or later?

A horse's muzzle nudged up on his other side. "I've dispatched riders ahead, by different ways," barked Colonel Wingate. The local magistrate was a corpulent man, but he sat his horse easy, as befitted one of Cromwell's lobsterbacks. He raised a hand to wipe road mud from a claret-reddened cheek. "Holcolme. Mill Hill. Totteridge." He gestured. "Constables will be roused. Citizens mustered. We'll catch this murderous swine. Have no fear."

He dropped back again, more comfortable with men of his own class and household, no doubt. Pitman glanced again at his son, weeping openly now. Josiah was rarely so wordless.

Pitman shook his head. His son's talkativeness back at the inn had led to this large accompanying party. Tending to their mounts, the boy had blabbed their purpose to a stable lad: the taking of the notorious Captain Cock. Within minutes, a large group of locals, sober and less so, had mobbed Pitman at his table. Their spokesman, this same Colonel Wingate, had informed him that only two weeks earlier they'd had the nabbing of Swift Jack, aye, and his hanging too, and they were damned if any thief-taker from London should trespass on their prerogatives.

Pitman had had but one recourse. He'd sat back, picked up his tankard and told them plain that he would not stir a foot unless they swore that the twenty-guinea reward for taking the highwayman would be entirely his. Otherwise, the men could proceed without him. Uncertain how to do so, they had grudgingly accepted his terms.

Even then, he had taken his time, partly in the hope that many would get too drunk to ride but mainly because he was certain his man was still somewhere on the premises. Indeed the captain could be among the pressing crowd, eager to hunt himself down. He had a reputation for just such bravado.

Now, as they reached a downward slope and he urged his horse to more speed upon it, Pitman sighed. This noisy mob. The corpse. Not how he'd meant this affair to go. Not when it began so well.

Back in the crowded inn, he had not hoped to single out his quarry—but he had easily spotted the man's mark. Captain Cock had a distinct modus operandi. He struck rarely and richly. A coach would be leaving later that evening, its owner Sir Griffith Rich, well-known firebrand of the king's party. His driver and footman, though large men, would not deter the bold captain; while the pretty wife, suffering the rough jests of her far older husband

and his brother, would entice any gallant knight of the road near as much as the jewels around her neck.

Would have enticed me once, he'd thought, wondering how she would look, naked by candlelight. Not as an ordinary man did, with casual lust. He'd smiled. Well, not *entirely* like an ordinary man.

"Have you sniffed him out, Father?" his son had asked, mistaking the smile for confidence.

"I've narrowed him down to three, Josiah, lad." He'd held up the sketches he'd made. "He will be one of these, I reckon." It wasn't true. There were a dozen candidates, more; former soldiers, hard men with steel gazes not unlike his own. He'd suspected Captain Cock for a military man from the reports, though he may have appropriated the rank.

His sketching stopped him drinking too much ale, calmed him too. It was a practice from before the war, when he'd thought to apprentice to an engraver. He had drawn the men as he'd waited for the coach to leave. He'd also sketched the lady. And her necklace; although seen briefly, it was hard to forget.

When the coach set out, he had not warned the member of Parliament. The party was well protected—an armoured lure, giving Pitman his best chance in a long while of a large reward. Besides, if there was a man in the realm he would wish a little discomfited, Sir Griffith Rich, the MP, was he. Not because the man was an ardent Royalist—Pitman had fought them in the wars and beaten 'em too. No, because of the type of Royalist he was—a Tory of the High Church who would harass and condemn any who chose to worship differently and worked ceaselessly in Parliament and out to secure their prosecution. Those, indeed, like Pitman and his wife.

Lord, let Captain Cock crow over him a little first, he'd prayed as they set out a few minutes after the coach. Then let me take him after.

Now, with his horse splashing through a little brook, Pitman prayed differently. Lord, he muttered, let me take this man before anyone else dies.

They came upon it suddenly, the second corpse, while they still dripped with water. This one was not arranged, Christ-like, but was a heap at the side of the track. The coach driver, by his livery. "See to him, some of you," he called, kicking his horse on. It was a huge beast he'd hired, which was necessary, for so was he, but it showed some speed now, as if also eager for this chase to be done. Perhaps it too could see in the twilight, as its rider did, his fellows up the long hill ahead, pulling the coach toward the summit.

The quarry was in sight. The horn sounded again. Men and hounds gave tongue. "Hi ya!" cried Pitman, setting heels to flank.

Perhaps the brass call succeeded. Perhaps the hill had sapped the coach horses, or they were less urgent since no driver snapped his whip between their ears. But the animals slowed from canter to walk. A hedge stood alongside the highway and the front horses made for it, to halt and nibble unchastised.

Pitman was among the first to draw level, and the very first off his mount. "Stay back," he shouted, his bellow cutting through the babble. "Hear me! I am an officer of the law and I will not be hindered. Allow me to proceed." He was an officer of the law, but not in this parish; he operated here under no one's jurisdiction but his own. Yet his size, bearing and the large pistol he now cocked gave him authority enough.

He walked up to the coach, gripped the door handle, took a breath, then opened the door just enough to admit the muzzle of his weapon.

He did not expect to see Captain Cock, like his namesake, crowing on a seat inside. But what he did see he did not expect either.

Three bodies. All on the floor, two men as close as lovers. The woman on top of them both, on her back, arms flung over her head as if reaching for the other door. The stench made him gag, and he shoved his sleeve against his mouth.

"What is it, man? Let me past."

It was the colonel behind him. But Pitman had obeyed men like him too often, for too long, during the late king's wars, and with the realm at peace, he was no longer a soldier. "One moment," he said curtly, not moving, blocking the interior with his bulk. He knew he had only a few moments, and he must use them, for he noticed things that others didn't. It was why he took more thieves than anyone else.

He breathed the stench again. Blood, pierced gut, a woman's fragrance—primrose. Some other smell also, sweet-foul? There, sliding down the door, yellow and thick as a custard. He reached a finger. The vomit was still slightly warm. He doubted it had come from any of the corpses: no yellow disturbed the pure crimson of their clothes.

Unlike the men, the woman had not been gutted. A single stab through the heart had done for her. So a different blade, the men's wounds different too from the cleaver that had killed the footman. An array of weapons, then? A butcher's set of tools? A surgeon's?

He looked at the woman again—at her eyes, half open. At her neck. He noticed an abrasion there, a scrape not caused by a blade. He reached a finger to a droplet of blood. He pulled the top of her gown slightly down. He had seen her display the necklace to the MP's brother, and so to half the tavern.

It was gone.

Anger came. So you killed her, Cock? Then robbed her, or t'other way about? Did she give you much of a fight?

The noise had faded behind him. Not disappeared, it was still in his ears. He heard the colonel demanding entry again as if calling from another county. But Pitman did not shift. There were other things here. He'd seen them in his first glance.

In the corner of one bench was a pistol. He picked it up, raised it into the little light. It was fine, with a brass plate showing Parket of London had made it. One of the victim's or—Then he saw the two letters carved into the butt.

CC. Captain Cock.

The weapon was uncocked. A sniff of the barrel showed it was also unfired. Pitman shoved it into his large pocket. Then he looked up, at another thing he'd noticed.

A scene was painted on the panel above one of the benches. Men walked with women beside a river, beneath willows and a sky that had once been cornflower blue and was now as red as a sunset that would gladden any shepherd. Yet something else marred the tranquility. Red numerals. Latin ones.

He was not an educated man, could read only haltingly his own language. But he recognized numbers: XII.XII. Even Roman ones.

"I insist, sirrah," came the voice again behind him, accompanied by tugging now, "I am the local magistrate and I insist."

Pitman was about to admit the colonel. Until he realized that there was one last thing he'd nearly missed, mainly because it was red, and so much there was red. It rested in the blood-flooded mouth of one of the men lying on the floor, the very recently deceased member of Parliament, Sir Griffith Rich.

With difficulty because it was slick and wedged between teeth, Pitman plucked it from the man's mouth. A stone, some kind of quartz. He pocketed it as well. Then, just before he backed out of the carriage, he did something he knew he would later struggle to explain. He wiped the Roman numerals off the panel.

Pitman had blocked the entire doorway and the man behind had to step off the running board to allow him out. "Well, sir?" the colonel snapped. "Will you now let me see?"

"Let me caution you first—"

"Caution, pish!" replied the man, shoving past. "I've been in more battles than you've had—"

As the cry came, the first hoarse half prayer, Pitman went to Josiah, who stood with his face pressed against his horse's neck. "Mount, boy."

"Should I not see, Father?"

"Nay, you should not." He helped his son up into the saddle. "Let us go home."

A few hours' rest, if no sleep, in the stable of the inn, and they left at the first hint of light. An hour's ride brought them to Cripplegate Without and the farrier's where they'd hired their mounts. Cripplegate itself was just being unbarred, so they passed through and walked into the City down Wood Street. Halfway along it, the pavement before some especially handsome merchants' houses was being washed down. This did not stop a man—drunk, no doubt, despite the early hour—from lurching out of an alley, preceded by his vomit. He collapsed onto the ground, moaning. Pitman and his son stepped around him. As they neared their home, church bells began to toll, the first summons to Sunday worship. Pitman could distinguish among them the distinct bass tones of Old Toby, which stood in the tower of St. Leonard's, their parish church.

The smile that always came at this sound of home went as he turned the last corner into Cock Alley and paused before their dwelling. We'll have to return to a single room and a poorer parish, he thought, if I don't take another thief soon.

They climbed to the first floor. She was awake, of course. One girl at her breast, two more round her feet. Ten years after Josiah, certain that God had withdrawn that blessing, Grace arrived. Then Faith, then Imogen. Blessings in abundance, and two more on the way.

"Success, Pitman?" Bettina asked.

He shook his head, too tired to speak. She sighed, and took the children into the only other room. The door closed softly on their son's renewed weeping.

Pitman walked toward his horsehair sleeping chair, then went past it, to the book on the window ledge. He drew Cock's pistol from his pocket and set it down before lifting the Bible. It fell open to his touch, as it always did, to the same page, for he had had this copy since his time with the Ranters, that mad sect of drinkers, cursers, smokers, and dancers he and Bettina had run with for a time after the wars. Ranters were much taken with this book especially, for the Revelation of St. John the Divine was the most sacred of all texts. Indeed, it supported one of their fundamental beliefs, for it spoke of the imminent end of the world. With that so near, the Ranters reasoned, why face it wearing clothes?

Revelation 12:12.

As soon as he traced the verse he knew it, as he knew many of them, by heart: "For the devil is come down unto you, having great wrath, because he knoweth that he hath but a short time."

He ran his hand over his shaven head and stared at the window before him, not seeing through it. He had something else in his pocket, but he was too tired to remember what it was.

3

THE BUTCHER

When he walked into the yard, there was a crowd around the well. He did not wish to wait and he never had to, for as soon as he was spotted, the cries began: "Why, look! Look! It's Abel Strong!" In a moment, they were all pressing round him. They knew not to jostle him, but their hands hovered near his smock.

He jerked his thumb over his shoulder. "It's there, good neighbours," he said. "Just inside the arch."

He continued to the well as the crowd ran past. Behind him, the scrapping began for the bounty he'd brought. Meat fell from his cart to the ground but was snatched up, wiped down. Nothing ever went wasted in Carrier Court.

Strong smiled as he lowered the well bucket, hauled up the water. They loves a butcher in St. Giles, he thought. No one minds how much water I pours over me. No one says nothing. He closed his eyes and let the cool liquid flow over himself.

The blood from the shambles covered him. So he kept dipping, hauling, pouring. The red water ran off him, onto the flagstones, into the gutter channel. A baby sat beside that, abandoned while the meat rush was on; she laughed at the flood, trying to stem it with skinny fingers.

As Abel scrubbed his smock with the stiff brush he always carried, he ran over the words again, trying to make them into a song. He'd always liked songs; they was easy to remember. Some of these words was hard to fit, though. Big words. Each had a colour and he matched them as he said each name.

"'The first foundation was ja-sper,'" he sang. "'The second stone is sa-ph-ire. The third, that's chalc-chalc-chalc-e-dony.'" He paused. He liked the sound of that one. "'A chalc-chalc-chalc-e-dony's quartz,'" he continued. "'Could be gre-een, could be blu-ooh. Could be a tiger's eye, aye, aye.'"

He liked that too. The tiger was a fierce beast, it was said. Could tear a carcass apart swifter than he could, and he was as swift as a butcher got. Perhaps I'm part tiger, he thought, and laughed. The baby looked up, laughed too. She'd found some scrap in the gutter and waved it about. He waved his brush back at her.

A last bucketful, a final good scrub, and he was done. Clean and shivering, still dripping, he walked to the stairwell. He passed children on the stairs, sprawled with kittens and puppies. He frowned. He didn't like animals. Perhaps it was his trade. He hated cats special.

He hadn't noticed her in the mob, but he heard her following him up the stairs. She caught up at their door. "'Allo, Little Spot," he said, not looking. He heard her giggle as he pushed into the room.

"That's Dot, not Spot—you know tha'." The girl followed him in and he saw that she had the baby from the gutter on her hip. She set her down by another on the floor and the two babes began to struggle for whatever the one still held.

He waited for the question that always came: "Save somethin' special f'r us, did ya, Mr. Strong?"

He made a little show of searching under his apron. Then he pretended to startle as he slowly pulled out a bone, watching her eyes widen. "A mutton leg," he said, handing it to her, observing her bend a little under its weight. "Straight in the pot, now."

He and Little Dot, her two sisters and their mother shared one of maybe five rooms in the whole of Carrier Court with a fireplace that still worked. Some of the other rooms held ten—fifteen people, if the inhabitants was Irish or gypsy. Mrs. Queek, Dot's ma, always had pots on the go, cooking for others. The coins from that, and the little he handed over each week, kept them separate from the crowd.

Dot stepped past the two babies on the floor, lifted a lid on a cauldron near as big as her and crammed in the haunch. "Ma, you should see what Mr. Strong 'as brung us," she called. "It's an 'ole sheep."

She laughed again. But all that came from the other side of the hanging blanket was a groan. Dot's smile vanished. "Our ma's not well, Mr. Strong. Not well."

"Is she not?"

Another blanket separated out his side of the room. He stepped behind it now. Nothing much there except the cot, a basin, other clothes hung on a hook.

He stared at them, till her voice came. "Are you ready for us, Mr. Strong?"

"Wait."

He pulled the apron over his head, hung it on a hook. The room was warmer than most because of the fire, but still he shivered in his wet clothes. Still, he wasn't ready to change. Not quite yet.

He sat down on the cot. "Come," he said.

A hand appeared, her pale face above it. "Will ya 'ave a look at 'er, Mr. Strong? 'As a terrible headache, she says. And the sweats."

"Afterwards."

She moved closer to him. "You're all wet."

"Don't matter." He patted his thighs.

She giggled, then sat on him. "Ooh," she said, wriggling a little. "Lucky the fire's goin'." She put one arm around his shoulder. With her free hand, she pushed a curl of wet hair from the forehead she then began to stroke. "Which one?" she asked.

"You know which one."

He closed his eyes. She began to sing:

The water is wide, I cannot cross o'er,
And neither 'ave I wings to fly.
Give me a boat that can carry two,
And both shall row, my love and I.

The singing was high-pitched, trembling, sweet enough, even if she pronounced the words like any girl from St. Giles. Tiny grimy fingers continued to stroke his forehead. She sang the verse three times, just as he liked, and then she sang, "'I leaned my back up against a young oak,'" so he could lean his back against the wall, while her hand on his face became another's. One that was not grimy at all but clean, gentle to touch. And the voice?

The voice also became another's.

"Mama," he breathed, seeing her, though he did not open his eyes. Her auburn hair flowed over her shoulders within her night-dress. Her dark eyes filled with love as she sang the next verses. For him. Only for him.

I leaned my back up against a young oak,
Thinking he were a trusty tree,
But first he bended and then he broke,
Thus did my love prove false to me.
O love is handsome and love is fine,
Bright as a jewel when first it's new,
But love grows old and waxes cold,
And fades away like the morning dew.

"'And fades away like the morning dew.'" He sang with her on that last repeated line. And though his mind cleared as the song ended and he knew where he was, still he wanted to linger with her. "Again," he whispered. "Sing it again."

But someone was calling them away. He could see the sadness in her eyes as she rose from his lap. "Don't go, Mama," he said, reaching out. "Don't go to him."

"I have to." Her cool, clean fingers were on his lips now. "I must obey him."

"I 'ave to," she said.

Not her. The other had returned. He opened his eyes. Little Dot was standing at the blanket.

"I 'ave to, Mr. Strong. Sorry, but Ma needs me. I'll be back, don't you fear."

She left. The blanket dropped back. He heard retching, then groans from beyond it. He stood, stripped off his wet clothes, dropping the rough shirt, the hand-knitted stockings and the wool drawers to the floor. Dot's ma would get to them in time. They would always be pink from his trade, he didn't expect white, but lye took out the worst of the stains. She'd scrub 'em, hang 'em on the hedgerows along Tottenham Court Road to dry. Ready for his next time in the shambles. Sick or not, she wouldn't want to let him down.

He dressed. The feel of these fresh clothes was good. Nothing fancy. Dry. Better made.

A hand reached round the blanket. "I'm back."

"Come, then."

She came, glanced up at him for a moment, then slipped little fingers under his doublet and began to hook it nimbly to the breeches.

He gazed down at her. Fleas crawled in her hair. Finishing the last hook, she spoke again. "Will you look at 'er now? She chucked, but I cleaned it up."

Silk on skin. Scratches on a shoulder, where a woman had raked him. Fleas on a girl's head. He felt dizzy, swayed, steadied himself against the wall. "I will," he replied.

She left. He scratched at the grey stubble on his head, then set his broad-peaked hat upon it, covered himself with a grey cloak, tied a scarf around his neck and stepped around the blanket. "Let's have a look," he said, passing between Mrs. Queek's crawling babies, now playing with kittens on the floor. Another litter? There were more cats in Carrier Court than rats. Toeing one aside, he put his hand upon the other blanket. "Mrs. Queek," he called, "may I enter?"

No reply. He tugged the blanket aside.

Little Dot is right, he thought. Her mother is not well. The eyes, which flickered open as he bent over her, were sunk deep in her fever-red face. "I'm sick, sir," she whispered. "Me bones are cold, but I'm sweatin'. And me 'ead—" she clutched it "—feels like some-one 'as knives in there."

He had no need to bend any closer. She had a stench to her that he'd smelled before, years before. Her blouse was open—for the sweats, he supposed—and he glimpsed a small oval mark on one vast breast.

He knew it was not a bruise.

He was still holding the hanging blanket. Stepping back, he let it drop before retying the scarf around his lower face. Then he reached into a pocket and pulled out a silver half crown. Dot's eyes went wide. He stooped to her, holding it up. "You know the apothecary's next to the Maid in the Moon?" She nodded. "Run there and buy a bottle called Dragon's Water. Give it your ma. Also buy some wormwood. That's to burn on your grate."

"Yes, sir. Oh, thank you, sir."

She grabbed the coin, but he did not let it go, looked at the girl over it. She might be lucky, he thought. If she is not, what will I do? He looked a moment longer, then released the half crown, realizing that he knew. In St. Giles, there would always be a little girl willing to learn songs for meat.

He turned at the door and spoke through his scarf. "Oh, and Little Dot?" he said.

"Yes, Mr. Strong?"

"Kill all the cats."

4

THE ACTRESS

May 10, 1665

When the prompter's whistle blew, everyone upon the stage froze.

Is it me? Sarah thought. Oh God, let it not be me *again*!

She looked at the other two players. Lucy Absolute's mouth was already twitching, about to rise into the smile that would inevitably lead to the giggles to which she was so prone; while John Chalker, her John, her rock on the platform and beyond it, was staring at her, the huge and bushy eyebrows scarce seen in nature but affixed to emphasize his character's bluster now joining and parting like a signal whose import was obvious. It's your line, they flashed. For the love of Christ, speak it!

She felt that familiar vacuum in her stomach. She looked out where she had just been seeking . . . what? The one gaze among so many that had unnerved her with its intensity. She could not find it there, nor rediscover the line she had lost in the faces that swam in the pit below her or shone like stars in the galleries above. The audience was rapt, set up by the prompter's whistle and keen to know which player had failed and in what manner this player would redeem themselves.

She glanced left—a mistake, for she looked into the royal box where the king himself leaned forward. She had learned over her three years of playing that Charles was perhaps the swiftest appraiser in the house.

A few seconds. A lifetime. Oh hell, she thought, forcing her gaze from the king. Open your jaws and swallow me.

A last, desperate glance at her husband. John Chalker was renowned for his skill at extemporizing. But even he failed her now.

"'Good my lord. You tax me with ingratitude.'"

There it was. Her line, sure. Clearly and precisely delivered by Williams, the prompter, from his nest, behind one wing, on which was painted a canalscape of Venice. As the stridently Welsh voice seemed to emerge right from the middle of the Rialto Bridge, some of the audience laughed, some hooted while all waited to see the culprit who would claim the line.

"'Good my lord. You tax me with ingratitude.'" Sarah declaimed, and discovered she knew what followed next. "'When you are the one who should be scolded.'"

And on she went. There was laughter, a touch of applause, which she acknowledged with a curtsy. In his box, the king leaned back. And that other gaze, the one she'd sought and in the seeking lost her line? She felt it lift from her, like a pressing hand raised from her neck.

Scene done, they swept from the stage. Thomas Betterton, the company's leading actor, muttered, "Distracted by a beau, Mrs. Chalker?" as he passed her. But John drew her deeper into the offstage darkness and whispered, "What's amiss, love? That's the third time tonight."

Amiss? Where in the catalogue do I begin? The rumours from their old parish, with the first houses daubed in red warning? The murders of the member of Parliament and his family, brutal even for London, which had set the town on a roar? No. She'd settle for the most recent fear. "He's back," she said.

Her husband stiffened. "Did you see him? Can you describe him to me?"

"No. He's in a box, I think."

"Royal?"

"No. He . . ." She hesitated. "He is returned, that's all I know. His gaze unnerved me."

Her husband's two false eyebrows contracted into one. Even in the ill-lit shadows beyond the onstage candles, she could see his face flush dark. "You find 'im out, Sar," he growled, "and I will 'ave words."

She took his hands in hers, drew his fingers to her mouth for a kiss. "John, it is my fancy alone. He, whoever he is, has done nothing but stare. I am an actress. I live to be stared at."

"Yet this is different. I've never seen you so thrown off."

"I know. I—" She broke off. Her husband's protection was the reason she had been able to rise as an actress in the Duke's Company without first lying back, the usual route to favour. But his temper sometimes made him punch before he thought. It had cost them before. "He may never approach. This may be nothing."

"Well, if it becomes something—"

"I will tell you." She released his hands. "Are you not on?"

"Aye, and soon. I need my coat. Sir Fidget cannot walk out during High Mall without a superfluity of French lace." He'd returned to his stage voice, as noble as any earl's, but now resumed his normal voice—as hers, as most players' from the streets not far distant from where they played, "I mean it, Sar. If you sense 'im among that crowd of fops and debauchers that will plague us after the play, you point 'im out to me. Never fear—I'll be most subtle. I'll dog 'im far from the playhouse before we 'ave our chat."

"Go on, you great goose," she said, kissing him, shoving him away.

He went. And she must too. The finale approached in three scenes and required a change of dress. Yet, for a moment she did not stir. Out there in the gloom, someone was still watching for her. She was not as gifted as her mother had been, the most cunning of the Cunning Women in their parish of St. Giles in the Fields. Betsy, on her best day, could probably have peered into the surface of a coffee cup and described the watcher's clothes. Sarah was used to being admired. Indeed, she craved it—the men's lust, the women's envy, a monarch's smile. But this regard had been different.

Shivering, she went to change her dress.

It was larger than usual, the mob that crowded in after the perform-ance, for the king had stayed. The party had been forced to spread from the smaller area behind the stage onto the platform itself and down into the pit. The musicians, persuaded to take up their instruments again, had the more drunken in the crowd gathered before them, swaying to the notes, sometimes breaking into a jig or a sarabande as the tempo required. The girls who sold oranges were also there, and their busy hands moved under cloaks, provoking, enticing some men away to darker corners or even the back alley, where they could more discreetly conclude the full transaction. Some of the sisters of the stage, if not so brazenly conducting busi-ness now, were certainly setting themselves up for trade later.

"Look!" cried Lucy Absolute, directing Sarah's gaze to the opposite side of the stage. "Sir Charles Sedley is trying again to pass Mrs. Sanderson something. What could it be? Coin?"

"Nay, Lucy. Mary's never been bought for mere silver."

"You're right. 'Tis paper. An assignation, do you think? Or the deed to some property? The king's been after her for all of a week now and we know Sedley is his pander. If Charles's image in silver won't open her knees, some of his land in Buckinghamshire might. Look how Old Rowley watches! His chin is so upon his chest he could catch flies in his mouth."

Both turned to regard the king—easy to do, since he dwarfed most of his companions. He was different from them in other ways as well. He wore a thin black moustache, unlike the shaven faces about him. His black wig was thick and richly curled, flowing over his shoulders, a neat contrast to the pearl white of his doublet.

"And can you believe he looks so hungrily when two of his mistresses—two!—are here present and circling like masked hawks?"

They swiftly spotted the vizards. Their masks might indeed conceal their faces, but gossip and their sumptuous gowns revealed them. Lady Castlemaine was one. It was said she had borne the king five children already. The other, by her full and shapely figure could be no other than Winifred Wells. She'd had at least one babe by him.

Lucy let out her famously coarse laugh and Sarah joined her. Then both sighed. Two hundred pounds per annum was a lot of money in exchange for a few regal caresses. Besides, bear him a child and a woman would be made for life. Charles was renowned as much for his paternal love as for his roving eye.

"Nay, look, Lucy, she's thrust the paper back. I tell you, Mary Sanderson will take no comers. She's only ever had eyes for our leader Thomas."

"What? Do you think that the title 'Mrs. Betterton' will keep the lusty monarch's hands off her? Thomas may be the prince of players, but in the end he is merely an actor."

"My John's an actor."

"Aye, but your John was also a soldier. Look at the size of his fists. All know he's killed with 'em. His reputation keeps you safe."

Sarah looked into the pit. John was there, a circle of friends and admirers before him. He was telling some ribald story, throwing his arms wide. Men laughed. "Maybe he keeps me too safe. Sometimes I think it costs me."

"How so?"

"Does our trade not require us to offer something on account, even if we do not pay, uh, the full reckoning? Perhaps my roles would improve if I was allowed a little more freedom."

"Kate Covey's roles have certainly improved since she let our manager Davenant place his ancient prick inside her. But did you hear her tonight? Like an owl, screeched the entire role, she did. It should have been your part."

Sarah smiled and studied her young companion. Lucy truly was a delight, the newest member of the company, whom Sarah had taken under her wing as soon as the girl had arrived. There was a freshness to her, the country glow still on her cheeks, a touch of Cornwall still in her voice. It made Sarah as protective as a mother swan. In her years with the Duke's Company she had seen others arrive with just this brightness, only to have it snuffed out. She was determined not to let it happen to Lucy. Yet she had not entirely succeeded in sheltering her. Lust could oft be deflected, but love was trickier to ward against—as the light suddenly coming into Lucy's gaze now proved.

"He's here," she said, her voice as charged as her eyes.

Sarah turned and saw the bringer of the light, the newcomer making straight for the king's party. He was younger even than Lucy was, and bounced across the stage with all youth's energy. No wig for him: his light-brown locks fell in waves down his back. The crowd parted so that the monarch's new favourite could be the more swiftly admitted to the royal bosom.

"Johnnie!" came the delighted regal cry. "My Lord of Rochester. You missed the play."

"You would have me listen to another man's words when I am brimful of my own?"

"Recite, Johnnie," commanded Charles. "Delight us."

"My words are too vulgar for the general ear . . . and thus perfect for Your Majesty. Draw close, all."

The men formed into a tight ball around the king and young earl. Yet the moment before he was quite sucked in, he glanced to where the actresses stood and winked at Lucy.

Sarah saw her companion's skin flush. "My dear—" she began.

"Nay, do not counsel me, dear Sarah." Lucy grabbed her hand. "Just be happy for me."

"I am happy for you now. It is for your future that I worry."

"Do not. My John will be as true as yours."

"But my John and I are married. Besides, we've known each other since we were children." She squeezed the hand that held hers. "You have known my Lord of Rochester a bare three months."

"Five." Lucy closed her eyes. "Four really, plus two weeks and two days, since he became enamoured of my role as Celia and presented me with violets picked himself, along with his first ode to me." She opened her eyes. "You do not know how well he treats me when we are alone."

"It is when you are alone with him that worries me." The girl tried to withdraw her hand, but Sarah held on. "I am afraid that as soon as he has his desire of you, he will be done with you. And then—"

"Well, you are wrong," Lucy interrupted, defiant. "Behold him still here. For me."

"You do not mean that you . . . ?"

"You see? You do not always know everything, Mrs. Chalker."

There was something behind the defiance now, something vulnerable. Suddenly Sarah knew for certain what she'd glimpsed and chosen not to fully notice till this moment. And it did not take a cunning woman to see it.

"Child," she whispered, "how long is it since you bled?"

Lucy eyes flooded. "Four months," she said, speaking over Sarah's gasp. "But it does not matter," she added. "My love will do the right thing by me."

"Lucy, he is an earl. He cannot marry you."

"I know that. Even though I am the granddaughter of a Cornish knight." This last flash of boldness was there, then gone. "But," she continued, "maybe I could be as . . . as one of these those vizards are to the king. I would not mind sharing the earl with a wife if he would be but kind to me and our child."

As the tears flowed, Sarah put an arm around her. "Have you told him?"

"Nay. I did not know if the child would linger. After your loss." She squeezed Sarah's arm. "I thought I might tell him tonight." She looked up. "Will you stay close, Sarah, when I do?"

Sarah swallowed. Two months since she had lost the child she'd carried and still that void when she remembered it. She took a breath, squeezed back. "Do you doubt it?"

The younger woman held her for a moment, then drew a hand-kerchief from her sleeve and dabbed at her eyes. "He says he likes my tears. But only a certain kind, I fear." She rose. "I must go and repair. Will you get word to him that I would see him below?"

"I will attempt it."

"What would I do without you, Sarah?" Lucy sniffed, then stood, tucking her hands under her busk, pushing the piece of whalebone up until her breasts were prominent. Now that Sarah knew, she could see how they had altered. "Am I repaired enough for a swift exit?"

"You are as lovely as ever, child."

Lucy was an actress and this was her stage. After picking up the glass she'd lately been sipping from, she swept across with a cry of "Nay! Here's a brimmer then to her, and all the fleas about her!" She stopped mid stage, threw the contents down and then started, as if only that moment noticing the king's party. They opened for her, revealing Rochester and His Majesty at their centre. "Sire," she said, her voice husky. "Forgive me. I did not see you there." She followed this with a curtsy that took her to the floor and her bosom into the fullest of views. She held the curtsy not a moment too long, and with-out even a glance at John Wilmot, Earl of Rochester, she was gone.

With all eyes upon the exit, Sarah was able to move discreetly closer. She had no idea how she would cut the earl from the pack, but she had promised to try.

"Now, there's a pair of oranges I would not mind peeling," declared Sir Charles Sedley.

"You'll have to sharpen your knife to attempt it, Charlie," replied the king. "For I heard yours is much, shall we say, dulled of late?"

Groans as well as laughter greeted the king's comment. Rumour had it that Sedley had recently taken the mercury cure for the pox.

Other voices arose from the group.

"I have a shilling here. 'Twill buy two such Sevilles in Covent Garden."

"Nay, gentlemen, they say this lady's not for turning."

"Tope's the word, all actresses can be bought, sure!"

"All women indeed. It is merely a matter of price," said Rochester, stepping forward. "Sometimes it takes but a shilling. Sometimes, with all due respect to Her Majesty, it takes a crown."

It was never certain with the king what topics were open for jest. Yet tonight it appeared that even his wife, Henrietta Maria, who never accompanied him to the playhouse, leaving that field to the vizards, was within bounds. For Charles laughed loudly, his courtiers swiftly joining in. "Ah, Johnnie," the monarch said, "the newest and already the most cutting of my wits. My queen placed in a sentence with players and . . . Beware, sir. I see the Tower in your future." He waved a finger. "Yet Young Rochester seeks to parry with his wit so that his own knife's actions are not discernible." Charles pressed his hand into his forehead. "Nay, sure we have cracked the wind of this poor metaphor. Let me then be as blunt as Sedley's blade." Over the laughter he continued, "'Tis Lord Rochester who's already had the peeling of those oranges. Aye, and has licked out all the luscious flesh too. For he has been occupying Mrs. Absolute these several months!"

Sarah was watching John Wilmot as laughter and jeering came. At least he blushed, murmured a protest: "Sir, that news was for your ears alone." But a smile grew as he received the slaps and congratulations of the crowd—none of which boded well for her poor friend. The sooner Sarah informed the earl of Lucy's new state the better. Corruption only awaited the young man in this circle.

A pop interrupted the laughter. Many in the group, the king included, had been soldiers, and several ducked. "Never fear, Sire," declared a newcomer, an older gentleman than most around the monarch, and twice the girth of any there, "for 'tis not bullets that I bring but Champagne."

"Clarendon," cried Charles. "You missed the play!"

"I did." Clarendon strode close. "Business of state kept me away from it and you. Hang it, sir, by appointing me your lord chancellor, you have robbed me of all my leisure." He sighed. "Still, I trust I will make amends with this."

He signalled, more pops sounded and servants moved forward to pour what had become in recent years London's most fashionable drink. Sarah wrinkled her nose; she couldn't abide the bubbles. But the courtiers were delighted, and eagerly held up their bumpers to be filled.

When toasts had been made, ladies pledged and the Dutch damned—war had been declared a little over a month earlier—Charles asked, "And does the business that has kept you from us, Edward, demand my immediate attention?"

"Good my lord, enjoy your night. We will speak anon."

There was something strained behind the casual words. Charles frowned. "Is it the Hollanders? There has been no battle?"

"Nay, Your Majesty, it is only . . . only some slight increase in the week's bills of mortality. Let us consider it tomorrow and continue tonight with—"

"Increase?" the king interrupted, raising his hand. "And the cause of this increase?"

Not only the king's party fell silent. It seemed to Sarah that the words "bills of mortality" had drawn the attention of many. Like all who paused to listen, Sarah leaned a little closer to hear the answer to the king's question.

Clarendon was now aware his audience had grown. He swallowed. "Perhaps, Your Majesty, we should ret—"

"It's the plague," interrupted Sedley, his words wine-slurred. "By God, it's growing, ain't it?"

A murmur arose, which Clarendon topped forcefully. "I said a *slight* increase and I meant it, sir. Also, the increase is where it has always been, in the outlying parishes, St. Giles and the like. A few more dying in such areas will not affect things much. It might even help. Remember the old verse 'St. Giles breed, better hang than seed.'" When no one laughed, he coughed and continued, "There are no deaths reported in the two Cities' bills, London nor Westminster. Not one."

There was a general breathing out at that, the relief clear. But not for Sarah. St. Giles! It was her old parish, her former neighbours, cousins even, being so readily dismissed. But she also knew, as all there knew, that deaths were reported for a variety of causes with plague the least acknowledged and most disguised—for the consequences of owning it were far too grave.

"Well," the king said, raising his voice so it carried, "though even the death of one of my subjects, wherever they live, saddens me, I am happy that the outbreak is contained. Our enemies will not be heartened and our friends will not fear visiting our ports. We will watch but not concern ourselves overly much." He lifted his empty tankard. "What concerns me more is the lack where once there was plenty. Champagne, sirrahs! Fill me up! And fiddlers, strike me up a less mournful tune, damn ye!"

A loud stamping reel started up and his cry echoed; mugs were drained, then raised again. Champagne was yet rare enough for Clarendon's—who as chief minister was able always to secure the best of all imports—to be the last of it. It was swiftly finished, and more sent for. Meantime, sack and ale flowed.

The group around the king fractured. Charles, despite his

bluster, had taken Clarendon upstage for a private, and intense, conversation. Sedley had produced some dice and gallants clamoured around him to have turns at Hazard. As Rochester was slightly on the fringe of the group, Sarah saw her chance to draw him aside. She took a step.

The soft voice came from near her shoulder; the touch, fingers at her elbow, was light. And in an instant, she recognized both touch and voice. Not because she had ever heard him, nor felt him, before. Yet she knew this for certain: the man who gripped her and spoke was the same whose stare had so unnerved her upon the stage. The man slowly turning her towards him now.

5

THE NOBLEMAN

He said, "A word, Mrs. Chalker, if you will."

As he spoke, before she turned, he looked down at his fingers. They felt warm—no, hot. Yet he'd been rubbing them all night in his box because they'd felt so cold.

Touching her had done that. Her *skin* warmed him instantly, even though he felt it through her costume. The dress that had appeared sumptuous from his box here showed itself frayed, cheap. This close, he could see that her hair was auburn, though some attempt had been made to lighten it. It was why he hated the theatre, its falseness, its front. Like the whole of society. He wanted to tear all that away, get to the essence. Beginning with the woman turning to him now, her elbow burning his fingertips.

"Sir," she said, finally facing him, and he could barely restrain a gasp. He had never been this near to her. Yet despite the cosmetics that all women applied—and actresses did to excess—she was no more painted than any other. True, the ceruse was starting to crack, the cochineal on her cheek losing its fire, and she was missing at least one beauty spot, pinkness now in the gap. But all that was mere appearance, for beneath the crayoning her eyes . . . oh, her eyes! They were of a blue he'd never seen, speckled with brown flecks as if thrushes flew across a cloudless summer sky. Yet far, far more shocking than their colour was what he saw within them. Oh, the light they held! A mirror for his, shining for him as his shone for her.

The relief made his knees weak. He'd feared. Because even if he'd loved her utterly and completely from the moment he'd first seen her walk out upon the stage three weeks before, how could she come close to loving him the same way, when she did not know him? Now he realized he'd been foolish to doubt, even for a moment. She *had* known him, even in that same blinding instant and then, in the weeks since, had acknowledged him in every discreet way she could—in how she did *not* play for him in his box so near to the stage, in the way her eyes deliberately did *not* seek him out. Because—and here was the pure beauty of it—she'd been saving herself for this moment. This one, right now, when she could turn to him and, ever so discreetly, remove her elbow from his grasp. Speak, with all the matter of their love in it, one simple word.

"Sir," she'd said. Her gaze moved over him, while his discovered a pulse in her neck that seemed to him almost a living thing, pushing against flesh walls, trying to break free.

He looked into her eyes again. He'd been silent too long. It was the problem of rarely being in company. Some things had to be spoken aloud, after all.

"Madam." He repeated his short half bow. "My name is Sir Roland, Lord Garnthorpe. Pledged to you."

He observed her closely. Sometimes his name affected people. However, she did not react, just said, "I am grateful for your approbation, my lord. It is always good to be admired for one's craft."

No! He wanted to yell at her, "You do not need to play for me." Yet she was probably simply being careful. Discretion was required in such a public setting. In private, though . . .

He took a breath. "Are you a Jewess, madam?"

It startled her, he could see. He was unused to the courtesies of conversation. He had been too blunt and had suddenly changed subjects, ever his faults. "It is only that the first time I saw you perform, lady, 'twas as a daughter of Zion."

"Oh, do you speak of the usurer's daughter?"

"I do. In Shakespeare's play. *A Merchant in Venice*, was it not?"

"Indeed I was her. But in play only. I am not Jewish."

She had embodied the role so utterly, her movements, her voice. Truly it would have been beyond wonderful if she had been a member of God's tribe. Like all the Saved, he revered the Jews and their holy books. But it did not matter. Nothing did now. Nothing except her and him.

He was surprised to discover he'd closed his eyes; opened them to apologize—and found that she was no longer looking at him. He followed her gaze, saw it settled on a young man gaudily dressed, laughing in a group of similarly clad fops and fools.

What was in her eyes now? Was it lust? Did she desire this youth? This damned debaucher who would visit whores, sicken with their diseases, then visit her and pox her too, killing her with his fouled desire?

"Madam," he barked. "Madam," he said again, more quietly when she'd turned to him again. "You are distracted."

"Momentarily, sir. I need to speak most urgently with the Earl of Rochester and I thought him about to leave."

So the dog had a name. He would remember it. "Let me caution you, Mrs. Chalker. Have nothing to do with such a sinner. He will seek only to corrupt you, to infect you."

"Sir, you misunderstand."

He did not wish to hear her excuses. He'd always known she was an actress. To raise her from her fallen state would require a little education. And she must be saved; he saw that even more clearly now. Saved from men like his own father, who'd brought his sin, his foulness, back to the marital bed. To his mother. A man like this Rochester.

He need not linger. There was but one thing left to do. He pulled a little velvet bag from his cloak pocket. "I have a small tribute for you. It would gratify me if you would accept it."

She took the bag somewhat hesitantly, squeezed out its contents. Drew in a sharp breath.

A large sapphire rested in her palm, exquisitely cut facets glimmering in the candlelight. She shook her head in wonder, and he smiled. He did not mind that she was so easily impressed. It would take time to remove the actress from the woman. He would spend that time.

She returned the jewel to the pouch. "No," she said, thrusting it back, "I cannot accept it."

This was not possible. She must have misunderstood. "Madam," he said, grabbing her wrist, "I insist."

She cried out in pain, jerked her hand from his grip. "No! I am a married woman, Lord Garnthorpe. I cannot be bought."

He was aware now of others looking. One of the king's party had turned. He whitened, feeling the chill surge from his stomach into his chest. He hated this public scrutiny. The cold reached his head. Another whiteness there. Blue white, but not like her eyes. Like a corpse stripped on a battlefield, left out on a winter's night.

Did someone murmur his name?

He looked at her hand holding out the pouch, looked up into her eyes—and saw the pleading there. Not here, they said. Not now. Later and alone. "No words, madam. I understand completely. Later. Alone."

"Sir," she began.

But he'd taken the gem, turned about, descended to the pit and marched through the playhouse doors onto Portugal Street. A few paces further and he was on Lincoln's Inn Fields. There he lost himself swiftly in the crowds.

It took him longer to lose his smile.

At first she could not breathe, as if the hand she'd felt earlier upon the stage on the back of her neck now squeezed the front of it. Then someone took her elbow again.

"Heh oops, and steady there," came a familiar voice. "Was your lover's offer so high that it causes you to faint? This is what comes of obeying your commandment to let you flirt with gallants, to the advancement of your career."

Her husband's tone was teasing, light enough to lift the weight that pressed her. "Oh, John," she murmured, and was the next instant in his arms.

"What's this?" He held her tight for a moment, then drew back to study her face. "It is not like my Sar to be so discomfited. Nor in such a public setting." They both glanced around. The king was still upstage in private conversation with Lord Clarendon, the gallants yet at their dice. Even so, she squeezed the arms that held her, stepped away. "What's amiss, love? Did your admirer affront you?"

"It was him."

John stiffened. "The one you've felt?"

"Aye. He made himself known to me."

"Did he?"

"Ah!" she cried out. John had taken her hand, the same one the lord had gripped. She pulled it from his fingers and rubbed at the wrist, a livid red mark upon it.

"Did he do that?" On her nod, he flushed. "By Christ, I'll . . . where is he now?"

She grabbed his arm as he made to go. "Nay, John, do not."

"Leave me! He must be corrected."

"For this? John, you spent a month in Clink last year for 'correcting' those two wherrymen."

"And would again when they presume to 'know' my wife."

"This is different. He is a nobleman."

John ceased pulling away. "He told you his name?"

"Aye. It was . . ." She had to close her eyes to remember it. For a moment, all she could see were his eyes, the frigid steel of them, like an unsheathed blade. "Garnthorpe."

"Lord Garnthorpe?"

"You know him?"

"Of him. He was one of those rare men—a baron who fought for Parliament in the late wars. He was especially brutal, so it was said."

"And was he not punished afterwards?"

"Punish all who were brutal and every tree in England would stand as gallows."

Something had come into his eyes. Something, she realized, akin to what she'd seen in Garnthorpe's when she'd spurned his gift. Unlike many, her John never talked of his time as a soldier. But she'd held him when nightmares sweated him. She ran fingers over his temple. "Let him be, love. You cannot hurt every man on account of my fears."

He caught her hand. "Well, I know where to find him if he troubles you again."

"In the House of Lords? Even you would not venture there."

"In a meeting house." He tipped his head. "Garnthorpe is known for something other than his cruelty. He's a Fifth Monarchist. You know them?"

"We did that play that mocked them, remember? *Cutter of Coleman Street*. They await the Apocalypse, do they not? All other monarchies overthrown by the return of King Jesus, whose kingdom shall last forever?"

"That's them."

"I thought they were all dispersed. Was there not a rebellion?"

"Aye, Venner's, four years ago. Easily crushed. But the Fifth Monarchy Men did not vanish entirely. And some do more than wait for the End of Days, which they maintain is fast approaching."

"How do you know that?"

"Because a former comrade, Blenkinsop, is one of them. He's a tailor in the City now, where he and his kind still meet. If I want to track down his lordship, it will not be hard." That look came into his eyes again. "And those streets are mine."

She lifted his hand to her lips. "Do nothing, husband, I pray you," she said. "My mind just runs on dark fancies. 'Tis these times perhaps."

Before John could reply, a voice interrupted. "Ah, the Chalkers," said King Charles, who had come downstage, "in love again upon this platform, just as you were earlier upon this same platform. Is life a play and a play always life for you?"

The couple parted. He bowed; she curtsied. "Damn me, what is that famous phrase of Shakespeare's?" the king continued. "It speaks to this far better than I can."

The Earl of Rochester struck a pose: "'All the world's a stage, and all the men and women merely players.'"

"Ah, youth! What it is to have a memory!" Charles nodded. "And did I detect, Mrs. Chalker, a certain lack in yours tonight?"

"Your Majesty is as keen as ever."

"Ungallant is what I am for alluding to it. 'Twas the fault of the play. This piece of Brereton's was a trifle, scarcely worth the remembering. Have you not something more substantial on the way?"

"Indeed, Sire," replied John. "We present a new work by Mr. Dryden next week."

"Dryden, eh? He can be good. Though all that praise he heaped upon the Commonwealth still rankles me." He sniffed. "What do you assay in it?"

"I play Leonardo, a soldier."

"Ah!" The king came closer, bending slightly, for he was taller even than the player. "Were you not in several battles during the late wars?"

"Some. I was at Cropedy Bridge and Edgehill for your father. And I was with you, Sire, at Worcester, in '51."

"Were you, indeed. We lost some brave men that day." The king's eyes went misty. "And I my one chance to retake my throne by force of arms." His eyes cleared, though one, as Sarah had noted when once this close previously, had a cast and so never quite shut. "Well, we look forward to seeing it played. And I will provide a handsome extra purse if I think the soldiery, what, martial enough?" He turned. "Yet now if all men and women are merely players, how much more so a king?"

"'When we are born we cry that we are come to this great stage of fools.' That's a king!" declared Rochester. "*King Lear.*"

"An unfortunate choice, given his fate," observed Charles. "While youth can become tiresome when they know everything."

Rebuked, the earl stepped back.

"Come, I must to another of my stages. Gallants away!" With a sweep worthy of a playhouse king, Charles and his entourage descended from the stage and exited through the theatre's front doors. The crowd waiting outside gave him a cheer.

As he paused to acknowledge it, Sarah, who had been following close, plucked the young earl by the sleeve near the entrance. "My lord, a moment, if you will."

Rochester turned, tossing his long auburn locks. They framed an angular face that would be more handsome were it not for lips that looked swelled by too much kissing, and a nose large enough to pass for French. "Yours ever, Mrs. Chalker."

"Charmed, sir. Though I'd rather you were ever my friend's."

"Ah, Sweet Lucy. How I wish that I had time to visit her now. Her curtsy—'slid, it did provoke me!" He sighed. "Alas, His Majesty has demanded another bout at Pell Mell with me. He has not forgiven me for taking a purse of crowns from him last week."

He turned to leave, but she caught his arm, held it. "She would most especially speak with you, my lord. A matter of urgency."

"Urgency? The king's business is urgent, a player's mere impatience." He jerked his arm free. "Tell her I may visit her later. If His Majesty can spare me."

Charles had entered his carriage with his first minister. As it moved away, a calèche drew up and Rochester made for it without another glance at Sarah. The earl, she thought, does not appear as much in love as Lucy believes.

Her husband was beside her. "Angry, love? Not with me, I trust."

"I am angry with young and careless men."

"Which excuses me on both counts." Someone shouted his name and he waved. "I am off to the Shoe Lane cockpits, sweetheart. Unless you are still upset?"

"Nay, go. I have my part to con again—as His Majesty graciously pointed out. Don't lose too much money."

"I?" He bent for a swift kiss, then joined his friends, a laughing group that merged into the larger surge. Only when he had disappeared did she realize she'd forgotten to tell him about the sapphire. Its price would have bought him a hundred fighting birds. Yet she had spurned it. Now she wondered why she had. Gifts were part of a game every actress played with rich patrons. A game that need not always end with the actress facing a wall, her skirt above her hips.

Then she remembered exactly what had made her refuse the gem: the look in Lord Garnthorpe's eyes. Shivering, she went back into the theatre.

Part Two

⊷✦⊶

FOR THE DEVIL IS COME DOWN UNTO YOU,

HAVING GREAT WRATH, BECAUSE HE KNOWETH

HE HATH BUT A SHORT TIME.

The Revelation of St. John the Divine 12.12

6

THE MONSTROUS COCK

May 15, 1665

Of the many things William Coke regretted in his life, the bargain he'd made with Dickon was certainly one. And he had never regretted it as much as he did that morning.

When he'd first discovered the orphan starving in his doorway, after two weeks given to the necessities of food, clothes and warmth, he'd thought that it might calm the lad if he learned to read. Words, like music, could soothe, it was said, and Coke had assumed, even though the Bible had not impressed him much despite his parents' and his tutors' urgings, that the holy book might tame some of Dickon's wilder jerks and lunges. But the boy remained uninterested; indeed, could not be made to sit even for a minute to trace with his finger the formation of the letter *I*. Coke had tried a basic grammar primer. Dickon had ripped out page after page by too forceful tracing, reducing it swiftly to so much "primer" for their hearth—a joke Dickon laughed at heartily when explained to him. Finally, in desperation, Coke had made his offer.

"Here's a sixpence, Dickon. Go to the booksellers in the crypt of St. Paul's and choose yourself a text you'd like to study."

The boy had whirled off—and returned as excitedly and fast. "Th-this!" he'd declared proudly, thrusting the purchase into Coke's hands.

It was a pamphlet. On its cover was a poorly executed woodcut of a woman with very large breasts, her arse offered up to what Coke supposed to be Satan, though his horns made him look like a bullock and his pitchfork was small enough for the eating of snails.

Yet a deal was a deal. Over a hard winter that kept them much indoors, Dickon learned to read—a little, at least, the choice of text always his. So he also learned rather more about some aspects of life than befitted an eleven-year-old, Coke felt.

Not all the pamphlets were about lust, though. Some were on the recent executions of notorious villains—a few of whom, like Swift Jack, Coke had known. Some combined carnal relations with other crimes. It was one pamphlet of this type that Coke held that morning; that caused him to groan and regret, for the thousandth time, his bargain with the boy.

The pamphlet was entitled *The Monstrous Cock*. The woodcut on its first page showed the interior of a carriage with three bodies heaped up, their torsos split open and what appeared to be yards of sausages trailing from each. Beneath these were the words "Captain Cock turns Bluebeard."

Dickon stabbed his fingers down upon the letters, trying to mouth each word—a feat made harder by his mouth being, as ever, crammed with nuts, his one true passion. He did not understand that he'd been involved in the events so inaccurately described and was delighting in each new word he mastered, yelling it out. Coke felt the ink on the pamphlet, testing its fastness, for it had probably been published that day, two weeks after the events depicted.

His groan was echoed from the other side of the wall, startlingly loud so thin was the horsehair plaster dividing his room from his neighbours'. A Dutch immigrant, his wife and three young children lived adjacent. The man had been moaning intermittently all the morning, sometimes loud, sometimes low. Once there had come a long cry in the man's own language, which Coke spoke a little. God was being solicited to relieve some agony.

Coke looked away from the wall, down to the pamphlet. "'Sa-sa-saw . . .'" stuttered Dickon.

"You saw this?"

The boy shook his head. "Sword!" A finger impaled the word.

The pamphlet had expanded the reputation of Captain Cock as a "knight of the road" through the assumption that the weapon for slaughter had been his rapier. But Coke knew that the tool or tools that had reduced the two men to carcasses had to be thick-bladed knives, perhaps combined with a cleaver. Only the woman had fallen to a thin point, which could have been a sword but was more likely a dagger. A single thrust into her heart.

He closed his eyes, saw her again, felt her hand wrap around his wrist as he groped for her necklace. What had she said—"pale horse"? Was she giving him a clue to her killer? That would not narrow it down much. Every third horse in England was pale.

A groan again. The Hollander or him? Both probably. "W-well?" the boy asked.

"Well enough. Read on."

Dickon turned back to the page, spluttering out the words. The text purported to be eyewitness accounts from several of the party who'd made the discovery. A local magistrate was mentioned, Colonel W. A local constable, one Geoffrey Boxer, of a place called Cuckolds Haven. And—Coke peered closer. A thief-taker, distinguished only as Mr. P., had led them to the site. He knew of several: Pockington, Pitman, Pears. Why did so many of that damned crew start with *P*? Yet this could be just another bit of information the pamphlet had got wrong. It did not matter—thief-takers from up and down the alphabet would be after him once they'd read, as he did now, the last paragraph:

> This monster. This demon in a cocked hat. He must be taken before more worthy citizens and ravishing ladies are brutishly butchered. And so the Honourable Company of Ropewrights offers this reward for said taking: not only the hempen cravat from which this dandy will dance the Tyburn jig, but the sum of thirty guineas for his speediest apprehension.

Coke rubbed his forehead. Thirty pieces. The original traitor's sum. Christ's bones, he'd sell himself for such. And though not many knew him, a few did. Three fellow "knights"—no, two: now Swift Jack dangled at Finchley. Maclean and O'Toole, Irishmen he'd worked with on occasion to their mutual profit, who would sell their mothers for a groat, let alone Judas's bounty. In sooth, O'Toole was the one who'd let slip Coke's name when they were taking Lord Carnarvon's coach on the Hounslow Road last December. The coachman had misheard it and reported it as "Cock."

"C-c-c-c . . ."

The captain glanced down. The boy was labouring over the name he'd just been thinking. "Cock," he pronounced.

"Cock-a-doodle-doo!" Dickon crowed, his imitation perfect.

"Aye, lad." Coke tousled the boy's hedge of fair hair and Dickon turned his head under the caress like a cat. "Though if we do not move soon, we may not have a chance to crow."

There was no question. He would have to leave the city. Probably the country, though he hated that idea. He disliked abroad. He spoke English, damn it, and had spent too long away, forced to learn French, Dago, Walloon, all because of his loyalty to the Stuarts. Yet when he'd arrived back, what had been his reward? Far less than thirty guineas. Certainly not the return of the Coke lands in Somerset, mortgaged to send three sons to war in the king's cause.

Maybe he would go to America. Did they not speak a form of English there?

Another groan shook him, joined now by a child's weeping.

He would need coin. A thought came and he seized the pamphlet, to Dickon's protests, and scanned the words again. No. There was no mention of the necklace. But that sort of detail would be included if known. Mind you, he thought, smoothing his moustache with two fingers, there's nothing about the pistol I left either, damn fool that I was. The thief-taker must have found that.

After handing back the pamphlet to Dickon, Coke reached up to a rafter. There, between joist and plaster, was a gap, and he pulled down the bag with the necklace. When in exile in Antwerp, he had spent some time warding a jeweller—it was either serve or starve—so he knew a little about gemstones. The rubies in the necklace were good, the emeralds better. The silver they were set in appeared of good quality too. He would not be cheated as to price, though necessity might force him to accept less.

He peered closer. He'd not noticed earlier, but the lowest silver loop was broken. So a jewel was missing at the very bottom, which would have completed the display.

It did not matter. There was enough of worth here to see Dickon and him clear. Where to, he would decide later.

Pocketing the jewels, he belted on his sword, swept on his cloak and took up his hat—from which, on a sudden urge, he removed the green ostrich feather, leaving it plainer. He picked up his walking stick, tapped Dickon on the shoulder with its silver-knobbed end. The boy immediately showed him a word: "Shambles," he said distinctly.

"Aye, 'twas. Now, listen. I am going out. I want you to pack up what we have. Most in the trunk, enough in a valise for a few nights on the road."

The boy was instantly alert. "A m-mark?"

"Nay, we do not go to work. We just go. Tomorrow, with luck. See to it."

Dickon nodded. Coke went into the corridor. He was surprised to find it busy at this time in the morning. Three families lived in the three rooms on his floor; four more in the rooms above, and the same below. Children, mothers, even men milled about. Then he remembered it was Sunday; the men were not at labour, and the better clothes showed that many were off to church. As he began to push his way through, the door next to his was flung open, and the groaning that the plaster had somewhat contained burst out, along with the Dutchman's three daughters. Their mother followed, leaned against the doorway and cried, "Dood! Dood!"

"What's she say?" The neighbour on the other side of Coke's room was asking.

"She says someone's dead, Mrs. Philips," Coke replied. "I regret it is probably her husband."

He tried to move on, but the rush of people, like crows to a corpse, held him before the door. Mrs. Philips and another lady pushed past the weeping wife.

"Merciful God in heaven," came the cry from two throats.

They came out fast, splitting for their respective rooms. "What is it, Mrs. Philips?" he asked, following her.

"Plague." There was terror in her eyes. "Plague, or I'm as Dutch as she is. My ma died of it in '36. I'll never forget the signs."

She'd whispered it—but enough had heard her and the word was carried from one person to the next the length of the corridor. People raised hands to their mouths, scarves if they had them. Catholics, hitherto concealed, revealed themselves in sudden crossings. Most of those gathered began to back away.

Coke did not. He'd got as far as Mrs. Philips's door, which she now flung open. Just as she was about to step inside, he grabbed her arm. "What are you going to do?"

"Do?" she shrieked, then dropped her voice again. "I am going to pack my family up and be gone from this place within the half hour."

"Why so fast?"

"Have you ever been in a plagued city, sir?"

He had. Bristol, during the siege. It was something he tried never to think about. Not when he was awake. When he was asleep, he could not stop her face coming to him as he'd last seen it. Swollen. Unrecognizable.

Evanline.

"As soon as this pestilence is known to the parish authorities, they will come and shut us up," Mrs. Philips continued. "They will board up the house. They will station watchmen at the door. We will not be allowed to pass, and half of us—more—will be dead within the month." She stuffed a hand into her mouth to stifle a sob, walked into her own room and slammed the door on him. He heard her turning out drawers.

He went back to his room. Dickon lifted the pamphlet. "Guts!" he said brightly.

"Pack," Coke commanded, and began to scurry. Dickon joined him. In sooth, it did not take them long. Two years he'd lived there, the longest he'd lived any place since the wars, and all packed up in less than twenty minutes. All they could not carry easily about them they flung into his trunk. With two satchels apiece, they left. He locked the room, though he did not expect to see it or the trunk ever again.

The corridor was empty now, quiet. Then, down below he heard a thumping on the front door. "Open here!" commanded a deep voice. "Open for the headborough of the parish."

"This way." Coke followed others down the back stairs, past the two privies, around the cesspit. They blended swiftly with people in the back lane.

They did not go far. Along Duke's Place, out the Aldgate. Just beyond it, on Houndsditch, was a coaching inn, the Hack and Horse. Access to a coach would be a good thing, he thought. Especially one that left for the eastern ports.

The inn was largely empty, it being Sunday morning. He placed Dickon in a corner, gave him coins for small beer and cheese. "Wait here," he said. "I will return in a few hours."

Dickon nodded. There was fear in his eyes now. He'd been abandoned too many times. "Read," the captain said, pointing to the pamphlet where it was stuck in the boy's breeches. "I will hear you when I get back."

"C-Cap'n," Dickon said, and settled on the nest of satchels.

As Coke left the yard, the Church of St. Botolph's Aldgate began to toll its summons to service. He paused for a moment. Where would he find a jeweller to appraise his wares on the Sabbath?

Then he remembered. The one he would visit did not attend any church.

He set off for the Jew.

"It is not that I do not want to help you, my dear Captain. It is that I cannot today."

"Mr. Ferdinando—"

"Please, sir. Call me by my real name. By the grace of Good King Charles, I no longer need pretend to be a *murano*." He laughed. "It was confusing for so long—the choice of being despised as a Portuguese Catholic or despised as a Jew. Let the confusion end and call me as I am."

Coke took a breath. The man indeed had shed all pretense. When first they'd met for "business" three years before, he had worn wigs, a beaver hat. Now his own curly, silver hair fell to his shoulders, topped with a small circle of leather. "Mr. ben Judah," he said. "You know I have never despised you or your kind."

"At least not to my face."

"Nor away from it. A man's faith means little to a man who has no faith himself."

"Now, there you sadden me. All men need faith. Faith is brother-hood. It is comfort in the darkness—even if that darkness lasts for centuries. Look at us Jews of England, exiled from the realm four hundred years ago. Some remained, adopted other names." He inclined his head. "Ferdinando, for example. And now we are brought out of the darkness. Returned from the wilderness. Yet how could we have survived so long unless with the faith that God would bring the light again?"

"Well, sir," replied Coke, "the late wars were fought at least partly for faith. For one man's vision of it over another's. Every day

I saw faithful men pray fervently for God to preserve them in the fight—and the next moment saw them ripped asunder by cannon. Saw others stripped of everything that made them human—nose, ears, skin—and heard them pray to God for merciful death. Saw that death withheld and agony continue, for days sometimes." He closed his eyes. But the vision of Quentin Absolute appeared behind them, so he opened them again and said, "I have only seen God do the opposite of what he was asked for. So you can understand why faith does not concern me."

"I can understand, even if I—"

Coke was not there for a pity. He never wanted that from any man. Briskly he changed subjects. "We are straying from the point, sir." He pushed the necklace across the counter. "I want a fair price for this."

"And you will get it. Only, not today."

"I am willing to take a little less today."

"And I would be happy to offer it."

"Then do so."

"I cannot." The Jew raised his hand to forestall the protest. "Captain, I am largely a gold- and silversmith. I know a little of jewels, but these . . ." He fingered the piece before him. "I do not know enough. Yet I have a cousin newly arrived from Antwerp. An expert. I will consult him, and then I will offer you a fair price. Bearing in mind the, ah, circumstances of its finding, yes?"

Coke flushed but kept his temper. Did this man know the details of its "finding"? It seemed unlikely—yet the Jews often had knowledge hidden from their gentile neighbours. Did he know already about people falling ill in the neighbourhood? Coke wondered. If plague had come, Isaac ben Judah was a man who would be much visited. Many would be trying to fund flight. Prices would go down.

The goldsmith put on spectacles and picked up the necklace. He held it up to the sunlight from the window. "This much I do know—it's lovely work," he said. "And good silver too. I can give you a guinea for that alone, and now. A pity the whole will have to be broken up. You can guess the reasons." He smiled at Coke, then glanced back at the necklace. "What's missing here, Captain? Did you keep a stone?"

"I did not. I discovered the necklace so."

"I see. Well, judging by the setting and by the size of the broken clasps, I would not be surprised if it were a sapphire that is missing. Perhaps the richest jewel of them all. Still—" ben Judah let the necklace drop, caught it just above the table, folded it into some pocket within his cloak "—the rest will fetch a good price without it. Leave this with me."

"May I return later today?"

"Tomorrow, Captain. Tomorrow." The Jew held out two hands. A guinea was in one.

Coke took the coin, shook the other hand. "I will be here at eight."

"And I will be here at noon. There's a feast tonight in my cousin's honour. There will be dancing. I may even drink some wine."

Jewish celebrations could be riotous, he'd heard, and the image of the dignified grey-haired man before him cutting a caper made him smile.

The Jew put a second hand atop their joined ones. "Keep the faith, my friend."

"I will keep the appointment, sir. No more."

Coke stepped out of the shop, and squinted into sunlight. The house opposite the Jew's had burned down some time before, so his was not in shadow, unlike the others in the row. Nearby, a bell tolled twelve. Coke had arrangements to make now, and perhaps a destination to choose. Then tomorrow, with fortune, he and Dickon would leave the realm.

So today, he would go see Lucy Absolute. He needed to, prior to departing for he did not know how long.

Decided, he took a few steps to the west before he remembered that today was the Sabbath and so she would not be at the Lincoln's Inn playhouse; also that there was no point seeing her unless he had some money. She was ever short of it, and he'd vowed to keep her purse full. She would never have to do what most actresses did to fill it, not if he could help it. This he'd vowed to her brother, Quentin Absolute, the comrade he'd loved—even if he could now not recall one detail of the man's face, only what it had become after case shot had scoured every feature from it on Lansdown field.

7

THE SCENT

"Off out, Pitman?"

"Off out, my love."

"On parish business?"

"No, chuck. The same business as yesterday."

"Well, I pray the Lord brings you more success today."

"And I that he hears both your prayers and mine."

"Will you take Josiah?"

His son raised his head from his place before the cold fireplace, like a hound hearing of a morning's chase. "I will not, sweetheart. I may have to meet with, uh, characters."

"Then best not." The boy lowered his head again and shivered. The hearth had been empty these few days, and spring yet cold. Bettina waddled forward, her stomach large before her, and dropped a thin shawl around her son's shoulders. "Good hunting, Pitman," she said, trying to smile at him, turning away quickly at the cry from the other room. Imogen, sick again, and no more money for fever pills than for fuel.

He stepped out into the alley, took another down to Blowbladder Street and turned left onto Cheapside. It might not be the swiftest route to his destination, but it would be far the brightest, and this morning he yearned for sun to warm him through—for Cheapside, unlike most other City streets, was wide enough that the jutties of the shops and houses did not near conjoin overhead to form a dark tunnel. The pavement was wide, well tended, the gutters constantly swept clean. And he did not feel the need, as he did so often, to hug the wall and challenge any who would force him from it. The richer merchants who dwelt in those fancy houses would not have shamed themselves by allowing their servants to empty chamber pots and other detritus from their windows.

He moved slowly, warming himself, hearing the growl from his guts. He had given most of his morning crust to his son, claiming he'd had sufficient. He had not. Taking a thief on a stomach near empty for three days was always harder. Hunger dulled. He would have to be careful.

Once more, as he headed east, he wondered if he'd done the right thing.

I would have bread, and Imogen medicine, and my son a fire to warm himself before if either the parish had paid me my three months' salary for my constable's duties or I'd taken Maclean yesterday and not let him go.

He shook his head. He would have received five guineas for Maclean, the Irish highwayman, as soon as he'd deposited him in Newgate prison. But Captain Cock's price had risen to thirty—so that pamphlet and the Company of Ropewrights had proclaimed. Five against the captain's former reward of twenty guineas and he'd probably have taken the Irish bird in hand. But the extra ten—that would do more than clear all the Pitman family's debts. That would set them up for a while. Till after the babes were born, anyway.

He'd considered kicking the truth out of the Irishman. But he hadn't. He couldn't risk an injury himself, not impossible from a cornered rat, especially one the size of the hefty Maclean. Also, information gleaned through pain oft proved false. And the truth was that though he'd put aside the dice and the cards when he married Bettina, he still liked a gamble. Five certain guineas against thirty possible? It was worth the hazard. Besides, he had gained something most useful in exchange for giving Maclean two days' start on the road back to Ireland. He had got a name.

"I heard him called it, Mr. Pitman," the highwayman had said.

"That's plain Pitman to you."

The Irishman had sat down again at his table in the low alehouse's corner. "'Twas two nights before the Hounslow robbery. We met in a tavern, the captain, O'Toole and me—the Devil, in Alsatia. Know it?"

"I know it. Go on," said Pitman, sitting close.

"Well, the captain did not. Had chosen it *because* he did not, to discuss the plan for the taking of Lord Carnarvon's coach. So he was not pleased when he was recognized."

"By who?"

"A buttock. A right low one too. Aye, aye, I thinks, that's odd. He always seemed uninterested in such women. In any women. O'Toole and me would ogle some tavern wench and he would not even glance. But damned if she was not the one what said his name."

"Tell me her words. Exactly."

The man's brow furrowed, lines of dirt in every crease. "Exactly? Well, I'd taken a couple of jugs aboard, but I do seem to recall . . . now, you did say three days' start, didn't ya, Mr.—I mean, Pitman?"

"I said two and I'll drop it to one unless you tell me the man's name now."

"She says, 'Why, Mr. Coke! I thought you never come west of Hounsditch.'"

"'Coke'? You are sure?"

"Sure as my ma sits to the right hand of God, sor. Remember it cos she had half her teeth missin' and it came out like 'Cock.' Least, that's what I heard, which I offers up, laughing about how she'd probably like some of his, you know." He chuckled, broke off at Pitman's unsmiling face, swallowed, then continued, "'I said Mr. Coke,' she says, clear as daylight, adding some gloss on both my country and parentage, like. But the next moment, the captain grabs her by the arm and drags her away. He was back fast, so if he occupied her, it was 'Whoops, Bob, and have ye!'"

"The trull. What was her name?"

The Irishman had cackled. "Who asks their names, sor? They're all Maggie to me. Hair like Satan's flame, if that's any good."

Pitman had considered for a moment, then noted, "You say 'Captain'—she said 'Mr.' Which is it?"

"O'Toole it was called him captain. He never said he was himself. Didn't say much, actually, especially that night. Just said where the three of us was to meet and left sharpish."

"Meet to take Lord Carnarvon's carriages? This was in December?"

"Aye. On Hounslow Heath, two nights later. It was then I called his name, by mistake like. He was furious. Levelled his pistol at me. I thought he was going to blow my head off. But he didn't." Maclean scratched at his thatch, flakes of falling skin glistening in the fire-light. "Leastways, I don't reckon so."

As Maclean laughed, Pitman thought about Mr. Coke's—or Captain Cock's—pistol, the one he'd found in the carriage, how he'd discovered it had charge but no ball in it. The man had never intended to kill. Not with powder, anyway.

"Did he seem mad to you?"

"Only when I named him. Oh, you mean because of the slaughter in Finchley? What about that, eh?" Maclean shook his head. "He was always a quiet bastard. Never said much. But lots of mad bastards about after the wars, aren't there? And it's them quiet ones you have to watch out for."

"His voice. How was it?"

"How d'ya mean?"

"Was he a gentleman?"

"He was a country cunt. West somewhere. Bristol?" He'd shrugged. "He used some fancy words so—"

Pitman had stood then. "Two days, Maclean. And then I'll be looking for you."

Two days now since Pitman had let Maclean go, but he hadn't verified if the Irishman had done so. Wouldn't, nor would he waste any time looking for a red-haired whore, because he'd thought of an easier way to track down "Coke," as he must now think of him.

He would look for the jewels.

It was noon exactly. The bells of St. Margaret Patton tolled the hour just as he arrived before the third most likely address nearest the Hounsditch, a gold- and silversmith's near the corner of Philpot Lane. One hand on the doorknob, he peered through the thick leaded glass, discerned a human shape within. The Jew, he presumed, and prosperous enough to have glass in his door.

He entered, a small bell set above the door sounding tinnily. Noon, and the light thus behind him, he saw the man look up, squinting. A hand rose to block the harsh rays.

"Well, Captain, you come most promptly upon your hour."

Pitman paused, his hand still on the door. The Jew removed spectacles, rubbed his eyes, looked up again. "I apologize, sir," he said. "I mistook you for someone else."

"A captain." Pitman laughed. "I am flattered, sir. Though I was a soldier, I only ever made corporal. This lovely morning's sun must have given me a glow."

"Lovely indeed." The Jew emerged from behind his counter and crossed to the door. He was small; Pitman gazed down easily upon his glossy hair, his leather skullcap. The goldsmith opened the door and stepped onto the threshold, then peered up and down the street.

"Are you searching for your captain?" Pitman inquired.

"I am. Captain Whittaker is a little shy. Some who do business here are, sir. I was hoping to call him in if he was about."

There had been no hesitation on the name, nothing in the man's smile or voice to indicate concern. But from his gambling days, Pitman had always been a good reader of others. When men bet, there was often some small gesture that gave their cards away. And this man, when he'd talked of the captain, had run his tongue over his lips. Pitman would watch for its repetition.

The goldsmith went back behind his counter. Pitman advanced to a tall stool before it. "May I?"

"Please."

Pitman sat. His height and girth meant that he blocked the sunlight from the small man's face.

"Now, sir," the Jew said, "how may I be of service?"

"You have been recommended to me as an honest man. A fair dealer."

"I am pleased to own such a reputation. By whom, may I ask?"

"Oh, more than one, sir, more than one. You are also prized for an especial virtue."

"Which is?"

"Discretion." Pitman leaned forward and the sun flashed in the goldsmith's eyes. "I am engaged by a . . . a certain gentleman. A nobleman. You understand, no names?"

"I understand completely."

"His lordship has lost something he prizes. 'Lost' is a loose term. He believes that one of his servants may have stolen this item and may be seeking to sell it."

"I see." The goldsmith shifted to his left until Pitman again blocked the sunlight. "And these friends who recommended me think that I may be a dealer in such 'lost' goods?"

It was spoken with no trace of his previous courtesy. "Oh, not at all, Mr.—ben Judah, is it? Not at all. No one would think you would knowingly deal in such items. Many honestly obtained jewels must cross this counter daily."

The man nodded. "All, as far as I am aware. As long as we are clear on that point, sir?"

"As clear as Buxton water, Mr. ben Judah. May I proceed?"

Tread soft, Pitman, he warned himself, then continued. "The *item* in question is a rather fine set of jewels, given to the duchess on the occasion of a twentieth anniversary. I hope, sir, I have not revealed too much about the man I serve. I rely on your reputed discretion."

"You may do so. Can you describe the jewels?"

"I can do rather better than that, sir." Pitman smiled broadly. "The duke had just commissioned the artist Lely to do a painting of his wife and him to celebrate their anniversary. Mr. Lely made some preliminary rough sketches—including one of the jewels. And here it is."

He'd always liked the way people were surprised in that moment when conjurers produced some object to astonish. And he had rolled the paper in such a way that when he produced it from his pocket, it unfolded suddenly. Pitman watched the Jew study the sketch then lick his lips.

Oh, I see you, thought Pitman.

The Jew pulled four small lead scale weights from beneath his counter and placed one on each corner of the sketch. Then he donned his spectacles and bent to study. Pitman kept still until, seeing the goldsmith about to look up, he leaned to his right. Sunlight reflected on glass. The Jew squinted, blinked several times, removed his glasses and shook his head. "Alas, sir," he said, raising one hand to block out the sun, "I will have to disappoint his lordship and you for I have never seen this necklace."

The devil you haven't, thought Pitman, and reached to take the man by his throat.

But his hand grasped only air, for ben Judah leaned hard back, then stood and stepped back a pace. In one hand he still held his spectacles. In the other he held a gun. "You will stand up," ben Judah said, full cocking the hammer, "and you will leave my shop."

"Sir," Pitman said, spreading his arms wide, "what do you mean by this?"

"You were attempting to lay hold of me."

"I was reaching for my paper."

"And you may take it up now." The gun barrel flicked slightly. "Take it up and leave."

"I will." Pitman lifted a corner of the sketch and pulled. The springiness of the paper made two of the weights drop to the floor. But the gun's aim did not waver. Tucking the sketch away, he said,

"Sir, I fear I have alarmed you. It was not my intention. Can we not discuss this reasonably?"

"There is nothing to discuss" came the reply. "I have not seen your necklace. I wish you to go."

Pitman moved to the door, opened it. The bell above jangled. He stepped into the street. The Jew followed, but just to the threshold. There was a moment when they were close enough that Pitman wondered if he could risk going for the gun. But glancing about, he noted many people on the street, several of them wearing the same leather skullcaps as ben Judah.

He looked back to find the Jew not looking at him but up the street. Then the goldsmith raised the gun, pointed it over Pitman's head at the charred remnants of the house opposite and fired.

The noise was not loud, yet people started all around. Pitman felt a spark land in his hair. He bent over, slapped the sudden sting. When he looked up again, it was to see the door slamming before him. A moment later came the sound of a bolt.

Why did he fire? Pitman wondered, still patting his smarting scalp. To warn me off? Or to warn someone else?

He swivelled, looking up and down the street. Men and women stared curiously at this large man wreathed in gunsmoke before the jeweller's. Pitman noticed no one out of the ordinary. Yet he had a feeling, as if someone's gaze, there a moment before, had suddenly gone.

Were you here, Captain Coke or Cock? So close? Here for your reward? Well, I will have you closer still. Will I not, Lord, by thy sweet grace?

8

THE LIGHT

Cursing, John Chalker watched Lord Garnthorpe vanish from sight.

"Damn you, Garnthorpe. Damn you and damn myself."

Chalker stared across the green at the meeting house, its whitewashed walls yellowed by twilight. He'd waited opposite Garnthorpe's columned portico in St. James's so he'd know exactly what the man looked like. Then he'd dogged him for two hours, all the way to this village of Newington, hoping for a quiet place to have his words. But now, just when he'd got close, his ignoble lord-ship had slipped into the sanctuary of his fellow Fifth Monarchist madmen. Saints, as they called themselves.

Thrusting his hands into his coat pockets, John gripped his blackthorn cudgel and his razor. Though he'd never planned to use them as more than threat, he did not think he would get even that chance now. He could hardly march into a Saints meeting and deliver a warning in word, cosh and blade. Yet he could not wait—he'd been told these meetings went all evening in prayers, visions, exhortations to action. Night was coming fast, and it was a long walk back to London.

Shite! He cussed, suddenly tired and hungry. Why had he not spent the Sabbath at home and content with Sarah? Why had he not heeded her caution to leave well alone? All they'd learned of Garnthorpe in the week since he'd approached Sarah at the theatre testified to a mad dog. The most brutal of soldiers during the wars, later the man had even spent a year in the same Bethlehem Hospital where his father, the first Lord Garnthorpe, had died, poxed and raving. Was not a Bedlamite hound likely to be distracted by the next thing, the next person who came to his scent? Garnthorpe had not returned to the playhouse, made no further attempt at contact. Perhaps Sarah was right and the man was merely infatuated, harmless.

Then John remembered the bruise on Sarah's wrist that had deepened in the days since and the fear that had lingered in her eyes. He'd known Sarah from a girl. He, a few years older, had watched her grow, admired her spirit long before he'd thought of her in any other way; marked her fight her way from the shit-filled streets of their parish all the way to and through the doors of the Duke's playhouse. He had never, not once, seen her as discomfited as when Sir Roland had gripped her so hard.

No. The man must be warned off. Maybe even punished, just a little. With all the plays that had to be learned and put on, John knew he would not get another chance till next Sunday, and maybe not then. He'd walked this far, damn it; he could walk a little farther—and did, across Newington Green to the meeting-house door.

"Greetings, Brother. God's blessing upon you."

After a few questions to establish his character—having played a Saint onstage, John could utter the terms with the required fervour—the large doorman waved him inside, others crowding in behind. The door was soon shut upon them. Well, he thought, seeking a place toward the rear, it has been a while since I attended any worship. Even the Anglican to which Sarah sometimes dragged him. He would be seeing none of that ceremony here. He knew that the Acts of Uniformity and Conventicles forbad any but the Church of England's worship within the city—but that did not prevent nonconformists meeting there in secret. More often, though, the banned sects gathered in outlying villages such as Newington, where they had a better chance of escaping notice and persecution.

Is this my chance to make my peace with God? To ask his forgiveness for my trespasses to come? He fingered his razor. "Thy will be done," he murmured.

Brothers were hushing one another as a Saint stepped into the pulpit. John looked at the man—who seemed for a moment to be looking right back at him. He had cropped hair the colour of autumn straw, and thin eyebrows visible only where they were slashed through with white. His nose had been violently broken at some stage, a scar across the bridge. Even at that distance, his eyes appeared pale. I know you, thought John, slipping into the shadows by a pillar. But where from? When he looked up again, the man had raised his arms and his gaze was above the congregation.

"'Our Father,'" the man began, "'who art in heaven . . .'"

The words were universal and John spoke his lines with passion, joined in the amens as loud as any. As the chorus of them faded, the man in the pulpit spoke on. "Brothers," he intoned, "today, this fifteenth day of the fifth month, I will recount to you a dream I had last night."

"Say it, Brother!" implored one Saint. "Testify!" called others.

"I will."

The man's voice lowered but still carried. An actor's delivery, John decided.

"I was alone in a great field of corn, without the walls of a magnificent city filled with many tall towers and great gates. I desired to see more clearly this shining place. So I climbed a tree that stood nearby, a mighty English oak, in full leaf, and through its canopy did I peer over the walls. There I beheld . . ." He paused, gazing over the upturned faces. "Streets filled with sinners. Heard voices raised in lamentation. But even as I watched, the gates were opened. First a huge pack of dogs came baying, and on their tails, sinners flooding out. Those sinners were a great multitude and all—all, each and every one!—did fall down beneath the tree in which I sat. Yet even as their bodies touched the ground . . ." Another pause, held longer. "They did vanish."

A sigh ran through the congregation, like a shiver of wind stirring that cornfield. The man next to him, staring up, whispered, "Is that Revelation?" John nodded. What else would the passage be? His former comrade, Blenkinsop, had told him a lot about these so-called "Saints" in which he was numbered. Their obsession with the Bible, especially that book of Revelation. Their rejection of "pagan" names for days and months. Their lack of prayers, saving only the Lord's. They awaited the imminent return of King Jesus. He would bring the Fifth Monarchy, the End of Days—which they would hasten, John reminded himself. Though they believed that this end was inevitable, they did not merely sit and pray for it. Since the king's restoration five years earlier, scarce a year had passed undisrupted by riot or even attempted revolt, these Saints ever in the vanguard.

The man in the pulpit spoke again. "Do you wish to hear, Brothers, the verses I found after my dream, opening my Bible at random, that no man could have predicted?"

"Read them!" the faithful shouted.

"I do not need to read them, burned as they are into my soul. Revelation. Chapter twenty-two. Verses fourteen and fifteen."

Nearby a church's bell tolled the hour. The man paused, all listened to this mark of time's passing. Then hard on the bell's eighth and final toll came another sound: a bugle. The congregation began to mutter and a moment later the man who'd admitted John to the chapel cried out, "'Tis Magistrate Chalmers! The militia's at his back. Come to arrest us!"

"Betrayal!" someone yelled. "There's a traitor among us!"

"Let's fight!" shouted another.

"Aye! Fight 'em!"

There were more shouts in favour than in dissent. From beneath coats, pistols appeared and men began to prime.

"No!"

The voice was from the pulpit. It rose above the shouts, and once more John thought, He's either commanded a playhouse, sergeanted a regiment—or both, as I have done.

"Do not fight, Brothers! Not now, when we have been betrayed and are in choler. We were called today to hear that the hour to rise is at hand, when the seventh seal, as prophesied, will be opened."

The horn sounded again, a drum joining it. The man at the pulpit raised his voice still louder: "It is soon—but it is not today. Too many of our brethren are in their foul dungeons—we need all to be free and ready. Oh, most ready in arms. For is it not also said, 'A man may as well go into the harvest without his sickle, as to this work without his sword.'"

He looked down—and John felt again that the man's gaze sought him out alone. "As for the Judas among us, know this: You will be discovered. You will be punished, even in the manner described in Holy Testament." Trumpet and drum sounded ever nearer. He raised his hands. "Go by separate ways, each to his home. Keep your powder dry and await the summons of King Jesus to the harvest!"

With this, the man leaped from the pulpit and ran to the back of the chapel. Other doors were opened, at the side as well as the front—through which was heard again and louder the strike of drum. John was about to run out this nearest exit—he had no wish to be mistaken by the local magistrate as a Monarchist man—when he glimpsed Garnthorpe rushing out a side doorway. Pushing back against the throng, he gained that same door and followed. Maybe he would get his chance for a word after all.

The congregation did not linger. By the drums, the militia was approaching from the north-east, so the Saints scattered in pairs, foursomes, all heading south and west, avoiding the direct road, taking to the fields. Ahead, alone, Garnthorpe crossed to Hollow Way, there joining the main highway down to the City. John, keeping his quarry ever in his sight as the bugles faded behind him, fell in with three hat makers, who shared some wine and bread with him. His lordship's pace did not slacken, neither for refreshment nor rest, bearing ever westward.

John parted from the hat makers near Clerkenwell. Yet Garnthorpe, instead of continuing south to Fleet Street and then on to the Strand— roads where householders observed the ordinances to keep a light before their door after dusk—cut west. And in a short time, John heard a sound he knew well. He smiled, for he had grown up within the clamour of the bell of St. Giles in the Fields.

He quickened his pace. Why did you choose this byway to your home? This is my world, not yours, my lord. As far from the splendour of St. James's as you can get, even if less than a mile apart. John did not come here often anymore. Why would he? He and Sarah had taken rooms—two of them, with their own privy, no less—in a house shared with only three other families, nearer Lincoln's Inn and the theatre. But the smell took him straight back to his childhood, a compound of stench found nowhere else in London—perhaps nowhere on earth. Like the waters Sarah concocted to freshen their rooms, it had a base note of something, other notes above it. Her base could be essence of orange, or ambergris, or lavender.

In St. Giles the base note was shit.

That sweet-sick smell was everywhere—for the people dwelt in houses built for one family, housing ten, twenty, with maybe one privy office between them. Maybe not, and if not—well, there were marshes on the outskirts where one did not tread without boots or iron pattens to raise up your shoes. Through these marshes conduits ran, though "ran" was not a term he'd use for creeks so thick with filth. The parishioners of St. Giles added other notes, their clothes and bodies rarely washed. Animals were kept in pens or wandered loose—dogs, chickens, pigs, sheep. Rats and cats. Fires burned everywhere, burned everything. Offal boiled in pots.

St. Giles in the Fields, John thought, breathing deep. It was good to recall the scent now and again; it made Sarah's orange water all the sweeter.

These inhabitants did not spend money on lights before their dwellings. The little that lit the alleys seeped through skins stretched over windows, or from open doors—and most doors were open, to let out the stench. Every seventh house appeared to be an alehouse, varying from a single room with nothing but a trestle and a cask within to larger taverns crammed with men and women. Before each, children begged for the coins that their parents would turn into liquor. Hands thrust at John, which he ignored; others grasped his coat, and were cast off. Behind the singsong of their plaints came other music: fiddles, and flageolets. Clogs stomped on wooden floors. People sang, out of tune and in.

He had done it himself, he and Sarah—played and sung in these taverns for small change. Unlike most, they had used the skills they'd acquired here to fight their way from these streets to others that did not stink so.

He had closed the gap with Garnthorpe to twenty paces, always keeping some bodies between them. It was too crowded to pull the man aside, but John knew he'd get his chance—especially as, for the first time, his prey was showing signs of distress, pausing at corners, looking about, shaking his head, taking longer to swipe off the scabbed hands of beggars. It was just as John's grandfather, who had come from the country and been a great poacher in his youth, had told him: "The trick with a deer," he'd said, "is not to run at 'im, for 'e will always run faster away. What you do, see, is sight one, leave 'im know 'e's sighted, then follow 'im, walking, walking, all day. 'E'll take you far, but by the end 'e'll be so dogged by terror 'e'll lie down and offer his throat to your blade."

John looked forward to laying his own blade to Garnthorpe's throat. He would not kill him. But perhaps a scar for him to see in his mirror when his servant shaved him? Or a sharp tap from his cudgel, leaving a bruise to match the one his lordship had left on Sarah's wrist? Warnings to remember.

Garnthorpe stumbled as he flung off some clinging urchins. Then, just past doors John remembered well, for they opened onto the Maidenhead Lane cockpit, the man lurched right and disappeared around the corner. His quarry had entered some especially noxious, ill-lit alleys—the perfect place to lay this deer low.

"John Chalker! Begod!"

The voice came sudden and loud from his right. He started, gripped his cudgel but then eased when he saw who had spoken.

"Clancy."

A big man detached himself from the doorpost that was hold-ing him up. John could smell the whisky on him, and the light spill showed a nose as splayed and bulbous as a red cauliflower. "It's been years, John lad. Look at you in your fancy garb. What brings ye back to paradise?"

"Business, Clancy. You'll excuse me."

A hand caught his sleeve. "Come, Johnnie. Let's nip along to the Cradle and Coffin. The Maiden's divils should stick together, eh? Yer buyin'."

He and Clancy had run in the same filcher's gang for a few years. He was everything John had left behind. Pulling a shilling from his pocket, John said, "You start," and placed the coin in Clancy's palm. "I'll take care of me business and return to join you."

He stepped away, Clancy's rough voice following him. "A shil-lin'? After all this time? You cheap whore stabber. See you return or yer name will be—"

John turned the corner. Clancy's voice faded and sudden darkness took his eyesight. He halted. Soon he saw just another shit-strewn alley, from the gloom of which came the sound of some object being kicked, a stumble, a low curse. He moved faster on.

The way twisted, circled back, into a deeper darkness. Then there was an archway to his right. He heard a noise beyond it, ducked through and was in a courtyard, open to the sky, a well at its centre, lit by fleeting moonlight. And no one there.

He pulled out his blade and cudgel, then stood unmoving in the shadows near the archway. It was quiet. Had he taken a wrong turn?

Had Garnthorpe given him the slip? Should he go back? Then, as he was turning, he heard a sound. And even though it was not the person he was pursuing, he could not help but listen.

It was a child. A girl. She was singing, her voice thin and high:

Lavender's blue, dilly, dilly, lavender's green,
When I am king, dilly, dilly, you shall be queen.
Who told you so, dilly, dilly, who told you so?
'Twas my own heart, dilly, dilly, that told me so.

He'd sung this song in his childhood, not three alleys from here. He could not tell where in the yard it came from. The gloom did not help him, pierced only sometimes by the beams from that waxing moon, which revealed a broken wheel here, a cracked jug there, the entrance to a stairwell, the cloud-wrack swallowing everything again the next moment.

"Hallo?" His own voice echoed, but no reply came; only, after several of his heartbeats, a childish giggle.

He took a step, but the moonbeam he was following vanished, and he barked his shin on some wooden thing. He cursed; the giggle came again, not where she'd been, behind him now:

Lavender's green, dilly, dilly, lavender's blue,
If you love me, dilly, dilly . . . I . . . will . . . love . . . *you*!

She dragged the last words out, not singing them, whispering them. And at their conclusion she grunted in a way that did not sound like a girl at all.

"You," he called. "I've a groat for you here, sweets. For you and your pretty song."

Silence. Beyond the quiet courtyard, he could hear the roar of St. Giles, and especially the roars from within the Maidenhead Lane cockpit, with which perhaps this yard shared a wall. He had begun his cock-fighting career there. Perhaps he should go there now, to light, to people.

Then he heard the footfall. It came from the doorway straight ahead, suddenly gilded by silver as the clouds parted again. He heard a man muttering. There was fear in the voice and, hearing it, John's own vanished. I have stormed breaches, he thought. I have stood in a field while Cromwell's guns plucked the man from my left and the man from my right, vanished them as if snatched up by the hand of God. I have been so drenched in blood it looked like I was playing Fallen Satan in the *Mysteries*. What am I afraid of? An effete lord? In my streets?

"Sir," he called, "are you there?"

The only reply was the sound of footsteps on a stair. He followed, through the doorway, into a dark that deepened with the next flight down, total and thick about him. He halted on a landing—then had a thought and straightaway . . . *acted*.

"Sir," he called again, pitching his voice a little higher than his own. "It is Thomas Wright 'ere, sir. 'Eadborough of the parish. I could not 'elp but observe your worship, and 'ow's you must be lost. I come to offer assistance. To guide you from the dark."

He liked that last—religious folk such as Garnthorpe were always seeking the light. And he was immediately rewarded with a moan. Terror in it.

He thought that perhaps his eyes were accustoming to the gloom, noticed a little brightness ahead; looking up, he glimpsed star shine through a tumble of timbers. A man leaned against them. "Help me," the man whispered.

"Oh, but I will," answered John, reaching.

The blow came sudden. A fist caught John on the temple and he saw light then, a lot of it, all whirling. He crashed back into a wall, the man following his blow fast, hands reaching for his neck. Dazed though he was, John shot his own hands up and wide, knocking the other's aside, the diverted force bringing the man's face too close to make out his features—but near enough to strike him. So John did, with his forehead. But he couldn't lean far enough away with the wall behind him and did little more than tap the bridge of the other man's nose. Still, it was enough to send the man back a pace, which allowed John to bring his razor and cudgel up before him. "Now, you dog," he shouted, and lunged.

The other man met lunge with lunge, his own hands rising to seize John's wrists. Fingers like steel bars bore in. For a moment the two men stood locked, force meeting force, neither giving an inch. John knew how strong he himself was, a strength bred in alley scrap and battle. So he was surprised when, after a time, he began to give.

No! It was not possible, this lord, this soft man, pushing *him* back. He cried, bent his knees, surged. But the other took the surge, held it. And John felt his wrists weaken. He tried to jerk them clear of the man's grip so he could slash up, gut him as John had gutted others. There was no question now of merely cutting him as a warning. He could feel the man's intent. This had become a fight to the death.

But the grip did not slacken. Instead the razor was bent back, its edge rising toward John's left eye. He loosed his fingers, let the blade slip onto the stone floor—a noise suddenly bright amid all the dull grunts. Then it was the other who released, just John's one hand, the one that had held the cudgel. *Had* held it, for now the other man did. Held it and swung it and John Chalker got his guard up too late.

The hard wood drove into the side of his head. Immediately there was light again, a lot of it. It dwindled to black, the fading accompanied not by grunts but by a voice he'd heard earlier:

Lavender's green, dilly, dilly, lavender's blue,
If you love me, dilly, dilly, I . . . will . . . love . . . you.

Another voice then. A man's. And John's last thought as the darkness took him was that it did not sound like a noble lord's at all.

"That's right, Little Dot," the man said. "Sing for us."

Light brought him back. His gummed eyes were hard to open and he couldn't rub them clear because his hands were shackled high up on the wall to either side of him. He was slumped forward, agony searing his shoulders. Taking his weight on his feet, he stood.

"Praise be," came a voice. "I thought I might 'ave 'it you too 'ard."

A soft chuckle. Nausea swept John and he vomited. He felt the wet warmth on his chest then realized he was naked. That thought made him buck against the shackles, which did not shift. He yelled, long and loud.

The man waited for him to finish. "They won't 'ear ya. There's a cockpit next door and the bets are down. And this cellar's two below the one we met in. Even if a bat squeak comes through, well, who pays attention to a scream in St. Giles, eh?" The man laughed again. "You'd never get any sleep."

John managed to force his eyes open, sticky though they were with what had to be blood. A little light issued from a gated lantern placed on the stone floor. He could see the man before him, but only from the waist down. The man was wearing some sort of leather apron. He held John's razor.

Seeing it, John moaned.

"This?" the man said. "Oh, no fear, friend. I'm not going to use this on ya." He flipped the blade, caught it. "Fit only for murder in an alley, this. Like you planned."

"I didn't." John spat, clearing his mouth. "Who—who are you?"

The man put the razor down and picked up something else. "Nah," he said, "no such toys for me." When he turned back, he held a long-bladed knife, which he ran up and down his apron. "For I am Abel Strong. Butcher of this parish. And I takes pride in my work."

9

KNIGHT ERRANT

May 20, 1665

"No, Lucy! I cannot. No, no, no!"

As he stared at her, Coke damned himself yet again for being a fool. Why had he not simply sent the actress a note of farewell, together with a promise of some money, forwarded when he had it? No written plea could have moved him to come if forewarned that such a boon might be asked of him. Once he'd heard from Isaac ben Judah that his cousin was in York and would not return for near a week and so be unable to value the gemstones—warned by him also in the same note, and by the gunshot that had sent him scurrying, that some huge man was inquiring after them, a thief-taker, no doubt—he should not have forsaken his room at the Aldgate coaching inn, let alone have ventured here. But no, fool that he was, he'd called in—and been trapped, as he had so often before, by Lucy Absolute. Not by her charms, which he noted but was never moved by. Not by her tones, similar to his own, from the West.

But by those damned familiar eyes.

Though he wanted to, he could not look away from them now. It was not her fault that they were the exact same shape and colour as her brother's. That he saw Quentin in them now, as he never could in mere memory. The man he'd loved, in every way a person can love—as comrade, as friend and once, on the eve of a battle they were sure would kill them both, as a lover. Lying in a ditch, shivering under one blanket, the youths had sought warmth in each other's bodies, life in the face of death. He had never, not for a moment, regretted the encounter. Indeed, sometimes he felt it was the only meaningful one he'd had in his life.

One of them had been right about death. On Lansdown field, a little after dawn, case shot had scoured every feature from Quentin's face. But Lucy's eyes, the Absolute eyes, blue-black as night, acted for him as a key to a casement; once he looked into them, memory opened and her brother's face was clear before him, and the youth alive again in her. He had sworn to Quentin as he lay dying that he would look after his infant sister. Coke had kept his vow over the years, had tried to be brother and protector.

But this? "Lucy, I came to take my leave *of* you. Not to undertake a quest *for* you."

"Pish, William. It is hardly a quest. I ask only that you see this letter delivered into his hand."

"These days, the Earl of Rochester's hand is rarely far from the king's. For many reasons it is best I do not go so directly into the public gaze."

Those eyes, so familiar, brimmed. "You know I would not ask it if my need were not great."

And what of my need? he thought. I have thirty guineas on my head. How can I do this? For what? A mooncalf passion?

Then her tears overflowed—and suddenly he understood that this was not mere May Day foolishness. "Lucy, you are with child."

She did not confirm his statement in words. Simply lowered her eyes and wept.

"By Chroist!" he said, anger bringing Somerset into his voice. "By Chroist, I *will* see this earl. And I will drag him back by his ear and hold him by it until he does the right thing by you."

Anger drove him to the door, boots stamping, sword sheath slapping against his legs. But Lucy was quicker to the door and placed herself before it. "I entreat you, no! You must not tell my John this news."

"Tell him? I'll beat it into 'e, the puppy."

"William. Listen to me. Nay, listen, you ox!"

She slapped his chest and he was so startled he gave back a pace. There was fire, not tears in her eyes now, her accent moving west also, even farther so, to her Cornish roots. "If you go crashing in there like an outraged brother, you'll spoil everything, you downser. Everything!" She shoved him but then continued more restrainedly, "He loves me—I know he do. But does he love me enough for . . . ?" She gestured to her belly. "That I do not know. And will not, unless *I* am the one to tell him."

"Lucy!"

"Nay, do not say it. Sarah Chalker has cautioned me enough: 'He is an earl. He will not, cannot, marry you.' That may be." She sniffed. "But if he loves me, truly loves me, then perhaps he will do right by me. Me and the baby." She wiped her tears away. "Yet I will only be certain of his love, or his lack of it, if I am the one to tell him first—for only then will I see the answer in his eyes." She held out her letter. "This merely beseeches him to come. Will you risk a little to put it into his hand? And vow—vow, I say!—that when you do, you will hint at nothing more?"

He looked down at her, at her brother through her. He had made him a promise. If he fled abroad, as he almost certainly must, this might be the last time he could honour that promise, for a time at least. He sighed and accepted the letter. "Content ye, lass. I will."

"Oh, Will!" She stood on tiptoe, grabbed him by the ears and kissed him full on the lips. "Now, if only you was twenty years younger. Heigh ho for a heart, eh?" Laughing, she twirled away.

He waved the letter at her. "There is still the matter of how I deliver this. If he is with the king, where is His Majesty?" He ran thumb and finger either side of his moustache. "And how can I approach without some kind of concealment?" He had not told her of Finchley, the pamphlet, the reward. Yet she was the only one in London who knew of his other life.

"I have taken care of that. At least, I can put you close to him." She bent to her table, picked up another folded paper. "I have been to see His Majesty's surgeon, Mr. Knight, at the sign of the Hare in Covent Garden."

He frowned. "Who are you—my Lady Castlemaine, with a brood of kingly brats—that you can afford such royal fees for your pregnancy?"

She laughed. "You simpleton. I did not go to consult. I went to get this. It is Mr. Knight's office that issues these invitations." She offered the paper. "His Majesty touches for the king's evil tomorrow at the Banqueting House. The Earl of Rochester never misses it. Says there is no better sport in town than watching the king's face while the scrofulous bend to kiss the royal arse—sorry, hand!"

She giggled, as Coke gaped. All knew of this "touching." Many hundreds would line up in the belief that such direct contact with the king would cure their various ailments, not just the scrofula that plagued so many. "Lucy, for mercy's sake. You know that I am trying to keep from view until a certain business is concluded. Yet you would send me to the most public place imaginable?"

"Aye. Where Rochester will be," she replied, waving the note. "Besides, don't you always say that the finest place to hide is in plain sight?"

"When I am drunk, I may say so," he said, reluctantly taking the paper. However, a rhythmic tapping at the door prevented further argument

"'Tis Sarah," Lucy said. "I know her by her knock."

As she heard Lucy approach the door, Sarah leaned her head against it and closed her eyes. So tired! Three nights with almost no sleep. She had searched for her husband all day when she was not playing, and each evening until darkness made the streets too dangerous. Three days he had been missing; and though he had on occasion stayed away a night and not sent word, he had never stayed away two. Anger drove her the first day—if he did not attend the theatre, to rehearse and to play, he would soon be replaced. Davenant, the manager of the playhouse, liked John, but he was a man of business as well as the theatre. Yet when Sarah's search of the usual haunts revealed not a trace of him, anger gave way to fear. Much could befall a man on London's streets, even one as capable as John Chalker. She felt fear for herself too—she only survived the way she did, as an actress unbeholden to anyone, under his protection.

As she leaned against the door, she searched for him with her other senses, inherited from her mother, who'd had them from hers. Yesterday she had burned paper with Hebrew words written on it, chanting them as she did. She had sought her husband in coffee grounds and in water poured onto a concave mirror. Now she simply looked out into the world through her closed eyes. She hoped that it was her mother's other sight and not her fear that had him living still. Alive and indeed not far away. But where was he?

The opening door caused her to stumble. "Oh, my dear," she began, then stopped when she saw that Lucy was not alone. A tall man was with her. He had long black hair—his own—curling onto wide shoulders, silver wound through it like filigree. He had grey eyes and a moustache, mainly black, which he was smoothing down with thumb and forefinger. His clothes were simple, dark, well made if not of the latest fashion, yet not so very far behind it that he would stand out. He held an uncocked, unadorned hat in one hand, his other resting on the pommel of a sword. Boots that rose to his knee appeared long worn.

"Sarah, you poor child, come in. Oh, and you must meet my Captain Coke."

The man bowed, his hat going to the side in a gesture somewhat older than the age demanded. "Mrs. Chalker. I have the advantage of you for I have seen you many times upon the stage. I am a great admirer."

"You are gracious, sir, and have not much advantage. For are you not the guardian Lucy talks so fondly of?"

"No guardian," Lucy said, "but a friend. To my poor dead brother first and now to me." Lucy took Sarah's hand. "My dear, you look exhausted. Come sit. I will fetch you some cordial. What's the news?"

Sarah regarded the captain. She did not want to discuss this business before a stranger, however dear to Lucy. So she settled for the common news. "I've been in St. Giles. There're more red crosses than last week. Three more houses shut up with all their occupants on Brewer's Lane."

"Fie, sister," replied Lucy, pouring out a glass, carrying it to Sarah. "I heard that the bills of mortality note only three dead of the plague in the whole City during April, and probably not many more in May. Did you not recently observe, William, that every year a few die of the plague?"

"I did." He thought of the house he'd fled the week before. He had walked past it yesterday and it was boarded, his former neighbours, who had not been swift enough to escape, now trapped within, hanging from the barred windows, begging for extra food from the constables. "Though I fear the contagion may be a trifle worse this year."

"Trifle?" Lucy replied. "Pah! I do not think even so much. Besides, that was not the news I was after. What of your husband?"

"I am sure the captain does not want—"

"Nonsense." Lucy seized Sarah's hand. "My friend here is seeking her husband, William. You must know him—John Chalker, our fellow player. Missing these three days. Could you not help her seek him?"

"Child, you cannot ask a stranger to undertake such a thing."

Lucy continued over Sarah's protests, "You said, sir, that you could not leave for a few days. And you know that there are places where a woman cannot easily go alone." She turned. "Besides, my dear, William is no stranger. He is my most especial friend." She leaped up and, while retaining Sarah's hand, grabbed Coke's. "And so he should be yours."

Sarah went to speak again, but it was the captain who now interrupted Lucy—after he laughed. "Mrs. Chalker, it seems that today I am able to deny Mistress Absolute precisely nothing. Only now I have agreed to undertake another quest on her behalf. Indeed, business will delay me in town a few days more. And she is also correct. There are some who are persuaded to talk more readily to a man than a woman."

"Persuaded—exactly!" agreed Lucy.

"Do you believe your husband will most likely be found within the boundaries of St. Giles in the Fields, since that is where you recently were?"

"I cannot say why, sir, but yes, I sense that he is."

"Then let me inquire of some people I know there. And since I have indeed seen John Chalker perform upon that same stage where I have so enjoyed you, I believe I would recognize him, or could describe him." He held up his hand. "Mrs. Chalker, I promise nothing. Except that in the little time I have, I will try."

Sarah opened her mouth to protest again but then closed it. She was desperate. She knew she needed both sleep and help. "I am most grateful, sir."

"Yes, thank you, dearest William," said Lucy. "If Sarah were not present, I would kiss you again."

"Dear heart, I live in the theatre. I have seen everything."

They all laughed. All stopped as suddenly. "I'll take my leave. Ladies." Tucking both Lucy's letter and the invitation to the king's touching into a pocket within his cloak, Coke bowed and left.

For a moment, the two actresses gazed at each other in silence. Lucy, as ever, broke it. "Did you like my captain?" she asked.

"I did. His eyes . . ."

"A unique grey, are they not?"

"They are, but it was not that." Sarah stared above her friend. "There is such pain in them."

"Only you would look beyond their beauty," Lucy chided. "But he has seen things, I know, that he would prefer not to have seen. And like many in the late, deplored wars, he lost land, family, fortune. Love. There was a lady in Bristol, I believe, who died of this same plague. And my brother, whom he also loved." She faltered. "Perhaps he will find your lost love."

"I pray God he may."

"Amen."

Then for a while even Lucy was silent, and the two friends sat and held each other's hands.

On reaching the street, the captain whistled. Dickon hopped out of a doorway.

"Guts!" he yelled, pointing out the word in that same foul pamphlet.

"Indeed. Now, put that away and come."

Coke headed for a tavern he liked hard by, the Seven Stars. As he walked, he cursed himself again for a fool.

Dickon, gambolling along, grinned up at him. He never minds owning his moonstruck state, Coke thought, whereas I? Oh, I am always so sure. Incur few risks and so keep my neck from the noose. Yet here am I agreeing to go into the court like some knight errant from a romance on behalf of his wronged lady. And after that, to go into the gutters of St. Giles—it took me two weeks to remove the stench the last time I ventured there—to chase down a man who probably has all good reason to be gone. And why? For eyes. For two pairs of eyes.

He shook his head. Lucy's eyes would always coerce him because of her brother. But Mrs. Chalker's? Which ghost did he see in their exquisite blue? Evanline? Nay, her eyes were green. No ghost at all, then?

Fool indeed. The very same one who as a youth had strapped on his father's sword and marched whistling off to a war that would take everything from him.

But oh, what eyes! Should have introduced myself beyond my old rank. I would she did not "Captain" me.

A few more steps and he paused with his hand on the door of the Seven Stars. Tomorrow he must go to the Banqueting House and "hide in plain sight." But how? Could he develop overnight the tuberous neck of the scrofulous? Paint a rash all over his back?

Dickon was before the tavern window, making faces at himself in the thick glass and spitting peanut husks at his reflection. The boy looked up at his captain, crossed his eyes. Studying him, a thought came to Coke.

Does this king also cure the lunatic?

10

THE KING'S EVIL

War had offered many sights to William Coke's eyes. Most, terrible.
A few, amusing. There had been a soldier in Sir Bevil Grenville's
Regiment of Foote, a Devonian by the name of Bulstrode. A pas-
sionate morris man, he had come to believe that it was the magic
of the dance that kept him safe. Well, some men wore amulets
with Greek or Hebrew letters upon 'em; some, dried lizard or toad
skins; others, half a dozen Bibles under their breastplates like
extra sheets of armour. Bulstrode danced. Laid down his pike,
picked up his jangling belled staff, wound his whole body with red
ribbon and capered before the ranks. The priests didn't like it,
because he usually did so after prayers but before battle, and they
felt it took men's minds from God's awful majesty and their duty
to him and their king. His comrades loved it, and many joined in,
especially as he survived battle, skirmish and fight, and ever in
the forefront. It was said that Waller's regiment, their constant
foes and rivals in the army of Parliament, would jostle to watch

Bulstrode before a clash, to the despair of their Puritan chaplains, even stricter than the king's; said too that their musketeers would aim away from him. He'd disappeared after the second battle at Newbury, but since no one saw his corpse—though many went unnoted into the mass pits—it was believed he had simply gone home, as many had. Or was now dancing for the devil—and making him laugh.

The man Coke saw as he and Dickon walked down the Strand toward the Banqueting House and the king's evil reminded him somehow of Bulstrode. At least, for a moment.

Dickon heard it first and stopped. "Wha-what's that?"

"What?" replied Coke, wanting to hasten on. Until he heard the sounds too: whips cracking, the frantic neigh of a horse. Glancing back, he saw a blockage where the roads met at Charing Cross. "Two hackney drivers fighting for the right of way is all. Come on!"

But Dickon did not move. "L-look."

Irritated, Coke turned again—and stared like his ward.

One of the coaches was now heading fast toward them, its driver standing on his box, whip in hand, flicking the metalled tip between his lead horses' ears with a crack like gunshot. And he was as naked as Adam before the Fall—more so, if the paintings were to be believed, with not a fig leaf to be seen. The only covering he had—which did not cover the essentials—were the reins wound about his body like Bulstrode's ribbons. He was laughing too, as the morris man had, while yelling words that became distinguishable as he sped closer.

"Flay me!" he screamed. "My skin! Rip it off!"

The coach skittered back and forth across the roadway. An elderly man and woman leaned out of the coach's flapping doorway, both shrieking. Coke and Dickon gaped—until the captain realized just how fast the vehicle was moving and dove back against a storefront, yanking his ward with him.

The vehicle passed within a yard of them. Swung back across the roadway, smashed into a stall; combs, fans and inkhorns flew up. The driver yelled, "All them bastards, burn!" just before the coach's right wheel got stuck and then ripped off. The body of the carriage flipped, slid for a dozen paces roof down, flipped again. Somehow the central bar sheared, slashing the traces, and the four horses, still yoked but free of their toil, galloped away.

Long moments passed before sound returned to normal. Dazed, Coke stood, took a wobbly step forward, followed by firmer ones. In a moment he and Dickon were running. They were the first to reach the wreckage, and Coke crouched to peer inside.

The old man he'd glimpsed was upside down in a corner, his neck bent at an impossible angle. His eyes were open but glazing. The woman was lying on her side, her face twisted in pain. Coke had just moved back to see if he could open the wreckage of the door, when a voice shouted near him.

"He lives! By Christ's mercy, help here, for he lives!"

Others arrived. One, a woman of middling years, cradling what had to be a broken arm, cried, "Mama!" and pushed past, while a younger man attempted to pry open the crumpled door.

The driver was alive, though how Coke could not reckon. "Water," the man cried. "Water for my head. It's filled with hellfire." They were spared the full extent of his nakedness, for the box of the coach had snapped off and wedged him in at the waist. Jagged splinters pierced his chest and back, blood oozing from a dozen wounds. As Coke bent to help pry him from the wreckage, the man's eyes, which had remained open, fixed on his. A hand grasped. "Put out the fire," he beseeched. "Put it out!"

Mercifully he fainted. The man beside Coke, who was trying to unwind the leather reins cut deep into the flesh, suddenly ceased and hissed, "What's that . . . ?"

Coke followed the pointing finger—and saw in the driver's armpit what looked like a black tennis ball thrusting from the flesh there.

"Is that?" the man said, drawing back his hand.

Coke rose, took Dickon's shoulder, began to shove him through the gathering mob. Yet before they reached the rear of it, that same man shouted, "Plague! He's got the plague!" Instantly handkerchiefs, sleeves, hats were thrust before faces, and people began to run—so did the captain and his ward. The pleading cries for help from the daughter with the broken arm, followed them a-ways, yet Coke only slowed to a fast walk. He pitied the lady, but he had undertaken to help two other women this day and that was enough for any man.

The road to Whitehall was busy. Within a few score paces, they passed from those who had seen, to those who had heard a little to those who strolled oblivious. Soon, the columned front of the Banqueting House was close, as was a line of people waiting before it. As a bell tolled ten, they joined that line, not needing to ask its purpose: the collection of the lame, the scabbed and most especially the scrofulous, with their goitres large and small, showed the line's purpose. Coke and Dickon were perhaps thirty back from the first, who stood directly before the doors. An hour to wait before they were admitted . . . and then? He had no plan beyond getting inside and delivering Lucy's letter to Rochester. He'd heard, though, that once the king touched the people, they waited and returned to have a gold token on a ribbon hung over their necks. In the interim between these two events, he assumed his chance would come.

People filled in behind them, chattering excitedly—or gibbering, depending on their state. All clutched the same paper invitation that Lucy had given him. Occasionally the king's guards walked down the line in pairs. He assumed they were looking for threats to His Majesty, and as he stood out because he was a head taller than most there and visibly healthier, when the guards drew near, he would crouch and fuss Dickon. The boy needed little to set him off in jerks and giggles. He writhed and drooled, and the guards must have taken his tall companion for attendee on the sick, as many in the line were, for they walked on.

I do not know why they fear, thought Coke, after another scrutiny. The English, unlike the French, Dutch, Germans or Turks, do not assassinate their kings. They kill them in public. In battle. Or right here.

When eleven sounded and the line began to shift, he considered. In front of these columns, they took his head, the king in whose cause I gave all I had.

He'd been in Holland when he'd heard. Those around him had wept, for they were Royalist exiles all. He had not. That well, he'd discovered, had long run dry.

"Bl-bl-blood!" exclaimed Dickon, pointing. Coke looked at the stains on the pavement. Could it be his late master's blood? Would not sixteen years of London rains have washed away all trace, howsoever royal?

They were now passing the street traders, many of whom had vials they claimed held that same regal fluid, collected that sad day; still others sold small sheaves of mouse-grey monarch's hair, bound in thread. Since some were bought even now, and so replaced, Coke assumed that Charles, the first of that name, must have had gallons of blood in his veins, and hair enough to furnish the city's thousand *perruqiers*. And since many thought Charles a saint, that miracle might be possible, like loaves and fishes.

The line shuffled through the gates and into the small yard, thence up the stairs into the Banqueting House itself. When he entered, Coke looked up first. He'd heard the ceiling was magnificent, and it was. An artist he'd admired in Holland had painted it, Rubens. He'd depicted the martyred king's father, James I, ascending to heaven; whither his decapitated son soon followed, the captain presumed.

So the father, the son—and now for the son's son. He lowered his eyes and gazed upon his monarch.

The room was not enormous and he could see him clear, knew his face anyway from closer studies. On the walls of Worcester and the eve of battle, they'd shared a bottle of Rhenish wine and talked of Spanish women. Five years later, in Antwerp, Charles had come to borrow money from the Jew whom Coke warded with his sword. That second time of meeting, he had stood by, silent, head bowed. If young Charles had found out Coke was English, he would have tried to borrow money from him too, such was the impoverishment of his exile.

He had seen him only once since his restoration, when Coke was among a crowd of returned cavaliers who petitioned the new king to restore to them their family lands, mortgaged for his cause. Charles had listened carefully, suffered obviously, and refused all but a very, very few—of whom Coke was not one. The captain knew why the king had done so. After the turmoil of twenty years, he wanted a settled land to rule over, a chance to refill the nation's treasury. He would not do that by taking land from those who had acquired it in legal purchase, no matter that it was for him and his father that so much had been given up.

No, thought Coke, taking a step nearer. I did not blame him. I do not now. I merely took the sole course left to a man with an education largely confined to blades and black powder.

At his side, Dickon, who'd been much taken with the surroundings and vocally intrigued with all the ailments manifested, was now staring to the dais ahead in open-mouthed wonder. At either end of it, two priests intoned the words for this ritual from the Book of Common Prayer. One held a bowl of water, the other a towel. In the middle of the dais was the third man, the centre of it all—indeed, the very centre of the realm.

If Coke had expected a weary reluctance, mere duty exercised, he was wrong. Charles did not just dismiss his supplicants with a brush of fingertips and averted eyes; he bent, whispered, *laid on* his hands like any healer in the slums. The scale of sickness did not deter him. Faces that disease had half rotted away, goitres with the circumference of wheels and the tautness of drums, the lame, the expectorant, the blind, all received the same royal care: both hands placed on the worst of wounds, a head lowered to an ear, a murmured phrase of comfort. It had an effect too: people left the dais weeping with joy, laughing, limps diminished and faces, however disfigured, held higher in hope. Yet the nearer Coke got, the more clearly he saw that the exchange was not one way. Charles's eyes were as ecstatic. He was a torch, bearing flame, and for the first time Coke wondered whether the king's touch might not indeed calm some of his ward's worse excesses.

The line proceeded slowly, until the captain and Dickon, his jerks already diminished by atmosphere and awe, mounted the last, small stair and paused at the top. Coke had no desire to be recognized, though he was sure Charles, with the thousands that he had met, would not remember him. Still, to distract all attention from himself, he bent swiftly and, while pretending to mouth calming words, dug his fingers into the boy's armpit.

Dickon exploded. "G-g-go!" he yelped, squirming sideways. Coke took a firm hold with one hand, removed his hat with the other; then, keeping his eyes and voice low, and returning to his accent of the West, beseeched, "This is my son, Majesty. Will y'elp him?"

"I will."

The king's attention was off him now, so Coke could watch as Charles reached hands to either side of Dickon's head. At first the boy shied, like a horse when something comes sudden at it; but soft words gentled him. His tongue withdrew, his eyes centred, he looked up into the dark gaze growing closer. "By the power that comes from our saviour Jesus, and only through his love, I ask that you be healed." The hands clasped, and Dickon, who usually hated to be held by any but his captain, stilled entirely. His eyes closed, his knees weakened and, for a few seconds, only a monarch's grip held him up. When Coke stepped in and took the boy's arm, he felt instant heat, like fire transferred through metal. He looked up. Monarch and highwayman regarded each other for a long moment. Then Coke saw those dark eyes narrow, as if the king sought a memory. So he pulled Dickon, meek as a calf now, gently clear of the royal grasp and down the side stairs to where a second line had formed, twisting around a roped-off area.

When he'd entered the hall, Coke had noted another group of men on the deep dais. Priests and guards had obscured them from the front, but here at the side he could see them more clearly—and soon spotted his quarry. The Earl of Rochester had been pointed out to him at the Drury Lane playhouse a few months previously, as the new man in town, the latest favourite. And there the puppy was. Today John Wilmot wore peach petticoat breeches, held up God only knew how, as they seemed to dangle untied and well below the hip, pulled down farther by a mass of multi-hued ribbon. His scarlet doublet was short, with a yard of canary linen puffing out of the gap at the waist.

The youth was just the sort of gaudy popinjay to catch a girl's eye—and more. And he was within earshot, the end of the dais being half a dozen paces to the roped pen where supplicants awaited their second approach to the king and their gold token. Giving up his place in line to the person who'd limped after them, Coke drew Dickon across.

"My Lord of Rochester," he called, not soft, not loud.

His was one voice among a multitude of intoning priests, chattering ill, gossiping courtiers. Rochester, amused in a conversation with Sir Charles Sedley—Coke knew him as another of the gadflies who hovered around the king—did not notice him. But one of the king's guards farther along the rope did. "Oy," he said, coming closer, his metal-shod pike tapping the floor, "don't bother your betters."

Coke ignored him. "Lord Rochester," he called louder, and this time the eyes, with lashes like heavy veils, flicked to him. "My lord, I bring you a letter—"

"What did I just say?"

The guard jabbed the butt end into Coke's ribs. Pushing the weapon aside, Coke finished his sentence. "From Mrs. Absolute."

The name got attention, if not from Rochester. "A billet-doux, by God," chortled Charles Sedley. "Isn't Absolute the name of that actress with the sumptuous tits? The one you've been tupping, Johnnie?"

"It is," said another of the group, "so perhaps not so much a billet-doux as a bill." He laughed. "Fellow looks like he could be her pimp."

The pike was now placed slantways across Coke's chest. "Do you know this man, me lord?" the guard asked.

At last, Rochester spoke. "I do not. Nor—" he hesitated for a moment "—nor this woman he names." He turned away. "Now, as I was saying, Charlie, the wager."

"Sir!" Coke called, pressing against the rope.

But the pike shaft, pushed hard against his chest, halted him. "You desist, my lad," said the guard, "or I'll throw you out. Then your idiot son won't get his token."

Dickon heard the insult and his eyes narrowed. He'd been known to fly at people who abused either him or his guardian. He also had the courage of a lion. The captain felt his own ready anger come; but he held it in and stepped away from the rope, pulling the boy with him. Keeping a firm hold, he moved out of the guard's sight. He waited, and as the pen filled with the ecstatic in a jostling line, he made sure he always shifted to the rear of it, with people ever ready to go before them.

At last, the healing was over. The final phase of the ceremony began. Holding on to Dickon, Coke moved slowly nearer. Finally, the last to do so, they climbed the small stair and stood again before the king.

He beamed at them, obviously relieved to be done. Behind him, the two priests waited with the bowl of water and the towel, while his courtiers jostled, eager to be away and about some other sport. "So, sir," said Charles, holding up by its azure ribbon the gold coin with his image upon it, "have I helped your son?"

Dickon was growling, glaring behind him at the guard who'd insulted him—and completely ignoring the king. "As you see," replied Coke.

The dark eyes narrowed at the terse reply. "Well, sir. I am better with physical ills. I never claimed the power of our Lord to cast out devils."

"That is obvious. Since you keep so many about you."

The words were not loudly spoken, yet all must have heard them, for even the gossips behind the king fell suddenly silent. The guard stepped upon the stair. Dickon's growling grew still louder.

"What do you mean, sir, hah?" Charles's one eye with the cast in it remained glazed. The pupil in his other eye contracted. "Are you some disgruntled Parliament man come here to insult us?"

"No, Sire. I fought for your cause and gave up much for it."

Charles leaned closer. "Do I know you?"

"*I* do." It was Charles Sedley who spoke. "This is the pander who just now tried to present our Johnnie with some buttock's bill."

"I am no pander, sir. And you should consider when you speak ill of a lady you clearly do not know."

He accompanied this with the lightest touch of fingers at his left hip. No sword hung there—none was allowed into the royal presence—but the implication was clear, and the guard grabbed his arm. Coke felt Dickon about to leap, so wrapped an arm around him. The boy wriggled but was held. Other guards moved swiftly closer.

"Stop! All of you!" the king commanded. Movement ceased. He pointed at the guard. "Unhand him." The man did and he continued, "And you, sirrah, tell me what you mean by this. To which lady do you refer?"

"*He* knows." Coke nodded at the man at Sedley's shoulder.

With the king's regard upon him, Rochester flushed the same colour as his scarlet doublet and muttered, "I think I do remember now. There is a lady. A woman. Ah, an actress."

"A whore," interjected Sedley.

"Sir Charles!" the king barked. "Since this woman, whatever her profession, is important to this gallant here, you insult her at your peril. And it is my wrath I am talking about, not his." He turned back. "What is this lady to you, sir?"

"Her brother was dear to me. Died in my arms, and in your father's cause, on Lansdown field. I promised I would watch over her and I have."

"I see." The king studied him a moment. "And what do you believe this earl is to her?"

For a moment, Coke wanted to blurt out the truth. Shame Rochester before the court—though how much shame would it be when the monarch's own bastards abounded, some also gotten on actresses? Yet he had his vow to Lucy. She must be the one to tell the man and see her fate in his eyes. So he swallowed, then brought her letter from his cloak. "I believe nothing, sir. I am simply a messenger."

He held out the letter. No one moved—until the king did. "Well, if you will not take it from him, you will from me." Charles snatched the paper. "Come, sir!" The earl accepted it. "Now, read!"

All watched as the earl broke the seal. His colour lightened as he read. "It is . . . it is only a summons."

"Is it?" The king tipped his head. "One you will answer. Yes?" At the earl's slight nod, Charles turned back. "Will that satisfy you, Captain?" When Coke started, he smiled. "Yes. Can't place where or when, but I remember you. And you have a captain's bearing."

Coke nodded. "'Twas at Worcester, sire. On the eve of battle. I had a bottle of Rhenish you were gracious enough to share."

Charles laughed. "Greedy enough to cadge, more like. I had precious little liquor of my own that night so I had to steal it from my soldiers. And your name?"

God's eyelids, thought the captain. He considered making one up. But His Majesty would probably remember his real one before long. "William Coke, Sire," he said, bowing. "Ever at your service."

"Cock!" yelled Charles Sedley, lurching forward again. "And a captain? Perhaps he's the Monstrous Cock whose story so diverted us at breakfast. The bloody butcher of Tally Ho!"

Coke closed his eyes. It was the king who spoke. "Don't be more of a fucking idiot than God and inbreeding have made you, Sedley. A murderous highwayman would hardly come to stand before his monarch on this occasion." He turned back. "I apologize for my drunken friend. Youth cannot hold it like us old soldiers, eh? As for my devil—" he gestured to John Wilmot, who was again reading the letter "—I will see he answers the summons. But now, sir, would you care to join us and let me repay the Rhenish I stole from you that night? I would like to hear your story."

That was the last thing Coke wanted. One could only hide in plain sight if one didn't stay in it too long. "Majesty," he began, without knowing what excuse he could give.

And then he was spared the need.

"The evil takes me! Cure me! Cure me!"

The shouting sounded from the doors, followed by the smack of wood striking wood. A tall man was charging into the hall. Whip-staff in hand, he had used it to strike down one guardsman's pike, ducked under a second's swing and now rushed toward the dais.

It was the driver from the coach crash. Still completely naked, though he appeared to have on apparel as scarlet as Rochester's, so covered in blood was he. How he was alive, Coke could not guess, but he had seen men in the wars walking around for three days with their guts in their hands.

He came on, shrieking. The guard who had held Coke descended the stair, pike at port. But the man didn't even attempt to fight. He dropped straight onto the wooden floor, using the velocity of his run and a body slick with his own blood to slide under the guard and right up to the base of the stairs. Then he was up and before them.

"Heal me!" he shouted, reaching up for the king, the buboes pregnant and all too vividly black under each armpit.

But Coke was between them. Shoving Dickon to the side, bending at the knee, he drove the heel of his hand sharp up. He hit the man under his chin, knocking him back and down. The coach driver fell hard, a last cry exhaled on a rush of air.

"Touch me," he wheezed, and closed his eyes.

Then guards were everywhere. Shod pike hafts driven down, kicks flying in to subdue. Coke suspected that they were unnecessary, that the man was already dead, though whether by plague, blows or blood loss he could not know and did not stay to verify. The dais was now a mass of soldiers, priests and courtiers, the king lost among them. Taking his chance, Coke seized Dickon's hand and fled.

11

FINDERS AND KEEPERS

May 22, 1665

As the church bell tolled noon, he heard the cry.

"Ass's milch! Fresh from the teat! Sweet as honey!"

Pitman rose. His son would arrive soon, and Josiah hated the small beer in this alehouse, which was sourer than most. Indeed, the whole place stank, the rushes on the floor unchanged in months, clogged with scraps of food thrown down and the street filth customers' boots had brought in. The alehouse's location was its only recommendation: almost opposite the goldsmith shop of Mr. ben Judah, with glass that could be seen through if eyes were not too far removed from it, thick enough so that the shape of the watcher would be but vague from across the pavement, let alone the whole street.

He would buy both himself and his son ass's milch. And he would take some back to Bettina. Emptying the remnants of the pint he'd been nursing to further sweeten the floor, then scooping up another tankard that had not been collected, he went outside. The landlord, a thin, scabby-faced fellow, grunted at him. Pitman may not have been a high-spending customer, but he was a steady one, having been there every day for five days now. And in the few hours when he was not, his son was.

He waited till a larger group was passing, stooped into it, followed the ass and its owner to the corner. There, with one eye still on the Jew's front door—the shop had not a back, he knew from exploration; its rear wall conjoined with another—he delayed the milch man and offered his tankards for filling. The man set up his stool, took the teats, squirted expertly into the vessels held between his knees. When one was full, Pitman drank it off, returned it for refilling. The milch ass let out a mournful bellow and flicked its tail, before returning its patient gaze ahead.

As the second vessel filled, Josiah came up. "Here, lad," Pitman said, handing over a mug brimming white. The boy slurped, but after a few big gulps, his father pulled his hand away from his mouth. "Save it," he said. "The new barrel of beer's even fouler than the last. Buy a pint of it later, but nurse the milk."

He gave the boy some of the metal tokens that passed for coins— few of the local shopkeepers had much small change, so short was its supply—and watched Josiah till he disappeared inside the alehouse. Then Pitman went down Love Lane and cut across some alleys to avoid passing the storefront, yawning widely. Ever since the Jew had fired that gun over him he'd watched the shop, from an hour before the goldsmith opened at seven till five in the afternoon when he closed. Josiah stayed for a couple of hours more, in case Mr. ben Judah—and more importantly, their quarry—returned. It allowed Pitman to attend to his parish duties as constable, till nightfall.

He frowned, thinking about those duties now. Only last night the first case of plague in the parish had been discovered in a house three streets over from his own on Cock Alley. With two other constables he had shut up the two families who lived there, hammering planks across windows, bolting the doors on the outside, daubing "Lord have mercy on us" in red upon one exterior wall. The wails of those within had been terrible, and indeed, to close up the sick with the well seemed a harsh thing. But the law was the law, and he saw the sense of it. Keep the plague in that one house and with God's mercy it would not spread farther . . . to his own dwelling in Cock Alley.

And if it did? Well, if his fortune held, he might soon have enough coin to move his family away from the City altogether. A few weeks with his wife's brothers in Kent, while the whole thing passed over, might not be too bad.

If his fortune held. Good fortune indeed, or rather God's blessing, to have spotted O'Toole, the second of Coke's accomplices in the Hounslow robbery, staggering from a tavern in Whitefriars, so drunk he could barely run and certainly incapable of fighting. He had not been able to tell much more of Coke than Maclean had, having not seen the captain since their joint endeavours. But the five guineas Pitman had collected for depositing O'Toole at Newgate, where he now awaited his short trial and even shorter rope dance, had enabled this watch to be tolerable and had bought his family some food and fuel for the nonce.

He looked down at the jiggling white of the milk's surface. Bettina would be pleased. More so, if Josiah sent word by a street urchin that Coke was in the shop, or followed him if he swiftly left. He'd trained his boy well in those skills. Once the murderer's lair was found, Pitman would be there in minutes and had hopes that the taking would be easy.

Still . . . Pitman shook his head. A vision of the interior of the carriage had returned. Someone who slaughtered like that? Who daubed the numbers for apocalyptic verses on the wall in victims' blood? That man would *not* come easily. For he was no longer a man. He was a monster.

Pitman spilled a little milk, cursed himself for his clumsiness. Yet he knew he would not be clumsy in this: he would be ready for Captain Cock, however he found him.

"'I am become, as it were, a monster unto many,'" he murmured, but for once the psalm did not calm him.

So he gripped his cudgel a little tighter.

"Monster," he whispered.

John Chalker dangled from the manacles, his hands high above him. Both shoulders were dislocated, but that had become a lesser pain among the many, many others. There was some relief in the unconsciousness into which he was slipping more and more, though nightmares always arrived fast. He'd had them since the wars. Yet all the horrors he saw in his sleep were as nothing compared to those when he woke. And what always woke him swiftest was the sound of footsteps upon the cellar stair. As now.

He had managed to rub the silk scarf again from his mouth. He could breathe easier through his mouth than through his smashed nose. Half the time he'd thought he'd drown in his own blood. Many times he'd prayed that he would.

When Abel Strong had discovered John, scarf out and screaming, he had cut out his tongue. He had laughed when he put the scarf back, knowing how useless it now was. But, for a brief moment, John had sensed perhaps some concern from this tormentor he could not see through the blindfold. For dangling there he had heard something—faint cries from the cockpit nearby, conveyed underground along some channel, through some crumbled brick. If he heard the gamblers, then maybe in their rare silences they might hear him. Maybe Clancy would come to collect that drink.

He hadn't heard them again after the butcher took his ears.

The footsteps stopped. His blindfold was jerked off. The flame within the gated lantern was low but still hurt his eyes, especially the one missing the eyelid. He could not see the face of his torturer beyond the little light; had never seen him, had only heard his voice, felt his attentions. Still, he would not look down. Since he knew he was dying, all John Chalker had left was defiance.

The lantern, its metal heated, was brought close enough to elicit instant pain to all the places he had been burned. "Well, you are a carcass and no mistake. Fresh meat, eh? Nothin' like it." The man sniffed. "She was very happy, Little Dot, with the stew I made. 'They don't look like pig's ears, Mr. Strong,' she says, when I flung 'em in the pot. 'Oh, but they is,' I replies. 'A right porker they comes from.'"

His lamp went lower. Chalker winced as heat neared his groin. "What I don't understand is 'ow you is a Christian, when I'd heard your wife was a Jewess."

John had guessed that his tormentor must work for Garnthorpe, the man who had led him into this trap. And Sarah had said that when Garnthorpe accosted her, he'd asked if she was Jewish. So this confirmed John's guess. Anger surged, and if he could no longer defend his wife from his lordship, at least he could defy the man's minion.

As the lamp rose again, he collected all the caked blood and broken teeth in his mouth and spat them full into what he hoped was the other's face. There was a satisfying cry. The butcher staggered back, the light swinging high to the ceiling. John waited for the punishment that would come, hoping he had done enough to provoke a violence that would end his agony. But he heard only the sounds of the lantern being placed on the floor, then wiping. Finally, a laugh.

"Well. Lucky I was wearing my apron, eh?"

John's chin was forced up. "As I was sayin', my friend doesn't like the idea that the woman he admires married out of her faith. Wants you, 'er husband—her *first* husband—to belong to 'er tribe." He sniffed. "Can't be formal about the ceremony. Don't know the words. But perhaps—" and here he reached down and took John's cock in his hand "—perhaps we can make you one of them in another way."

He released him. The lamp spill came halfway up the blood-ied leather apron, and through his one ever-open eye, John could see the man's hand dip into his pouch. He tensed, waiting to see what new horror would be drawn from it. And when he saw his own razor, the one he'd planned to use to mark Lord Garnthorpe, he could not hold back his moan.

"That's right," Abel Strong said, "I've finally found a use for your little tool."

Dipping her quill, Sarah wrote the third of the locations on its own piece of paper. She lifted it, blew lightly and, once sure the ink was dry, rolled it and placed it beside the other two. Then she mixed up the papers, looked again. The three tiny scrolls, no longer than her little finger, were identical. She could not know which had which name upon it.

She took the first of them and pushed it into the hollow end of their lodging's large door key. Then she inserted the key in her Bible. The quote it touched from Matthew had seemed suitable: "Again the kingdom of heaven is like unto treasure hid in a field."

She uttered the shortest of prayers: "Guide me, Lord." Then did something of which no priest would approve. Thinking of whom she sought, she spoke.

"Where are you, John?"

She picked up the Bible, waited. But it remained steady in her hand. So she drew the paper from the key, did not unfold to read it, put it carefully aside. She did the same with the next scroll. Still no response. Before inserting the last scroll, she hesitated. If nothing happened, she did not know what she would do next.

She lifted the Bible. Nothing happened; she had not been answered. Then, just as she went to lay it down again, she could no longer hold it. It was as if her fingers were forced open. The book fell hard upon the table, the key spilling out. She reached for it, removed the scroll, laid it beside the others. Even though only the last gave the answer, she opened the first scroll first, hoping.

It said "Dice House."

So John was not gambling.

With trembling fingers, she opened the second scroll. Exhaled the word—"Whorehouse"—on a relieved breath.

He was not lying in some brothel.

She knew what was upon the third paper, but she reached for it anyway.

"'Cockpit,'" she read aloud.

She had already been to his favourite one that afternoon, a swanky establishment in Shoe Lane. Women often waited outside the doors of such places, demanding their men, and other men conspired to hide their own. Then a baronet's son she knew a little from the theatre undertook to search for her at the cost of a kiss and a fondle. She let him, and he returned shortly: no John Chalker within and not seen there for many a day.

There was one other place to try. This one she'd have to enter herself.

She rose, pulled her most worn black cloak over her plainest brown smock. She didn't think it would do much good—only a certain type of woman ever ventured inside a cockpit and whatever her clothes, she would be assumed to be one of those. Yet go she must. Anything was better than sitting and waiting for the news that John Chalker's body had been pulled out of the Fleet.

Using the key for its proper purpose, she locked their door and began walking up Sheere Lane. She would take High Holborn and stay better lit as long as she could, before she once more entered the gloomy alleys she'd grown up in.

As she swung up Maynard Street, she caught again that unique savour, the stench of St. Giles, and tucked her nose into her cloak. She rarely went there, though she lived less than half a mile away, unless she had to. As now. Soon enough she was standing before the cockpit in Maidenhead Lane. John used to frequent it when they still lived near, before they were taken on at the playhouse.

It was the cocking time of night. Nine by the toll of the old church, answered by a hand bell rung within. No one was paying any attention to the door and she slipped inside.

It was an old warehouse, cavernous and dark except in its very middle, where it was near as bright as noonday due to the number of candles studded into an iron candelabra. It must have only just been hoisted, for it still swung to and fro, lighting the sanded arena and the raised benches that bounded it on four sides, four rows high on each riser. Every inch of bench was taken, with more people seeking to perch a buttock on each end. People pushed to reach the sand, or climbed on the shoulders of a neighbour to see. The swinging light lit now one side, now the other, each filled with the jostling, yelling crowd. Large men patrolled the squared perimeter of knee-high wooden boards, and if anyone fell over the barrier, they quickly lifted him and threw him atop the crowd wedged into the corners.

Everyone was shouting—some the changing odds, some the exchange of bets, some encouraging the two cockerels now being brought in from opposite sides. The birds were held firmly around their middles, their shrouded heads bobbing on long necks, already scenting their opponents, despite the stew of smells.

Sarah, perched up on a splintered wooden pillar, scanned the ranks for John Chalker, to no avail. Behind her, back from the benches, the few women present were waiting for the fight to be over, adjusting their blouses to reveal their bosoms more fully, ready to celebrate with winners or console losers. Some took the chance to cram food down; others drank from flasks.

One looked up just as Sarah noted her and in a moment was across. "By the pox, what you doin' 'ere?" She pulled Sarah down, scanned her clothes. "We don't like amateurs 'ere."

"It's not what you think," replied Sarah, freeing her arm. "I'm looking for my, for a man. His name's John Chalker."

"I don't give a floozie's fuck who you're lookin' for. You get out now." She jabbed a finger into Sarah's breast. "Get out, or I'll—"

Behind her, the shouting had built to a crescendo. The bell rang, the whore turned to it—and Sarah slipped fast away, disappearing into the shadows against the warehouse walls. She could still see into the cockpit, and searched the benches she had not been able to scan before.

In the arena, two birds leaped high, wings beating, feet lashing, candlelight glimmering on the spurs attached to their ankles. John had trained cocks; she had seen the equipment lying about. The curved blades, four inches in length, were sharpened to a razor's edge. If the bird struck right, it would cut off an opponent's leg. Or worse.

As here. To screams of delight and despair, both cocks fell to the sand. One bird was up in a moment, crowing, head raised, wings flapping. The other was squat on the sand, blinking at its own severed wing.

Immediately the benches cleared, as the gamblers retired to the wider area to consider the printed list of combatants, check odds, drink—and some to seek other pleasures. Sarah could see the women among the men, their brighter colours like a cock's comb.

She shut her eyes, leaned against the back wall—and just as she touched the stone, a feeling came, a stab in her chest painful enough to make her clutch herself there. "Is that you, John?" she murmured. "Are you near, my love?"

She heard a voice then, one she recognized. Not her husband's.

"There she is!" said the whore who'd noticed her earlier. "That's the bitch tryin' to cozen us."

A hand closed over Sarah's arm, pulled her out of the gloom. A man looked down, sweat shining in candlelight on his pudgy, pockmarked face. "You were correct, my Lizzie," he said. "She's a pretty one, all right." Fingers twisted into her flesh, yanking her face nearer to his, cheap whisky wafting with his next words. "A prime pullet, sure. Not a pox mark on her." He said this to two men just behind him, who muttered agreements. The man took his lower lip between stained teeth, appraising her. "You could do well here, my Lizzie. But you'd need protection. No lady works alone."

"What you doin', George? I brung ya to warn 'er off, not recruit 'er. Let me."

Without releasing Sarah, barely glancing, the man backhanded the whore across her face. "You go back to work now," he spat. "I want a crown from you tonight before you take one penny 'ome to your brats."

The whore slunk away. "Don't worry about her, my Lizzie," he said, "I'll protect you from 'er and all."

Sarah jerked her arm from his grasp. "You have mistook me, sir," she said, stepping away.

He caught her elbow, wrenched her back. "Everything's for sale here, my Lizzie," he said, his voice harder. "Everything and every-one. But I'll need to check your qualities. My customers demand it. You're pretty enough to be a boy under all that cloth." He grinned. "And they pays less for a boy."

She'd known where she was coming, the risk of it. But she did not take the risk unprepared. She'd grown up on these streets and escaped worse than him. So she struck fast.

He looked down, at the line of red oozing across his knuckles. "She's cut me! Bitch has cut me!"

Sarah palmed her knife, tried to move away. But one of the cron-ies had stepped around, and he grabbed, pinning her. The man she'd cut bent, prised the weapon from her grasp, held it up. "A perfect little blade," he hissed, then nodded at the man who held her. "Take her in the back. No one cuts Gentle George and gets away with it."

Wrapping arms around her mouth and chest, they began to drag her toward a dark corner.

"Though someone must. Get away with it. Now and again."

Sarah had heard the voice before but could not place it. As she turned her head to the sound, she saw a flash of metal, felt some-thing pass her ear, some whoosh of air, followed by a grunt as the man who held her let go of her mouth, released the arm around her chest. She stumbled forward, glanced up in time to see Captain

Coke, his sword drawn fully now. Realizing that earlier he must have drawn it just enough to drive its pommel into her captor's skull.

That man was down, groaning in the rushes; the other had vanished. Only Gentle George stood there, sucking his bleeding hand, his other groping his belt, at Sarah's knife thrust in there. But just as he touched it, the captain's sword rose and stopped a finger's width before his eye. Could the man see, she wondered, even in this gloom, how the steel tip wavered not at all?

"Now, why would you want to do that, sir, when the birds are about to have at it?"

The bell had rung. The man's hand hovered, then moved slowly away from the weapon. He took a step backward. "We'll meet again, my Lizzie," he said.

"I would not hope for that," Sarah replied, jerking her blade from his belt, "for next time I might take more than a little blood."

He glared at them both, then turned swiftly about and made for the tumult.

"Come, Mrs. Chalker." Coke sheathed his sword and nodded toward the entrance. When Sarah hesitated, he added, "Your husband is not here. I searched for some time before I noted your arrival. Please. Else Gentle George might muster both courage and friends."

She slipped the knife up her sleeve. "You have been kind, sir. I would appreciate your kindness still."

"Well." He nodded again to the entrance. They got to it just as the hand bell ceased ringing, as the last great shout for bets sounded, followed hard by the shriek of fighting birds.

The gates of the warehouse closed behind them, shutting out some of its noise. A light rain had begun, together with a fitful wind, bringing a slight sweetness to the streets. She breathed it in, trying to clear her nose of the stench of the pit and the air. With all that had happened within, she felt giddy. She swayed into Coke. "I am sorry, sir," she said.

He reached up and held her. "How long is it since you have eaten, madam? How long since you truly slept?"

"I do not recall either with any clarity."

"Then let me suggest that you do both straightaway. Leave me alone this night to inquire, to explore certain other places where a man can easier go *alone*."

She heard the emphasis he gave to the word. Like a player, she thought. "You are right, sir," she said, standing upright, stepping away from his arms. "I need a little food, a little sleep, before I resume the search. Both can be had at my lodgings."

"I will escort you there."

"That will not be necessary. It is not far and—" she looked around "—we grew up on these streets, John Chalker and I. I do not fear them. And if you are willing to keep to the task?" She hesitated, then added, "I sensed him, sir. Before. In there. I feel he is somewhere near."

"Then I will seek him here."

"Thank you, sir. Well then, good night and good fortune." She started to go, realizing just how exhausted she was. Then a thought turned her back to him. "I am curious, Captain, as to why you undertake this. You are a gentleman and this—" she glanced around "—this cannot be your world."

"They might surprise you, madam, the worlds I inhabit. As to why?" He ran finger and thumb over his moustache. "Well, Lucy is as dear to me as you are to her. So—" he coughed "—so there we have it."

"Do we?" She smiled. "Then come to me at any hour, Captain. With news, I hope."

"As do I. And please, next time we meet, do call me William."

He removed his wide-brimmed hat and bowed in that old-fashioned style. Like something off the stage, she thought again, as she walked away.

12

LOSERS AND WEEPERS

He stood with hat in hand, enjoying the rain on his face, which ceased even as he did so, though the gusty wind continued. He watched her till the lane's bend took her. Why, indeed, was he helping her? Was it her eyes, their beauty reaffirmed even in the darkness of a St. Giles street? No. A fool he might be, but a romantic fool he was not. Was it that he wanted something to do while he waited for further word from the Jew as to the value of his gems? More likely. After the gunshot, and the news that one of the thief-takers was that close, the sensible thing would have been to keep to the room in the Aldgate tavern after he'd accomplished his mission for Lucy. Yet he knew his nature; he could not lie low. Though Dickon was surprisingly good at Gleek or Ombre, they were not games that two could play for long. And though the boy always had coins about him, it never took more than an hour for Coke to win them all before he gave them back.

"She's a viper, that one. Always was. Gentle George was lucky to lose only a little blood."

Coke turned. A large man was leaning against one doorpost of the cockpit in a jumble of attire: two doublets, one atop the other; some wide breeches held up with rope; boots with soles that yawned. Strangely, strapped to those was a shiny pair of iron plattens to lift him above St. Giles' cobbled mire. They made him a good head taller. His face, under his cloth cap, was a red beacon even in the poor light. "You know her, sir?"

"Know 'er? I've 'ad 'er!" He let out a loud belch. "Many did, before Chalker reserved her special for 'isself." He leaned, spat, wiped what he'd failed to expel into his beard. "Chalker! Tight-pursed as a Jew. Can you believe it? After all these years he gives me a shillin' at our reunion. A shillin'!" He looked to spit again, thought better of it. "When Chalker and Clancy was friends from this 'igh up!"

He held his hand at knee height. But the movement unbalanced him on his plattens and he tottered forward, his other hand reaching out to steady himself on Coke's shoulder. The captain inhaled the man's mix of scents. Cheap liquor predominated. Casually Coke asked, "Was this reunion recent, Mr. Clancy?"

The eyes narrowed. "Who told you my name?"

"You did. You said this woman's husband and you were friends."

"Oh, right." His beard rasped as he scratched it. "What's it to you when I last saw Chalker? Or should I say, what's it *worth* to you?"

Coke pulled out two coins. "Shall I match his shilling and make of it a pair?"

"Make of it a threesome and I'll tell you what I know."

"You can say where he is?"

"Mebbe." Clancy stared a moment, then shook his head. "Nah, I don't. But I can tell you the hole he went into, not five days since."

Five days was a long time. But it was the only sighting Coke had heard of, and after his wife had last seen him. "I will give you these for that information. No more."

"All right." Clancy snatched the coins and shoved them in the folds of his mismatched clothing. Then he stood tall and beamed. "He went around that corner. I thought it odd, because the lane leads nowhere but to Carrier Court, the filthiest tenement in St. Giles. Only one way out, the same he went in, but he never come back, though I watched a few hours, on account of how he said he'd buy me a drink. Never came back." He wiped his streaming nose. "Strange, though, I was down in the cockpit and I thought I heard him whisperin' me name, two days since." He jerked his thumb over his shoulder. "Maybe he was callin' his whore. Must have one down there. Well, you would, if you was married to St. Sarah the Viperous."

"I thought you said you'd had her."

The bigger man shrugged. "Yeah, well, 'twas a long time ago."

It would not take much to thrash the drunkard for his insults—and take back his two shillings. But a fight always drew a crowd and would mean delay. He would act immediately on this small piece of information.

So he walked away. Behind him, Clancy mumbled something, but when Coke glanced back, the doors of the cockpit were banging shut again. The two shillings would be on a bird in moments.

He entered into the alley and even more gloom. Doorways on either side showed nothing but empty, foul-smelling and roofless rooms.

He nearly missed the entrance to Carrier Court. Only detected it by sound, so in shadow was it. Voices turned him. Children's.

He felt the outlines of an archway, walked through it. From darkness he emerged into the relative brightness of a large courtyard whose width meant that the near-full moon, emerged from the driven clouds, shone here.

The moonshine lit a well at the courtyard's centre. Children danced around it, seven or eight of them, boys and girls, singing a rhyme as they twirled:

Pat a cake, pat a cake, baker's man
Bake me a cake as fast as you can
Roll it, pat it, mark it with *B*
Put it in the oven for baby and . . . me!

On the last word, they let go of each other's hands and dropped to the ground, where they all made sounds like a mewling baby. Then one, the smallest girl there, cried, "Again! Faster! Faster!" and they were all up, linked, moving the other way, faster indeed, chanting the same verse, till they dropped again.

More laughs, more shrieks. But whether he moved or moonlight touched him, someone saw. "The devil comes to take us!" screeched that same small girl, and though he came forward with arms raised in peace, every child disappeared in seconds into the dark of stairwells and doorways, and silence swallowed their screams.

He walked twice around the perimeter of the courtyard, calling softly. None answered. He began his third circuit—and noticed it. Just another ooze among the many there. But when he knelt, touched, then smelled his fingertips, he recognized it.

Blood. It was like an arrow, pointing into the deeper darkness of one stairwell. He took a step toward it and straightaway that distinct iron tang deepened. There were other smells mixed in, none of them pleasant—and exactly like the smell of the coach in Finchley.

He drew his cloak across his face, his mouth flooding with spit. It could be a dog, he thought, or a pig, fresh butchered by the dwellers of Carrier Court. It could be . . . someone else. Whatever the stench, surely its source did not have to be John Chalker?

He had to find out, for Sarah's sake; find out now. Yet he realized, with all the relief of delay, it was foolish to try and find out in the dark.

After scratching a cross on the arch's lintel with his dagger to make sure he could find the court again, he walked swiftly out the alley and back up Maidenhead Lane to Holborn. Better dressed people walked there. "Link boy!" he called when he saw the shimmering torchlight.

The lad came running fast on bare feet; he was younger than Dickon, as thin. "Light your way 'ome, sir?" he cried.

"Nay. But how much for a link?"

Coke did not bargain much, merely parted with near his last sixpence. The boy maintained he was giving up a portion of his stock in selling the link, though truly a willow wand with some wax-impregnated wool wadded at one end was scarce worth tuppence. Coke was allowed to choose and chose the thickest waxed. A light from the boy's, and he was on his way back, down the same lane, threading the same alley, to stand at last before the same entrance, the rough-etched cross marking it.

The children had not returned to the courtyard. Crossing it, he halted at the head of the stairwell, where the stench had not diminished a jot. If anything . . .

Gagging, pulling the cloak again before his face, he descended.

There were three flights, any trace of moonlight gone after the first one, his own paltry flame enclosing him in its flickering pool. At the bottom of the second flight was a door, old and rusted, which nonetheless opened almost noiselessly to his push. Another stair led to another door. This one was heavier, thicker, but its weight was not why the captain paused so long before it. The smell made him pause, its source a shove away. Taking a deep breath through his mouth, nosing deeper into a fold of cloak, he shoved the door open.

It gave onto the centre of all foulness.

His light glimmered upon the stone of an old cellar—and upon shackles on one wall, loose and opened. It also shone on a sconce, a rush torch in it, which, on closer examination, was scorched but not burned out. Holding his link carefully to it, Coke let the pitch catch, then blew the flame gently to life. It flared suddenly, a sun compared to the moon he carried, which he now snuffed out with licked fingers, saving the remaining wax for his return.

He didn't see the body at first because it was tucked into the corner, blending with the shadows at the base of the wall. When he did, he knew that it was a man. What had once been a man. Naked, he was curled up like a child, knees to chest. The face was to the wall, though the rest of the body was turned into the room. Torchlight revealed what metal and flame had done to flesh. But it was the head Coke focused on. He knew, by sight and by description, that John Chalker had long, curly, black hair—rivalling, it was reputed, the finest wig that His Majesty ever laid upon his dummy at night. For a moment, Coke felt relief—for this hair was not curly, but straight, hanging lank down the back. Then, as he stooped, as he touched, he realized the hair was indeed thick and would indeed be curly, if blood had not so soaked it and laid it flat.

He had one more thing to do, for himself, for Mrs. Chalker. He turned the head from the wall.

There was not a face to be recognized, only a mass of blood, cut and scab. Yet in its nothingness, he saw the face that case shot had scoured away on Lansdown field. Even in the one eye that stared at him—stared because the eyelid had been cut away and so could not help its gaze.

This is not John Chalker, he thought, though somewhere inside him he knew it was.

No. What Coke saw was Quentin Absolute.

So it was his friend's ruined face that drove the captain from his knees, lurching to the reed torch to smother it in his cloak, to put out the light on this abomination; his friend who drove him out of the cellar, slamming the door behind him, slamming the next one, tripping and stumbling in the darkness because he'd forgotten to grab either link or torch to light his way.

The children had returned to the courtyard. They were moving hand in hand around the well again, but slowly, and wordlessly now. This time they did not scatter at the sight of him, as he burst from the stairs and ran past them. Perhaps the game, their quiet attention to it, was simply more important than a running, vomiting man.

13

LONDON RACE

Pitman rubbed his eyes. He'd dozed off. Then he rubbed the ale-house window, where his breath had fogged the glass. Its thickness did not give him more than blurry sight. Still, it was clear enough to note the figure that twitched for several moments at the gold-smith's door before pushing it in. The tinkle of the bell above it came faint to his ears, though it was like his regiment's trumpet calling him to battle, for he was on his feet in an instant. "Keep it," he said, spinning his last florin to the alehouse keeper at his trestle. It was a shilling more than he owed; but he or Josiah had sat there for five days and nights nursing the execrable beer, picking at the mouldy cheese. Also, he was certain now that his pocket would soon be filled with coin again, because although Captain Cock had not come, his boy had.

The boy, Pitman thought, blessing his five wits as he crossed to the door, hefting his dagger stick, feeling for the weight of his cosh, hearing the clink of his manacles. He'd only thought of the boy two days earlier, as he went over yet again all he knew of the captain, especially as he thought back to the conversation he'd had with Maclean, the accomplice. The Irishman had said that he and his countryman O'Toole had held guns on Lord Carnarvon's coachman and footmen, front and rear, letting Cock handle the niceties of the actual robbery with his polite demand for all they had—gold, gems, fobs and watches—"while his idiot boy held the bridles and spat nut shells at the horses." Pitman had been too busy questioning the highwayman as to his leader's accent, his manner, and had forgotten to return to the bridles, and their holding, and the nut spitting. By the time he'd remembered, the man was gone, eager to use every minute of the two-day head start he'd been granted.

Pitman half-opened the door, keeping in its lee, until he saw the blind on the Jew's door come down, heard the bolt shot, distinct despite the vendor crying, "Buy my fat chickens, alive-alive oh!" in the ashes of the burned-out building beside the tavern. Isaac ben Judah was closing for a special customer, unusual for a man of trade in the middle of a busy day. More unusual that he closed for a boy of around eleven years, full of the jerks and shuffles of one plagued by his own demons.

Pitman waited till a group was passing, stooped into it, merged into another about the chicken seller, from where he could observe. He even started bargaining. They looked like plump and healthy pullets. If the afternoon went as expected, he would receive an advance from the constable of Newgate prison when he dropped Coke off, then return and buy the plumpest. Bettina had been craving roasted bird, and the pigeons Josiah had trapped of late had been scrawny.

The transaction between boy and Jew did not take long. Blind up, door ajar, the goldsmith glancing up and down the street before the boy slipped out. He stood for a moment at the door, threw something in the air, caught it in his mouth and then began to gambol away. As Pitman passed the door, he glanced down: some hazelnut shells lay before it. Coke's boy, certain.

Pitman followed. His quarry walked briskly down Buttolph Lane, making for the Thames. Pray God, not the bridge, Pitman thought. Let his rendezvous with the captain not be in Southwark. He was a north-of-the-river man entirely, and considered most who lived on the other bank barbarians. Not the foreigners who clustered there, who were mostly French or Dutch fleeing their homelands' oppressions; they were sober and religious in the main. It was the native southerner, corrupted by the liberty of Southwark, which housed more sin within it than the rest of London combined. Cockpits, the lowest taverns, bear baiting, bull fighting, and a brothel beside each one. First a man wanted booze, then blood, then—Pitman shuddered. He could deposit Coke in the Clink jail, but the jailer was a sot. Besides, Pitman preferred Newgate prison and the men he always dealt with there. He also didn't fancy dragging the Monstrous Cock through half of London; for although he'd told Bettina that the thieves he took usually came as gentle as lambs, he knew it was not a lamb that had wrought such slaughter in Finchley but a wolf.

Pitman clutched his weapons a little more tightly and held his breath when the boy reached the corner of Thames Street. If he turned right, he'd be heading for the bridge and all the trouble that would yield.

The boy turned left, cutting sharp right down an alley, entering a maze of them, bearing east and south. Smiling, Pitman closed the gap between the boy and him to fifteen paces, for the crowd was growing ever thicker as it neared the river, its warehouses, its traffic, all its trade.

That was when Pitman caught the first good reek of fish, fresh and not so, and realized where the rendezvous would take place. A place where ships called all the time and a man seeking to flee the country could find passage out.

"Billingsgate," he murmured. "Easy, Captain. Come easy, I pray you."

Coke waited on the dock at Flounder Stairs, rope in one hand, holding the skiff against the pull of the tide, the skiff man in the stern of the vessel, splicing rope and softly singing some song in whatever language a black man sang. The captain would have preferred it if the man he'd hired for two hours rather than a single trip had his hands poised on oars and was not about his weaving. Still, he was big-shouldered, his forearms were braided steel, he had the cross-brand of a former slave upon his forehead and so a legacy of labour. He would get them away speedily enough. And speed, Coke thought for the umpteenth time that day, was required.

Why was he so unnerved? He'd tried to convince himself that it was still the shock of Chalker's body from the previous night. But he had seen such grisly sights before. Was it because it had so utterly taken him back to the—*destruction*, it was the only word for it—of Quentin Absolute? He shook his head. No. Though it had ravaged his night with foul dreams, nightmares and exhaustion could not account for the heaviness about his heart. Something was going to happen this day; he simply knew it. Something to do with the man Isaac had warned him off with gunfire. The note he'd finally received from the goldsmith had been a summons, short on detail. His cousin had returned. The offer was fair. Be cautious on collection. That was why he'd sent Dickon, who, despite his failings, was also steady in the breach. Yet . . .

Coke placed the heels of his hands into his eye sockets. I'm tired, he thought, tired from too much scanning through this frantic mob of Billingsgate market. Through crowds of porters unloading the fishing boats, silver mackerel flashing in the sunlight as hoisted nets were emptied into barrels, as baskets brimming with sardine, sprat and eel were lifted onto shoulders—or onto heads, the fishwives of the market sporting their famous flat caps to accommodate the loads. Fishermen endlessly split, salted, trayed and shoved herring into smoky ovens; tossed larger skate, salmon, pollack and codfish onto fishmongers' slabs to auction away. The noise tired him too, the constant roar, the bargaining, the selling, the shrieks of "Clear away! Clear away!" the insults when they didn't, the laughter when one fell attempting it.

He'd booked passage for Dickon and him on a boat at Gravesend. France first and then who knew? He did not like sea voyages, but this one he was looking forward to. To be in silence for a while. To sleep.

He took his hands from his eyes, focused, and saw him: Dickon, fifty paces away, gliding through the mob, agile as a sardine in a sea. But Coke saw too, and immediately, a different kind of fish following—large, no less fast, with no need to dart or shift, clearing the way with his bulk, undeviating as a tunny.

"To oar," he cried, and the black man laid down his rope and slid oars into the rowlocks. Coke put one leg upon the skiff, dropped in the rope, turned and shouted, "Run!"

Despite the tumult, Dickon heard him and sped up. But so did the giant behind him, his stride doubling in length, his mouth wide to bellow, "A thief! A thief! Make way!" Some did not hear, nor clear; others froze. One porter stopped directly in the path and Dickon slid under his arms, skating, barely breaking step. His pursuer could not duck so low, nor slip around, and his velocity was too great on a slope slick with scales and guts. He smashed into the porter and both went down.

Dickon ran into his captain's arms. "Fish! Fish! Fish! Whish!" he cried, laughing.

In a moment Coke had him swung into the skiff. The next he followed, and shoved them off from the dock, nearly capsizing the boat as he leaped in. "Heh," yelped the rower, struggling with his oars. Then he had them right, and a few strokes pushed them away.

Not too soon. Heavy boots thumped onto the jetty. Coke looked at the man, even larger now he was so close, anguish on his heavily bearded face as he stretched an arm out at them. But he said nothing, just wheeled and began seeking something. A skiff himself, Coke suspected, but did not see as they steered around a fishing boat coming in and the market was lost to his sight. Indeed, it was frustrating what a devious route they were forced to take, swirling around vessels swirling in, others of every shape and size also heading out, his boatman in constant argument for right of way. At last they emerged from the chaos, his man pulling strongly for the centre stream, and Coke could look back. Criss-crossing traffic still obscured everything. Then it cleared, and he saw a wherry shoot out between other boats. There were two men rowing it, and when one turned for direction, Coke saw again the bearded face of his pursuer.

He regarded the blackamoor. Gravesend was a two-hour row at the least. They would be overtaken, undoubtedly. Overtaken before they reached the Surrey shore! Cursing, he looked the other way to the bridge. He could see the turbulent water between its piers. London beyond. His streets. "There!" he shouted, pointing.

The oarsman, in the midst of swinging the stern downriver, glanced where Coke pointed, then jerked his head the opposite way. "Grave-es-end," he said, his voice a bass rumble.

"Change," Coke replied. "Savoy Stairs."

The man looked again, then shook his head. "Tide turn. Now race too strong under bridge." He shrugged. "We can die."

Coke kept one gold sovereign sewn into the hem of his cloak for only the most pressing of matters. He ripped the stitching away, squeezed the coin out, held it up. "Savoy Stairs?"

The man's eyes went wide. But he shook his head. "We can die," he said again.

"We can always do that," Coke replied, and drew a pistol from within his cloak. "Go."

The man spat out a word in his own language. But the half cocking of the gun made him move. He swung the oars to steady his craft and turned the stern to face London Bridge. Glancing back, the captain saw his pursuer make the same adjustment.

The blackamoor began to pull hard. They would reach the bridge first, be the first to run the race. Beside him, Dickon could barely keep himself on the cramped bench but lifted and dropped, lifted and dropped, till Coke laid firm hold of him. The boy squirmed, giggling with delight. His guardian kept him tight as the bridge got rapidly nearer, as he felt the push and tug of water under the bows. Coke knew they both could swim—and that swimming would not help them here at all.

From the middle of the bridge to its northern end was a large gap where fire had consumed the houses some decades past. But before that end one building had been rebuilt and in the arches nearest it, wheels turned to pump water for the New River Company. They revolved furiously now and it was at the empty arch nearest to them that his boatman aimed, closest then to the City shore, though to Coke this arch did not look to contain any less a maelstrom than did any of the others.

The tide now had them. Uncocking his pistol and then putting it away—the boat could not be more committed than it was, nor the boatman—he wrapped a second arm around Dickon.

"Whee!" the boy yelled, as the shadow of the bridge fell over them and water surged around.

Pitman watched his quarry slip under the arch, vanishing in spray. "Pull harder!" he shouted.

Instead the man lifted his oars from the water. "Can't go in from this side, friend, not now," he said. "Too bloody dangerous."

Pitman stared at him for but a moment. "Can you swim?" he asked.

"Nah. Bad luck for a wherryman to swim. Cos then he might 'ave to."

"Well, can you float?" As he asked the question, Pitman hurled the oarsman from the boat. He nearly followed, so violently did the vessel tip. Terror helped him right it—he certainly could not swim, and he doubted he'd be lucky enough to grasp the tangle of nets and spars where he'd thrown the man. He'd sink like Jonah, with no whale to take him into its belly.

"I'll be back to compensate you," he called as the man scrabbled onto the flotsam. Using the oars, Pitman righted the craft, pointed it again at the same arch Coke had disappeared through. He'd been an oarsman on the Thames when he first came to the City. He'd shot the race several times. But looking back over his shoulder as he steered into the surge, he realized he'd never done so when the tide was so perfectly on the turn.

God preserve me, he prayed. And Lord? Let Bettina be carrying boys this time.

With that, Pitman put the boat into the race, shipped oars and closed his eyes.

There was an immediate grinding of wood on wood as the skiff scraped the starling that girded the pier. A surge of water lifted the boat high and his eyes jerked open just in time to save a smashed skull as the wherry shot toward the stone roof. The boat dropped as suddenly, with Pitman hanging in the air before plummeting, to miss the bench and end up half on the canopy that sheltered passengers from rain—and whose crest impaled him now between his legs. With a mighty effort, he threw himself forward, and landed on hands and knees on the strake.

Someone screamed. He looked up and saw above him, as if on a higher shelf, a skiff going the other way. A man and a woman gazed down, horror on their faces. Their vessels scraped, seemed to stick, parted as if discharged from a cannon. Then there was light where gloom had been, and his boat shot out into it, its bow dipping once to splash enough river over him to fill a dozen tubs.

He shook himself, wiped water from his eyes and looked about. The river was calmer this side, but that did not mean he did not feel the draw back toward the arch. Miraculously the oars were still in the bottom of the boat. "Praise God," he cried, seizing them.

One rowlock had snapped off, but he leaned an oar against its ruined stanchion, found the other, steadied the vessel and gave a few strokes. Only then did he see, pulling hard about a hundred paces from the bridge, the fox he followed.

Curses came now instead of prayers, as Pitman rowed in pursuit. He could not go as fast as two had, nor as one if that one had had a brace of rowlocks. Still, he did not fare too badly. They passed the Queenshythe, Wood Wharf, Baynards Castle. As they passed the place where the Fleet River discharged its filth, a deeper brown ooze in the Thames, his arms began to tire.

"Where are you going, Captain?" he wheezed.

Then he saw the other vessel swerve and make for a jetty. Two wherries had just departed it and his quarry was able to glide immediately alongside. But they only stopped long enough for the captain and his boy to leap out. In a moment they were running up the stairs, their skiff already pushed away behind them.

Pitman used curses he thought he'd long forgotten under his wife's influence. "Alsatia," he muttered, as the boat bumped into the dock. He was out in an instant, aware of the injuries he'd sustained in the race as soon as he took weight upon his leg. He glanced at the skiff that had just pulled away, its black boatman, something golden glittering between very white teeth. Then he began a hobbling run.

"Alsatia. Give me Southwark any day."

14

THE WARREN

Alsatia, Coke thought with a shudder, striding into the shadows of the first crumbling warehouse. He had lived here once. When he was first back from the Continent and his purse could run to nothing else, '61 and part of '62. Left as soon as he was able, on the proceeds of the first successes of his new career. You didn't keep gold about your person in Alsatia. Not when you shared a room with a dozen other people, some of whom could sniff it beyond the stench that smothered the place like a fog.

Thrusting his nose into his cloak's neck, liberally doused anew with sandalwood, and keeping one hand in Dickon's collar to prevent dawdling, Coke advanced deeper into the warren.

Though he'd been away only three years, he was soon lost. Alsatia shifted constantly. Hastily made shacks thrown up from the collapse of others, built as single rooms, then built on above and again above, three ill-joined storeys and sometimes more, forming the new laneways that they leaned over, conjoining above to shut out near all the light. Trapping the air too on this warm after-noon, making the street fetid. These shacks were a front for others, erected in the same manner by people desperate for space, every row linked by shifting narrow wynds scarce the width of a wide man's shoulders. My big thief-taker will have to go sideways, Coke thought, and one arm would be easier to deal with than would two, if it came to it. Though he doubted he was still pursued. If he was lost, his pursuer was bound to be.

Glimpses of the sun and the slightly rising slope from the river gave him a rough north. A few twists and then he would go straight. Five minutes and he would be among the strollers on Fleet Street. Fifteen and he would be at the Lincoln's Inn playhouse.

He thought of the note he'd arranged to be delivered to Lucy at the time when he believed he would already be a-ship. Well, now he would see her briefly—Mrs. Chalker too. His note to her, for delivery at the same time, informed her only that her husband was dead. He would not wish that havoc in anyone's mind before it had to be. He did not wish it in his own. Yet he had also given her the corpse's location. Too many widows in the late, deplored wars had been unable to mourn fully without the body of their beloved. She would have that much of him back, at least.

The increasing narrowness of the lanes had forced him to let go of Dickon. Now at a crossroads, the boy halted to offer hazelnuts to an urchin in a doorway. Coke seized the boy's hand, spilling some of his precious nuts to stuttering protests. The thief-taker might yet be somewhere close.

He took the narrowest lane, heading north. Five minutes and they would be clear of Alsatia. Soon clear of London. Clear of the whole damned country.

—

Five minutes, thought Pitman, pausing at yet another crossroads. Only five that I've been in this hell pit and I am already lost. Worse, I have lost him. And if I have, I have probably lost him for good. No medicine for Imogen. No food for Josiah. No provision for the babes to come.

There was movement near his feet. A crippled child, legs twisted underneath him, was crawling a few paces toward some tiny things brighter than the muck they lay on. Just as the boy reached them, Pitman bent and seized the child's hand in the very act of picking one up.

The child squealed. "It's mine! I sees it! Mine!"

Gently Pitman prised the begrimed fingers open. There was a hazelnut in the hand, more scattered about. Releasing him, Pitman said, "Did someone drop these?"

"Yeah. Boy. Crazy boy."

"Which way did this crazy boy go?"

The child popped the nut in his mouth and then pointed. "There."

"Good lad." Pitman pulled out a groat. It had few companions in his pocket, yet he gave it to the boy before taking at speed the lane indicated.

It was narrow, stalls and carts on each side. He twisted, dipped, did not slow even when he barked his shin. His pace paid off. As he rounded a bend, he saw the captain and his boy twenty steps ahead. At the same time Coke turned and saw him too.

Pitman sped up. He preferred a more measured pace but could sprint if he must. He noted that the boy was not as fast as either man, with a stutter in his gait. Coke was slowing to keep with him.

Fifteen steps now and closing. Another junction approaching, three splits there. But his prey must have known as well as his hunter that the chase was soon up if it continued this way. Pitman saw him bend down, put his mouth close to the boy's ear. The lad jerked his head up and down; then, at the junction, he went left, while his captain ran straight on.

The thief-taker didn't hesitate. While the boy was probably old enough to hang, or at the least be transported to Jamaicy to work the sugar, there was no money in him. Besides, the thought of that slaughter in Finchley, of the dead lady in particular, drove Pitman and made him do two things: speed up to apprehend her murderer, and make sure his cosh was fitted to his hand.

They were both running full out now, as far as the passage allowed—a trip would cost either of them the race. People stared, slid into doorways, did not interfere, and Pitman did not cry out. A yell of "Stop thief!" upon Fleet Street, which they were rapidly approaching, would bring the thief-taker aid from the gentry who walked there. In Alsatia any aid would go to the thief. So he kept his voice silent and his pace fast and waited for his prey to burst out upon that avenue, drawing near.

However, his quarry must have realized what lay ahead too, for he darted right down the last alley he could. Pitman followed, cursing as Coke swung back into Alsatia. The man was heading straight past a crowded tavern, its doors wide to the heat of the day, a large group drinking and smoking before them. Many began to cheer like spectators at the races as the men hurtled toward them. Pitman recognized the place immediately; he'd found Coke's confederate, Maclean, there. He had got useful information and given the fellow two days to quit the town in exchange for it. So he was surprised as he ran up to spot the man standing there, a tankard in his hand, shock on his face. Escalating shocks: the first for the man only now passing him; the second for the man in pursuit.

Pitman was close enough now to see the progression from surprise to fear to cunning. "Look lively, me lads!" Maclean cried, stepping onto the alehouse's stoop. "For that's the Monstrous Cock what's just run by and there's thirty guineas for the man who takes him. Dead or living!" And with that he vanished into the interior.

I'll pay you in hemp, Maclean, Pitman thought, but did not slow, nor turn as the hue and cry began behind him, along with the noise of tankards dropping, of men running. Perhaps the captain heard the ruckus too and it made him falter, for he slipped and fell into a oyster stall, scattering shells and meat. He was up in a moment and running again, but Pitman had gained five paces. Now he was a bare five behind.

A swerve right, a dart left, ducking under hanging clothes and close enough now to hear the man's breaths coming in whoops, an echo of his own, audible even above the shouting behind them. The captain took another alley left—but this came to a dead end at a coopery, its doors open, barrels stacked up before. The cooper froze, his mouth full of tacks, hammer in one hand, as Coke raced past him and inside, three steps ahead of his pursuit. Pitman wrenched the two doors shut, rolled a huge barrel into their centre and then sat on it.

Not a moment too soon. There was an almost immediate banging, shouted demands to open. When Pitman did not move and pushing could not shift him, the men retreated a little while plans to force entrance were loudly discussed. Pitman noticed a wooden bar to the side, lifted it and then dropped it into hooks either side of the door.

He knew he did not have long. "Are . . . are you there, Captain Coke?"

The reply out of the shadows was equally breathy. "I . . . I am."

The voice drew him, and Pitman could now make out, through the shafts of sunlight that filtered through gaps in the walls, the figure standing a half-dozen paces from him. "They'll hang you here, Captain, and drag your corpse after to a magistrate for the reward. Come easy and I may be able to get us out. At least you'll live to see a trial tomorrow."

"And Tyburn the day after. It is not much of a prospect."

"And your son?"

"My son?"

"Come easy and I'll see he has ale to toast you with 'neath the gallows tree."

A soft laugh. "He'd prefer a bag of nuts. But mostly he'd prefer not to see me hang at all. So I have another idea." The man passed through bars of sunlight, though his face remained hidden. "Let me talk to the mob. They like a bold dog in Alsatia."

"But not a mad one." Pitman had got his breath back—enough, anyway, for what he must do. "Your foul murders have put you beyond even their regard." He stood, readied his cosh. "So you must accompany me."

Someone smashed an axe into the wood behind him. It stuck, was wrenched out. Pitman took a step, then stopped, as the man before him moved into a larger patch of sun—which glimmered on the barrel of the pistol he held. Even with the shouting outside, the sound of it pulled to full cock was loud in that space.

"Do you think that after the bridge race, all that water, all that running, you still have powder in the pan? Dry powder?" asked Pitman. "You have scarce had time to reload."

"I never needed much. I learned to reload fast in the late king's wars."

A memory came. "I thought that Captain Cock never put ball in his pistol."

"You know that? Well, today I did. I felt I might need it. As for the dampness of powder . . ." The barrel flicked slightly but did not waver, not a jot. "Are you a gambling man, Thief-taker?"

"I was. No more."

"Well, you must hazard on this. We both must, for I will pass."

"You will not."

"Alas, then!" Coke took another step forward. A beam fell slant-wise on his face now, and Pitman saw him fully for the first time, his black hair streaked in silver, his grey, troubled eyes. "Yet before you die, I would you knew this. Outside of those wars you will be the only man I have ever killed."

With that, the captain pulled the trigger.

The spark of flint striking the steel was tiny, lost in a sunbeam, the fizz of powder scarcely audible. In Coke's face, Pitman sought signs of further resistance, readying the cosh. Noted only the slightest of smiles.

"Now, that is just how my luck has been of late," Coke said. Then he flipped the gun in the air, caught it by its barrel and held it out.

Letting go the breath he had not realized he was holding, Pitman stepped forward again, his attention on the other man's right hand, for a sword was at his hip. But the captain let him have both that and the pistol, made no other move except for the closing of his eyes.

"I've got a length of rope for him! A rope for the Monstrous Cock!" The cry was louder than the axe blow that followed it, and taken up by others.

Many others. Pitman frowned. He'd once intimidated a score of looters at Soudley Churchyard by sheer size and bravado. But this mob had its blood up and might steal his prize. Unless—there was a loft above, with a stair leading to it. "Go," he said, pointing with his chin. The captain, with a glance at the splintering door, shrugged and went.

In the shadows under the eaves was a smaller door. Pitman kicked it hard and the door burst open. The scent of livestock wafted through, a faint lowing confirming the adjacent warehouse's use. "Are you game, Captain? Die here or have that extra day and a chance to make a brave last speech?"

That slight smile again. "I've had one long prepared. After you?"

"Nay, sir. Gentlemen always first."

Coke slipped through. Just as Pitman followed, the doors below crashed open and the cooperage filled with angry men.

The shouts faded behind them as they ran around the loft, which lay above three pens with a cow in each. The far wall had no door, but the slats were old, rotten; Pitman demolished them with a few kicks, then peered into yet another warehouse, by its acrid smell and the clucking a home to chickens. Another loft, but this one ended in wood far more solid and no door. There was, though, a gap in the roof. Hoisting himself up, Pitman thrust his head out into the air. Conjoined roofs moved away in all directions, chimneys disgorging the smoke from cooking fires.

He dropped back down, heard the clear sounds of pursuit, men following the only passage through. He jerked his head above him. "Are you still game?"

"How far? I weary of this chase."

"A noose over cobbles is more tiring, man," Pitman replied. "Not far. Confuse the hounds and they may lose the scent."

"Then let us go."

They were neither of them small men, Pitman especially so, but after much squeezing the captain was through and he after. The slates were at least dry, for it had not rained in an age. They traversed several roofs before Pitman halted them. "There," he said.

It was a casement, standing proud of the roof like a doorway. Perhaps in the late queen's time this had been a splendid mansion; now it was a wreck like most others, converted to lodge a hundred, or for commerce, or both.

"Through," commanded the thief-taker of the thief, and through he went, the bigger man following close; taking a stair that doglegged down; stopping just inside the first room, his hand wrapping around the other's arm to pause him. This ceiling was solid, no sunlight through the slates. The walls too, though Pitman could make out broken lines of light at the front wall. "Shutters, I think. Wait here," he said, pulling the door to and walking with his hand stretched out before him.

It pushed into something, something soft. Between his fingertips, he felt it: fur, a dangling fur that swung away, swung back. Other furs brushed his face and hands as he crossed to the shutters. Reaching them, he put a finger under one slat, pushed it up, saw a group of men running past, shouting.

"I think we should rest here awhile, Captain." He was forcing up the slats as he spoke, more light admitted with each one. "If you are willing," he said, "I've some sausage, a flask of ale."

He turned, stopped speaking. He could see only the captain's boots. Above them, all was obscured.

By cats.

They were everywhere, hung from cords tied around their tails, so close that they touched each other, so many that they filled the entire attic. The cats swayed in the breeze of his passing, like so many inverted corpses upon a vast gallows tree.

Part Three

AND I SAW AN ANGEL COME DOWN FROM HEAVEN,

HAVING THE KEY OF THE BOTTOMLESS PIT

AND A GREAT CHAIN IN HIS HAND.

The Revelation of St. John the Divine 20.1

15

ARRANGEMENTS

Lucy Absolute heard the hall door slam and rose from her chair into the sunlight by the window, as she had half a dozen times already that afternoon. He would see her first backlit by fire, her golden hair aflame. She would draw him dazzled into the light to dazzle him further with the eyes he had so praised in verse. His would then drop, drawn to her breasts. Like every other man, she thought. How he had enjoyed them, with almost a child's wonder, when first he'd gained admittance. She'd had to teach him much, she the elder by four years. He had been an apt student.

Footfalls upon the stair. Placing her hands under her bosom, she lifted and compressed. She was wearing the new dress she'd borrowed from the playhouse, a countess's castoffs acquired by Davenant, for the nobles who attended the theatre to watch versions of themselves portrayed liked to see those versions sumptuously clad. The gown, of cerise silk and trimmed with finest lace, had been too large for Lucy when she'd first coveted it. It was not too large now.

The footfalls reached the landing. How softly he walked, the slim young man she loved. How graceful, like a cat moving through seashells on a mantel. She felt a clutch inside that spread below, nothing to do with the life growing there. If hearing him caused this, she would flood when she saw him. A month had gone by now, and she had never wanted anything so much as his hand reaching beneath her gown, up her shift, parting the folds of her underskirt. Pushing her down onto the divan . . .

A knock. A soft one. Was it the shy earl who came this day? The lovelorn, the country swain, innocent of the ways of the Town, keen to be educated? Well, she had some tricks she had not yet worked upon him. He would like them. And when she had practised upon him, on that smoothest of skin, when once again he lay like a lamb folded in the embrace he called his paradise, she would tell him what she had to tell him and see the answer clear in his eyes. And in that moment, with him about to walk through the door, she knew what his answer would be.

"Enter," she called, turning her face again into the sunlight.

The door opened. "My dear," came the voice.

Not his voice. Lucy sagged. "Sarah! Sister, what make you here? You know I am expecting Rochester. You must go. Quickly."

"I forgot. Forgive me."

Sarah turned to leave, but Lucy immediately noticed how exhausted her friend was, her usually shining skin sallow, creases lined with grime, her auburn hair limp, her bright eyes dull and swollen. "Dearest," she said, crossing to catch Sarah's hand. "What's the news with you?"

Sarah's eyes brimmed, overflowed. "My John is gone."

"And has been these many days."

"You misunderstand." She withdrew her hand from Lucy's—just as the street door opening sounded from below.

"It's him," Lucy cried.

"I will go."

"Nay, I do not want you to pass on the stair. I do not want him to sense any conspiracy." Lucy dragged Sarah across the room. "Wait in here. Do not stir—no matter what you hear." She opened the second door, pushed Sarah into the bedchamber. "Wish me fortune," she whispered.

"Fortune," Sarah said, the word drowned by the slamming of one door, the hammering upon the other.

Lucy hastened to the window. "Enter," she called.

The door opened forcefully enough to swing in and bang upon the wall. The bold earl then, thought Lucy.

"Sweetheart! I am here at your summons and at the command of His Majesty."

The drunk earl too, she realized, hearing the slur in the words. Well, he was a merry drunk in the main—and in some ways easier to manage.

"My Lord of Rochester," she said, sweeping into a deep curtsey. He would pay little attention now to her fiery hair, her subtly highlighted eyes. His attention would be elsewhere.

"Sweetheart," he said again.

He was upon her quickly, hands under her elbows, mouth stooping for hers. She smelled the sweet sack on his breath, turned her head aside. His lips found her cheek. "My love," she breathed into his ear, "the door?"

He crossed the room and slammed the door shut. When he swivelled around, she was sitting upon the divan, one arm along the back, the other lifted to him. "Come, my sweet," she said. "And tell me why I have not seen you this long while."

Rochester flushed. The delay in closing the door, her poise, had sucked away his urgency. "I have been busy. The king, you know." He waved his hand before him in a vague gesture. "'Twas he commanded me to see you today."

"Is it only your sovereign's orders that brought you here?" She leaned toward him as she spoke. "Did love not have *any* sway?"

His gaze lowered, as did his voice. "You know I am ever your servant, madam."

"Are you? Truly?" He nodded. "Then obey me in this. Come sit." When he had, she leaned close till she could breathe the words into his ear: "Make love to me."

Though he was a little drunk and rushed, the command she'd always had over him she asserted now, slowing his caresses, delaying his advances, forcing him to take time, to pay attention to her. She knew such lovemaking would be better in several ways. For her, yes, but more importantly, afterward he would lie meekly in her arms, like a kitten after consuming a platter of fresh cream. Only then would she tell him that she was with child.

They were kneeling on the floor in the end, she before him with her arms braced on the divan, for she knew that would be easier in her state. And when he spent with a great shout, she squeezed him and thrust back, her cries urging him on to further, final effort. He was so young his strength did not diminish, and soon she joined him in pleasure as he pressed her deep, his lips on her ear, their fingers entwining as she cried out.

There were men she'd known—few, it was true, for she had known but three before him—who would withdraw as soon as they were done because they believed that for a woman to conceive she had to reach her height too. Her Johnnie was not like them. He stayed inside her until both realized the pain in their knees. With groans and giggles, they disengaged and climbed onto the divan.

There he did indeed lie easy in her arms, laughing softly while she put on the accent of her childhood and played the Cornish milk-maid shocked by the young squire's attentions. While she prattled, she ran fingers through his long, silken hair, disentangling all the knots. Then, after a silence, she took his head in her hands and looked into his darkling eyes.

"There is something I must tell you, my sweet."

Sarah could not help but hear it all. Indeed, there was a pleasant distraction in listening to people in love and showing it. She and John had not been like that for years, indeed if ever. They had been like brother and sister for so long that being husband and wife had at first been hard. They had enjoyed each other sometimes, of course. But the last time had been a while ago now, for the result of it had been her pregnant and then he hadn't wanted to come near. And when she lost the baby, she did not tell him because *she* did not want him near, not for a while.

And now she would never have him near again.

She did not know the why of it, the how. She'd had no news, from the captain or anyone. Yet she was certain that the final evil had befallen him. Up to the day before, she'd *felt* him in the world. Now she did not. And she knew she would not sleep well again until she found out both who had done it and why. Someone had murdered her John. She would look that person in the eye.

Somehow, as the noise in the next room subsided to murmurs, she dozed, exhaustion taking her to a troubled sleep. She awoke, uncertain where she was until Lucy opened the door.

"He is gone," Lucy said, sitting on the bed. "Gone to make arrangements." She took Sarah in her arms. "Oh, my dear," she said, "all will be well. He even talked of eloping with me and damn his family." She laughed. "Can you imagine me, my dearest, a real lady? I have played so many of them onstage perhaps I might carry it off."

She cried then, Lucy Absolute. For relief. For joy. And Sarah Chalker held her and cried also, for her own reasons.

It's been a lively day and that is always fun, thought Dickon, as the handsome young man came out of Sweet Lucy's house. That's what the cap'n always calls her. *Sweet* Lucy.

He watched the handsome man step straight into a chair, a uniformed footman at each pair of poles lifting it and setting off at a trot. I'd like to ride in one of those, Dickon thought. But it would not be like the *whee* and the *whoosh* of the water this morning, not like shooting the race of London Bridge. That was the most fun—*most fun!*—they'd had in the longest time, on account of the cap'n being so worried and so not playing as he could. And they had not robbed in such a long while, not since that time in that place, wherever it was, that had ended badly, or so the cap'n said, telling him to forget it so he had. Mostly.

He liked robbing, for the cap'n always let him do things and he liked to be useful, liked to earn his keep. Then the cap'n was happy to buy him things, like Afric peanuts off the docks, and cobnuts when they were in season. They'd gone to Kent to pick them off the bushes—when was that? Last autumn? The one before it? One of the two. Had to be one of the two because before that was before the cap'n. And he didn't remember much of that time at all, and not because the cap'n had told him to forget it. He forgot it all by himself. He knew it had not been nice. No nuts, no *nothing*, really. Just hungry and shivery. Alone too.

He shivered now just thinking about it, though it was hot. Also, he'd finished his hazels. But he could not leave and get more. He might miss the cap'n, who had told him when they were racing that man to go ahead and wait at Lucy's. Excepting he was not sure if "wait at Lucy's" meant wait in the doorway opposite or wait up in the room. Sweet Lucy would give him nuts and a sip of ale. But he'd waited too long not sure, and then the actress had gone up and not come down, and then the handsome man had gone up and had come down and gone off in the chair at a clip but not so fast as a boat under a bridge.

Should he go up now? The cap'n had said, "This is the arrange-arrangeme-arrangement!" That was it. He'd said the "arrangement" would be to meet at Sweet Lucy's. He would give the slip to the bearded giant who'd chased them on water and up the lanes and then he would come. And Dickon would be waiting.

No, he thought, settling back down after standing to see how fast the chair moved—not very fast, was the answer. He would not leave this doorway. The cap'n would come. The cap'n was probably coming now. With nuts.

Dickon pulled out the pamphlet, its pages ripped, its ink smudged. Still, he could see some words clear. He'd learn more of 'em. That would please the cap'n when he came.

"Slaugh-ter," he said. Now, what did that mean again?

"Mr. Palmer. Are you certain that this superfluity of lace is essential?"

The tailor, kneeling at his customer's knee, sighed and took the pins from his mouth. "I repeat, my lord—quite essential. That is, if I am to obey his lordship's instructions—to transform you into a man of mode. Now, be still, sir, I pray, and let me pin you."

Garnthorpe stiffened, anticipating yet another jab. Damned fellow had already stuck him twice, his apologies half-hearted on each occasion. He swivelled slightly, provoking a grunt of reproof and, yes, a prick to his knee. At least the coxcomb's mouth is occupied and so I am not subjected to his ceaseless prattle, mainly concerning his other illustrious clients, reaching even to Whitehall now. Merely an excuse to charge ever more outrageous sums for the attentions of the Duke of York's own tailor. Truly, Garnthorpe did not mind the expense—he knew he could buy and sell the duke and still have change for oranges—but what was the expense for? This?

He turned so he could gaze at himself again in the tailor's full-length mirror. He was even more appalled. The lime ribbons Mr. Palmer was engaged in fitting at the knee contrasted sharply, vilely, with the breeches—*petticoat breeches*, he reminded himself they were called. These were magenta, and that colour was continued to the item that he wore under his unbuttoned dark blue doublet—what had the tailor called the damnable thing?—his *tabby*, that was it, a kind of waistcoat, its nauseating red standing out clearly against the cream of his billowing lawn shirt.

He shook his head and saw curls sway. Another disaster, surely, though Mr. Palmer had insisted that since the king wore just such a wig, all gentlemen above a certain age must as well. He'd even sent him to the king's own *perruquier*. A fortune spent on this monstrosity.

At his knee, Mr. Palmer went back on his haunches, took a last pin from his mouth and began to sing under his breath. There was something about the song, something familiar.

This was absurd. *He* was absurd. Garnthorpe could clearly see now what a mistake it had been to compare himself with the coxcombs and noble fops, and the preening, strutting players who were Mrs. Chalker's daily acquaintance. To believe that she would be easier with him if he appeared before her in this fashion. Ridiculous! He'd seen what was in her eyes, that incandescent look she gave him when she first noticed him from the stage. When he'd been plain, ungilded. What she so instantly loved, surely, was Garnthorpe himself, the natural he, unadorned.

Mr. Palmer, still humming, was leaning forward to place his last pin. "No!" Lord Garnthorpe declared. "Cease your fumblings, sir. I will no longer submit to them." He pulled off the infernal wig and threw it to the floor.

"My lord!" Palmer protested. "Think of the cost. Why, the styling alone—"

"I care not for its styling or its cost, puppy." He seized the tailor by the elbow, pulled him up. "Nor for any of these embellishments."

"My lord! You are hurting me!"

Without releasing the man, Garnthorpe jerked the lace away from his breeches. They gave with a satisfying rip and soon joined the wig on the floor. "Now, sir," he said, shaking the man to further whimpering, "you may finish the doublet since I've already paid for it and its colour is none so vile. I will even concede to this style of breeches if you match the colour to the doublet's and hang no poxy ribbons upon 'em. But as for this infernal whatchamacallit—" he tapped the tabby "—it is to go. A plain beige waistcoat will do."

He released the man, who retired three paces, clutching his elbow. "Beige? My lord, I could not hold up my head among my peers if it were known I allowed—" he shuddered "—beige!"

"I care nothing for your peers, fool. My only concern is a lady."

"If she is indeed a lady," the tailor replied, some of his hauteur returning, "and of the fashion herself, she will want—"

Garnthorpe took a step and the man shrank back, hands raised, the last pin held like an absurd miniature sword before him. "The lady wants *me*. Unadorned. In a simple wig. In plain clothes—they can be of good cut, certain. In boots."

"My lord!" said Mr. Palmer, who'd now moved behind his cutting table and regained some composure. "If you keep these, my breeches most *au courant*, you cannot wear those boots."

"What's wrong with 'em?"

"They are country boots, sir, not even fit for elegant riding in Hyde Park. Further, they are worn and—and stained, sir. Horribly stained."

Garnthorpe looked at the boots, which lay by the door. Now that the puppy mentioned it, they did appear stained. London's streets would do that, for he disdained to affix onto them the iron pattens that kept most above the grime. Looking closer though, he saw that not only the brown of London's foulness had besmirched them. Those stains were red, a deep, blackened red.

What was the damn song the tailor had been humming?

While you and I, dilly, dilly, keep ourselves warm.

"My lord? My lord? Are you quite well?"

Garnthorpe blinked. "I will attend to my boots, sirrah. I will wash them."

"Indeed, my lord. And now that I know what you want, shall I, uh, continue?"

Garnthorpe grunted, let the man unpin him and carefully remove the clothes. He then went and donned what he'd shed earlier: plain black breeches, wool shirt and stockings, his black velvet doublet. Lastly, he pulled on his boots. The man was right in this: they were *horribly* stained. He would not like to appear before Mrs. Chalker at the theatre next week wearing boots so thick with blood.

16

OLD FOES

"They kill the cats," said Coke, pushing a feline body dangling near him. The skin, tanned on the inside, knocked the one next to it, which set the next swaying too, and for a few moments all Pitman could see was the man's dark face, now there, now not, revealed and then hidden by swinging fur.

Pitman reached out to steady what swung. "I have never understood it. They kill all the cats, and the small dogs too, both easy to catch. But then the rats, which they also have condemned but are harder to lay hold of, multiply." He let go of the furs, which now spun in place.

"I suppose the authorities must act if they believe the plague has come."

"It has come. I am a constable and have had the shutting up of several houses in my parish, may God forgive me." He sighed. "Yet perhaps between the shutting up and the killing of all vermin, the disease will be curbed."

"Let us hope so, Mr.—?"

"Pitman. No 'Mr.'—plain Pitman to you. And you are Coke? Are you a genuine captain or is it just your title of the road?"

"A genuine captain once."

"Good, then."

They eyed each other. From outside, shouts came. "They're in the brewery. Someone saw them. Let's go!" Metal-shod boots clattered over cobbles.

"A brewery should keep them busy," Pitman said. "And they will be about it awhile. That damn Irishman has set the hive a-buzzing."

"Irishman?"

"A friend of yours. Maclean. He saw us run past the alehouse and named you."

"Maclean, eh? No friend to me." Coke let out a low whistle. "I'll pay him for that if I get the chance."

"You may not. But I'll pay him for you. I gave him two days' grace to go back to his land, in return for certain information he provided me regarding you. He must have seen me see him and thought the hue and cry would protect him."

"He was right. Thirty guineas was the price he called. There's not a man in Alsatia wouldn't sell three of his children for that."

"Aye."

More shouting. Both men listened, then this mob ran off too. "So, Captain," continued Pitman, "you heard my offer. An easy time while we wait for them to go or . . ." He raised the cosh.

Coke studied the man for a long moment. He truly is enormous, he thought. His face. His hands. If need be, though, I will fight him. But I will hope that a better course presents itself. "You said something of sausage and a flask?"

Gentle as lambs, Pitman thought, once the game is up. Yet a memory of blood came, and though he sat when the captain did, he kept his cudgel in his hand.

He passed the flask over. Coke drank, grimaced—the beer was the same sour stuff from the tavern opposite the goldsmith's. The dried sausage was better, and they both chewed upon it for a time in silence, as men ran to and fro below.

"This thirty guineas," Coke said at last, pulling a bit of gristle from between his teeth. "I may be able to match it. To better it. If you let me go."

"The necklace went for so much?"

"I do not know. I never got a chance to see what Di—what my boy brought me."

"I cannot take tainted money."

"Your conscience will not let you?"

Pitman smiled. "My wife will not. We are redeemed, sir. By God."

"That must be nice for you. Baptists?"

"Nay, we are of the quiet people."

"Quakers? I know little about them. But then, I know little about God. I leave him alone and he leaves me."

"Forgive me, but he does not. God watches over you always and will judge you for your deeds." Pitman shook his head. "And I cannot but think that he will judge you most severely."

Coke chuckled. "Yet was not the thief crucified at Christ's right hand forgiven and admitted to paradise?"

"He was not a murderer."

"Neither am I."

"Captain—" Pitman swallowed, then continued softly "—I was the next man into that carriage in Finchley."

Coke started. "So you saw."

"I did, God help me. The first to see what you had done. But not to reckon it." He leaned forward. "I could comprehend killing in the heat if they resisted you. But the footman? The coachman? All three within? Especially the lady. In that fashion?"

"So you think you know me because you think I did that?" Coke passed his hand across his eyes. "Oh, I know what you saw. I saw it first, remember. But I did not do it." He saw the denial in the other's eyes. "I did not."

"Sir, I have tried to understand. Indeed, it is the curse of my nature that I *need* to understand. And when you say you did not do these deeds, perhaps I take your meaning. For I saw many men in the late wars, uh, translated." Pitman cleared his throat. "I do not believe in the devil as one outside ourselves, seeking our souls. But I do believe that each of us has demons within that, given the opportunity, will come out. Will come out *because* they are given that opportunity. Wars provide it. During them a man does some things, some terrible things, simply because he can."

Coke stared for a moment. "You were in the wars?"

"I was. A corporal in the London Trained Bands. I served throughout."

"As did I," Coke said. "My captaincy was in Sir Bevil Grenville's Regiment of Foote."

"An honourable band of men, I heard. Cornish, are you?"

"From Bristol, I. Near it, anyway. But my father had connections." He paused. "Did we fight against each other? I wonder. I was mainly in the West."

"And I in London and a little in the Midlands. And once I fought as far north as Marston Moor, by York. Were you there?"

"I was not. Though I was at Naseby."

"As was I."

Naseby, thought Coke. The ruin of the king's cause.

Naseby, thought Pitman. That awful triumph.

For a few moments, while men ran in the streets and cat skins swayed in the warehouse, both men were not there. They were upon that field both had tried to forget. Both had only ever partly succeeded.

Does that explain it, then? Pitman asked himself. Things witnessed on a battlefield? The horror? Slaughtering others before they slaughter you? The first man you kill, terrible; the second, a little easier; by the third, a habit formed? But at every death the terror never leaving you? Knowing that unless you stick a pike in their guts, they will stick one in yours?

He looked again at Coke. His face was calm—and that made Pitman suddenly angry. "War might explain your actions a little, Captain. But it does not excuse. Not what you did. Not that." He saw the interior of the coach again. The lady. The blood. How it was used. It further fuelled his anger. "And you claim to leave God alone? When you blasphemed him by writing his words in the victim's gore upon the coach's walls?"

"What you are talking about?"

"What you wrote from Revelation. 'For the devil is come down unto you, having great wrath, because he knoweth that he hath but a short time.'"

"That was written there?"

"The numbers were. Chapter and verse."

"I did not write them."

"Of course not. It was your demon who did." Pitman's anger went as swiftly as it had come. "But they will hang you," he continued, "once for a madman, once for a murderer—and justice will be done."

Coke opened his mouth to deny again—then closed it. He studied Pitman's face, the righteous anger there. You *need* to understand me, he thought. Is that what you said? And now you think you have done so? But I *do* understand you. For you are not merely a thief-taker. You are an angel of justice. And there my hope lies.

Instead of denying further, Coke said, "I will acknowledge that I may be hanged as a thief. The laws of the land demand it—even though those same laws did not prevent the stealing of my family lands. Never mind that. But you speak of the justice that sees the highwayman hanged. What then of the murderer?"

"You hang as both. You are equally dead and equally punished."

"Am I?" Coke tipped his head. "Any man who saw the slaughter in that carriage would want to have the true culprit apprehended. If the wrong man is hanged for the crime, the slaughterer who did those . . . those things lives to do them again. More guts will be spilled—and the lady we both, I suspect, admired goes unavenged. If you have even the slightest doubt that I am the murderer of Finchley—and surely the fact that you have not coshed or shackled the mad dog shows you must have that tiny doubt—you must give me the chance to prove that I am not he."

"The judge will give you your chance."

"Come, you have been to court, sir. You know the judge will do only what the mob demands—that the Monstrous Cock dance the Tyburn jig before them. I will be lucky if it is only that, that a charge of treason is not somehow laid and proven, so the people can watch me hanged, drawn and quartered. Or that my crimes are not labelled witchcraft so they can see me burn." He shook his head. "Nay, sir—you claimed before that you would not accept tainted money. How much more tainted will your thirty guineas be when innocent blood washes it? When the true murderer lives, perhaps to murder again? Could you live with that?"

Pitman saw then in his mind's eye his home, his hungry children, his wife's belly swelled by the two yet coming. But then he imagined his wife's face, heard her voice: "You have to do the right thing, Pitman. God will not keep blessing us if you do not."

He drew a deep breath. "How can you prove you are not the murderer?"

Coke paused before he spoke. "By taking you to his latest victim."

"You mean your demon has killed again?"

"I mean, sir, that the murderer has. It is clear to me only now, in this conversation with you, that the two crimes are linked. The carriage and this cellar where the new victim lies. *If* he still lies there. He did last night and I can only hope he has not yet been disturbed."

"Where is this cellar?"

"In the parish of St. Giles in the Fields. Not far."

"I know where St. Giles is." Pitman chewed at his lip. Curse the fellow, he thought. Coke had made him doubt—which he had to admit he did already. For despite the evidence of that night, nothing he'd known of Captain Cock led him to believe the man capable of committing such crimes. Nothing he'd discovered in their conversation today had changed that opinion. "Even if you prove you are not a murderer, I could still hand you over for a highwayman and collect my reward."

"You could. Perhaps you will. Let justice be done."

Pitman raised his eyes to the heavens. Why, O Lord, why? "We will wait a little longer, for the chase to die away. And then you will take me to this cellar. Only then will I decide your fate." He reached into his cloak and pulled out manacles. "But you and I will be joined by these, Captain. I do not ask for your pledge. What man would not escape the noose if he could, despite the giving of his oath? But I'm damned if I am doing any more running this day. I'm too old for it, by heaven."

"As am I." Coke sniffed. "Though I hope we may leave soon. These cat skins may have been tanned, but how they reek!"

"They do. It is strange, is it not, what they say? That there are many ways to skin a cat. I can think of only one." He spun one of the furs. "But there are many ways to prove a man a murderer, Captain Coke. As you shall see."

They left an hour before sunset, the manacles that joined them, left wrist to right, concealed beneath Pitman's cloak, slung over their arms.

As they walked, Coke tried to tell a little of why and how he'd discovered the body they were about to visit, stating that he was on a mission for a lady, whom he did not name. But Pitman merely grunted, so Coke went silent. The thief-taker still thought he was the murderer.

From the murky warren of Alsatia, and after a brief time on the wider, better lit streets around Lincoln's Inn, they entered the equally twisting lanes of St. Giles. Before the Maidenhead, a low tavern whose crudely drawn sign depicted a frowsy lady most unlikely to have retained hers, a gang of link boys were dipping wands into a tub of molten wax. At Coke's insistence, Pitman bought two links, lit them, then went with the captain down an especially dark alley.

They stopped before a crumbled archway. "Are you sure this is the place?"

"Carrier Court." Coke raised his link. "Here is my mark."

His flame lit the scratched cross. "At least it is not painted red," said Pitman. "No plague here."

"None that is owned. Come."

Though evening light yet lingered, it did not do much to enhance the courtyard, still as grey and dingy as it had been the day before. No children danced around the well today; indeed, save for a piebald dog that rooted in the rubbish of one corner and ran off snarling when they entered, nothing stirred. Yet Coke still had the feeling they were observed, thought he heard a girl's giggle from the shadows.

"Well, sir?" said Pitman, shaking the manacles. "Where do you lead me?"

"Over here," Coke replied, setting off as he said it, though his feet dragged a little, as if they too were shackled. A small part of him hoped that the body was gone. A day had passed; surely someone would have nosed out the fellow. Coke`s proof would be gone. But he would be spared the sight again.

As soon as they stepped into the dank stairwell, he knew differently. The scent had been ripening before. Now it was ripe. Instinctively he raised a hand to his face—bringing Pitman's up with it.

"I do not think you can run from me now," the big man said, handing over his link so he could unchain himself from Coke, then chaining Coke's wrists. "As long as you go first," he added, taking his wand back, gesturing down.

It threatened to unman them both, the stench beyond the last door. Indeed, if either had fled back up the stairs, both would have done so. But neither did, and taking a steadying breath, foul though it was, Coke and Pitman entered the cellar.

"Where is he?"

Coke's reply was to wave his link toward the corner. Pitman approached and crouched. "I cannot see," he called. "Bring your light over here, man."

"I can do better than that." Coke remembered now the snuffing of the reed torch when he'd fled before. He lifted his flame to the charred reeds and blew. They glowed, flared, and a dancing light filled the cellar.

"Did you place that there so you could better work, Captain?"

"I found it. When I found that," he replied.

"Him," corrected Pitman. "Take this," he said, holding out his wand. "Stand close so I can view him properly and still see you."

"You will not wish it when you do," replied Coke softly, but moved nearer nonetheless.

Strangely, the stench diminished at its source. Or rather, Pitman realized, sight overwhelmed scent. Nevertheless, he was careful in his study. Noted the missing ears and single eyelid, the burns, the slashes, the wounds that had opened up the cavity, the guts drawn out. And yet, in the carnage he saw the same order that he had seen in the coach. Some of the havoc was indiscriminate, but some was precise. Done by someone who knew how to open up a body.

"Do you know how to dress a deer, Captain?"

"I do not. We hunted them, of course. But our servants prepared them." He ran his tongue over his lips. "I never even liked to watch."

Pitman rose. "Show me your hands."

"Why?"

"Show me."

Coke put the links into the sconce beside the reed torch, then held out his manacled hands palms down. Pitman turned them over, his own hands moving delicately despite their size, so lightly that Coke's skin tickled. "They are soft, Captain. Almost feminine."

"I wear gloves near all the time. I do not like to—"

"Labour with them. That is clear. Your labour requires you to hold a gun, does it not? You do have sword calluses on the palm of your right hand, on your index finger. Are you good with blades?"

"I am sufficient."

"A modest reply." Pitman sucked in a breath. "Tell me, did you ever study for a surgeon?"

"I did not—though I extracted a musket ball from a friend's back once. Near killed both of us."

"Hmm." Pitman released the man's hands. "You know, Captain Coke, whilst that same hanging judge might not believe me, I would testify that you did not slaughter this man. Nor, I believe now, those unfortunates in Finchley."

Coke felt the relief in a cooling of his brow. "And why do you believe that now?"

"Because whoever wrought this will have the hands of one who uses tools regularly, have knowledge of how bodies are put together— and how they are taken apart. His hands are stained permanently, as yours are not. A surgeon or a butcher—though from what I witnessed in the army there was little to tell the two professions apart."

Coke shook the restraints on his wrists. "Then if you believe me innocent, could you?"

"Not yet, sir. If I no longer think you a murderer, I have yet to decide what to do about the thief." He knelt. "Bring those lights back, if you please."

Coke did. Pitman was turning the body this way and that. The captain watched as he opened the man's jaws, using both hands and some force to counter death's hardening. There was a crack. Coke looked away, mastered his stomach's heaves, and then heard Pitman's cry of "Found you!"

When Coke looked back, he saw an oval lump in the thief-taker's hand; not, he was relieved to see, of flesh. Lights reflected in it, more so when Pitman rubbed it on his cloak before holding it up again.

"You found that in his mouth?"

"I did. And if I was yet a gambling man, I would give you short odds that it is a sapphire."

"Do you have knowledge of gemstones, sir?"

"No. But I know my Bible. I pulled a stone from the mouth of that member of Parliament in the coach."

"Did you, by God? A sapphire also?"

"No. That one was a jasper. And the book of Revelation speaks of an order to such stones."

"Revelation again." Coke frowned. "Why is that of concern here?"

"Because of those numerals I mentioned, daubed upon the coach's wall. And in that book it is written that gems will adorn the cornerstones of the new Jerusalem, which is Christ's returned kingdom upon the earth." He intoned, "Chapter twenty-one, verse nineteen: 'And the foundations of the wall of the city were garnished with all manner of precious stones. The first foundation was jasper; the second—'"

"Sapphire?"

"Which makes me suspicious of you anew, Captain. For I believe it was this very sapphire I glimpsed, aye, and sketched too, around the lady's neck in Finchley. Part of the necklace you already admitted to stealing. What makes it here unless you brought it?"

"I . . ." Coke was trying to remember something that Isaac ben Judah had said to him the last time they met. "The Jew thought that a jewel was missing from the necklace. He said he thought it might be a sapphire!"

"Convenient for you."

"If you don't believe me, we can go and ask him."

"I am not sure I want to see that Jew again. Last time I did he shot a gun near my head."

While the thief-taker continued his examination, another memory came to the highwayman. A face. A voice. "The lady," he said. "She was not dead when I found her." Pitman glanced up sharply. "Beyond any aid, sure." Coke hesitated. "But she said something just before she died."

"Did she? What?"

"She said, 'Pale horse.' She said it twice." Coke swallowed. "It made no sense to me."

"It does to me." Pitman gazed into the flames of the torch. "'And I looked, and behold a pale horse; and his name that sat on him was Death.'"

"Revelation again?"

"Aye."

"So the murderer, what, *quoted* as he killed her?" Coke felt anger flush him, the first warmth in that cold cellar. "By Christ, if I could have that man before me now!"

"Easy, sir. And perhaps this fellow will help you to that meeting." Pitman put the gemstone into a pocket. "Do you know his name?"

Coke hesitated. Reveal that and he'd reveal Sarah too, and so far he had not named her. His note would not have reached her yet. Yet somehow, whatever decision Pitman would make about the highwayman, he felt sure the thief-taker would bring no harm to the lady. "His name is John Chalker. You may know him. He is—was an actor. With the Duke's Company at Lincoln's Inn. He and his wife are quite a famous pair."

"I would not know them. Bettina and I do not approve of the playhouse, though we will watch the puppets and jugglers at Smithfield on fair day." He looked down. "Was he a soldier?"

"A famous one. But an enemy of yours. It is said he held Cropedy Bridge alone against a troop of lobsterbacks. 'Cropedy Chalker,' he was known as for a time."

"Is this the man?" Pitman gave a low whistle. "Well, sir, we left too many, old foes and friends, all jumbled in pits on the fields of Mars. Each deserves his own grave. Can you spare an old comrade your cloak?"

"Will I get it back?"

"I doubt you will want it. By your leave."

Pitman unclasped the cloak, then reached underneath the corpse, rolled it onto the cloth, covered it. "Do you know the mortuary in this parish?"

"I do not. But I can inquire. Shall we go there?"

"I will. You fetch his wife."

Coke lifted his manacles. "Like this?"

"Ah." The thief-taker took off the manacles, replaced them on his belt. Then he drew the captain's sword from the same place and held it out.

Coke regarded it a moment. "You are letting me go?"

"For now. And I do not even ask you for a pledge." When Coke took the sword, Pitman bent, lifted the cloak-wrapped corpse, carried it to the door, paused there. "Yet this I do say, Captain. Return and you may help me catch a monster. You may help avenge not only your lady in the carriage but both Chalker's widow and a man who was if not my comrade, then an adversary worthy of my respect. Indeed, you may help to overcome true evil." He left, and his voice echoed from the dark. "How many of us ever get a chance to do that?"

Coke rubbed his wrists, listening to the footfalls on the stair, soft for a big man despite his burden. When he was ready, he went to the reed torch and put out the light.

17

RESOLUTION

"Open the coffin."

The mortuary man looked past the woman to the two men who stood behind her. He pulled out a soiled square of linen and dabbed his damp face. "Sirs, I appeal to you. You know what is within this wooden box. A wife does not need to see it."

"But a widow does." Sarah laid her hand on the wood before her. "Open it. Or lend me chisel and hammer and stand back."

As Pitman stirred, Coke said quietly, "Your husband is not there, Mrs. Chalker. His soul is departed, we hope, for a better place. What remains is corruption. Leave it be."

"John was never much of a churchman. Rarely on his knees, unless to throw dice or introduce a cock into the ring. So I have no expectations of seeing him anywhere else but here. Open the coffin."

The man looked a last appeal at Pitman and Coke. When they said nothing, he sighed and picked up his tools.

Sarah folded her hands before her. "Gentlemen, you may leave me," she said.

Pitman's eyes widened. "Nay, lady."

Coke laid a hand on the larger man's arm. "We will wait for you outside, Mrs. Chalker. However long you wish."

"Thank you."

At the first hammer strike, Coke and Pitman departed. Sarah pressed herself to the cold stone wall as the fellow went about his task. The nails had been driven in deep, and the coffin's sides splintered under the blows and levering, while the lid cracked wherever he prised out a nail. When he finally lifted the top, its left panel split off at the one tack he'd forgotten to remove. The man, muttering and wiping his face, stacked the two broken pieces to the side then left. A long moment after the door's soft close, Sarah came forward.

She'd been forewarned. Not so much because of what the captain and the other man had said but because of how they'd avoided her gaze, a shadowed complicity between them. So she knew it would be bad; and it was, worse than she ever could have imagined. Yet when the first shock passed, weakening her knees so she had to rest both hands on the coffin's edge, the next was as powerful.

Relief. It overwhelmed her. For this wreckage could not be her husband.

The body was wrapped in a shroud, the wounds beneath it clear, lines like bloody stigmata running across the grey linen. The face was uncovered—and nothing about it was familiar. Indeed, no face was there, just a mass of blood, pooled and congealed around slashes. And how could that be her John's hair? His had always been thick and curled to excess, not this lank black sheet. And the eyes? Someone had put a penny over each one, and despite all the shaking in opening the coffin, they had remained in place. She would make certain of him by eyes as black as his hair. "Gypsy blood, you'd say, sweetheart, wouldn't you?" she whispered. "Or Black Celt. Whichever story you were spinning. Though once you confessed to me that you thought your mother had had knowledge of that Italian puppeteer Orsino, even if he was near a dwarf and you—"

She stopped talking. Since it was not John Chalker, why was she prattling at this man so? This shrunken, bloodied stranger.

She bent, lifted one penny. The eye was open; there was no lid to close it off. And she saw him. Knew him. Began to weep for him.

At the first cry, the three men started. The keening rose. It did not sound quite human, and the mortuary man crossed himself three times, tapped out his pipe on his boot heel and left the small yard.

Coke and Pitman glanced at each other, taking solace in the tobacco the man had given them, sucking hard upon their pipes. Then both sought for embers in the clay, while each sought for words.

Pitman spoke at last, loud to reach over the wailing. "I will need to speak to her. Later. There is so much I do not understand that she may be able—I mean, why him? Why an actor? A strange choice of victim after that MP in the coach."

"You are certain that the same man killed both?"

"You saw this body and all those in Finchley?"

"Aye, but many know the butchering trade or the surgical one."

"But few kill so precisely. The slashes just so, the guts *placed*, not simply extracted."

Coke raised a hand. "Your favour," he said, then leaned against the wall, taking breaths, spitting.

"You have a weak stomach, Captain. You vomited in that coach in Finchley, did you not?"

"I did. I nearly always do." He wiped his mouth. "I would be grateful, since we both know what we saw, if you did not dwell upon the details."

"Very well. Yet, other details lead me to think the murderer is the same man."

"The jewels in the mouths?"

"That, certainly. And what was written—and spoken, you say—in the coach. The verses from Revelation."

"Were there verses also in the cellar? I did not note any."

"There were not. But there were other things." Pitman pinched the bridge of his nose. "'The first foundation was jasper,'" he declaimed. "That's a type of quartz. 'The second, sapphire; the third, a chalcedony.'"

"And what is that?"

"An agate. People call it tiger's eye."

"And it was jasper found in the mouth of the MP?"

"Yes. While this sapphire—" Pitman pulled it out of his pocket, held it in his palm "—came from Chalker's mouth."

"So the next victim will have a tiger's eye?"

"If we do not find the murderer before he kills again, that will be his next stone. And there is something else." Pitman glanced at the door from behind which the keening came louder. Still, he lowered his voice. "Chalker was circumcised."

"Truly?" Coke frowned. "I would never have taken him for a Jew. A gypsy, perhaps."

"You mistake me. Or rather, I should have said that Chalker was circumcised *recently*."

"You mean . . . ?"

"I do. Among the many wounds, that."

Coke could not hold himself. Afterwards he leaned against the spattered wall, shallow breaths coming, which he was eventually able to deepen. He spat, stood straight. "Are you saying then that his killer is a Jew? You'll be telling me next that the murderer is stealing Christian babies to drain their blood." Red suffused his paleness. "Man, the Jews have been accused of such calumnies for centuries. All lies. You voice this suspicion and there will be blood on the street, on your hands."

"Captain, rest easy. I do not accuse any of that tribe. I know you have befriended them."

"Some. They have always been kind to me. One especially."

"Isaac ben Judah. The man who shot at me."

"*Over* you. Then if a Jew is not to blame, whom do you accuse?"

Pitman sucked his lip. "There are those who like the Jews as much as you do. Indeed, they revere them. To these men, the Jews are God's first chosen people, and they agitated strenuously for their re-admittance to the realm. Succeeded too during the Protectorate. Those I speak of believe that they cannot establish the new Jerusalem without including the inhabitants of the old one."

"Who do you mean?"

"The Fifth Monarchy Men."

"The dreamers of Apocalypse? I have heard of them but know little of them."

"I know much," Pitman replied. "Since I was one myself."

"You were?" Coke started. "You do not strike me as a Bedlamite."

Pitman shrugged. "I have been mad enough. The wars did that. The fighting—and the freedom that was unleashed. I was a great sinner in my day." He looked at Coke. "Before I was a Fifth Monarchist, I was a Ranter."

"Ranter? So you lived in a colony and spent your days and nights naked, smoking and drinking, cussing and fornicating?"

"Not only that. Sometimes we danced."

Coke laughed as he imagined the large, sober man before him cavorting. "By heaven, I'd have liked to know you then."

"You would not have, sir. Even less so, perhaps, after I ceased my sinning to be saved. When I believed I was one of the Elect, that I would be washed clean—burned clean!—by the floods and fires of the Apocalypse." A light came into Pitman's eyes as he continued. "I believed that the last of the four monarchies since Christ was about to be destroyed. That the fifth was upon us, when Jesus himself, in person, would descend and rule the wide world as sole king." He nodded. "It is all prophesied."

"Let me guess—Revelation."

"Aye. In Daniel also. Jeremiah. Deuteronomy. It is why the Saints love the Jews so much. All is foretold in their ancient books."

"Saints?"

"It is what the Fifth Monarchists call themselves. After Daniel 7:18—'But the saints of the most high shall take the kingdom and possess the kingdom for ever, even for ever and ever.'"

"But when shall they possess it?" Coke, who had been trying to relight the little tobacco left in his pipe from a taper, gave up, stamped out the flame, knocked the ashes from the bowl to the ground.

"Even now," replied Pitman. "Do you not know that the End of Days is upon us? Revelation tells how the Great Beast shall bring it. Its number is 666. What year cometh, Captain?"

"Sixteen sixty-six. Ah, I see. And you think the murderer is not content to await its coming?"

"Many are not. Apocalypse is coming, sure. And it can be hastened."

"Why do the authorities not arrest them all?"

"They've arrested many. But these people are not all Bedlamite, as you call them. Most are ordinary. Tanners, weavers of silk and wool, brewers. Butchers." He paused, then continued, "They are hidden everywhere, awaiting the trumpet."

"Why do they not await it in the Holy Land?" Coke lowered his voice, for the keening had finally stopped within the mortuary. "Surely King Jesus will arise again there."

"Some think so. But most believe that England is the chosen land, the English the new Elect. A nation that could topple a king— aye, and top him too! Who allowed, for a few short years at least, such freedoms that had never been seen anywhere before—and to the common people, mind! Freedoms of action, word, deed. The return of the king only put a bung back on the bottle. Inside the beer again ferments. Ready to explode." He shook his head. "It is the English who will lead the world into the Fifth Monarchy. Here it will happen. Here it is foretold. The Saints are preparing."

Coke stared at the bigger man. "Do you still believe in this End of Days?"

"Not since I met a woman who changed my beliefs. Who showed me enough heaven on earth. I believe in our saviour. I just do not believe he is coming in person to redeem us. Not next year, anyway."

"But our man does believe that?"

"I am sure every atrocity he commits is for Christ." Pitman's face was grim. "We met a few who committed horrors for such beliefs in the wars, did we not, Captain?"

"We did."

The mortuary man had returned to the yard and was standing with his ear to the door. "I have other customers coming," the man said. "Many others. There's a lot of death about these days. Should I?"

He raised knuckles to the door. From behind it, they all heard her voice: "You may enter now."

The other man did so but Coke pulled Pitman farther away from the door. His voice was low. "Do you think we can find this killer?"

"Perhaps. It may be that Mrs. Chalker can help us uncover some link between what happened in Finchley and her husband's murder. It may also be time to reacquaint myself with the Saints."

The door opened and Sarah emerged. "Mrs. Chalker," Pitman said, "I am so sorry for your loss."

"Thank you, sir." She gazed up at him. "May I ask who you are?"

"I am Pitman, ma'am. The captain here brought me to your husband's body."

"I see." She glanced at Coke. "Are you a constable of this parish, then?"

"I am a constable, but not of this parish. I am, uh—" he hesitated "—I am also what is known as a thief-taker."

"Are you? Well, exercise your profession, sir. For a thief has been here. He has stolen my husband's life." Before he could speak, she'd turned to Coke. "Captain, I thank you for your help. You have gone far beyond the bounds of all friendship to find my husband for me. I suspect you would rather not have seen him like that and I am sorry that you had to. But your duty is done. I release you from all obligation. Gentlemen, both."

She went past them. The nearby church bell was tolling. By its eighth and final strike, she had reached the yard gate. "Mrs. Chalker?" Coke called. She halted, her back to him. "Mrs. Chalker, I do not consider myself released. Not until the person who did this is discovered. And I believe my, uh, my friend here feels the same way."

"Why?" Sarah returned to stand before them. "Why are you concerned? Beyond a charity that you have both already displayed."

Coke looked at Pitman, received a nod. "Your husband was not the first murdered in this way. The first deaths touched us both. This second? No one deserves to die like that. No one who does should go unavenged. Nor will, if I can help it. You may trust me on that."

"There are some questions I would ask you," Pitman said. "Another hour, of course. After you have had some time to mourn."

"If it helps you catch this villain, I will answer any question you put to me as soon as I am able. But now I must go to the theatre."

Coke caught her arm. "They would not be so cruel as to make you play tonight. Let me walk you home. Or better, let me take you to Lucy."

"Lucy is at the playhouse. As I must be. And we do not play at night, sir. We rehearse. I cannot afford to miss any more time." She glanced back to the mortuary's door. "Since I have lost my protector, the only way I can protect myself is by winning acclaim for my performances. Perhaps that will start with *Othello*, which we revive next week." Suddenly she lifted Coke's hand to her lips and kissed it. Tears filled her eyes. "I thank you again, sir. You have been most kind. Yet if you are undertaking this cause, not for me but for what is right, know this: I will not rest until the man responsible for the slaughter of my husband is dead. You may trust *me* on that."

She crossed the yard and was gone. After a silence, Pitman said, "An extraordinary woman."

"Indeed."

"She reminds me of my Bettina. Lorks!" He slapped his forehead. "I had forgotten Bettina in all this. We have barely a crust in our larder and I—" he felt his pockets "—I spent the last of my coin on those damned links."

"You have a sapphire in your coat that Isaac ben Judah would give you ten gold pieces for right now."

"I told you, Bettina does not allow us to prosper on tainted money." He looked at the captain. "You have cost me thirty honest guineas, sir. That's a labourer's wages for a year!"

"Well, I am sorry for it even if my neck is not. Yet surely the reward would be yours still if the real murderer were caught."

"If guilt could be proven. But that will not stock my larder this day."

They were exiting the yard, when Coke gripped Pitman's arm. "Wait! How much is Maclean worth?"

"That betraying swine?" Pitman scratched his beard. "Five guineas."

"How are your legs after all that chasing?"

"Not so weak that some ale would not restore them."

"Then what say you if my tainted money supplies that, at least? And then," Coke said, grinning, "what say you if we pull our scarves about our faces, return to Alsatia at midnight and snag the rogue?"

"I'd say you were a bold fellow—which I always knew. But would you not feel badly about betraying one of your brethren of the road?"

"Brethren?" Coke snorted. "That Irish dog hallooed me on the street—aye, and he'd have plaited the noose to see me dangle above it. I'll take him for the pleasure alone, and you can keep the entire five guineas."

"A bargain, Captain." Pitman held out his hand. "Thief and thief-taker. Who could stand against us?"

Coke clasped Pitman's hand with both of his. "Thief and thief-taker. I think that between you, me and the actress, this murderer had better watch his back."

18

THE TESTING

June 5, 1665

Brother Simeon was halfway across the river, when the screaming stopped him.

He moved to the parapet and let others pass him. He looked
back up Ludgate Hill, to the great square tower of St. Paul's.
People were coming from the church to cross Fleet Bridge. When
they reached its midpoint, the more sharp-eared heard what he
had heard.

Faces changed. Men and women each took the sound differently—with a wince, with a curse, with—if they were papist—a furtive
sign of the cross. Most shrugged it off. London had become a city of
screams and you could not think too long upon each.

Simeon left the bridge and cut riverward beside St. Bridget's
Churchyard. Soon, he thought. Soon every citizen's ear will be filled
with nothing but the weeping of the ungodly, the gnashing of their
teeth, the lamentations of the judged. Ignore those, if you can.

Then he turned into Bride Lane, and the sound hit him full, halting him again—for the screams were coming from the very house he was making toward, and it was not the ungodly who dwelt there but one of God's true Saints.

Four other Saints gathered about the door, including the man he particularly sought this day. He hurried to him. "Brother Roland," he said, "is it one of Hezekiah's family who cries thus?"

"Nay, Brother S.," replied Lord Garnthorpe, "it is Hezekiah himself."

"Alas. I am sorry for it. May God have mercy on him."

"Amen."

Brother Roland's face showed no expression. A sheathed blade, Simeon thought, so reserved. Hard sometimes to remember him as the dashing commander, the noble who'd fought for Parliament, the man who'd led their regiment in the countercharge at Marston Moor. Harder still to recall the roarer Simeon had recognized only two years before in Bedlam's general cell, covered in his own excrement. But Simeon was ever glad he had noticed him that day, indeed had saved him from his degradation. For Lord Garnthorpe's blade was not always sheathed. Indeed, after that famous charge, he ordered the execution of six Royalist knights. Two had died by his own hand; the corporal of their company, who was speedy in such things, had killed four—for he had been in his civilian life a butcher. Simeon had been thinking of him especially of late. "Tell me, Brother," he said, "have you recently seen our old comrade Abel Strong?"

The man glanced up, a light in his eyes. "I have—" he began, but a different shriek from above and the sound of feet thumping down the stairs interrupted him.

A woman ran out. She paused as she saw the group before the door, then her face lightened when she noticed Simeon. "Master," she cried, seizing his hand, kissing it. "Thank the Lord you are here. My husband is sick with . . ." Her voice dropped to a whisper. "My sons cannot hold him for the doctor to treat him." She tugged Simeon toward the house. "Please, Master, help us."

"I am no master, Sister. We are Hezekiah's brethren and we will come." He gestured to the others to precede him. They did not move.

"Brother S.," one murmured. "It sounds like Hezekiah suffers from—"

"Hush!" Simeon held up his hand. "It matters not what ails him. Know you not that all our days are numbered in God's great book? If you are marked to die, you will. Now you will come to answer a sister's plea."

They obeyed, though snail-like. Only Lord Garnthorpe moved briskly, his eyes empty again.

Inside the lodging, the stench derived of various things, none pleasant, and all there threw cloak edge or cuff before their faces and breathed through their mouths. But they did not shade their eyes, could not look away from the horror on the floor. Their brother Hezekiah Chambers writhed upon a mattress. Black ovals a finger's length covered his reddened skin, as if inky fat slugs crawled over him. One youth was trying to hold the man's flailing arms, another his legs with as little success.

When the Saints entered, Hezekiah ceased thrashing to lunge up. "Brothers!" he screamed. "God's mercy but you must help me! They wish to, wish to—No!" He fell back, his eyes fluttering shut. His sons seized his limbs again.

Simeon turned to the woman. "Sister, what would you have us do?"

Instead of replying, she gestured under the eaves. Someone who had merged with the shadows stepped from them now and every man in the room fell back, several crying out in terror—for the figure was from a nightmare. His long black robe glimmered with wax, cracked in various parts. White cowhide gloves wrapped his arms up to his elbows. But it was his head that was the worst—for below a high black cowl was a bird's face with a long, moulded beak.

"Be you the devil?" cried Simeon. "What make you here?"

The voice came muffled from within the leather mask. "No devil, sir, though I have been called that and worse these past weeks." The creature gave a slight bow. "I am a doctor. This is my uniform and I would be about my business. Many are waiting to receive my treatments if this man will not."

"Tr-treatments?" one of the other Saints spluttered. "Why must you wear a demon's face to treat the sick?"

"I wear it to prevent their sickness infecting me." He tapped his beak. "This is filled with sweet herbs to prevent the miasma of contagion from reaching my lungs." He drew closer, moving awkwardly like some great buzzard. "And I say again, if this man will not yield to my remedies, I must haste to those who will. I am paid by the patient and time is money."

Simeon spoke. "What must we do?"

"Hold him. Spread his limbs so I can apply—" he was delving within a large leather bag "—this." He pulled out a bottle with a glass stopper.

"Is it a medicine?" asked Simeon.

"For him it can be. If I am not too late. The buboes, sir. The putrefaction must be emitted. If it is not, he will certainly die."

Simeon turned to his fellow Saints. "An arm and leg each, Brothers. Swiftly."

The boys relinquished their father's limbs to the men. Each knelt, gripped—and averted his eyes from the blackened, distended balls of skin protruding from the man's groin and each armpit. Simeon went to Hezekiah's head, taking it onto his lap.

Hezekiah's eyes shot open—and the first thing he saw was the approaching doctor, bottle in hand. "The devil comes for me!" he shrieked, flinging off a man at one arm, seizing Simeon by the collar. "Do not let him touch me, Brother! He wishes to do something *down there*." He hissed this last, his tormented gaze toward his groin. "It cannot even be touched, not a finger laid upon it for the agony."

"'Tis only a salve he puts there, Hezekiah. Have faith. Pray to God as I do. You will be healed." He looked at the others. "'Our Father,'" he began, "'who art in heaven.'"

The prayer filled the small room, with wife, sons, brethren joining in. It stilled the patient a little. He closed his eyes, murmured the words.

From the bird's beak came a chuckle. "Only a salve," the man said, "I like that."

Then he stooped and poured acid on the bubo.

The scream could have been heard in the nave of St. Paul's. Hezekiah bucked up, his eyes wide, threw off each man. Only Lord Garnthorpe retained the arm he held; indeed, endeavoured to grab the other that flailed free.

The savour of burned flesh filled the room. The boys and their mother wept; three of the Saints turned their faces away, one to vomit, the others to continue the Lord's Prayer.

The doctor said, "Spread his limbs and let's be done with him."

"No! No! No! No! No!"

The men held tight again, faces averted, eyes closed despite their comrade's pleading, his thrashing, But they could not close their ears to the sizzle of corroding flesh, nor their nostrils to its sweet-sick stench. In their grip, Hezekiah bucked each time the liquid dripped, until at last he fell back to writhe and scream no more.

Simeon lifted one of the man's eyelids. "I think your salve has killed him, Doctor."

The bird-faced man was stoppering his bottle. The beak swung back. "If he is dead, it is the plague that has killed him, God that has taken him, not me." He picked up his bag and without another word he left the room.

Simeon put his ear against Hezekiah's chest. After a while, he looked up at the man's wife and sons and shook his head.

They all knew what it meant: when the doctor reported the plague, as he must, the house would be shut up, along with any found within it. Simeon, dispatching three of the Brothers, told them where to meet again later that night. But he kept his hand on Lord Garnthorpe. "Walk with me," he said.

They made for the river, to a coffee house on the water. Both sipped at chocolate; neither spoke until their hearts slowed. At last, Lord Garnthorpe murmured, "Are we all to die like that now that we have been so exposed?"

"We do not know," replied Simeon. "My sister lived in a house not three streets from here where a dozen died in '47. Yet she did not contract the disease. Others never venture near one with the plague and yet are stricken straight. It is, as all things are, what God wills." He lifted Brother Roland's hand from the table. The man stiffened but did not pull it away. "Yet I say this: if the plague has truly come to take London, it is both a terrible and a glorious thing. Yea, glorious! For does not it say in Numbers, 'The wrath of the Lord was kindled against the people, and the Lord smote the people with a very great plague'? Is it not foretold in Daniel, in

Revelation, that before the Fifth Monarchy can be established such disasters will—must!—come? These are signs, Brother. Terrible signs. Glorious signs. They assure us that God is hastening the End of Days, that the hour of King Jesus is nigh—and that even now his Saints must prepare." He squeezed the man's hand hard. "Do you believe that?"

"You know I do. I am the Lord's soldier ever."

"You are. And all his soldiers are needed now, yea, now more than ever." Simeon released Garnthorpe and picked up his chocolate to sip again. "I asked you, before the tragedy of Hezekiah intervened, how is our old comrade Brother Strong?"

"Busy at his butchery, I believe."

"Is he?" Simeon studied the man before him, then nodded. "Because we have need of him." Three merchants entered and sat down nearby. Simeon lowered his voice. "We have a Judas among us. Hezekiah had found him out and was going to tell us his name this very day. He died before he could." He glanced at the merchants. "I would like you to take over this good work. Find out this traitor."

His gaze still on the table, Garnthorpe replied, "Why me, Brother? I do not move so easily among the Saints. Some resent that I am of the nobility."

"They do not matter. For will we not all be Christ's nobles when he returns to rule over us? I ask you to do this for two reasons. The first is that with Hezekiah's death there is an empty place now among the Six of the Council of the Great Ones. You could fill that place if you prove yourself worthy."

"You do me much honour."

"The second is that once this Judas is found out, our friend Strong will be needed to *converse* with him. We must discover if the traitor works alone. Then after he must be punished." He nodded. "Strong has the sapphire still, does he not?"

Garnthorpe met Simeon's gaze. "No."

"No?" Simeon frowned. "How can he not have—" He broke off. There was no point questioning. Only Strong would know the answer. And the butcher of Harrow Alley was not there. "Then he will need this, though it was meant for another." Simeon held out something on his palm. "Do you know what this is?"

The amber showed strongly within the copper. "It is a tiger's eye."

"Also called?"

"Chalcedony."

The pale man ran a finger across the scar that bisected his nose like a cut of light. "Should not this traitor carry this gemstone in his mouth?" he said.

For a long moment, Garnthorpe stared at the small stone in Simeon's palm. Then he took it up, put it in his pocket and replied, "If that is the Lord's will."

"Oh, it is, Brother Roland. Doubt not but it is."

19

THE GAMBLE

"Off out, Pitman?"

"Off out, my love."

"Will you take Josiah?"

His son looked up, hope in his eyes.

"I will not, love. I need him to be with you, in case you fall to labour. He knows where I am bound and will run to fetch me then."

"I've told you, it is not going to happen till after the Sabbath. At the earliest." Bettina came to the doorway, wiping her hands with a cloth. "I have had enough of them to know."

She gestured back onto the room, where the whole tribe was busy—Josiah, Grace, Faith, even little Imogen had a cloth in hand and was scrubbing. Since the house four along from theirs had been shut up the previous Sunday, each day they cleaned every surface with vinegar in which Bettina had steeped rue, valerian and clove. Every part of their bodies had a soaked cloth passed across it daily. Any coin brought into the house they dropped in a bucket of vinegar to steep—though there had been few enough of those since he and the captain had taken Maclean three days earlier, the Irishman proving hard to find in the stews of Alsatia.

The five guineas had gone fast for rent, food—and the ingredients in the pot now steaming on the hob. "And I still need those last items for my mother's plague water," Bettina said. "You can never remember them."

"Nay, sweet chuck, but I can. Angelica, bay, campana roots. Uh, juniper. Mace?"

"Pitman, you lump! I made you learn them by letter because you don't like reading my notes. You've jumped from *c* to *j* and skipped such essentials as gentian, hyssop." She slapped his arm. "And that's why you shall take Josiah with you. He will be your memory. Will you not, boy?"

"I will, Ma," their son replied, leaping up. "After mace there's myrrh, penny-royal—"

"There's a bright lad. But don't tell me—tell your father when he is at the apothecary's. Fetch your coat."

As Josiah scurried away, Pitman bent to speak softer. "My love, it might not be suitable for the boy to accompany me."

"Why?" Her eyes narrowed in concern. "Do you go to take another thief?"

"No. At least, I do not think so." He dropped his voice still lower. "I am going to the theatre."

"The *theatre*?" The word *whorehouse* would not have received more disdain. "We have not enough coin to buy unguents for Imogen's rash and you are going to spend what little we do have on depravity?"

"Nay, chuck. I have been vouchsafed the ticket. By an actress."

He wanted the word back as soon as he said it. But it was too late.

"An *actress*?" His wife grabbed his arm and pinched it hard. "Have you turned lunatic, man? Next you'll be dancing naked down the street, save for the bells on your ankles, crying, 'Once a Ranter, always a Ranter!' What are you about?"

Pitman looked over her head at their offspring, who looked back with fascination at the comet rarity of their parents fighting. Discomfited, he lifted Bettina as if she were a doll, not a woman about to put forth twins, and placed her behind him in the hallway, then closed the door on the amazed faces of their children. "Hush, love," he said, "I didn't tell you before because you are so near your time." Impatience was colouring her face a red to match her hair, so he hurried on. "I am on the trail of something big. Thirty guineas big."

"Captain Cock? I thought he was lost."

"He may not be the one I seek. I have a possibility. Otherwise I would never venture into such a temple of Sodom as a playhouse."

"Though there was a time . . ."

"A time for both of us, aye."

"Shh!" Bettina glanced at the door, from just the other side of which came children's whispers. "We do not speak of that time now, Pitman."

"I know." He pulled her into his arms. "Though sometimes I dream of that summer and the camp by the Great Ouse. Of the whole Ranter crew. The singing. The drinking. The moonlight on your naked skin after you left Arise Evans and gave yourself only to me."

"Hush," she said, "you daft ha'porth." But she did not pull away, and when he bent to kiss her, she opened her mouth to him, her whole self, as she had always done, moonlight or none. After a few moments she stepped from his arms, laughing. "Get on with you, then. But listen. I assume the thirty guineas depend on the taking of this pigeon, and it's not yet netted, nor will not be tonight?"

"You assume right, my love. I have confederates—"

"Does this mean a shared purse?"

"Nay, love." He thought of Mrs. Chalker and Coke. The actress sought only vengeance for her husband's murder. The highwayman? A strange fellow, whose company and skills he'd appreciated in the hunt for Maclean. The man had enjoyed the chase, the capture—and was morose afterwards, as if all his joy was in action alone. Both Mrs. Chalker and the captain had sent him notes, which he had labouriously pieced together, being unable to ask Bettina for her usual help in deciphering. Both had said they would rendezvous at the playhouse to discuss the greater hunt. "These others aid me only, sweet. They desire no part of the reward."

"Citizens about their duty, then? Good. Then you'll take Josiah—" she raised her voice against his interruption "—as far as the apothecary's. He'll bring back the ingredients I require for the plague water. I can bottle and be selling by noon tomorrow. We're likely to need the cash—" she winced, placed a hand on her swollen belly "—by the Sabbath indeed, if their blows are anything to go by."

He placed his own hand there. "Hard kickers, eh? Boys, you think?"

"Arise Evans would give you short odds." She slapped his hand away. "Now be off, you great simpleton, and I'll send Josiah." She stood on tiptoes and pecked his cheek. "Go take us a thief."

I'll try, my love, he thought, watching her waddle away. Though it's not a thief I am after but someone much worse.

His son found him staring at the front door, his brow creased. "Off out, Father," he called.

"Off out, Son."

They emerged to a mad carillon of bells. These did not sound with the solemnity of the toll for the dead, near continuous this past week.

"What mean these bells, Father?"

"'Tis said that the English fleet has sunk some scores of Dutchmen off Lowestoft. To hear the talk, it is a victory near as famous as Old Bess's over the Great Armada."

"Is that not good for us, Father? For the realm?"

Pitman sniffed. "Perhaps. I care little for the realm these days. My parish, my neighbours, my family are realm enough for me."

Coke looked slowly around the seven faces that floated over the green baize. Though they were in the back room of Lockett's, with a clientele that professed to the genteel, he didn't think he'd seen a scurvier crew of sharpers in the lowest den in Alsatia. They were better lit—the establishment had cut-glass chandeliers suspended above the tables, studded with candles. Yet better lighting only more clearly revealed the smallpox scars, no matter how painted or patched the face; revealed too those who had suffered from the other pox, the great one, and had attended the mercury baths to cure it—though whether the disease or its attempted remedy had ravaged them so, Coke did not know. All he could see were several men with only half their teeth their own, the other half a gleaming, false white, some below nostrils as mangled as if gnawed by a rodent.

He continued his study, and finally halted his gaze on the man opposite him, the spokesman for the group, the one in the eye patch. This was not the customary sober black item but emerald green, and studded with sparkling stones in the oval of the missing eye beneath. "Well, sir, do you call?" drawled this fellow, resting his hands upon the raised soft cushion that edged the table. "Really, sir, call your main or pass the dice. You have left, what? Five guineas of your original stake? It has been an enjoyable hour, has it not? But truly, sir, would it not be wise for you now to pass?"

Each "sir" he uttered with the same tinge of derision. Coke did not wear the clothes that these men did, the latest fashion displayed in colour and cut. When he'd ordered wine, someone had laughed at his Somerset lilt, someone not brave enough to emerge from the dark beyond the candle spill. Now they were all silent, waiting for the captain to pass and walk away.

He never walked away. "Seven," Coke said, and picked up the ivory dice.

Eye Patch smiled. "Again? Your number of fortune, eh. Well, it has failed you so often tonight it must come good soon, what? And how much of your remaining five would you wager, sir?"

Coke smiled back. "All of it."

"Very good. We shall take that wager, shall we not, gentlemen?"

A murmur of assent came from the other six who made up "the bank."

"Then roll, sir. Roll. And may the devil dance in your dice."

Coke opened his hand, spat on the dice, then flung them across the table, thinking hard as they tumbled: seven or eleven, seven or eleven, seven—

"Five," called Eye Patch. "The gentleman rolls chance."

Two, three or twelve and he'd have lost. Seven or eleven, won. Five gave him the chance to roll again, at least—though now he must not hit his main. Seven and he would lose. Five and he would win, and stay in the game.

He reached for the dice, but Eye Patch picked them up first and held them out with that same smirk on his face. Coke took them, staring into the one eye. There were as many sharpers at Lockett's as upon any dirt floor in the slums. Perhaps more.

The weight felt the same. Palming one die, he passed the other lightly between his forefinger and thumb, rubbing each surface. During the wars, he'd had a soldier in his company who'd worked in a shop that made false dice. A tiny end of boar's bristle, wedged in, sticking out, imperceptible to the eye but not to the touch, could give the result desired, the opposite of what Coke wished for. The maroon velvet doublet of the one-eyed man could conceal a multitude of pockets, each with a pair of dice to give any result required. Yet as Coke rubbed the first and then the second die, he did not feel the telltale prickle. Eye Patch, knowing what Coke did, simply kept smiling.

The captain lifted the dice into the light. He'd noted something on one of the treys—there! The slightest fleck of blue on the ivory, like a tick to the dot. It recalled to him the exact blue of Mrs. Chalker's eyes. The dice were good, and the same ones he'd used for the past hour; won a little, lost much with. He raised them. Five, not seven. Five. Coke saw it, and her eyes again, just before he rolled.

The first die stopped on a trey. Two, he thought, two, watching the other spin on a tip for what seemed an age. At last it halted.

"Four," called out Eye Patch. "There's your lucky seven. Just when you didn't want it." He leaned across the baize, snatched up the five gold guineas. "Is that indeed your last? Do you pass? Or do you have perhaps one final coin about you to give us?"

There was a faint buzzing. Around him. Within him. He had heard it every day for the three days since the taking of Maclean and he'd had nothing else to focus on. He could not rob again for he could not in all good conscience continue the hunt with Pitman—a hunt that would begin today after the rendezvous at the playhouse—and be a thief under the thief-taker's gaze. So he had sought to reduce the buzzing in customary ways. At the cockpits. At the prizefights. At dice. And he had marvelled at how swiftly the profit from a rich necklace could be disposed of.

An impatient hum. "Come! Do you cede the table, *sir*?"

He focused again. Not on the true eye. On the false one that glittered beside it. "I do not," he declared, then looked to the back of the room. "Dickon!" he called.

The boy was perched on two legs of a chair, leaning precariously against a wall. He looked up from his latest pamphlet, his mouth agape, the shell of a sunflower seed clinging to his lower lip. "Bring me my money, boy."

The boy brought the two chair legs crashing down and stood. Then, instead of obeying his captain, he turned and ran.

"Dickon! Come here!" Coke bellowed. But the only reply to his command was the sound of the boy's boots upon the stairs.

"Your idiot son does not heed his father, *sir*. Maybe not such an idiot after all."

Coke would have stopped and perhaps had more than words with the fellow. A finger jabbed in the man's one good eye would make him mind his "sir"s. But that could wait till after he had thrown the dice at Hazard one more time. And that would only happen if he caught the fleeing boy.

Derisive laughter accompanied him out the room and down the stairs. Reaching Lockett's entrance, he looked left, then right, spotted the sheaf of wheaten hair bobbing at speed up the middle of Fleet Street, where all walked to avoid getting close to any walls. "Dickon!" he roared, his sword sheath clattering between his legs as he ran, near tripping him twice. For a time he seemed to be gaining—the boy had one gammy leg, after all—but the lad could still move fast, his size letting him duck and dart through gaps in the crowds that Coke had to run around. When after fifty paces he'd made no real gain, the captain slowed, then stopped dead. He shook his head. The buzz that had beset him had diminished. In a short while, he would be free of it entirely.

"Dickon," he said, with no hope of being heard. The boy had done exactly as ordered: kept the last coins they had from his captain. The rent on the rooms they'd taken near Lucy's was paid for two months. They had an ample supply of various nuts. But they still must eat more and drink until something else arose.

Until something else—The very last of the buzzing left him, displaced by the nearby Bridewell's bells. Noon on a Thursday. The playhouse doors were opening; yet he had no need to rush there, for Mrs. Chalker had someone holding a place on the pit's benches for Pitman and him. He hoped that someone was big. Pitman in the pit? It seemed an apt place for the giant. A rare character, sure, with a nose like a beagle, proved when he was tracking through the reeking country of Alsatia in search of Maclean.

The only thing Coke regretted now about the Lockett's episode—aside from the finger jab he still owed Sir Eye Patch—was the bumper of Rhenish he'd left beside the dicing table. He still had a thirst but now no coin to slake it. Dickon would avoid him till after the play. Perhaps Pitman would arrive early and stand him a jar.

20

THE BLACKER DEVIL

"My lord! A pleasure to see you, as ever. Will you follow me?"

The attendant led him up the stairs, then along an ill-lit corridor. Three-quarters of the way down the man parted thick drapes, and what had been a dull murmur of voices changed to a loud buzz, borne on a waft of heated air. Garnthorpe did not enter. "This is not my usual box."

"A thousand apologies, my lord. But there was such excitement to see Mr. Betterton attempt the Moor, and Mrs. Bracegirdle the tragic Desdemona, that every seat was fought over. A foolish colleague gave your customary box to the Earl of Sandwich before I could intervene." The man cringed and gestured Garnthorpe in. "I hope this will do."

"We shall see." Garnthorpe entered. The box was farther from the stage than he liked. His eyesight was not what it once was and he wanted to see the player's faces clearly. One especially. At least this box, like his customary one, had some depth, some shadows; it was also farther from the giant cut-glass chandelier that lit others so well. In them sat those who liked to be observed, indeed attended for that purpose far more than to see the play.

Or the players.

"Tell me, Master Aitcheson," he said, sitting without any further acknowledgement, "does Mrs. Chalker have a prominent role this night?"

"Indeed, my lord. She plays the maid. The villain's wife." The man darted a tongue over his thin lips. "Are you an admirer of hers?" When no reply came, he coughed and continued in a lower voice, "Would you care to have her visit you here after—or even during—the performance?"

"Is that possible?"

"Sir, she is an *actress*. And a widow now."

The man's tone irked. He obviously did not know of whom he spoke. "Do not presume, sirrah, to know what I may want until I inform you of it."

The attendant swallowed. "Of course, my lord. May I fetch you some food? Oranges? Wine?"

"Bring me a quart of Canary. The best, mind you." Garnthorpe pulled a gold coin from his doublet. "And you may keep what remains of this if you are attentive this night."

"Good my lord! You are as generous as ever."

The man withdrew, the drapes falling behind him. Garnthorpe leaned on the box's railing and gazed down. There was indeed a throb in the playhouse today, a more than common excitement. In the pit, the orange and nut girls were competing more vociferously—and displaying more than a customary amount of breast. As for their clients, the well dressed moved among the benches or squeezed themselves upon them, while the even better dressed took their seats in the boxes above. The largest of those, closest to the stage and with purple curtains lined in gold cloth, was empty; for now but not, he suspected, for long.

Then he felt it—someone regarding him with as keen an eye as he regarded. He looked into the pit and saw the man immediately. He would perhaps have noticed him sooner or later. Partly for his dress: the brown coat, the simple faun doublet, a sober contrast to the peacock gaudiness about him. Partly for his size: he was a head and a half taller than the next biggest man present. Mainly for the intensity of the stare, directed straight at him.

He sat sharply back. When Aitcheson returned with the wine, he said, "There is a fellow below. I would know his name."

"If you point him out to me?"

The attendant leaned, then yelped as his lordship's hand closed over his wrist and jerked him back. "You do not need to see him yet. I would not have him know I inquired. But you cannot miss him. He is a giant among pygmies, thick bearded, with a shaven head and the tallest man in the house, even when the king gets here."

He released his grip, and the attendant backed out, rubbing his wrist. "I will find him out for you, my lord."

Garnthorpe remained in the shadows, his gaze fixed on nothing across the auditorium. Soon enough there came the rustling of cloth behind him. "Well?"

"He was indeed easy to discover," Aitcheson said, entering the box. "He is known in the City, though I have never seen him here. His name is Pitman. He is a constable in the parish of St. Leonard's."

"A constable?" Garnthorpe took a sip of wine. "Very well. You may go."

The man hastily withdrew. Garnthorpe considered. Why did you stare at me so, Mr. Pitman? What make you here?

—

What make you here? thought Pitman, staring at the vacated rail of the box above.

He knew the man who'd looked down. Had seen him before; twenty years before, in a battle—or rather, in the aftermath of one. He had hoped never to see him again. He now discovered that twenty years had not diminished that hope one jot.

So lost was he, failing to dodge his memories, that it took him a while to note the persistent poking of his arm. His eyesight cleared and he glanced up into the familiar face of Captain Coke.

"I think you'd better insert yourself on the inside of the bench, sir," Pitman said. "My size has already been much abused, and if I assume that position, we will be the target for orange peel throughout the performance."

"I am hardly small myself, sir. And there is no space there."

"Oh, but there is." Pitman pushed hard sideways. Two people popped up farther down, and a yelp came from the far end of the bench.

Coke dropped into the small space, widening it with determined thrusts of his hips. "'Twill do," he said, looking up at the bigger man. "I was tapping at you for a while. You seemed to be in a world you like none so well." He took in the riot around, the cries of "Orange-orange-oh!" and "Fine ales!" and "Nuts! Nuts! Nuts!" rising from the cacophony of names called, insults traded, reunions noisily greeted. "Is this too much sin for one so godly?"

"Nay, Captain." Pitman glanced again to the box above. "I have just seen a ghost."

"Have you, by God. Whose?"

"Lord Garnthorpe's."

"I do not know him."

"No? He was perhaps more notorious on our side of the wars than on yours. A colonel with the London Trained Bands, he had . . . a way of dealing with those who displeased him."

"Harshly?"

"I once watched him whip three deserters to death. He wielded the whip until he tired, then had a corporal carry on, a brute, name of—" He squinted. "Nay, I forget his name. I had mercifully forgotten Garnthorpe's too until just now."

"Many terrible things were done. Many that I would forget and cannot." Coke shook his head. "The best way I've found is to drink them away. What say you to a bottle of strong ale?"

"If you are buying."

Coke placed thumb and forefinger and rubbed down either side of his moustache. "A slight problem. I have no money."

"What happened to the forty you had of the Jew?"

"Gone." Coke sighed. "Five was my hazard and I rolled my main."

"Captain, tell me you did not lose forty guineas at dice?"

"Certainly not. A considerable portion went on a cock, Diavolo, whose name was the fiercest thing about it. Then there was a fighter named Glazier, whose jaw was also made of glass." He clapped the other man on his shoulder. "So, Pitman of the Pit, it's your round."

"You will scarce be surprised how stale that joke already is. The alderman of my parish, who sits yonder and was most astonished to see me here, would not, like a dog that returneth to its own vomit, let the phrase alone. Still, it cost him, for the parish owed me three months' wages and even that paltry little adds up." He delved into a pocket, produced a florin. "Do not tell my wife. You fetch the beer while I hold this place."

Coke took the coin, slid out. In a short while he was back with two bottles. Both men forced their bungs out, then toasted each other.

"Now, sir," Pitman said, wiping froth from his beard, "as to the hunt for our murderer, I have had some thoughts on how we should proceed."

Yet before he could share them, there was an upsurge of twittering in the house. A man in crimson livery had appeared in the largest box. Now he bellowed, "All rise for the king!"

Charles entered, arms raised as he beamed at the acclamation, the huzzahs and the impromptu rendition of a popular song:

Here's a health unto His Majesty
With a fa-la-la-la-la-la-la
Confusion to his enemies
With a fa-la-la-la-la-la-la
And he that will not drink his health
I wish him neither wit nor wealth
And yet a rope to hang himself
With a fa-la-la-la-la-la-la.

Charles bowed, then helped a lady to the seat beside him. She wore a mask, and behind fluttering fans the crowd speculated on whose face was beneath it. Most decided that the woman, wearing a pea-green dress cut to emphasize a sizable bosom and the slimmest of waists, was Frances Stuart, the new favourite of the king's, rather than the older Barbara Castlemaine, whose figure was differently shaped, having already borne the king five bastards.

After Charles had helped her sit, and before he himself did, he took a long look around the house, with a smile of equal warmth for both ladies and orange girls, all curtsying revealingly low. He acknowledged the occasional gentleman with a nod—and paused a fraction longer when he saw Coke, the slight dip of his head showing that he knew exactly who he was.

"He truly misses nothing," the captain murmured, as first the king and then the audience settled, though the gossip was only suppressed by the clarion blast of a trumpet, followed by the subtler tones of viola, violin and flageolet. The ensemble played eight bars and then from behind one of the wings, on which was painted the Rialto bridge of Venice, stepped Thomas Betterton. His face and hands, as befitted the role he was about to perform, were painted a mahogany brown. Yet it was not in the character of Othello that he spoke now but as the leading actor of the Duke's Company:

Like savage beasts that in their jungles lie
To leap and rend unwary passersby,
So we, the lions in this city's glade,
Seek so to ambush lady and gay blade.
Alas!

Coke had never liked these prologues, which appeared to offer modesty and crave forgiveness, when truly they puffed up both player and audience. "'The play's the thing,'" he murmured. "For mercy's sake, let's to it."

"Do you know this piece?" whispered Pitman as Betterton concluded, people clapped and the small orchestra struck up again.

"No," replied Coke, "and I confess I find Old Will dull. I'm for a comedy and a dance when all's said. Why, last year at Drury Lane, I saw—"

He did not finish, for two players walked in from opposite entrances onto the forestage, acknowledged the applause with a bow, turned their bodies square to the audience, their faces to each other and began to converse.

The play proceeded, though oranges were still sold, their sellers groped, and beer bottles popped explosively. "She does not have so much to do, Mrs. Chalker," Pitman said at one scene's end. "She is the villain's wife, the mistress's maid and nothing more?"

"She told me her main part is later. Now hush! For here comes Mrs. Absolute."

Lucy entered and the crowd laughed. It was partly her gait. She played the role of Bianca, the courtesan, but not in the usual style of scheming vizard. This courtesan had paid a price for her lasciviousness: a belly swollen by it.

"She has it pat." Pitman laughed. "My Bettina has been waddling so these two months."

Coke did not laugh, knowing that the padding was not much and the walk near her natural gait. He glanced up at the boxes near the sovereign's, inhabited by Charles's closest cronies. But Rochester, the man responsible for the waddle, who had vowed to make amends, was not among them.

Coke had been distracted. The scene had ended and Charles was rising, applauding, so the rest of the audience did too. A break was being taken. King, courtiers and commoners would go to their separate stations, be it commode, closet or convenient wall, to void. "Come," the captain said, "shall we go see the ladies?"

"Between acts? Is it done?" asked Pitman.

"Aye. It's where the king's going. Betterton will feed him, and offer him a more discreet place for the royal piss."

It was unfortunate that they arrived backstage after His Majesty. The royal party and those who ogled them formed a barrier to progress. Coke himself had no desire to see Charles, nor be seen by him—their interchange at the Banqueting House had been more than enough. Pitman, however, resisted Coke's tugs to go around the mob. Indeed, for a man who'd spent a considerable part of his life trying to defeat the king's cause, he seemed inordinately fascinated by the king himself.

"Amusing, is he not?" Pitman whispered.

"Hilarious," answered Coke. "Now, if you would—"

"Hark! Betterton's just praised him for being the one who allowed women on the stage—an addition I do think good myself. Let's hear what he has to say, eh?"

"Saw 'em on the Continent during our exile, didn't we, Jamie?" Charles was addressing his brother, the Duke of York, who nodded. "The French have had women players for years. My brother monarch Louis maintains it has led to a notable decrease of sodomy in his kingdom!" Cheers arose, which the king loudly topped. "Now, while I admire a comely lad as much as the next man, I do not desire one. I require a woman with whom to fully explore my feelings. Is that not right, my heart?"

Charles asked this last of the masked lady at his side. Rouged lips beneath the gold vizard shaped a smile. The voice was husky. "I cannot speak to your feelings, sir. Though, God's my life, I know all about the exploring of your fingers."

The loudest laughter came on this. Coke gave up pulling at Pitman and left him there gawking, going solo in search of the mistresses Chalker and Absolute.

He found them by the open rear door, in an enclave whose walls were made of racks of dresses. They were sitting on stools, Sarah with her arms around the younger woman, who looked pale. He bowed, then sat beside Lucy, taking her hand. "Lass, are you well?"

Sarah answered for her. "She was—until she realized Rochester was not with the king. He has never yet missed her first performance in any play. Yet no note has arrived, no messenger."

"I am sure he has his reasons." Lucy's voice was weak, quite unlike her courtesan's upon the stage. "All will be well, I am certain."

"I will see that it is well," Coke growled.

"Ah, my gallant," murmured Lucy, squeezing his hand.

Sarah passed Lucy a glass of cordial. "Drink, my dear."

Coke rose as did Sarah just as a man stuck his head through the dresses and said, "Mr. Betterton has given us the nod. A few minutes, ladies."

"Mrs. Chalker."

"Captain."

Sarah led him a little way apart. "You need to know, sir. Lucy is ill."

Coke stiffened. "It is not the plague?"

"Nay. It is her woman's state alone. But the worry does not help. I fear that the earl dallies with her. He promised her much last week and since has made no contact."

Coke sighed. "I feared as much. I know Lucy has hopes of him, but a nobleman and an actress? It never ends happily. The most she can hope for is a settlement, which I shall strive to get her. Should we not persuade her of this and begin to ease her toward her new situation? I doubt she can remain much longer upon the stage."

"We should. But not today." She took the captain's arm. "Let her believe what she will for now. She will know the truth soon enough." They both glanced at her hand upon him and she drew it away. "Do you enjoy the play, Captain?"

"I do. Though not as much as Pitman does. He is enraptured."

"Ah, yes. I noted him. Hard to miss, isn't he, our Pitman in the Pit?"

"It is not an analogy I would belabour. He is already mightily sick of it."

"I am sure."

Both laughed. Both fell silent. Then, "Are you recovering, Mrs. Chalker?"

"No," she replied, "but I am sustained. With the hope that you will keep the pledges you and Pitman made to me last week and aid me in finding John's killer."

If he'd had any doubts in his constancy to this cause—and he had—they vanished in her presence. "Indeed, madam, Pitman has some ideas of where such a search could begin."

"I have been thinking much on this. This may be nothing—but there was a certain lord who was bothering me, whom John—"

She was interrupted by a young male voice. "Shelter me! Hide me! For mercy's sake, sanctuary!"

The rack of dresses burst apart. Thrusting gowns aside, panting and sweating heavily, was the Earl of Rochester.

21

THE CLOSING

"Johnnie!" Lucy rose, stretching out her hands to him. "Whom do you flee? Oh, come to me."

But whatever sanctuary he sought, it was not in Lucy's arms. "You?" he cried. "No, it is the king I need—the king!" He swung around. "Majesty, where are you?"

"Here!" Through the dresses the earl had parted, Coke saw Charles step from around some furniture. "Well, sir? What means this clamour?"

"Sire!" Rochester threw himself down at the king's feet. "You must protect me!"

"From whom? Get up, for pity's sake."

But the earl did not move and then did not have to answer, for through the rear doors charged three large men. "We have you!" the first of them cried, as the trio strode toward the prone noble-man. Men equally large intercepted them: the king's bodyguards, interposing themselves between hunters and quarry.

Seeing their way was blocked, the earl's pursuers began shouting, demanding him. The crowd below and a new one forming on the stairs, drawn from the theatre by the noise, also gave tongue.

But one voice above them all bellowed a single word: "Silence!"

Immediately the king's command was taken up. "Silence for His Majesty! Silence!"

"What means this uproar?" demanded Charles. "For God's sake, Rochester, get off my boot, will ye! Stand and face your pursuers, man. I will not let them take you. I do not know who they are. Who are you, damme?"

The first man, his large face heated to a carrot red, now fully realized in whose presence he was. "Sire," he said, removing his hat, "we are constables of the parish of St. Martin in the Fields. And we have come to arrest that villain."

"No villain I," shouted the earl, standing at last, "unless love be a crime, I am none."

Some of the courtiers cheered this, some people on the stairs too. Charles waved a hand. "This is the Earl of Rochester, Constable. By what right do you pursue him?"

"By the right, begging Your Majesty's pardon, that he has committed a heinous crime in our parish. A most heinous one."

"And have you a warrant drawn for this crime allegedly committed?"

"I require none. For the outrage was committed not half an hour since and we are even in pursuit of him from the scene." The man drew himself up still taller, not much intimidated by the royal presence. "He will be indicted once we have him in Newgate."

"But what has he done?" demanded the king.

"Not twenty minutes since, by Charing Cross, he tried to abduct Elizabeth Mallet!"

A gasp arose at the constable's announcement. Obviously some there knew the name. Coke did not and raised eyebrows at Sarah. "An heiress," she whispered. "Very young, I believe, but possessed of two and a half thousand a year when she comes of age."

"Is this true, Lord Rochester?" The king's tone was severe.

"Sire," the earl answered, "it cannot be a crime, surely, when the victim is willing."

"It can if she is below the age of consent. The crime is not against her but her parents. They are the ones you robbed. Failed to rob, you double idiot!" He shook his head. "I warned you off her, Johnnie. Time and again I told you, do not—Ach!" He put a hand between the earl's shoulder blades and pushed him. "Take him, Constables. Do your duty, since he knows none."

The king's bodyguards and the courtiers gave back. Only one stayed quivering in the path of the advancing men. "Ma-Majesty," stuttered Sir Charles Sedley, "you cannot let one of us be put in—" he swallowed, his prominent Adam's apple bobbing "—Newgate."

"Why not?"

"You cannot! Unhand me, oafs!" squealed Rochester, as men took his arms. "Sire, I beg you! Do you not rule here?"

The king pivoted, his one walleye appearing even glassier. "I do, Lord Rochester. And I have vowed to see that the laws of England apply equally to every man." He glanced up. "Here is someone arrived who will confirm me in my opinion. Is that not so, my Lord Chancellor?"

All turned. Standing on the stair was Sir Edward Hyde. "I am sure you do not need my confirmation on anything to do with the law, Sire." His voice, oft likened to dry leaves rubbed, barely crackled.

"But would value it anyway. If you feel able to give it, Edward— you look exhausted, man."

"I have been up these several nights upon a matter I would speak to you about with some urgency. It is why I am here. It is *your* opinion I need, Majesty." Sir Edward sighed, pinching the bridge of his nose. "What is the crime for which they would take you to Newgate, my lord?"

"Love," shouted Rochester.

"Abduction. Attempted, anyway. Of a minor," said the king.

"A capital offence, then. You could hang, sir." Hyde lowered his hand. "However, since you are a nobleman, you can claim the axe rather than the rope. Indeed, since you are a nobleman—" he yawned "—you can claim the Tower over any other prison."

"The Tower?" Rochester ceased struggling. "I'll take the Tower. That's where nobility lies."

The chief constable spoke. "If I can have him before my justice of the peace back in St. Leonard's, and he says it's acceptable, I'll turn him over to the king's justice and the Tower."

"Very well. All settled. So it is prison for you, my lord, one way or t'other, and no more than you deserve." Charles looked around. "And now that we have had quite enough drama off the stage, shall we return to the professionals? Can my opinion wait on this other matter, Edward?"

"It cannot, Sire."

"Very well. Mr. Betterton, please give me a few more moments. 'Uneasy lies the head that wears the crown,' eh?" He smiled. "That's Shakespeare, ain't it?"

"It is, Sire. And well spoken, may I say."

The king nodded. "Then I will talk with my good chief minister while you, sirrah," he turned back to Rochester, "away!"

The earl, who now appeared quite recovered, shook off the men who had held him and walked between them toward the rear door.

Yet he was not halfway to it, when a woman's cry rang out. "But love, love, what of me?"

Lucy pushed through men to seize the earl's hand. He raised hers, kissed it swiftly. "Do not fear for me, sweetheart." His voice rose. "Be assured, everyone. All will be well." Then, jerking his hand from hers, he swept from the playhouse.

Lucy dropped to the floor. Coke and Sarah were at either side of her in a moment, but Lucy had swooned and they had to carry her to a stool. There, they held her while another actress ran for some sal volatile. Over her lolling head, Coke and Sarah looked at each other. "He did not even notice her here," Coke said, his voice low.

"I know," replied Sarah. "We will have to persuade her of his indifference."

As Sarah bent to Lucy with the small bottle the player had fetched, Coke stood—and recognized the voice talking low on the other side of the rack of dresses.

"There can be no doubt, Edward?" asked King Charles.

"None, Sire. I have brought you the bills of mortality from not just one parish but from five. From Whitechapel across to Westminster. The figures are clear. They have risen tenfold in two weeks."

"It is certain, then. The plague is upon us."

"It is. May God have mercy on our souls."

"What is to be done now?"

"Proclamations must be issued forthwith. The first must be the closing of all places of gathering. Bear baits, taverns. Theatres."

"May we not at least see the rest of the play? There's some good deaths, I hear."

"Death is in this house already, Majesty. If you are willing to allow it a few more for your entertainment, sir, then by all means see the end of the piece."

A harsh intake of breath. "No, very well, very well, Edward. I would not have that. But let me speak to Betterton and try to do this calmly. No doubt he can extemporize some speech. Should I send the queen straight to Syon House, think you?"

Coke did not hear the reply. The men moved away, talking low once again. He turned to Sarah and Lucy, whose eyes were now open. "Listen, both," he said. "You must put on your own clothes—and swiftly. The plague is come."

Pitman, who'd appeared quietly and unnoticed, heard him. "So they are at last to admit what many have known this month and more?"

Coke nodded. "And you were so enjoying the play, Pitman. I am sorry you will miss the end of it, for they will close the playhouse immediately."

The large man shrugged. "Bettina would say it is the just reward of sin. So be it. But what do *we* do now?"

His gesture encompassed the other two, but it was the third person there who spoke. "My John is arrested. I must see him. I must!"

"Child!" Sarah put her arms about Lucy again, restraining her. "You heard why he was arrested, didn't you, love? You understand?"

"I do." Lucy wiped away tears. "He has forsaken me."

"He has, dear heart." Coke knelt. "You must forget him."

"Hard to do when a part of him so swells my belly."

"Something for which he will still answer to me. But in the meantime—and especially in this time—we must make plans around you, not him."

Lucy moaned. "He kicks, the little earl." Her eyes went wide. "I would go home."

"Indeed. Mrs. Chalker, her dress? Let us get her back to Chancery Lane."

"You misunderstand me." She gripped his arm. "Home."

Sarah sat, keeping her arms around Lucy. "I think, Captain, she means Cornwall."

"I have two sisters, each with a brood apiece. They will know what to do." Lucy's large eyes opened wider. "Will you both take me there?"

"I will. Since my livelihood is to be put aside." Sarah reached for the captain's hand. "But have you the leisure toward us?"

Coke glanced up at the man standing silent above them, the question in his eyes.

"I believe all business will become personal for a while," said Pitman. "Maybe even his whom we pursue. Can you return soon?"

Coke nodded. "Immediately. I vow it."

"Events have indeed overtaken us," Sarah said. "Yet my husband's ghost still walks and will not sleep till he is avenged." She turned to Coke. "How long will the journey take?"

"When this larger news is made general, coaches will be hard to find. I know where I can obtain horses, if I move swiftly."

"Never mind the coach." Lucy sat up straighter. "I was born a-saddle." Her voice rose above protests. "If we do not go at a full gallop, I warrant I shall do well enough. Pshaw! I am only six months gone. And if he's a bastard within, at least he's the bastard of an earl. He may as well learn to ride in the womb."

All laughed. Pitman put a hand on Sarah's and Coke's shoulders. For a moment, all four were linked.

"Birth and death," said Lucy. "Is there a play in it, do you think?"

"That fellow," said the man on the stair, looking down, "who clings onto Mrs. Chalker. His name?"

Aitcheson followed his lordship's gaze. "Pitman? I have already pointed him out to you, my lord."

"Not him. The kneeling cavalier. With the moustache."

The usher peered among the heads and shoulders of people forcing their way back to the theatre. Above, a drum beat a solemn rhythm. Mr. Betterton was calling for silence, which even he was not finding easy to command. "I do not know him. Shall I inquire?"

"Do. Discreetly. And those others—" he waved "—what was the stir about? With the actress and the earl?"

"Oh sir, 'tis the talk of the theatre. The king's new favourite impregnating Mistress Absolute." He leaned closer. "It is said that she has taught him all the carnal vices. She—"

"The whore!" Garnthorpe snarled. "Mother of harlots and abominations of the earth . . . filthiness of fornication. She—"

The attendant was startled enough to interrupt. "But sir, she is an actress."

The lord grabbed the man's shirt front. His voice was much quieter but had lost none of its vehemence. "Do not link the Widow Chalker with a poxed whore. One who corrupts and is corrupted by a foul knight."

Aitcheson tried to prise the grip from his collar. "Sir, I did not refer to anyone. Others are watching. My lord, I beseech you."

Others were indeed. Garnthorpe released the man. "Find out what I have asked of you," he went on more calmly. "As for this earl and his strumpet—" he glanced down again at the group below "—God has them marked in his book already, fast filling with such whores and blasphemers."

Before Aitcheson could reply, a powerful voice came from above.

"Your Majesty! My lords, gentlemen, ladies!" Mr. Betterton called from the stage. "Prithee your attention. Pray you, silence!"

The hubbub decreased and the actor continued, "Alas, playing is suspended for the night. For the next little while, I fear." The crowd's voice increased anew, but the actor's rose over it. "There are reasons, my lords. Sirs. Ladies. *Grave* reasons."

Part Four

>⊷∙○∙⊶<

AND I WILL SMITE THE INHABITANTS
OF THIS CITY, BOTH MAN AND BEAST:
THEY SHALL DIE OF A GREAT PESTILENCE.

Jeremiah 21.6

22

SMITTEN

July 10, 1665

London had never smelled sweeter.

Pitman inhaled deep through both nostrils, something he would never do on a normal July day. On a normal day the heat would conjure all the city's worst smells, and this July was hotter than most. The sun would beat on every house's unemptied cesspit, drawing foul steam from the mounds. Fish heads would roll in the gutters, vegetables rot in piles, heated bodies give off rank odours through clothes rarely washed. Rats would nose among the garbage, cats and dogs piss against walls, hackney horses drop their piles alongside those of the sheep, cattle and pigs driven daily down thoroughfares to the various shambles.

Yet this July Londoners emptied the cesspits daily; no householder allowed garbage to collect before the door, for fear of fines that were finally enforced; while the gutters were flushed every few hours. And people *washed*. Themselves, their clothes, their front steps, their houses. The acrid tang of vinegar was everywhere, softened by whatever had been steeped in it, all manner of botanicals: rosemary, rue, sage, lemon balm.

No meat animal could be herded through the streets. The hackney carriages came infrequently, their best customers having fled the city—and if the carriages were discovered to have carried a sick person, they had to stand idle for a week. All the cats and dogs had been slain. Which made for more rats, thousands more. Pitman had always felt the expression "smell a rat" to be inaccurate. A wet hound stank a hundred times worse!

Nay, he thought, if you do not die from it, there's something to be said for the plague.

He shook his head, breathed deeply again, strode farther into the parish of St. Leonard's toward his home. There *were* people dying of it, he understood—the ceaseless tolling of each church's bell announced yet another parishioner dead. It was just he did not know any who had passed; so far he'd shut up only strangers. Sometimes he'd see a new face at a food stall, a different boy at the apothecary's, an empty place on the bench before theirs at the meeting house. But many had left the city: if they could get the certificate—and if they could afford the price. He saw fewer rich people around, that was certain. But his fellow poor were still by, still living. Mostly. There were times when he heard the carts rumble in the night, when he'd look out his window to see one pass by, a cloth over a fleshy mound, an arm dangling from beneath it.

He heard a familiar tap, tap, tapping upon the street stones and stepped under the awning of a saddlery to let the group go by. There were six of them, each clutching a white stick that they struck upon the ground. Their physician walked behind them, distinguished by his red stick, his waxed gown, his self-satisfied smile—and by the bird-beaked mask hanging from his belt. Men and women trailed him and he spoke to them in whispers. The people with white sticks had been cured of plague. His advice was sought, his remedies—he had a large supply of small glass bottles about him—purchased. Pitman wondered about his other patients unable to walk by. Hard to give a testimonial from the grave.

While the doctor conversed, his patients chanted verses that Pitman knew well:

"'Thou shalt not be afraid for the terror by night; nor by the arrow that flieth by day.'"

Psalm 91. He nodded, and as they passed him, he joined in the next verse: "'Nor for the pestilence that walketh in darkness; nor for the destruction that wasteth at noonday.'"

The psalm was one of his favourites. He took it as a sign and it made him feel even better. For was not all going well? To be a constable in times of plague was to be, for the nonce, regularly paid—the parish could not afford to anger the men who enforced the edicts. Who else would supervise the shutting up of people who needed to be quarantined? He knew there were officers who took bribes, let some escape before their windows and doors were hammered closed, or assigned watchers who were also corrupt and would pass over a share of the exorbitant prices they'd charge the unfortunates for their necessities.

But I am not one of them, he thought proudly. Only by enforcing all laws would the plague—that monster in the labyrinth of London—be tamed. Only by honesty would he and his be saved—that and by the grace of God, of course.

"'A thousand shall fall at thy side, and ten thousand at thy right hand; but it shall not come nigh thee.'"

It shall not come nigh me, nor mine. Besides, between my salary and the coin Bettina earned from that first batch of her ma's plague water, we are far better off than most. Money for medicines and meat broth for the new mother and her two healthily squalling babes—strong boys, as she had foretold. And if there was not an abundance for the other things they would like—the two rooms had looked small before the new ones' arrival—well, perhaps that would be sorted as early as tonight.

"'Only with thine eyes shalt thou behold and see the reward of the wicked.'"

He had been busy with his one business, but that did not mean he had forgotten his other. Nor neglected it entirely. The wicked could not, must not, be allowed any rest. Their reward—the killer's reward—must be by taking. His own reward would come after the taking, with forty guineas now offered for the Finchley slaughterer, also the slayer of John Chalker, actor, the two crimes linked in the public mind by their skilled savagery.

Forty guineas! Why, that would buy Bettina a house big enough for the whole brood. His, if the word he'd heard this day was proven true.

The plague had driven not only the wealthier from the city, but also most of the priests. Pulpits stood empty, the people deprived of God's word when they needed it the most. Yet men had arisen to fill the void. Or rather, they had returned. For the Act of Uniformity and the Act of Conventicles, banishing dissenters from practising within London's walls, were being ignored. Not overturned; unenforced. If the Church of England would not minister to the people's spiritual needs, others would.

Baptists. Muggletonians. His own Quaker brethren. Every other sect and creed. No longer did they have to hide in the dark. They stood in the light again, drawing crowds into it. Drawing crowds . . .

There might be a crowd there tonight, which would make the taking of the murderer more difficult. For people were not only lured by sermons of salvation. The promise of Apocalypse, of which plague was only the first sign, also attracted them. It was seductive, the increasing catastrophe, the deepening darkness leading to the eventual and all-revealing light.

Aye, Pitman thought, the Fifth Monarchists have a power that cannot be denied.

All Hallows the Great, on Thames Street, was one of their chapels, one of the few he hadn't visited. And near all London's Saints would gather there tonight. Something was afoot, Tobias Sym had told him, a man who'd once been his fellow constable and was now an agent in the government's pay.

They'd met by chance, gone to a tavern, and the man had passed on to Pitman a whisper he'd heard at a Saints' gathering—a whisper of murder. Could even remember who had done the whispering. "He had a sabre scar across his nose—and the coldest eyes above it of any man I've ever seen," Sym had confided. "He turned them on me when he thought I'd heard, so I pretended I hadn't." He'd shivered. "Still, if you're interested, why not sneak in with me tomorrow night and hear their madness? A fellow your size could stand me in good stead if'n I get frightened again."

He'd laughed, and Pitman had bought him another beer. "The man with the sabre scar," Pitman had queried. "Was there anything of the butcher or the surgeon about him?"

Sym had said he hadn't noticed if there was.

They'd agreed on a place and time to meet. Pitman knew his own gifts; the one he sought would give himself away, even in a multitude. There might be too much blood on a shirt cuff. A boning knife in a belt.

"'Ware fire!'"

The shout sounded from around the corner before him. Pitman, along with everyone else nearing it, halted. This was the last corner before the row that contained his dwelling. Yet there was no reason to be afeard. Part of the sweet scent of London was the fragrant smoke of guns and stink-pots frequently discharged on the streets. That was the surest way, the king's physicians had announced, to disperse the miasma that contained the evil.

The explosion came; a cloud engulfed him. He sneezed thrice. He had never minded the smell of brimstone. Faith, he had filled his lungs with it on enough battlefields as the musketeers and can-noneers vented their gunpowder. This smoke he recognized, for his neighbour Brown the Brewer always savoured his pots with pepper, his own hops and lavender.

It was the smell of home. Wiping his nose on his sleeve, he rounded the corner, speaking another line of the psalm: "'There shall no evil befall thee. Neither shall any plague come nigh thy dwelling.'"

He stopped when he saw the men. They had instruments similar to those he had just used on Paternoster Row: ladders, planks, ham-mers and nails, a bucket with paint. Red paint. It took him a moment to realize that the house they were attending to was his own.

Two of his daughters, Grace and Faith, were leaning out of the casement on the first floor, begging the constable with the paint-brush to cease his daubing of their door. Which he did, since there was nothing more to add to the writing above the ragged red cross: "The Lord have mercy upon us."

Pitman nearly rushed forward—to plead, pull aside the hands with their hammers, even attack those who would imprison his beloved in the house of death. Not an hour before, he had been just so beseeched, so assaulted, even as he drove the nails in. Instead he lurched back around the corner. Forced himself to breathe deep the traces of sweet smoke that remained.

Think, Pitman!

If he ran forward, what would he do? Drive off his fellow constables, gather his family of small children and babes and run? They would be cried in the streets in moments. Or should he be shut up with them? To suffer what they must as a family, to pray as a family to avoid it. It was a temptation.

Yet he did not yield to it. He knew what could happen to families locked up with the monster. It devoured many of them, the cruelty of the practice much criticized for herding together the ill with the hale, and oft causing both to die. He had seen it in houses he supervised.

What if he stayed free?

He pushed himself away from the wall, his first steps weak, his next more assured. If a neighbour should happen upon him there and cry him out, he would have no choice: he would be shut up with the others. It was in so many ways his heart's desire. He must not give in to it.

He took a narrow alley to his right, the next right again; followed a twisting route that would lead him to the house directly behind his own, with which it shared a wall.

I will not join them. Not yet. Not unless Bettina tells me to.

Words came again; the next verse to the one he'd spoken just before he'd seen the horror: "'For he shall give his angels charge over thee, to keep thee in all thy ways.'"

Keep me, angels, he prayed.

"Pitman, do not be more of a fool than the Almighty made you."

He could see only part of her face in the hole he'd gouged in the attic wall of the house that backed onto his own. Bettina's eyes were bright with both her fear and her certainty. "What good can you do for us in here eating twice your weight in food each day? Out there you can help us."

"I can try," he said, "though they will be looking for me as well. I cannot—"

"Then," she interrupted sharply, "you must avoid them." Her tone softened. "Pitman, love, I know you fear for us. I fear too. But we will put our faith in God."

"Amen."

"And in you free. You are a clever fellow, chuck, for all your lack of reading. You will find ways to aid us, I am sure. Better food, ingredients for my plague water."

"Who is't that's sick?"

"The Dutch family, in the basement. Mother and son, I hear. But two floors below us." She placed her fingers on the edge of the hole. "Listen, Pitman. We are shut up, but we can also shut out. The only thing getting into our rooms will be the bucket of supplies hoisted from the street—and I'll wash everything in vinegar before I admit it. We will keep what's left of our plague water for ourselves, till we brew another batch, whose remaining ingredients you'll fetch us."

"Have you any money left?"

"Maybe four crowns. You?"

"Three shillings. We'll need more, for my wages will be stopped." He laughed without humour. "They pay us to halt the plague, not carry it."

"Which you do not, Pitman," she said fiercely. "Not a member of my brood does." She shook her head. "But we could use more money, sure. Forty days is a long time to be quarantined without it, no matter how generous your fellow constables might be."

"There is—" He stopped himself. He did not tell Bettina much of his other trade. She'd only fear for the danger of it. And she had enough to fear now.

But she had heard the hope in his voice. "You have a mark?"

"I think so. That same murderer. Maybe e'en tonight. And he's worth forty guineas now."

She whistled. "Then you do the Lord's work, as well as ours." He reached his fingers up to hers as she continued, "If you are successful in that, why—" he could not truly see, but could hear the smile in her voice "—I may even let you dig out this wall, come in and stay awhile." She looked away. "Josiah is calling from below. The babes are crying again." She pressed her fingertips against his. "Take care, chuck," she said, then moved away.

He listened till the attic ladder in the other house ceased creaking, wanting that much of her. Then for another moment, he did not move. How can I take care? he wondered. He was the tallest man in the parish.

There were different ways of hiding, though. His bulk might be hard to conceal, but if people looked directly at you, they often mistook you, howsoever tall. If you walked differently. If . . .

By the time he'd descended to the ground floor, he had his plan. He knew the man whose shop occupied the street level of this house. A seller of metal goods, pots, pans. Blades.

"All well?" the man inquired when Pitman entered the small room behind the shop.

He had not told the fellow why he wished to visit his attic. As a constable of the parish, he did not need to. "All well, Mr. Tombes. I wonder, could I borrow some shears and your razor?"

The man went to fetch them and some water. While Pitman waited, he stroked the thick hair that ran far beneath his chin and all around his face, even up to his cheekbones. The fashion was against it, but he had had a beard ever since he could grow one. He wouldn't recognize himself without one. He doubted anyone else would.

The man returned with all Pitman had asked for, and left him to it. He'd brought no mirror, few could afford one, but he'd polished some of his trays to a brilliant shine and Pitman could see enough of his face to get by. Placing the shears into the knotted hedgerow that was his beard, he started to cut.

23

THE MURDERER

He didn't notice him at first. He'd been looking for a tall man ever since the Judas had told him, reluctantly at first, soon not reluctantly at all, everything; volunteering a babble of words, mostly pathetic pleading but some of it interesting. Including the name of someone who was hunting a murderer among the Saints—a man who could be a butcher or a surgeon.

Then he'd realized that the fellow lurching along Thames Street to All Hallows *was* tall, indeed very tall, but only when he'd noticed how contorted the man had made himself, bending so at the middle that his nose was close to the cobbles, at which he shouted every few paces. Indeed, like most other good citizens, he'd immediately glanced away from the ranting drunk in distaste. Besides the height, the traitor had told him that his pursuer had a heavy beard and this piece of human filth did not. In fact, his face was as smooth as a Pell Mell ball. And *that* was what made Strong look sharply back. He had his spectacles on, which helped him see the rawness of the cheek skin, a startling white compared with the man's fore-head; see the little flecks of red where a razor had recently nicked. And seeing that piece, Abel Strong saw the whole.

"Pitman," he whispered, withdrawing deeper into the shadows of the church portico. He'd noticed him before, couldn't remem-ber where. The man glanced up as he passed, shouted something, shambled on. He himself was invisible, Strong felt sure. Yet since this was the thief-taker—come to take a man who was *not* a thief!—he knew he should not remain there. Pitman would return soon enough. And it was too early and people too much about for their encounter to happen outside.

He pushed the door open behind him and silently slipped back into the church.

Soft summer sunlight poured in through the glass cupola in the ceiling, burnishing the tall cedar cross upon the simple altar. The Saints had brought the crucifix; for the Anglican incumbent, when he'd fled, had removed all that was valuable: altar cloths, com-munion vessels, the bronze cross. Wise, for the godly would have sold any trappings left behind. They required no luxury to medi-ate between themselves and the Almighty; needed only their faith, their prayers and some rough wood. Strong found it strange to be back inside a church that had the remnants of the established faith. He'd been raised in one, of course. But All Hallows was older even than the Reformation chapel he'd first worshipped in. And the way the sun fell now, so directly onto the wall behind the pulpit, he could see those ancient papist paintings that whitewash could not entirely conceal. Faint, but distinct still, the stations of the cross. And he could not help but reverence the Christ who had walked to Golgotha under his burden of wood, the blood that ran from his crown, the blood that marked in lines the scourging of his near-naked body. Yet even as Strong admired, the sun sank a hair, the picture faded, then vanished entirely, as if by a magus's trick. Or by a miracle.

He climbed the stairs of the pulpit. They were wood within stone and they curved, so he could not see the body till he was near the top. As scourged as Christ's was. As crowned with blood.

He'd forgotten, when he'd finally killed him, to do the last that he always did. He'd had to get outside in case this Pitman arrived early. He knew he had but a little time now. However, this part, unlike the killing, never took long.

"'The first foundation was jasper,'" he intoned, "'the second, sapphire; the third—'" He dug beneath his apron, to a pocket in his smock, his finger closing over what he wanted. "'The third, a chalcedony.'"

He turned it several ways, admired its striping of brown, yellow and green, the flash of the "eye" in its centre. "Tiger's eye," he murmured, pleased with the stone's other name. "And that's for you." He shoved it between Tobias Sym's torn lips. "That'll stop your babbling."

He laughed, then sat, his back to the pulpit's inner wall, his legs straddling the body. I'll need an emerald next, he thought. Expensive. Perhaps my noble lord will get us one. Perhaps he'd be so generous.

He did not even hear the door. But there was the faintest creak of floorboard.

Yet you do not need it now, Abel Strong, he thought, as he reached for his walking stick. You do not need it for the thief-taker. No, indeed. You have something different in mind for him.

Pitman paused just inside the entrance of the church. His one footfall had sounded like musket shot to him. While he waited, he considered. The man who had approached him when he'd returned to the front of the church had thought him a fellow Saint and had told him that the meeting was postponed a day. He was there to wait and tell the others, though he was an hour early for his task. Pitman had said he would assume that role and the man had departed happy. Not so Pitman. He'd felt relief: did he not now have an excuse to shamble away, keep on playing the stooped and shouting drunk, reappear on the morrow? The relief lasted until he thought of Bettina, their children, about to spend their first night in a shut-up house that the monster had touched with its blackening claw. He needed his reward—and he would get it. For when he'd passed the church's shadowed porch the first time, he'd noted a faint light reflected in glass, and the scent of fresh blood on cloth, not faint at all.

He could smell it now, mixed with the incense that impregnated the walls, the smoke of ten thousand candles burned over centuries. There was the sweet smell of bird too, which he noted even as he heard one begin to coo softly—a pigeon that had made a nest up in the cupola.

A party of men singing drunkenly passed outside. He used their noise to move up the nave toward the altar. When their song began to fade, he stopped, steadying himself against the pillar of the pulpit stair, then frowned, withdrew his hand, rubbed fingers and thumb together.

They were sticky wet.

The noise came sudden from behind him. He swivelled just in time to see the walking stick falling from the ceiling and the pigeon, at whose roost it must have been thrown, bursting out of the cupola with a fast flapping of wings. And it was these two things he realized he should not be looking at, when the cudgel hit him, wielded by the man who'd silently and swiftly descended the pulpit stair, a man whose face he glimpsed even as the blow caught him beside the right ear, full force. His legs gave and he sank to the floor, unconscious before he reached it.

The flaring light woke him, its flames reddened by eyelids that would not open at his bidding. While he struggled to see, he listened to the voices that jabbered nearby.

"He holds it still!"

"Aye. The blade as wet with blood as 'is 'ands are."

"Christ! The stench!"

"Gutted 'im. That's the fellow's guts you're stepping in now."

"Shite! Oh Jesus, a church! Forgive me, Lord, but 'ow—'ow come 'e lies there still? Can a man with his belly slit still strike a blow?"

"Must 'ave. There's 'is cosh. Took the knife in the belly and struck back e'en as 'e did."

Pitman groaned. He heard the men scramble back. "Careful now," the one with the deepest voice called, "stand ready with your staffs. He's a big bastard."

Pitman reached a hand to unstick his eyes. There was something in it, which he let go.

"'E's dropped the knife!"

"Kick it away!"

"You kick it. I ain't goin' near the brute."

As Pitman put fingers into his eye sockets and wiped off the blood, someone nearby toed the dagger away, at the same time shoving a stick into Pitman's chest. He batted it off, looked up in time to see the stick withdrawn—only to be brought down hard. He deflected it from his head at the cost of pain in his wrist.

"Are you going to fight us, bastard?" said the deep voice again. "We'll beat you if you try. There's six of us here, constables all."

Pitman raised a hand, partly in peace, partly to block out the flaring light that probed his head like a blade. "No fight," he groaned. "Nothing. Done nothing."

Someone laughed. "'E's denying it!" another man said. "Found 'im with his blade in someone's guts and 'e says, 'Not me, friend!'"

Other laughs, until the deep-voiced man cut them off. "Quiet!" he commanded. "Respect for the dead."

The dead. Until now Pitman had tried only to fend off his persecutors, to clear his eyes, to not vomit. But now he felt something other than his pain. He looked down—at his other hand, resting against a corpse's chest. At the corpse's eyes, Tobias Sym's eyes, staring somewhere above him, glazed in death.

He cried out, used his feet to drive himself away, not halting until his spine hit the pulpit stair. The six men—he could see six now—followed him, sticks raised. "Now, you can come easy or you can come hard," said the man with the deep voice, better spoken than the others. When Pitman continued to just stare up, he demanded, "Where's that fellow who found him?"

"Went outside to puke. Not come back."

"We don't need him anyway. I've never seen anything more obvious in my life. One of you, pick up the knife. Two more, get this body down to the mortuary. And you—" he jabbed Pitman with his stick "—I ask you again, you coming easy or are you coming hard?"

"Where—" He had to spit, clear his throat before he could respond. His voice came in a rasp. "Where are you taking me?"

"Where murderers go, of course. Newgate."

No. He could not go to Newgate, the place where he had delivered so many to justice. People died in that fetid prison long before they saw a length of hemp. Especially now. The prison stood in the very centre of the labyrinth that was London. In its dank foulness, the monstrous plague ruled entirely. And what of his family if he was lost?

"No!" he roared. But his head burst with pain, his eyes filmed and he couldn't get off his knees. So not many blows of the constables' staffs were needed to tumble him back into unconsciousness.

He did not, however, fall into it alone. Someone came with him.

The man was not one of these who wielded their sticks with more enthusiasm than skill. This man had hit him but once and had a face Pitman had seen before.

The dark took him before he could remember where.

24

THE RETURN

July 20, 1665

The shrieking had risen to a still higher pitch. To Coke, lying with his sore feet in the Thames, where they awaited the barge that would carry them the last stage back to London, it seemed that they were competing in this too. Striving for the highest note. The boy had the advantage of fewer years, the actress her trained voice. Yet the noise was incidental to the main event: the height that each would reach while vaulting. The lowest branch of the oak beneath which they leaped provided evidence of success in snatched leaves. But most had been cleared in the ten minutes they'd been at it. They needed to reach higher. And surely, Coke thought, they must be tiring.

Evidence for this appeared with Dickon's next leap. His hands slapped lower on Sarah's back, pushing up her skirt and revealing a flash of calf muscles that had browned considerably during this month of journeying in the sun—instantly hidden as youth and lady collapsed, both screaming with laughter.

Sarah dug herself out from under and then strode over to Coke at his tree, planted herself before him, hands on hips. "Truly, sir," she gasped, "Leap the Frog is better played when there is more than one frog to leap."

"Kiss the Frog is more my game, mistress," he replied. "It can be done without much movement on my part." He stretched his arms and leaned farther back against the willow. "And who knows? It could turn even me into a prince."

He raised his face, puckered his lips. But her lips never touched them. All that came was her throaty laugh, followed by renewed shrieking. Sarah was shoving Dickon to a position beneath a branch they had not yet attempted to reach; then she walked a dozen paces back. What would I have done had she kissed me? Coke wondered. Kissed in return? Retreated as I have ever done with any slight advance from her, as she has done whenever I casually ventured?

There had been moments—few enough, and so distinct in his memory—when the ease that they felt with each other could have tipped into something more, perhaps. These had mainly been on the way down to Cornwall, when they all had, with unspoken agreement, decided that plague, pregnancy, vengeance and all things awful should be put aside and they should enjoy this journey through an England now in full bloom. Lucy had led, a wildness to her gaiety, drawing Sarah, Dickon and him in. If she could forget her situation, her swelling belly, the greeting that awaited her at home, could they not forget theirs: a husband murdered and unavenged; the gallows that threatened him for ghastly crimes that he did not commit?

No, he thought, tipping his head to the faintest of breezes from off the river. Not forget, not entirely; never that. All was ever there. Intruding most in those moments that could have moved onto something more—a hand snatched as it aimed a reproving slap, held a second too long. An amused look in sky-blue eyes, sliding into a question neither he nor she dared to study, let alone answer.

The journey down had taken two weeks, near half of that on the rougher tracks that passed for roads into the Cornish wilderness, and Lucy slowing, her laughter fading, the nearer she got to Zennor, the place she'd left as a girl and to which she'd vowed never to return—especially in disgrace. But the greeting was not as she'd feared. True there had been many oaths, much vowing and clashing of steel from an assortment of uncles and cousins, determined to ride forthwith to London and spit the seducer on their swords. Thwarted by her silence, the one she'd also sworn them to, never naming the man who'd corrupted her. The women, her grandmother, her two elder sisters, had said little. Simply led her away from the bravado and set about the plans for her delivery.

A louder shout from Dickon. Coke half opened his eyes. The boy had given up leaping imaginary frogs in the finding of a real one. He held it up by its body, showing it to Sarah, its webbed feet kicking.

She liked the boy, for all his stutterings and shambles—perhaps because of them. He'd told her about Dickon—finding him, saving him—one night in a Wiltshire inn, on the road down.

"You have a kind heart, Captain," she'd said.

"William," he'd replied, the first time he'd again offered his given name, though Lucy, asleep at last across the room, used it freely. "Or Will, if you prefer. I haven't been more than a captain of the highway these many years."

"But were once, uh, William?"

"Aye."

"In the late wars? And for the king's cause like my husband?"

"He fought most gallantly, I heard."

"He did." A silence came between them, bringing memories of the mangled corpse of John Chalker. Sarah cleared her throat. "Do you think he was gallant at the end? In that cellar?"

"Bravery needs an opportunity. I doubt the murderer gave him much of one. Yet I suspect that he was."

She'd nodded. "I suspect you were gallant too, were you not?"

"On occasion. When given little choice."

"Does a man not always have such a choice?"

"Not really. I know that as often as I chose to stand I often chose to run."

"But were not, perhaps, the first to run?"

"Marry, perhaps not the *very* first."

Her face changed utterly when she laughed and he'd thought at that moment—and maybe it was the first time—that he'd like to banish that other face entirely. Then she'd said, "And you knew Lucy's brother, did you not? Knew him and loved him, I understand."

He'd stared at her, seeking any colour to the word "loved." Yet in the end, he'd decided it did not matter if there was. He and Quentin just were. He'd loved him, sure, as he had loved Evanline, in Bristol; they'd both died badly, and as he'd looked away from Sarah, he'd thought that it was best for him not to love her either, since loss was the way love ever ended for him.

He glanced back now. She'd hiked up her skirt to wade alongside Dickon in the shallows of the river. The game had changed again; she and the boy were snatching at minnows. Again he noted her brown calf muscles, water drops caught like jewels in the faint down on them. Then beyond Sarah and Dickon he spotted the donkey, the man leading it, the rope that ran from its saddle. The next moment the prow of the barge itself was in view, steadily dragged toward the jetty that thrust into the Thames here at Sunbury. The others had not noticed it yet, so intent were they on their game, and he did not call. He would let them have their last carefree moments.

The care had been their choice. In Cornwall, Lucy had used all her skills to persuade them to stay, to not risk death in the centre of its domain and return to London. Coke had tried to persuade Sarah, and Sarah had tried to persuade Coke. Neither had succeeded, though they had dallied several days more—for what drew them back was more powerful than any contrary argument: not least a compact made with a thief-taker that justice would be done.

Yet he wondered: if she had been persuaded to stay, would he have too? Was it her determination that drew him back? Or was it, simply, her?

He watched her now, saw her notice the barge, raise a hand against the sun to study it; noted the way her shoulders set. There would be no persuasion that would unset them now. The boy saw the boat also, and took longer to realize what it meant. When he did, he jerked around to seek Coke, and calmed when he found him. Dickon they'd not tried to persuade to stay in Cornwall; they'd simply left in the middle of the night, hoping that Lucy, whom he loved, would manage to keep him there. But Dickon loved his captain more, and he'd run for a day and a night back along the road until he'd caught up with them. It had taken all Coke's skills and Sarah's caresses to soothe the lad, together with the vow that he would never be abandoned again. Whatever dangers lay before them, be they plague, murder or the noose, Dickon would face them all at his captain's side.

She strode from the water to speak to him. "Is this the vessel we await?"

"Aye. This barge will take us to Teddington and we'll find a boat there for London."

"Thank the Lord for the river," she said, dropping her skirt. "I do not think I could walk another ten steps."

"Yet you can run and leap the frog?"

She pushed loose hair from her face. "The boy wanted it so."

Coke raised his feet from the water and reluctantly put his boots back on. They were meant for riding, not walking, and because they'd trudged most of the miles from Cornwall, and taken near four weeks to do it, his feet were a sorry affair indeed. His mare, Dapple, had injured a leg running in Cornish fields and had to be left, while their little coin had not run to horses, whose hire had trebled in price since the plague had come, nor coach fares raised for the same reason. There had been an occasional wagon going their way.

"And what awaits us in London?"

Death, he thought, but did not say. "Pitman," he said instead. "By now the thief-taker will surely have some paths for us to follow. He may have already identified the villain. I would not put it past him, for he seems most able." Coke tried to smile. "Perhaps we will regret the haste of our return if the murderer already dangles at Tyburn."

"The only thing I will regret, Captain, is if the words you speak are true. For I will not consider John Chalker avenged until I have looked his killer in the eye. Until I have had some hand in his taking."

He sighed. She had "captain-ed" him again. And there he was once more, John Chalker, the spectre ever between them. He rose, with nothing else to say save, "Then let us speed you to that, ma'am. To London."

Even in the short walk from Wood Wharf to Sarah's lodgings, he could see how the metropolis had changed.

Almost no one walked on the streets, most unusual on Sabbath's eve. Each tavern, wine-house, alehouse and ordinary they passed was closed, when usually at this hour they would be overflowing. Though some would still be open in the dingier back alleys, despite his thirst Coke did not seek them out. Both Sarah and Dickon were exhausted, while he was determined to get to Pitman before the City gates were locked for the night.

However, it was not just the lack of people, the shuttered inns, the many houses blossoming red crosses like roses, nor the near silence broken only by the bells. "Look," Sarah said. At first he did not see, until she added, "The grass."

Then he saw it. Between the always well tended paving stones of the Strand, knee-high plants bent in the wind of their passing.

At her lodgings, they protested when he went to depart by himself. "I go for information alone, not action," he said. "I will return with the dawn." He left them fallen together on the one bed as if slain.

He chose to swing slightly from the direct course, crossed the Fleet on Holborn Bridge, bore through the Churchyard of St. Bartholomew the Less rather than enter the City by the gate nearest Pitman's address. For that entrance was Newgate, and it was part of the prison of the same name. He'd always avoid it if he could, ever since a gypsy had discovered on his palm that he would only see its outside thrice more before he saw it from within. So instead he took lanes and alleys that roughly paralleled the Wall until he reached the next entryway, Aldersgate, the extra distance costing him, for the guards had begun to shut up and only a shilling from his scant supply made them pause to admit him. The steeple of St. Paul's, the highest spire in London, its tip gilded by the setting sun's last rays, guided him down St. Martin's Le Grand.

With few about to ask, and those few scurrying away when he tried, he discovered Cock Alley by sound rather than sight. Around a corner, he found the source of the wailing he'd heard: noise and destination, one. There, before the very house he sought, a hand cart stood with one man carrying a body out the door while another held back a woman on the threshold who was weeping and trying to get to the corpse. A third figure stood by, an older woman in a ragged grey cloak. She was as still as the others were active and to the screams offered a sound more awful: a low laugh.

Fear flushed him; he knew this house was Pitman's by the distinctive gable the man had described. Still, he advanced, just as the wailing woman was shoved forcefully back inside, the door was slammed upon her and the bolts affixed to its outside were shot into place. "What happens here?" he asked.

The woman jumped two paces back, hands raised against him. "Eh?" she screeched. The man who'd been bolting the door turned fast, hefting a cudgel.

"Peace, friends!" Coke raised empty hands, as the second man finished dumping the body on the cart and turned too, also armed. Seeing she was warded, the old woman stepped back, into the light spill of the lantern above the door.

Dank hair, inexpertly dyed blond, pressed into a brow that was white due to the layers of lead paint plastered onto it. Here, as on the rest of the skin, great fissures had cracked the ceruse, splitting under a single mouse-skin eyebrow; the other eyebrow was absent. A cloud of cochineal reddened each cheek, disappearing into the hollows of skin that folded over a mouth missing most teeth. Beauty patches had been randomly applied over pox scars. Most were plain orbs and half moons, though a cat chased a carriage toward the missing eyebrow.

All this Coke saw in the one swift glance before he retreated. Yet he did not run, with that opportunity soon taken when the crone cried, "Seize him!"

The men grabbed an arm apiece. "Easy, friends," Coke said, gauging their strength. He would fight if he had to. The reek that rose off them showed that all three were drunk on Guinea rum, which would make any fight easier. But that would not serve his purpose: to find Pitman. Though the plain fact that his house was plagued might mean there was now no Pitman to find.

The old woman smiled toothlessly at him, thrusting her face close. "Well, well," she breathed, "is this the missing 'usband, then? Shall we unbolt and throw 'im inside?"

Coke, gagging a little at the proximity of her, said, "Madam—" To an immediate chorus of jeers. "Madam," he continued, "may I know who it is I am addressing?"

"Oh, so polite! What a gennelman!" The woman looked down her nose. "You is 'dressin' Mistress Proctor. I am the searcher for this parish. I sniffs out the sick. I slams them up in their 'ovels. I carts away their dead." She slapped the wagon beside her, causing a corpse's arm to drop and dangle outside the canvas covering. "And who might you be, sir gennelman?" She thrust her face still closer. "Are you the 'usband? Are you this Pitman?"

"I am not." He let his western accent thicken. "I am a cousin, come from the country to seek his kin."

"Country cousin?" she shrieked, falling to wheezing laughter, joined by the two men who held him. "Country fool, more like! For who would leave 'is native pure air to breathe pestilence?" Her face was now so close their lips almost met. "I think you're lyin', sir gennelman. Not even a fool willingly enters Hades, eh? You're Pitman!"

The man on his left arm spoke. "Nah," he mumbled. "That bastard was bigger. Arrested me once, just for the beatin' of my own daughter on the street."

"A daughter!" Coke was near enough to see the thought enter the gummy eyes. "'Course! One way to find out. Swing 'im over 'ere." She stepped to the cart and the two men gripped tighter and shoved Coke forward. "For what father will stay as stone when he sees . . . this!"

As she said the word, she jerked back the canvas. There, on top of two other corpses, lay the latest addition: a girl, perhaps two years old. It was one of her arms that swung over the side of the cart; her other arm was flung back, as if desperately reaching for the house she'd late been ejected from. Even in the poor light of the lamp, Coke could clearly see the distended armpit and the black oval tokens covering her skin.

He could not stop it. Never could. He vomited, partly onto one of the men who held him there and who now threw him off. The other man let go as well, leaving Coke to void bile onto the cobbles.

Fingers like claws dug into his arm. He looked up—into those eyes under their one eyebrow. "Puke tears," she hissed, "but not sorrowing ones. A father would rage over 'is dead daughter, wouldn't he?"

"I tell you, s'not 'im." The man who spoke peered up from his attempts to wipe yellow vomit from his breeches. "Bastard's covered me, though. I'll give 'im a beating for that."

A cudgel was in his hand. Coke, already bent over, reached to the dagger in his boot cuff. But a screech halted them both. "You will not!" shouted the crone. "It's late, and there's money to be had of the beadle of St. Leonard's for these three if we hurry. I wants a drink. You—" she pointed at the man with the vomit "—will stay and keep the watch." She flicked the canvas back over the corpses, tucked in the dangling arm. "And you," she said, pointing now at Coke. "I'd not linger 'ere if I were you. Go 'ome, *cunt*ryman."

With that, she gestured to the cart's arse and the other man went to it, heaved. "Bring out yer dead!" she suddenly cried, her voice sharp and clear in the silence. "Bring out yer dead!" The man still wiping away puke followed, whining that it was not his turn.

They'd got to the corner, were just about to turn it, when Coke felt something hit his shoulder. He glanced in time to see a ball of paper fall to the ground. He picked it up, unfolded it. One side was printed, a call to buy the world's most effective plague water. The other side had words scrawled in charcoal. By the lantern light he could just make them out: "Next street at bak. Empte Ironmongers. Attik."

The captain went fast, the opposite way to the death cart.

Three houses down there was an alley on the left. He took it, turned left again. Crossed cutlery was nailed above a door. He pushed this, and it gave with a squeal of rusted hinges. "Hallo?" he called, his voice bouncing back from emptiness. There was only one lantern back in this alley. He returned to the house. It was silent, its inhabitants no doubt asleep. He fetched an empty barrel, stood upon it and carefully unhooked the lantern from its spike, then descended and returned to the ironmonger's.

The little light the lantern gave revealed a room as empty as its echo: a bare counter, some broken pots, a fallen chair. At the rear of this room was a doorway and Coke went through it, climbed the narrow stair beyond. The only memory of life he found was when he stumbled on something, bent to feel what it was, grasped cloth. He lifted the object into his little light, saw the flaxen string hair, the button face of a poppet. He dropped it.

There was a ladder on the last landing, rising into the roof. It creaked as he climbed it. When he stuck his head into the space above, he heard another sound. A whisper in the dark.

"Do not come any closer, sir."

He lifted the lantern, placed it on the attic floor before him. It did not light much beyond the trap.

The voice came again from the darkness. "Who are you, sir? Do you know my husband? Do you know Pitman?"

"I do. Let me draw closer."

He made to push himself up, but her sharp cry stopped him. "Do not! Even there, the sickness may reach out and take you. How do you know my husband?"

"My name is Coke."

"He told me of you. The captain. You are engaged on an enterprise together."

"We are. I had hoped to find him to continue our work. I—" He broke off. Pitman had said he recounted little to his wife, to save her from fretting. What could Coke say now?

"If he lives, sir, you will find him in Newgate prison."

"What? How so? For what offence?"

"Murder." She continued over his cry. "It's three weeks since. Caught by the All Hallows watch, his dagger in a man's guts, they told me. They were happy to tell me." A sob, restrained, and she went on. "I have not had another word."

Within this appalling news was something that did not make sense. No one accused of murder remained in Newgate three weeks without a trial. It was usually done within a day or two. "Are you sure he is not . . ." He stopped.

She must have sensed his doubts. "He is not hanged, sir. He cannot come to trial because the courts are suspended. Prisoners must wait for the plague to pass before they can be brought to justice. And most will never face it. Because if there is one place in this entire pestilent city that is the very centre of disease, that place is Newgate. Yet I believe he lives. Those who keep us shut in would delight in telling me if he did not."

She sobbed again, and he bit his lip till blood ran. This was the ruin of all hope. What could have happened? Pitman was not a murderer. Had he come upon the real killer and been forced to kill him? Could that not be proven?

"Madam, what can I do for you? Can I free you? I could cut away the lath in these walls. Your family could escape through."

He'd half raised himself onto the floor again, when she stopped him with a shout. "And go where? This is a house of the plague, sir. I have lost a daughter this night, a babe last week, have another son sick below." He heard her choke back her tears. "We must wait for God's judgment, and pray that he will decide he has punished us enough."

"Can I at least bring you food? Medicine?"

"Yes, perhaps that. Yet, sir, what would truly sustain us is this: find out if Pitman does still live. Take our prayers to him. Bring him word of us. Tell him that Imogen and Little Jeremiah sleep with the angels." Another sob, swiftly pulled back. "And tell him that by God's good grace he will be brought back to us soon."

"I will. And will return with some food for you on the morrow. Goodbye for now, madam."

He descended the ladder, passed down the stairs, out onto the street. Without thinking, he remounted the barrel and placed the lantern again upon its hook. As he did so, the stub of candle within it flashed bright, then died.

Newgate, he thought, swaying there. So the place I most avoid is the one I must go to now.

25

THE HOUSE

Ignoring the screams from the cellar, Lord Garnthorpe looked around the room.

Is it *too* austere? he wondered again. He had instructed his upholsterer that it be decorated plainly, for the room was to function as much as a place of contemplation as a chamber for daily living. The man had obeyed, whitewashing the walls to obliterate the crude scenes of country life painted on them in case any should lift the woven hangings he then hung from ceiling to floor. However, since their weave was of a uniform brown, they made the room appear even smaller than it was. The only things that relieved the uniformity were the oak door, the window cavity from which all the glass had been removed save one small panel, and the single decoration he had allowed: a painting of some saint in the very moment of her martyrdom, her body still in the grip of her ravishers, her soul already moving to salvation.

If she sits in the single straight-backed chair and contemplates that, he thought, breaks off only to read from the solitary book upon the table—the Bible, a newish copy purchased that morning from his bookseller's in St. Paul's Churchyard, with suitable passages marked—surely her mind will be the more swiftly calmed from her other life's concerns.

Yet something troubled him. He saw her again in that other life. Such a different world from the one he would bring her to. Perhaps he should ease the transition a little.

"Flowers."

His body servant, Maggs, was standing silently by the door. "Flowers, my lord?"

"I want some. On the table beneath the saint. Beside the Bible."

"Yes, my lord. What kind?"

"Nothing gross. White and red roses. Marigolds—" He broke off. "What do I know of flowers, man? Go to Gurle's nursery in Spitalfields. Buy what you can for a gold guinea."

"A guinea?" Maggs's usually immobile face cracked in wonder. "Will that not fill the room, my lord?"

"I do not know, simpleton!" Garnthorpe shouted. "Ask Gurle, not me. If there is excess—" he considered a moment "—then we will put it upon the grave in the churchyard opposite."

"Which grave?"

"You know which one, dolt. The one I ordered you to clean last week."

"Oh, that one. Oh yes, indeed, my lord. I'll be off." As Garnthorpe's eyes narrowed in suspicion, Maggs retreated from the room.

Garnthorpe leaned on the straight-backed chair. He felt a little faint. He understood that women liked flowers. His mother had, would pick enough to fill rooms with their scent. Would *she* like them?

Maggs slammed the front door behind him, a habit no amount of curses and blows could make him desist from doing. Immediately the screaming got louder. She had stopped for a while, two hours after he'd locked her in the cellar, her eventual silence achieved by no harsher expedient than ignoring her entirely. It was doubtful her sounds carried much beyond the walls. Even if they did, they would be ignored. London was a city of screams these days.

He crossed to the Bible. It was open to Daniel; one of the texts she must know if she was to stand beside him when King Jesus came. And she did not have much time, judging by the way the world went.

And yet? There was another text, something his mother had read him long ago.

He hunted for it. First the chapter, then the verse. And when he finally placed his fingers upon the passage, a shock went through him. His father had discovered him reading it as a youth and broken two sticks on him for straying from the very few texts the man found acceptable—when he was sober enough to read and guilty enough to pray. But his father was long dead. So he found his voice was calm when he read the words aloud: "'Rise up, my love, my fair one, and come away. For, lo, the winter is past, the rain is over and gone; the flowers appear on the earth; the time of the singing of birds is come, and the voice of the turtle is heard in our land.'"

He turned the pages back to Daniel, walked out the door, up the stairs. The cries redoubled at his footsteps, but by the time he stood in the bedchamber they were gone.

Yes, he thought, looking about. This room's beauty will make up for that other's plainness. The panels of emerald silk, hung from battens to cover the oak walls; the colour picked up in the curtains that close in the bed. The rich linen sheets on that; the coverlet embroidered in silken threads.

What was that other verse, he thought, in the Song of Solomon?

"'By night in my bedchamber I—' No! 'By night on my bed I sought him whom my soul loveth,'" he declaimed.

He went to the window, pushed it open. A breath of wind came and he closed his eyes to it. That is what she will say, he thought, after she has spent time in the room below. After she has learned the lessons, after she has come to God, then will she come to me. By night will she seek me.

Somewhere near, a hand bell rang, a familiar cry with it: "Bring out your dead!"

The End of Days was fast approaching. He had work to do, God's work, as Brother Simeon directed him. He would see him shortly for prayer, for instruction. But first, he had a soul to redeem.

In the corner of the room was a table, an inkpot and quill upon it. He sat in the single chair. The paper was already sealed, not with his own crest of Gryphon Rampant but with another he'd had made for the purpose.

He dipped the quill, then wrote the words swiftly, in letters that leaned hard to the left: "To Mrs. Chalker, Percival Buildings, Sheere Street. From John Wilmot, Earl of Rochester." He hesitated, dipped anew and added, "On a matter of great urgency."

He blotted, scattered some sand, blew. Outside, the cart of the dead creaked closer, while from far below came again the faintest bat squeak of a wail.

Sarah sat at the window of her lodgings, the road below her as empty as on the Sabbath at church time. Only occasionally did someone pass by, and nearly always in the same manner: nose thrust into a bundle of herbs, moving down the very middle of the way. Sheere Street was as overgrown as any other, knee-high grasses obscuring its cobbles. Yet though its pavement would have made for easier passage, no one now drew close to anyone else's walls. The plague might be behind them, red cross or none. And rumour spoke of some victims who would reach out to breathe upon and so infect the unwary. For if more sickened, did not that make the chances for survival of those already smitten a little better?

Movement came, but not human. Rats, a thousand at the least, emerged from the cellar of the abandoned house opposite, then ran up the street, their progress shown by the shifting of grasses, the column vanishing into the cellar of another empty dwelling.

"Rats!" Dickon had approached silently behind her. "L-lots more of them now."

"They killed the cats and dogs that hunted them. They feared they carried the plague."

"But what if the r-rats do?"

He returned to the day bed and the play script she'd given him: *Cutter of Coleman Street*, a drama they'd performed in the early days of the Duke's Company. The plot was a thick one, of murder and conspiracy, set among the Fifth Monarchists who'd attempted to rise in '61 and been defeated on the streets after a bloody battle, their leaders shot then or hung since. She studied him as he mouthed words, wondering what he made of it all.

The loud knock upon the street door made both her and Dickon jump. He ran out of the room, down the stairs. Whoever had arrived was hidden beneath the awning of the glass blower's shop. She listened to bolts being drawn, then a murmur of voices. She hoped it was the captain she heard. For five weeks she'd seen him safe every night. One apart and she was worried.

It was not him. It was a stranger. He wore livery of purple and green. After taking off a feathered cap, he bowed briskly and removed a letter from his sleeve. "His lordship's compliments," he drawled, holding it out.

She took it, glanced at the seal on the back, then turned the paper over, saw the address. "My Lord of Rochester!" she exclaimed. "He is released from the Tower?"

"He is."

She broke the seal, unfolded the vellum, read the note twice, looked up. "The earl wants a reply?"

"If you would be so kind." The insolence was not concealed: Rochester's servant, delivering a note to an actress. "I'll write it for you if you wish."

She flushed. "There is no need for ink. Tell him I will come at the appointed hour."

"You know the place?"

"I can find it. Can you find the door?"

His eyes bulged at her tone. He went, Dickon following. The noise of bolts sounded again, then some louder words. She assumed the man was insulting the boy more openly than he had her, but she was wrong.

"L-look!" said Dickon, running in ahead. Following close behind was Captain Coke.

"Well, sir," she said, more sharply than she'd intended, "you are late."

He peered at her, surprised at her tone. "I warned you that I would get caught by the city gates. Then I needed to see someone this morning, if he was still there. He was." He reached into the pocket of his cloak, pulled out a cloth bag, threw it to Dickon. "For you, lad. The first cobnuts of the season from Kent."

With a yelp of delight, the boy caught the bag and in a trice had the drawstring opened, a nut placed and jaws crunched together.

"Now, share some with the lady, you puppy," Coke said. Dickon dodged him, crammed in another nut, sheltering the bag from the man's reach.

They jostled until Sarah called, "Really, sir, I do not need a nut. I need news."

She could see by the way his face changed so completely that the report would not be good. He led her to the window seat, leaving Dickon to sit upon the bed and continue working his way through the bag.

"Tell me swiftly, sir. What of our enterprise? What of Pitman?"

He told her. She heard it all silently. When he was done, she sat for a moment staring ahead, then said, "He is innocent, of course." She looked up at him. "But that does not help our cause. What can we do now, Captain?"

Their journey was truly over. She was indeed back to calling him captain. "To begin, I will do what I promised Mrs. Pitman: I will go to Newgate this very afternoon—though it is the place in the whole realm I would most avoid. My word to both Pitman and his wife drive me to it." He dug again into his cloak, produced a second cloth bag. "My visit this morning was to my friend Isaac ben Judah. I was surprised and happy to find him at his shop, not fled like so many others. But he said to me, 'My tribe took four hundred years to return to London—how can we abandon her again after less than eight?'" Coke gave a smile, but it left his face quickly. "His tribe is paying for such steadfastness, though. As many Jews are dead as gentiles, proportionate to their numbers. Still, he was kind. Though I could offer him nothing as collateral, nor future service—coaches do not travel the King's Highway laden with gems these days for me to acquire—he agreed to make me this loan." He shook the bag, which clinked. "It means I was able to deliver some food to Pitman's family and will take some to Pitman himself when I visit." He swallowed. "If he lives."

"Do you think he does?" Sarah asked.

"His wife believes she would know if he did not."

"And do you believe that he will have learned, before his incarceration, of the man we seek? The true murderer?"

"If any man knows him, Pitman does. Here," he said, holding up the bag, "I will take enough for the bribing that will come. I'll leave you most of it."

"Why? Will you not return?"

He caught a note in her voice, saw the concern on her face. "Nay, lady, of course I will. But since I go into the largest gathering of criminals in England, it would be safer not to go full pursed. A lamb might as easily walk through a valley of famined wolves." He smiled. "Faith, is there not a psalm in that?"

He dumped the contents of the purse upon the bed. Then she saw again what she had put aside. "Captain," she said, raising the letter, "there's some matter else. This is from the Earl of Rochester." She passed him the paper. "He is released from the Tower. He says here that his imprisonment has given him much time for contemplation, that he realizes now the wrong he has done our Lucy."

"Does he indeed. The dog!"

"*And* he wishes to make her amends. He asks that I go to a house he owns off Little East Cheap, to consider if it might make a suitable lodging for Lucy and the child, and to discuss whatever other provision I may deem fit."

"He does not know that Lucy is in Cornwall?"

"He asks that I come alone, so perhaps he does."

"Alone? Well, I will accompany you, sure. When is the rendezvous?"

"At five o'clock today."

"Five? The noon bell just tolled. That does not leave me much time at the prison. Perhaps I should put the visit off till tomorrow."

"No!" She surprised both of them with the vehemence of her shout, so she took his hand in both of hers. "Let us not leave our Pitman one hour more than is necessary in that terrible place without hope, food, some news of his beloveds. I will wait for you here till four. If you do not arrive, I will go on alone." He tried to free his hand, but she held tighter. "You may join me there if you are late."

"You would be alone? With that rake?"

"That *boy*. Truly, sir, though I may act the gullible maiden, I assure you I am not one. I am versed in dealing with such bucks."

Coke stared at her a moment, then nodded. "Well, you will take Dickon with you. For all his simplicity, he is used to hot action, and keeps a steady head when it comes. Leave him outside the house, and send him fast to find me if you have need."

"Agreed, sir. Shall we shake on it?"

They did, easy since they were already holding hands. Then each retained the other's a moment before they parted.

Coke sorted among the coins on the bed, pocketing a few and finally selecting a gold crown. "Have you water? Some vinegar?"

"I have both. But would you not prefer an ale?"

"I would. Have it ready. First, alas, I must eat. Fetch me what I have asked for, I pray you. And a basin."

She brought a jug of water, two bottles, a little wooden bowl. He dropped the coin into that, poured water and vinegar atop it. She bent to study it. "A strange meal, Captain. What are you about?"

"This." He popped the bung from the beer bottle, licking the froth as it bubbled over the rim. Then he rubbed the coin vigorously in the bowl, before lifting it out, holding it up to glimmer in the sunlight. "I have been in jails before. The searches can be most thorough. There is only one way I know of to escape discovery—and clean gold is the best for it." He lifted the coin into the light, shook off the last drops. "So, as they say among the Dutch, *Prosit!*"

Then, to a shocked cry from Sarah and a delighted one from Dickon, he popped the coin in his mouth and washed it down with ale. It took a while, and the bottle was near empty before he was done.

26

NEWGATE

"Is 'e dead?" A stick was shoved under his chin, his head lifted. Of course, it could not move very far, what with his ears nailed to the board.

Pitman would not open his eyes unless the jailers forced him. Show them life and they might beat him again. Or worse. For all his agony, he was better off as he was.

They removed the stick, only to thrust it hard into his stomach. He could not restrain the groan.

"Not quite dead yet, then."

"Not long for it mind, I'd say," added the other jailer. "I said you 'it him too 'ard."

The first man laughed. "Wozzit matter? Dead of a beating, dead of the plague, he's still fucking dead, ain't 'e?"

"Yeah, but Briggs don't like to put beatings down on the bill of mortality, you know that. Maybe we should say 'e . . ."

The voices faded. Only when he was sure that the men were

far gone did Pitman carefully open one eye. His tormentors were on the other side of the yard, poking into a pile of rags. The body within them did not move. A harsher jab and still nothing stirred. One of the jailers now turned to two prisoners, waiting a few paces behind them, eyes down, bodies folded in on themselves. He gestured with his stick and the two immediately seized the limbs of the dead man, dragged him toward the prison entrance. Before it stood the cart of the dead. There were bodies in it already, and this most recent corpse was swung atop them.

Pitman let his head sag, chin to chest. Like most things in life, there was a trick to it; the balance point where the head could hang without the nails further ripping the flesh. Fortunately for him, his jailers had nailed both ears at the top. This meant he could just rest the tip of his chin on his chest. It relieved some of the ache in his neck.

"'The Lord is my shepherd; I shall not want,'" he muttered. "'He maketh me to lie down in green pastures: he leadeth me beside the still waters.'"

Waters! When had he last had a drink? In the dungeon, a few sips late last night just before the man attacked him for the bread? He didn't think he'd killed the man, but he had hit him hard enough to. He'd had no choice—if he hadn't, he could have been killed himself. And then what of his family? "'Yea, though I walk through the valley of the shadow of death, I will fear no evil: for thou art with me; thy rod and thy staff they comfort me.'"

No! He'd left out a verse. He had done that too many times now. It was his weakness. He was growing weak. Three weeks in Newgate; three of beatings and starving, for he had only received the tiny bit they gave the prisoners who could not pay for more. Bread, a little gruel, fouled water. Yet what he would not give for a taste of any of those right now! A bite would be a banquet. But how to get it? If he "awoke," they might free him from the stocks; but then they would return him to Limbo, the dungeon below the gatehouse that gave the prison its name, a place for those sentenced to die. And even though he had not been condemned, because the courts had not sat since his taking, still he was accused of murder, and that foulest of cells was reserved for murderers, for traitors, for witches—for all whose only judgment would be hemp, blade or flame. It was a hell of scant air, scant light, and foul with prisoners' waste, warmed more than any other part of Newgate by this summer's terrible heat. Here at least there was air, only slightly less foul from a place that made the three surrounding parishes reek.

No. he would live off air for now, and when he could bear his thirst and hunger no longer, or when sleep threatened to take him and so rip the nails through his ears, only then would he awake.

"'My God, my God, why hast thou forsaken me? Why art thou so far from helping me, and from the words of my roaring?'"

No! That was not the missing verse. That was not even the right psalm. And he had roared it. His two fellows in the stocks started to shout. Those manacled on the ground nearby took up the cry. Some prayed. Some cursed. Through one blood-clotted eyelid, he saw the guards turn to look.

Lower the head, Pitman.

Then he heard a different sound. Not the guards kicking and cursing their way toward him, but the sound of the gate opening. Pitman risked a glance. The guards had turned back, part of a crowd now moving toward the gate, prisoners and warders, the latter beating back the former; clearing the way so that the visitors could enter. Each inhabitant of Newgate hoped for something from those who came, the family members or friends who could bring food, or coin to buy a little better treatment.

Pitman knew he should not hope. Yet he did. Perhaps his house had been shut up in error. Perhaps Bettina was among those entering now, lining up to pass the expectant guards. She would give them the bribe they required, suffer their pats and pinches. She would walk across the yard, carrying her husband a bottle of ale, an apple, a chunk of cheese.

He gazed, yearning. But only a small group of men was there. No Bettina. No succour.

He was about to lower his head to the chin point again, to close his eyes, to try to recall the verse of the psalm he'd meant to recite, when something about one of the visitors made him look harder. The man was taller than most there; his clothes were less shabby. There was colour too, in the plume on his hat, its vivid green almost painful in a world so grey-brown and drab. But it was the way he held himself, near all the weight on his back leg, like a swordsman, that made Pitman realize it was him.

"Captain Cock," he said, and despite everything, smiled.

"You, sir! Do you come to visit a prisoner?"

The head guard, whose girth seemed all the vaster in contrast to the shrivelled wretches still pressing around, was beckoning Coke closer.

"I do."

"Name?"

"My name is Robert Bartholomew."

"The prisoner's, sir. I care not a jot for your name."

"Pitman."

"Given name?"

"I never knew it. He goes only by Pitman."

The jailer spat on the cobbles beside him. "Jesu, man! There are four thousand here and much coming and going." He jerked his chin at the dead cart behind Coke. "Very well. Describe him. Begin with his crime."

Yet before Coke could start, another guard stepped close and whispered in the jailer's ear. He listened, then turned back to Coke. "It appears that we do know him. A notorious murderer. We can take you to him directly. But first you should consider this." He cleared his throat. "This Pitman was brought in by the All Hallows watch with nothing. So clear was his crime that he would have been sent to hang straightaway had the courts not suspended that very day. No one has been to visit, so he has been living on our charity. In plain words, sir, he has cost us. Do you wish to help your friend?"

"I do. I have brought him food."

Coke put the basket on the table. Half the contents disappeared immediately into a box behind the jailer. Coke saw three of his six apples taken, one of the ham hocks, one of the two loaves. The man lifted a bottle. "What's this?"

"Whisky. I was sure you'd have been kind to him, hence a gift?"

The man grunted. "I'd have to confiscate it anyway. No liquor allowed in here but what we sell. So I'll keep that." He tucked it behind him. "Now, have you any coin? He's had no bedding, just straw to sleep on. For a crown . . ."

The rest of the transaction went swiftly. Coke had coins secreted about his person, and only handed over all that remained in the purse: three florins. The man grunted but seemed satisfied enough. "Your sword, sir," he said. As Coke unbuckled and passed it across, he continued, "Any other weapons?"

"None," he replied, feeling the small dagger pressed against his spine.

"Well, we have to believe a gentleman, don't we?" He swept his hand in a gesture of welcome. "Enter, sir."

Coke took a step. "Pardon me, but where will I find him?"

"In the centre of the yard."

"Near the stocks, then?"

"Very near them indeed." The man nodded, his face impassive. "I am sure he will be all ears."

Laughter exploded from those standing by. Coke frowned, moved off. There was no obvious path to the stocks, so he threaded his way through the sprawled prisoners, most lying with their tongues out, panting like dogs in the sun. Many sat up to beseech him; with several he had to wrench his cloak from their grasps. One of the guards was trailing him, still chuckling. When Coke reached the stocks, he placed one foot upon its platform and searched about him. "I do not see him," he said to the guard.

"Then you are blind," was the reply.

Coke searched again, his gaze passing over the three unfortunates actually in the stocks, two with their arms just fastened in the holes, the worst off with his ears nailed to the board as well.

Then Coke gasped. He had not recognized him because Pitman was so changed. It wasn't just the rags. The vast, neat beard was gone, but some rough growth hung from the chin, merging with chest hair that glistened with blood. There was hair too, on a head that before had been shaved as bald as a Pell Mell ball. Mostly, though, the sheer diminishment of the man shocked. A giant did not hang there. A lanky scarecrow did.

"Pitman," Coke called out. The other man's head lifted slowly. Coke turned back to the guard. "May I free him?"

The guard looked to the gatehouse. The officer who'd examined Coke there was watching. He nodded. The guard turned back. "You may. But it'll cost ya."

Coke did not want to delve into his clothes, revealing that he had more concealed coins, so he pulled his timepiece from his doublet pocket. "Will this do?" The man sniffed but accepted it. "Will you now free him?" Coke asked.

"For a poxy clock?" he said, "Nah. But you can." He threw down some pliers and walked away.

Coke snatched up the tool. He examined the ruin of flesh before him.

Pitman opened one eye. "Welcome to hell, Captain Coke."

"Easy, my friend," he said, and put the pincers over the nail head.

He had never done this before. A gentle wiggling caused Pitman to moan. Cursing, Coke got a good grip of metal on metal, placed his other hand on the board of the stocks and wrenched.

Pitman gave a great cry, his head flopping over to the still-pinned side. Coke stepped across, placed, jerked. The other nail came free. Pitman sagged, held up now only by his wrists in the stocks' holes. Swiftly Coke moved around, pulled the pin out, threw up the bar and was around in time to catch Pitman just before he fell. "Easy," Coke said, lowering him till the big man could put his back against the post. Then Coke looked about. There was a well nearby. He went to it, picked up a bucket on a rope. A different guard there looked to the officer at the gate. Another nod. Coke lowered the bucket, pulled it back up; detached it and carried it over to the stocks. There was so much blood that he did not know where to begin.

Pitman did. He took the bucket, raised it to his mouth, drank most of it off, then lowered it to peer over its rim at Coke. "What

277

news?" he rasped. Then he saw the basket Coke had set down. His eyes went wide and he reached.

Coke picked up the basket in one hand and helped Pitman rise with the other. "Here, man. Let us get you out of the sun."

The two of them made a halting progress to some shade. The yard, which had gone near silent while Coke freed his friend, now burst into noise again, with cries, with pleadings, with laughter and drunken song from the prison tavern they collapsed before. Someone within it was tuning a fiddle.

Pitman ate two of the small, bitter apples whole, stem, core and all, and tucked the third apple within his rags. He chewed every scrap of meat from the ham hock; though the bone, thrown aside, was still fought over by three men and sucked hard by the victor. The bread was swallowed in four bites, and only when it was gone and the empty basket shown to those hovering near did the crowd give back.

"What news?" Pitman asked again.

Coke kept his recounting short. There was little he could do but tell the truth, certain that Pitman would recognize a comforting lie. He was silent until the tale turned to his house and Coke's meeting with Bettina.

"My Sweet Imogen? And the babe Jeremiah?"

"Aye. I am so sorry for it."

A tear ran down the grimed face. "And Josiah?"

"Lives. Sick, but lives. That is all I know."

"I see." Pitman went silent then, and Coke took the chance to pull out his *mouchoir*, dip it in the bucket, and try to dab the worst of the blood from the torn ears. Pitman ignored him, until he suddenly gripped Coke's wrist. "I also have news for you. I have seen the face of the devil."

"Pitman," Coke replied, "how could you not, when you live in hell?"

"No, Captain. It is why I am here." He told the story of the church, of Tobias Sym and of glimpsing the face of the man who'd struck him before oblivion came.

"Did you know him?" Coke asked.

"I . . ." Pitman touched the side of his head. "I cannot remember. It was but a glance before he hit me and I had never, never been hit that hard before." He rubbed his temple. "That blow has blurred everything. But this I can say. I saw blood."

"On the victim?"

"No. On the man who hit me. An apron covered in it. Like a butcher's."

"You are certain?"

"No."

"Yet you are certain it was our killer and not another?"

"Aye." He jerked his head to the jailers at the gate. "They have delighted in recounting the tale. The butcher of Finchley and St. Giles, caught at last. The jewel found in this victim's mouth as in the others. I am famous here. It is why I receive special favours." He touched an ear. "His face . . . I think I do know him. But I cannot remember." He groaned. "I cannot."

Coke put his hand over Pitman's. "Easy, my friend. We old soldiers, there are things we forget."

"I will remember. I will!" He swallowed. "Now, tell me of Mrs. Chalker."

Coke told of their journey to Cornwall, of leaving Lucy, the long walk back—and of the note from Rochester, the rendezvous that had been arranged—which he must depart for shortly. At this Pitman frowned. "The Earl of Rochester has not been freed from the Tower."

"He has. The news cannot have reached here yet."

"I tell you, man, we would have been the first to hear of such a thing. There is a fellowship of jails, where every common villain thinks himself the kin of any nobleman because both view the world through bars. Word would have come at the freeing of one so famed as John Wilmot."

"Then who sent the—?" Coke flushed cold, stood. "I must go."

"Go, then."

The captain looked down. Pitman was in a sorry state: starved, his body a mass of bruises, cuts and flea bites, his ears torn. He had just been told of two dead children, another sick, a family in peril. He was about to be left hopeless. In hell.

The bell of St. Sepulchre's struck the hour. Three of the clock. Coke had a little time. "Here," he said, crouching. "You might find a use for this." Keeping his movements small, he slipped the dagger from its spine sheath, slid it over. "And these—" he dug out the coins from all the little pockets Sarah had sewn for him "—might keep you for a while, until we find a way to free you."

"Free me? If I last another week, it will be a miracle." He coughed. "And if that miracle happened, what then? I would survive long enough only for the courts to sit again, before I'll be doing the hemp jig on the Tyburn tree."

Coke could not think of a reply. Then in the tavern at their backs, one song ended and another began, a famous ballad. About a highwayman. "Well, since we are speaking of jigs and since they are now playing 'Whisky in the Jar,' shall I buy us one with the last coin I possess?"

Pitman considered for a moment. "When I made my wedding vow, I swore to leave off both cursing and spirituous liquors." He spat phlegm and blood. "But fuck, man, a whisky can't hurt me."

"I'll fetch them, then."

As the captain entered the tavern, the song reached its chorus. To distract his mind, he joined in under his breath:

Musha rin du-rum do du-rum da, Whack for my daddy-o,
Whack for my daddy-o, there's whisky in the jar.

The swaying, singing crowd was mainly men, a few women. It was even hotter within the room than the yard, the stench different, that sweet liquor note to it equally foul. Coke, who'd raised his scarf on entering, now dropped it to speak. "Two whiskies," he said, handing over his coin to the large man sweating hard on the other side of the trestle, who poured tots into two chipped mugs and swept the shilling into a tankard.

"No change?" Coke asked, but the man just laughed and went to serve someone else.

Coke sniffed. What was within the vessels made his eyes water. Christ, he thought, I'd scarce clean my sword with it.

The song, so popular the first time, had immediately been struck up again, from his favourite part—the bold highwayman betrayed by his lover. The fiddler's not bad, he thought, and looked into the man's face. Knew him, in the instant that the fiddler looked into his, and knew him too.

Coke had dropped the mugs and was already at the door, when the fiddle screeched a foul note and stopped. "Well, look there," the fiddler cried, "and if it isn't my old comrade Captain Cock."

Coke was out of the tavern, walking swiftly for the main gate, trying not to run. But he was never going to beat that Irish voice. "Remember me, guards, and treat me special," shouted Maclean from the doorway, "for there's thirty guineas on that thoroughbred's head and I wants me share!"

Twenty paces to go, and Coke thought he might make it, until the two guards blocked his path. He was moving fast though, and they were uncertain, so he ducked under the one's spread arms and hit the other with the heel of his hand under his chin. Ten paces now to the gates, and he could see the cobbles of Giltspur Street beyond. But what he didn't see was the flung cudgel, though he felt it strike him behind his right ear. Somehow he kept going, though his legs were not working so well, indeed one knee dipped, touched the ground. He forced himself up, managed one more step, when someone landed on his back. Then he was looking closely at a cracked paving stone, with the man on him shouting, as if from far away, "Got 'im!"

Sarah, he thought. Must warn her about—

The darkness took him, and the only words left were from the chorus. He didn't like them so well now:

Devil take the women for they never can be aisey . . .

27

GILDED CAGE

Lord Garnthorpe stood before the mirror in his dressing chamber at St. James's, turning about. Dissatisfied. Though he had curbed his tailor's worst excesses, was even the little he'd retained not too much? Sarah loved him as he was: plain, honest and only as handsome as God had made him. So there must be no artificiality in their exchanges. Nothing false. She'd known that before he had. It was the reason she had so demurely declined his offering of the sapphire.

A knock. "What?" he snapped.

"A visitor, my lord," Maggs called.

"Of what estate?"

"He would not give his name. He's plainly dressed. Not a nobleman."

Garnthorpe snorted. Maggs had all the snobbery of a manservant. Was he not noble and yet as plain as any other man? Then a thought: "What is the colour of his hair?"

"Such as there is, my lord, is fair."

Garnthorpe turned from the mirror. "Does he have a scar across his nose?"

"He does."

He knew who waited below. He had been neglectful of the man in the past week. Of all his brothers. And in neglecting them, he'd also neglected God.

"Ask him to wait in the parlour. Give him what he wants to drink. Inform him that I will be down shortly."

"My lord."

He considered himself again in the mirror. If the woman who loved him wanted him plain, how much more so the old comrade, his fellow Saint? He began to strip off the petticoat breeches.

"Brother S.," Lord Garnthorpe said as he entered a few minutes later, "did my servant not provide you with something to drink?"

The straw-haired man shook his head. "I want only this: to speak with you, on a matter of great urgency." He looked around the room. "It is richly furnished, your house."

The words had not been uttered as a compliment. "My father's house. I have not enriched it since he died. You know I care nothing for exterior show." He gestured to his sober clothing to emphasize the point.

"'In my father's house are many mansions,'" the other man quoted. "'I go to prepare a place for you.'" He stepped close, took Garnthorpe's elbow. "We have been preparing many places, Brother. There is still so much to ready for what is nearing. Yet we have not seen you these several weeks. At prayer. At meetings. After that Judas was dealt with, you were meant to come to me. To take your place among the six on the Council of the Great Ones. You did not come." He gently shook the arm he held. "What have you been about?"

"Matters of my own."

"Your own?" Suddenly he gripped Garnthorpe above the elbow, his voice no longer gentle. "There are no matters beyond the one great matter: that the End of Days is nigh! That Jesus is coming to be our King! He himself in the flesh!" His fingers bore in and Garnthorpe cried out. "You know this—and yet you speak of your own *matters*?"

Garnthorpe jerked his arm free. "I do know this, Brother. And I have been remiss. But I am the Lord's sheathed sword still, believe me. Draw me when you will."

Brother Simeon stared at him, silent. Garnthorpe saw the scar across his nose pulse with fire, though he knew flame had not laid it open but a cavalier's blade; knew because it had happened right beside him when the king's cavalry had charged Parliament's lines at Naseby. For the first and only time, over years of battle, Simeon Critchollow had dropped the regiment's banner. But two very different men had picked it up: the nobleman Lord Garnthorpe and the butcher Abel Strong. Rallying the regiment, driving off the royal horse, helping turn defeat into the most famous of victories.

Perhaps this close the other man saw what he was seeing. For the darkness in his gaze lifted. Simeon smiled, and when that powerful voice sounded again, it was as smooth as before. "You ever were the Lord's weapon, his fine shining blade. And is our old comrade as apt? Or is Abel Strong also about matters of his own?"

Looking down, Garnthorpe murmured, "I have not seen him these three weeks. Since he dealt with the Judas. Yet I believe—nay, I know—he is ready."

"Praise God." The pleasure in the voice made Garnthorpe look up as the man continued, "I was thinking of when and where we were reunited, you and I. Long after the wars. Do you remember?"

It was not a time he ever chose to think about. Though this man sometimes made him. "And do you remember," Simeon went on as if the answer had been yes, "the verse you were reciting that day in Bethlehem Hospital? The one that made me stop, before I even recognized your voice. It was as if—" he gazed at the ceiling "—as if an angel spoke to me out of heaven. Which in a way one did. For you revealed yourself with that verse, did you not? It enabled me to raise you from the pit. To release you and then with your help release our brother Abel Strong." He smiled. "Say it with me now." He reached out, placed the other's hands in a position of prayer, his own wrapped outside them. Their two voices rose together: "'But the saints of the most High shall take the kingdom, and possess the kingdom for ever, even for ever and ever.'"

"Yes," continued Brother S. "I knew you then, even in the disguise of your filth, your degradation. Knew you not simply as my old comrade but as a brother Saint, a Fifth Monarchist man, even though you were little acquainted with them. But I taught you about them, did I not? Brought you into that light?"

"You did." Garnthorpe swayed. The verse they'd spoken, this man's presence—they always made him weak for a while. Until they made him strong.

"Good. Perhaps now I will take that drink. Do I espy some sack?" He went to the table, uncorked a bottle. "There is something I need you to do for us. Both of you." He lifted an eyebrow—Garnthorpe shook his head. He poured a tot into a crystal glass. "And you will have time for your own matters also. The gathering does not happen for a week."

"What gathering?"

Simeon sipped, regarding the other man for a long moment. "You understand this plague that kills so many is an instrument of the Lord's wrath. A sign of the coming end, though not the end in itself. That the mark of the beast will not be upon us till the year of his number, next year, 1666."

"I understand this."

"More must happen before the Ancient of Days comes and the Saints possess the kingdom, as written of so gloriously in the Book of Daniel. Yet there is much we can still do to prepare for that glory—the most important being to strike at the heart of the Fourth Monarchy that yet rules over us."

"How?"

"By killing one close to it."

Garnthorpe gasped. "The king?"

"Nay. He is too well guarded. And a chance to kill a king does not happen more than once a century, I fear." Brother S. smiled. "Not him. Someone close, though."

"The Duke of York?"

"You have him. And he is not so closely protected."

Garnthorpe frowned. "But is he not with the court in Oxford, fled this plague like all the coward Stuarts?"

"He is. Except for one night next week. Next Tuesday he attends a meeting at Whitehall. Some fellow in the navy office, name of Pepys, arranges it. We have a brother in that same office who tells us all the details." He raised the crystal into the sunlight at the window. Rainbow shafts lit his face. "Many forget, with all this death on land, that there is also death at sea. That the war with the Dutch continues. The duke is head of the navy, so—" he lowered the glass, sipped "—he comes to give them their orders. By boat on the Thames to Whitehall Palace, meet, then return on the next morn's tide." He drained the glass, placed it on the table. "Do you attend the meeting at All Hallows this Sunday. We will pray. And then talk of ways and means."

He moved to the door. "Ah! I almost forgot. You will need this. Or rather, our friend Strong will. You must give it to him." He returned to the table and laid a velvet purse beside his empty glass. "Till Sunday, then. Peace be with you."

"Praise God."

Simeon left. Lord Garnthorpe heard the front door slam after him, Maggs's uncorrectable fault. Next Tuesday we are called, he thought. That's seven days about my own affairs. Will that be time enough to bring the sinner to God? And then to myself?

He picked up the velvet pouch, put it into a doublet pocket. He did not need to look at the stone to know it would gleam, greener than crystal, in the sunlight.

The walk from St. James's to Simeon's destination near Charing Cross took little time with the streets so empty, which was unusual at this time of a weekday, usual at this time of the plague. There were still some hawkers about but far fewer than normal, their customers gone, one way or another.

Beggars, though, had multiplied. Many were new to the trade, their clothes a little less torn than the experienced ones, the wounds some had given themselves a little less well done. Many wore the last castoffs they'd received before their employers, fine lords and ladies, fled because they could afford to. One servant might be retained to brave the city and guard the house. The rest were thrown onto the streets.

It is the poor's plague, sure, Simeon thought, as he pushed past another set of reaching hands, hearing the mumbled cuss as he did, seeing the dull hatred in so many eyes. The poor who starve and sicken, the rich who, in the main, survive. But that very hatred was a force to be harnessed, he knew, like Thames water driving the wheels in the arches of London Bridge. Channelled like that water, it would power the second revolution in England in twenty years. They had come close, so close, to establishing a truly godly republic, only to be betrayed by those who led, who had not the faith nor the will to go as far as was required. This time they would not let it slip. This time, they would set a flame that would bring Christ's fiery cross, his everlasting kingdom. On the ashes of Babylon, Jerusalem would rise.

He was passing the Eleanor Cross on the Strand, a spluttering torch upon it, when yet another hand tugged at his coat. He was about to thrust it aside like all the others but glanced up – and was startled by eyes as green as the emerald he had just left behind in St. James's. They belonged to a youth scarce twenty, whose face would have been hand-some had not hunger and shame so reduced it, and whose big frame in better days could have hefted a pike. Halting, Simeon reached into a pocket, pulled out a shilling. Yet he did not hand it over straightaway.

"What is your name, my young man?" he asked.

"Daniel, sir, and it please you."

Oh, how it did! Daniel, the prophet he had only just been quot-ing to Lord Garnthorpe. The holiest of flames that guided the Saints. "Your voice sounds gentle. Where are you from?"

"Aylesbury, sir."

"And your station?"

"I was a servant in a rich house. Mostly, I played the flute for them but they—" the youth gave a little sob, swallowed it down, "—they abandoned me when they fled for the country."

Simeon smiled. There was no coincidence in the holy plan, no thread astray in God's exquisite tapestry. "Have you heard the good word, my son?" he asked. "Have you heard that King Jesus is coming in the flesh to rule us all?"

"I, uh, I have not, sir."

"Then attend ye All Hallows the Great this Sunday. There to hear the word. There to receive blessing—and bread too." He pulled out another shilling, then put both coins in the youth's hand, closed his own over it and pressed. "Will you join us there, Daniel? Will you be saved?"

The beautiful eyes brimmed. "I will. God bless you, sir, but I will."

"Praise be." With a last squeeze, Simeon moved away, pushing through others who had noticed him stop, who quickly arrived to beg a share. Another recruit, with something special about him. Simeon could see that, and something else too. What he himself had once found: light in the dark.

They had already gathered in the underground room, their murmurs fuelled by liquor and impatience. "Where have you been?" demanded the landlord, keeping his voice low as well. The large inn he ran was shut up like all gathering places. But the cellar beneath it was crammed. "I've already taken their coin, sold them drink. They grow restless, and the watchman I bribed has been asking for more. They expected you an hour since."

"Other business," Simeon Critchhollow answered. "I am here now."

He elbowed through the crowd to the last arch of the long cellar, edged behind the drapes there, climbed the five stairs to the platform. A lantern's light showed him that all was as he'd left it. It may not have been as well appointed as his usual place of trade, but it would do. Even Saints had to eat.

When the landlord thrust his head through, he nodded, then reached. The drapes below him were pulled back. He blew a long vibrating blast on the small trumpet fixed on the frame before him.

Whistles, a few claps; then they, along with all murmurs, ceased as he lifted the marionette from its stand and walked it to the middle of the small stage.

"'Eh! Eh! Eh! Here am I, Punchinello!'" he cried, his voice high-pitched, his accent an exaggerated Italian. "'Eh! Eh! Eh! 'as any one seen thata fatta beetch, my wife, eh?'"

Laughter filled the cellar. Simeon smiled too as he reached for another set of strings.

It was plain, the room Rochester's servant showed her into, in the house on Priest's Alley. Woven brown hangings covered the walls, no decoration upon them save a portrait of some half-clad female saint gazing heavenward, some devilish shapes lurking nearby. That and a simple wooden cross were all the adornments—save for the flowers, oxlips and violets in the main—that the room possessed.

She was surprised—Rochester had a reputation as a man of gaudy tastes. Then she realized that he'd probably rented this house for his leaving of the Tower, only a few streets away; that it could belong to merchants who had fled the plague, foreign maybe, sober, religious folk. She doubted he planned to stay in it long before he joined the court in Oxford. Or maybe he meant it for Lucy. He would not be aware of her going to Cornwall. Perhaps he intended more than just paying her off. Perhaps he was truly penitent, and this place was a haven he intended for his mistress and their child.

As she bent to study the painting more closely, from somewhere nearby she thought she heard a sob. It was ever so faint, yet it made her reach to her hip to touch the knife that rested against it.

John Chalker's knife. That and Dickon in the churchyard opposite the house her twin comforts.

Footsteps were descending the stairs from the upper storey. Her answer approached. "My Lord Roch—" she began, even as she started to curtsy, stopping both words and movement when the man who entered was not John Wilmot. She didn't see his face clearly at first because he was already sweeping into a bow and his hat obscured it, an expensive beaver, with an outsize blue ostrich feather curled into the crown, a vivid contrast to him and this setting, a dazzle of colour against the drab.

He straightened. "Come, don't you know me, Mrs. Chalker?" he said, after a moment. "Nay, you are being coy with me." He smiled. "For how can you not know the man whom you have secretly loved this many a day?"

She did know him, of course, and everything that had been murky in her mind came clear. Her husband had not told her what he was about the day he disappeared. But it was only days after she had confessed her fear . . . of the man who stood before her now. John had vowed to deal with this lord who so disturbed her in the theatre, who'd gripped and bruised her wrist. But her John was the one dealt with. By this man. Never in her life of seeing things that were there, and those that were not, had she been more certain of anything.

All this thought flashed in near a second; the same one that had her snatching out the knife, driving it at his face so fast that only a jerk of his head saved his eye, at the cost of a cut along his temple. She pulled the blade back, but his hand fell upon her, fingers like metal wrapping around her wrist, instantly squeezed so hard she had no choice but to drop the weapon. She shot her left hand up, fingernails reaching, but his other gripped her as she struggled, jerked, kicked, could not break free. The man was as strong as she'd ever known. Stronger even than John Chalker.

The memory of her husband, how she'd last seen him, took her strength; she sagged, ceasing her struggles. He dragged her across the room, dropped her onto the one chair. As she rubbed her agonized wrists, he stooped to pick up her knife, at the same time pulling a square of linen from a sleeve to press against his temple. The white *mouchoir* crimsoned immediately. "Well," he said, "I do not blame you for this. You were startled, that is all. And it shows you are a woman of courage, of spirit. That is good. You will need spirit for the week we will have together in this house—" he dabbed at the gash "—and for the time beyond its walls. You will need it to survive the End of Days that is so swiftly approaching. Which you and I shall face hand in hand."

He crossed to the table, placed his fingers on the book that lay open there, beneath the martyred saint, leaving a trace of blood on the paper. "Spirit, and faith also," he continued. "I suspect you have not been instructed in the truest words of God, those found mainly in the prophecies of Revelation and of Daniel, have you?" That half smile again. "No matter. It will give me the greatest pleasure to instruct you."

She'd regained enough breath to propel herself to the door. It was not locked. She flung it open. Maggs stood on the other side. When she tried to push past him, he seized her arms, shoved her back into the room.

"There is something else," Lord Garnthorpe continued, as if she had not moved. "Someone else. A great sinner, full of filth and degradation. Yet one who was corrupted by a devil in the guise of a lord. It is our duty to King Jesus to save them. Just as I shall save you."

He left the room. Maggs stared down, his face blank. She heard Garnthorpe cross the hall, a second door open, feet descending. That sob came again, louder, then it stopped. Sarah heard Garnthorpe returning and the sound of something being dragged.

He entered, hauling someone behind him. "Behold," he said, "the mother of harlots."

And he threw Lucy Absolute onto the floor.

Part Five

✦

AND I . . . SAW THE HOLY CITY, NEW JERUSALEM,

COMING DOWN FROM GOD OUT OF HEAVEN,

PREPARED AS A BRIDE ADORNED FOR HER HUSBAND.

The Revelation of St. John the Divine 21.2

28

LEVELS OF HELL

One week later

"Coke? Captain Coke? Are you awake?"

The whisper entered his dream. It was not welcome.

He was in a bath, the one his sisters had drawn for him when he'd visited home after three months in the field. They'd teased him for the colour he'd turned the water. Murkier than a pond, they said. A habitation for frogs, they said. He told them he'd eaten frogs when he'd followed the prince to France, though he thought that strange, since he'd only gone to France after his sisters were dead. Still, he began casting around in the warm murk for anything living. Right now, a frog fried in a parsleyed butter would be the best thing he'd ever tasted. A raw one would do near as well.

"Wake, Captain. 'Tis time."

Captain? Hadn't he asked her to call him Will?

"Sarah," he said loudly.

"Hush, man!" A finger was placed on his mouth. "You'll rouse them all."

He brushed Pitman's hand from his face. "Leave me be."

"Then I would also have to leave you in Limbo. Rise. Macready's here."

"I am. Still alive! Still alive!"

There was little light there during the day, just what the cracks in the stones of the gatehouse floor, directly above, admitted. The only way to tell day from night was when there was no light at all—as now. But Coke heard the distinctive *huh-huh-huh* wheeze of the Scotsman, like a magpie's mocking laugh, could picture his ragged face. The nose half gone, bitten off in a fight, he said. The black crossed eyes. The toad skin he wore on a string around his neck as a ward against the plague. Perhaps the talisman had worked, for Macready was most distinctive in this: he had survived in Limbo for nearly six months. Three months longer than any in living memory. The guards made bets on his longevity, and many were happy to hear that wheeze each morning. Some fed him a little better, like a fighting cock they kept alive for sport.

The wheeze came now. "Are you ready for this folly, lads?"

"Ready," replied Pitman.

"And I," said Coke, sitting up.

"Then set about what ye must do. Have you my reward to hand?"

Coke felt for the gold guinea, the one he'd swallowed as a precaution before he ever set foot in Newgate, and which had done its journey through his guts to eventually emerge bleached but whole. "I do."

"Don't you forget to leave it me. I have such plans for it!"

Macready laughed, but the laughter quickly dissolved into wet coughing. "I'm not sure you'll live to spend the gold," said Coke, leaning away. "Is that a plague cough I hear?"

"Plague?" The man snorted. "You're such a new one here, Captain Cock." He sniffed, a long wet intake. "What I have, sir, is jail fever! A superior form of sickness entirely. I've got weeks of life in me yet. Time to spend that gold while you two are being chased down to Tyburn gallows by the Black Dog hisself."

Coke shivered. The Black Dog of Newgate. He'd scoffed at it, this story to frighten children to sleep. But after one week there, he could swear he'd heard its paws padding above the dungeon each night.

"So look you do not try to cheat me," added the Scot. "Now, about it, boys." He wheezed off.

"This *is* folly, Pitman." Coke coughed. "Entwining ourselves with plague victims. How shall we 'scape the fell disease ourselves?"

"Many dwell side by side with the dying—nay, lie in the same bed and never catch it. Others do and yet live. Only God decides who he takes."

"Very well," said Coke, rising. "Let us see if we can cheat the Black Dog a little longer."

Immediately they set about it. "They will go to lengths not to touch you," Macready had told them, "if they see the plague marks clear. And they will not study them close, for fear they will be studying them closer still—on themselves."

Spit, piss and charcoal made a fair black dye, they'd discovered, in the little light that arrived with day and the rare opening of the dungeon's trap door. Pitman now daubed oval rings—darker upon the outside, lighter in the middle—first on his own throat and chest, then repeated and varied the patterns on Coke. They did the backs of each other's necks.

Then it was the captain's turn. With the knife he'd brought and the rats he'd killed with it, he fashioned oval pouches of the skins, which he then stuffed with fetid straw blackened with that same charcoal mix. He pressed them into Pitman's groin and one armpit. They'd pass as buboes if the observer did not study them too long. After tying them in place with dyed, plaited straw, he let Pitman tie others onto him.

Now there was only the waiting.

"Where will they take us, do you think?" Coke whispered.

"I heard the city cemeteries are all full. They're digging pits beyond the walls now."

"That means longer in the wagon?"

"Aye."

"But what if Newgate is the first call, not the last? We'll be in the bottom of the damned cart."

"You'll still have to bide as you can."

"Christ, this I pray: that I am not thrown first into the cart. Indeed, I pray most of all I am not under you. You may be shrunk from what you were, but you are still a great ox, for all that."

Pitman smiled. "My only prayer is they place us so that for the entire journey your Royalist nose is up my Puritan—" He broke off. "But whatever happens, man, cling to this: if you do not escape, whatever danger Mrs. Chalker is in continues. If I do not, more of my chicks will die. And I jest when I speak of my only prayer. My true one is that the Almighty preserve us a little longer, to do his will and catch the fiend."

"You still do not recall his face?"

"His face, aye, but not the name that goes with it. If—"

"Huh-huh-huh." The wheeze was close in the dark. "They come."

And they did, as always, with the scrape of the iron bar run along stone and thrust into the metal hoop, with the squeal as it was twisted, lifted. Immediately there was light, flaring torch light, which had all below holding their arms before their eyes, at the same time crying out—for pity, for water, for their God, however they knew him, to deliver them.

"Macready," the jailer called, "are you alive, ye hound?"

"Ow, ow! Still alive, Cap'n, still alive!" the Scotsman howled. "So that's another tanner you owe your corporal."

Laughter mingled with some curses until the voice sounded again. "And what's the bill of mortality in Limbo this night, Macready?"

"Ah, the Black Dog has run among us, sure," was the reply. "There's one dead of fever as I can see, one choked—did you know there was murderers down here, Cap'n? It's shocking!" More laughter. Then the Scot added, "And the plague's taken two."

The laughs ceased. "I'm sending down for the corpses. Clear away, do not any paw them or none will get their bread and gruel."

The Limbo dwellers who'd started to crawl onto the stone stairs hurried aside. Four other prisoners—mere thieves, no doubt, their clothes a little less ragged, their faces swathed in cloth—scurried down the steps, pausing on the last one. "Blade? Fever?" one asked, and Macready pointed. Two bodies were removed, then the men returned. "Plague?"

Pitman was the first they picked up, amidst much swearing at his weight; the two men then carried him away up the steps, his long arms dragging. Then they came back for Coke. "Shite, look at that buboe," one of the men said.

"I'd rather not," said the other, his voice a little more genteel. "Now, grab his arms, sir, and let's be done with him."

"You grab his bloody arms," the first said. "I'm not going near that scab."

Coke was halfway up the stairs, when the hiss and cough reminded him of the last thing he must do to ensure escape. Carefully he unclutched his hand and let the gold guinea slip.

"Thank you, Cap'n. Ow! Ow!"

"What are you thanking me for, Macready?" the officer asked.

Coke didn't hear the answer; he was out of the cell and being run through the gate. It appeared that his bearers wanted rid of him fast. He risked the half opening of one eye—then wished he hadn't. He was being borne toward a cart piled high with bodies. In a moment, he was thrown atop them.

The gates slammed shut. Two men mounted the bench of the cart. "Bring out your dead! Bring—"

"Belay that, ya fool," said the second man, taking the reins. "One more body and this starved nag ain't moving. Get on, ya bitch!" He cracked a whip and the cart lurched.

"Where to?" asked the first man.

"Moorfields," the second replied. "They dug a new hole yesterday. 'Alf filled it already."

Coke could not help the laugh that shook him. He was out of Limbo! Then he felt scratching under his left thigh. Too consistent to be a flea. He looked around, down.

Into Pitman's face. The man did not open his eyes but had a finger across his lips in the gesture of silence. But Coke found it hard to obey when he saw that it was in fact the Puritan who had his nose pressed up the Royalist's arse.

Between the swaying of the cart and the shifting of the bodies as it did, Pitman was slowly able to free his own limbs from the tangle. Though his head was close to a living man, it was the dead around who concerned him. He felt them pressing him all over—a child's arm over his thigh, a woman's breast at his belly. He could see the oval plague token clear on that by moonlight, which was bright as a noonday sun to him after Limbo. He needed all his will not to burst from the middle of the pile and run screaming into the night.

He knew he must not. They had discussed it, Coke and he, every day in that darkest level of hell, and had agreed: though death was on every street in the city, in such numbers that the ink to note it was running low, even so every man's death must still be recorded in the parish ledgers. If the notorious murderers Pitman and Coke were to rise from a death cart and flee into the night, there would be such a hue and cry that they would soon be caught and returned to prison. Already *dead*, they had a chance to do what they must to save those they loved.

Yet they had also discussed this: to be fully dead, they had to be buried.

The cart had left on the city side of Newgate, down the road that bore its name. So it was down his most familiar streets that he was taken, and he found comfort in naming them, distraction from his situation. As he peered between limbs stiffening and blue, for a moment he thought he might even glimpse the spire of his parish church, St. Leonard's, wondered if he'd be able to restrain himself as the cart passed within a stone's throw of his shut-up home. But he was spared the temptation. The vehicle turned left up Butcher Hall Lane, right onto Bull and Mouth Street, and then paralleled the Wall as far as the twisting lanes allowed, past Cripplegate to Moorgate, where the gate guards averted their eyes from the grisly cargo and waved it through.

Moorfields was the destination the driver had stated; but it was not at the lower, nearest walks that they stopped. Mounds of earth, their crests thick with quicklime glistening silver in the moonlight, showed there were no vacancies. On the cart trundled, into Upper Moorfields; at last, it halted.

It was time. The cart was backed a little way onto the grass. Then its rear bars were unhooked and a body near the end pulled. The entire fleshy mound slid, Pitman with it, arms above him to try to guide putrefaction from his face. He was not at the bottom of the pile, but neither was he at the top. He rolled, struggled to breathe. He had lost touch with Coke, hoped the highwayman was keeping as still as him.

Then the body atop him cleared and hands grasped his wrists. The bubo at his armpit ripped clear and the dyed rat skin fell away, but the men were too occupied to notice. Cussing both his size and parentage, they half carried, half dragged him along the grass and tumbled him into a pit.

The fall was not far, the landing soft. He contrived to roll as naturally as a dead body might, so that his face was not up to the sky and the next corpse. But sudden cursing made him freeze, one arm stretched awkwardly across his head, and before he could move it, another body fell, to land full upon him.

Instant agony, searing white pain from his shoulder through his skull. He could not help the groan.

"Did you 'ear that?" one of the carters said. "That moan?"

Pitman did not writhe, though his whole body surged in fire. "Nah," the second man said. "It was you yourself, you fool. Let's get this done. I need ale and a whore before me bed. Gives you a thirst and a hunger for life, all this death, eh?"

More bodies were flung in, fortunately not near him. A sound like seeds being sown followed for a while—until he heard the first carter call, "Where's the rest of the lime?"

"I thought you 'ad it."

"I thought you did."

"Shite!" The man spat into the pit. "They'll 'ave some over there, at that next mound. Suppose I better go, what with your leg."

"I'm not staying 'ere by meself. Bastard might moan again."

He heard them walking away. He had to move. They were coming back with quicklime to throw on the corpses; that was the seeding sound he'd heard. During the wars, after battles with too many killed for individual graves, he had seen how those flakes would devour flesh. He did not wish any on him, not for a moment. He began to shift, though every small movement was agony.

A whisper came. "Pitman? Where are you?"

"Here!" He thrust his good arm up through the bodies above. "Can you see me?"

"No. Yes!"

Pitman felt him through the shiftings of the dead. In a few moments the man was above him. "I am hurt," he said, "my shoulder."

"We must be swift," said Coke.

"Move this fellow."

"Get away!" Coke snarled.

"Who's there?"

"Crows. They are pecking." Pitman felt the shaking above. "Away, you beasts."

"Leave them."

He heard Coke's groans as he heaved and shifted. Then there was brighter moonlight, a clear sky. Pitman wriggled, and between their efforts, he was freed from the dead's embrace. When both were on top of the pile, they began a slippery crawl and scramble to the pit's edge. Crows rose, screeching protests at this disturbing of their feast. At last they gained the edge, fell over it onto unshifting ground.

"Do I look as bad as you?" Coke asked, getting onto his knees.

"If I am streaked with lime, covered in blood, pus and shit and have rat-skin buboes dangling from my armpits, then yes, you do."

"I simply must change before I attend the theatre." They heard voices: the carters returning. Coke grabbed the bigger man's good arm. "Let's leave."

They ran toward the hedge that lined the road. No one shouted, so after an instant they climbed it, Pitman with difficulty, then knelt again in its lee. "What now?" Coke asked.

"My invention did not go much further than this moment. But we cannot proceed looking as we do. Ah! I've a thought. Come."

He rose, crossed the road. "North?" said Coke. "Away from the city?"

"Just a little ways. There's a pond at the edge of Bunhill Fields and it's a fine night for a naked moonlight swim."

"Once a Ranter, eh?" Coke began to laugh. "Truly, I feel like I have drunk a quart of double double ale. A swim? Why not? And after?"

"There's a tenter field close to the pond. Clothes will be hanging there to dry."

Coke laughed again. "Did you not hear in Newgate? They've added stealing clothes to the list of offences for which you may hang."

They'd reached the pond, its water reflecting moonlight through the surrounding reeds. "They can't hang us," said Pitman, ripping off his rags, which even using just one hand fell away easily.

"And why not, pray?"

"Because you and me, Captain, are already dead."

29

BORN AGAIN

"You have been most diligent in your studies, Mrs. Chalker."

"I am glad you approve, sir. I warrant it is a comfort to me to know I receive your approbation. Yet . . ."

"Yet?"

Sarah hesitated. The role she played required the finest calculation, was far subtler than any she had ever ventured in the playhouse. And she had overreached before in the week they had been at it, too eager to please him. Then Lord Garnthorpe's forehead would furrow, he would lean forward and slap her—once upon her face, twice upon her thighs—and bellow, "Do you take me for a fool?" and she would have need of all her playing skills and womanly skills to coax him back to calm. If she did not so soothe him, if he left the house in a fury, Maggs would continue the punishment, deny her food and water, lock her for hours in a room with no windows. She did not mind so much for herself, the darkness, the heat, the hunger. But she minded for Lucy, who would also suffer thus. With the baby almost due Lucy required sustenance more than ever.

Lucy. Were it not for the girl so near her time, Sarah might have attempted escape. His lordship came and went. Maggs was not always watching closely within the house, and if he opened the door, as he sometimes did, she knew she could outrun the two drunkards who kept guard outside. But Lucy could not. Lord Garnthorpe had made it clear: if Sarah was not diligent, the punishment would not be hers alone. If she escaped, she knew the consequence for Lucy—death almost certainly—before Sarah could return with help. The man had not revealed much of his life, so focused was he on her redemption. But sometimes when Lucy cried loud, his eyes would narrow and he would spit out words of hate. From them Sarah gathered this little: that such a whore had corrupted his father; more, had poxed him. And his father had in turn poxed his wife, Garnthorpe's beloved mother.

A sob came now and she saw his head jerk to the door. Thoughts had distracted her, a product of her exhaustion. She had to pull him back to her, away from Lucy.

He had asked a question. Ask him one back, she thought. She had never known a man who did not welcome a chance to look superior, and Lord Garnthorpe, for all his madness, was no different from other men in that—and in other ways.

"Yet, sir," she said, softening her voice, raising her eyes to a point above his head, "when the Bible says, in Revelation 18:2, 'With whom the kings of the earth have committed . . . *fornication*—'"

"Revelation 17:2, child."

"Ah! Yes, thank you. Seventeen, of course. 'The inhabitants of the earth have been made drunk with the wine of her *fornication*.'" She looked him straight in the eyes. "Are all womankind condemned for the act of procreation? Are all of my sex guilty of the harlot's sin?"

She put her hands on her thighs and pulled up her dress a little. She saw him flush. "Nay, child," he said, leaning closer to her. "In your ignorance, you have mistook the word 'fornication.'" He cleared his throat. "That is an illicit act between people unmarried, a carnal satisfaction only, abhorrent to God and his saints. But to come together, as husband and wife, to lie in a bed such as the one upstairs . . ." He coughed. "That is not a sin. That is legitimate. And necessary, for the continuation of man."

Yes, she thought, and I would go to that bed with you e'en now if you wished it, and lie with you upon it, let you lie upon me, even though I am certain you are the man who killed John Chalker. For if I managed it well—as I know I can, for I have—perhaps afterwards you would doze and not notice me moving toward your sword.

She lowered her eyes in case he read her hatred in them. "I thank you, sir, for telling me I am no sinner. For I have only ever *lain* with one man. And that only after holy banns were read."

She held her breath while she waited for him to take the lure.

Which he did. "There is something I have not told you. You mention holy banns. I took a precaution because I knew . . . because I felt certain you would indeed profit by my instruction. That you would see, and come to God."

"What precaution, sir?"

"In my church in St. James's I have caused the banns to have their first reading." She made her cry joyous and his voice rose above it. "That Sarah Chalker, widow, might marry Sir Roland, Lord Garnthorpe, bachelor of this parish."

Another sob. Lucy again. Yet for once, he did not take his stare from Sarah until the bells of St. Dunstan's briskly tolled. "Five of

the clock," he said at the final strike. "I have something I must do."
He stood. "An important personage to see."

There was danger in it; she could tell that instantly. At the beginning of her imprisonment he had said they had one week for her "studies." One week to the day, she had been in the house. Now her role there demanded something more. For herself. For Lucy. For John Chalker.

"Sir," she said, rising too. "Tell me you go not into peril."

The words were almost the same as in a play she had once performed. She could only pray Garnthorpe had not seen it.

"It is true, madam. I am about something wonderful. And yes, there is danger in it. I may not—"

"May not return?" She took his hand then, squeezed it. "Tell me it is not so."

"It is. I—" He broke off again when she lifted his hand, kissed it. "Mrs. Chalker, you weep?"

"Call me Sarah, I beg you. And I cannot help my tears, sir." She looked up at him, eyes welling. "I know you have doubted me. Thought me a sinful woman, ignorant of all save pleasure. But my time here has changed me. Your kindness has, in teaching me." She gestured to the Bible under the saint's painting. Her face, she knew, wore a look near identical to the martyr's. "And you were right, Roland—may I call you so? You were right also in this. That first moment our eyes met I also knew, though I have tried so hard to deny it." She wiped tears away. "Revelation speaks of the End of Days fast coming. Do not let me face it alone, I beseech you."

The next moment he was in her arms, his mouth on hers, and she opened to him, let his tongue penetrate her. A different church's bell sounded, these tolls slow, and for their duration he held her, kissed her, and when he pulled back, she kept his body close.

"I must go. To help a friend in a . . . an enterprise at the palace. Yet I have always triumphed in the cause of King Jesus." He stared into her eyes. "If I do return, shall I cause the banns to be read the second time?"

"Do so!" she cried. "And then I shall count the hours till the third reading and we can be—Oh, Roland! That we did not have to wait!"

She saw it then, in his eyes, heard it in the husk of his voice, felt it in the heat of his body pressed against her. "Maybe we do not. For will our troth not be plighted in the eyes of God?"

"Of course it will!"

She had only one fear now: that he was so far gone in lust he would try to take her immediately. But then his eyes changed and he slipped from her grasp. "I will return . . . Wife," he said. "Tonight. Be ready for me."

"Sir," she called as he reached the door, "can you send your man for some ass's milk or goat's milk? My friend weakens."

He considered, then nodded. "Maggs must remain to watch. But I will send one of those outside."

"Thank you, sir. Roland. Husband."

He stared at her a moment longer, then bowed, left. She heard him issue commands, heard the front door opened and bolted behind him. Her knees gave; she sank onto the chair—until another cry had her up, out, moving down the hall.

"Open it," she ordered before the cellar door. Maggs took his usual exaggeratedly slow time despite the moans from beyond it. When the key turned, Sarah pushed past him, ran down the stairs.

Lucy was not on the truckle bed. She was standing, leaning on a wall. "So hot!" she moaned, as Sarah rushed to her, sagging into her friend's arms at the first touch.

"Hush, child," Sarah said, struggling to hold the younger woman up. She was not as strong as she had been and Lucy was much heavier than ever she was. "Here."

With an effort she half lifted, half dragged Lucy across to the bed. She fell heavily upon it. Then, when Sarah had raised the young woman's legs up, took a step to pick up the bolster that had been thrown across the floor, Lucy gave a louder cry and fastened on her arm. "Do not leave me," she begged, "do not. He will come when you are gone."

"Nay, child, he has gone out. Let me fetch—"

"No!" Lucy's voice rose to a shout, the fingers dug deeper. "The baby!"

Despite the pain in her arm, Sarah went still. "You are certain?"

"I cannot think this hammering is anything else. God help me!" she screamed. "For my head feels like it is to burn right off."

What has birthing to do with the head? Sarah thought. Yet truly, what do I know of birthing? And even though it was useless, still she asked herself for the hundredth time, why is Lucy not in Cornwall?

She knew why: another forged letter, a false Rochester seeking forgiveness, offering a house, protection, maybe more. So a strong-willed girl had moved her seafaring family to secure her a berth in a Falmouth packet; the westerlies had blown her faster to London than feet could carry her friends through England. And why had the family not sent one of those sisters to help her? To be here now as Lucy gave another sharp cry, to know what to do as Sarah did not?

Questions were useless. She was all there was. And she had watched her own mother give birth several times on the floors of various hovels. That not a baby had lived beyond three months did not matter. God decided that—but there were things she could do to influence his choice.

She climbed the stairs and banged upon the locked door. "What?" Maggs drawled from the other side.

"It is Mrs. Absolute's time," she called. "Open straight."

The key turned. Sarah flung the door wide and pushed past the man. He grabbed her. "Oy! Where are you going?"

"To fetch linens from the bedchamber."

"You can't go—"

"Hear me," she said, her voice steel. "My friend is about to bring a child into the world. You will help me. Or if you prevent me, I will see to it that you are arrested for both her death and the child's. And if you don't swing for that—" she grasped his fingers, twisted them off her "—I promise you, cock, I'll swing for you myself."

For once, Maggs had no mocking response. He took back his hand. "What must I do?"

"Fetch me hot water. Lots of it."

She moved to the stairs. Maggs looked to protest again, but at a great cry from Lucy, he turned and made for the kitchen.

Sarah climbed to the level above, where Garnthorpe had never allowed her. Two of the rooms were empty of any but the most basic furniture. The third—she halted in the doorway, stunned by its opulence, fresh colours, plush appointments. The bed itself was a vision of luxury, the bolsters plump, the sheets beyond the lace curtains of richest linen. For a moment she wondered what it could mean. When she realized, she shuddered, then ripped off the sheets.

As she went back downstairs, the cries built to a shriek. And then she heard a thump. She ran into the cellar to find Lucy off the truckle bed again, trying to rise from the floor. "Here, child,"

Sarah cried, flinging the bed-stuffs down, pulling the horsehair mattress from the frame onto the floor, helping Lucy to roll atop it. The girl lay back with a long-drawn groan, legs spreading wide, her skirt billowing out. The garment seemed constricting at the waist to Sarah, so she yanked it off. Lucy had only her shift on now.

It was soaked. "He comes?" Sarah asked.

Lucy, panting now, her brow shiny with sweat, looked up. "In haste," she replied, "in a manner most like his father, the earl. Aye me!" she yelled, bucking from the mattress.

"Water!" Sarah shouted, turning—and there was Maggs in the doorway, a small saucepan in hand.

"I had some on for my tea," he said, setting it down on the floor.

"More!" snapped Sarah. "Much more! Hot and cold."

Eyes averted, the man ran out. "Breathe slower, child," Sarah said. "Deeper."

Sometimes, in the next minutes, Lucy heeded her; sometimes she didn't. Sometimes she flung back her head and howled; sometimes she lay still and almost calm. And it was during those increasingly brief moments that Sarah used a knife she'd fetched from the kitchen—which Maggs, humming loudly to himself and engaged in cleaning a matched pair of pistols, had wordlessly let her take—to cut up the bed linen, using some to replace that which Lucy soaked, for her whole body was venting sweat; some to steep in cold water to lay across Lucy's boiling brow, and her breast, spotted in a red and angry rash.

And then the child came, in a rush, with Lucy risen to a squat, bearing down, her arms around Sarah's neck. Sarah had one arm about her and the other fortunately free, to catch the slick babe as he burst forth; catch, nearly lose, then secure him, while Lucy, with a last great cry, slid down to lie entirely upon the mattress. Sarah was acting on instinct now and memories a decade old; she scooped up the glistening bundle up and placed him at Lucy's breast, where the child, until then deafening them with roars, went to silence as he filled his mouth.

"Is it . . . ?"

"A boy, as you always knew."

"A boy!" Lucy sighed. "Does he resemble the earl, do you think?"

"I do not know. He has the black Celt hair of your Absolute cousins, sure," she replied, adding, as the child removed his lips from the breast to wail again, "and the Absolute playhouse lungs."

Then they were both laughing, and crying, and laughing more. The babe seemed to startle at their noise, pause in his, then renew louder as if seeking to outdo them. A nipple placed quieted him, and as Lucy lay back and closed her eyes, Sarah happily set about the tidying, the cutting of the cord, its tying, relieved the birth had been so easy, when most of her mother's had not. After all was done, she cut another sheet into strips and, while mother and child slept, took the infant, washed him, then swaddled him in linen. Moving quietly so as not to wake either, she sat upon the one chair, clutching the bundle tight and shedding tears again, for another cause; her own, in thinking then of John Chalker, of the baby they'd made and lost, not six months before. Tears fell, dried; the babe did not stir but snored as gently as his mother did on the mattress. Her own eyes drooped, and she slept too.

She did not know how long. The light beyond the shutter seemed different—and then St. Dunstan's tolled seven. She looked down—babe and mother were gone. "Lucy?" she called, rising.

"Up here."

Lucy was in the parlour, on a chair, wrapped in a sheet. She was feeding again. "It's nicer here than in that cellar, don't you think?"

Sarah knelt beside her and Lucy squeezed her shoulder. "All's well," she croaked. "Except in my head. It aches horribly still. And I feel nauseous. Is that common?"

Sarah placed a palm on Lucy's forehead. It was feverishly hot. "I do not know. You have just given birth. I am sure there are many different ways that affects one." She went back to the cellar, dragged the mattress up. "Do you rest again," she said, laying it down. "I will fetch you some broth. A new mother needs feeding too."

"I will. So tired," said Lucy, passing the babe over, lying straight down.

She was asleep on the instant. Holding the child in one arm, Sarah bent to pull her friend's shift over her exposed breasts. She grasped the cotton—and stopped. The fever was not only in Lucy's head; the rash Sarah had seen earlier now ran from neck down . . . to where? She lifted, the cloth sucking away from the dampened skin.

Lucy's entire torso was covered in furious red bumps. Sarah laid the baby down upon the mattress. Then she lifted the shift from its base, pulled it up. The rash went from the ankles all the way up to—

No! It cannot be, she thought, moving fast away till the wall stopped her and she sank down. I have mistook. I must have.

But she knew she hadn't.

Someone came in behind her. Saw what she had seen, the black oval mark. Named it. "Plague token!" Maggs cried. "She's got the plague."

"She does not!" Sarah stood. "Yet even if she did, we must—"

"No!" the man yelled, stumbling back, a hand thrust out at her. "The plague! I'm not staying. You can't make me stay!"

He ran into the hallway, flung the front door wide. "Wait!" Sarah cried, following. "You must fetch us medicines. A doctor!"

The door slammed in her face. She reached for the knob, twisted it—just as the key turned. "Stop!" she shouted. "Come back, you dog!" She pressed her ear to wood but heard no reply, just Maggs's voice raised and two others, the footmen Garnthorpe kept outside his house, questioning, followed by the footfalls of several pairs of boots rushing away. "Come back!" she cried again, beating upon the wood till her hands ached, words of fury lost in tears and terror. Finally, exhausted, she slumped down with her back against the door and wept.

Between her sobs and the child's from the other room, it took her a while to hear the scratching. Then the voice that went with it. Not Maggs returned. Another's. This voice was choppy, unrefined— and infinitely sweeter to her ear.

"Sa-Sarah," said Dickon. "Are you there?"

He'd remained outside his lordship's house for a week, faithful to his captain's orders, stirring only to void, drink and buy such food as Coke's last coins allowed him. But those had soon gone, and he'd had to be away a little longer each day, to scavenge and to check back at their lodgings. The cap'n had gone somewhere to see the giant Pit Man; that much Dickon knew. Where, he did not; nor could guess why he had not returned.

Until earlier when the cap'n had appeared at their lodgings, all in . . . motley! This new word Dickon had learned from Sarah's play script, and he'd been pleased to use it so appropriately too— for the captain had been dressed most strangely, in a variety of coloured cloths and textures and what his ward was quite certain was a woman's shirt, which looked especially odd considering the stubble on his usually shaved chin. But he'd not been allowed to laugh for long, seeing that as soon as the cap'n was changed, they'd had to go straight to the house where Sarah was.

Most of this he now managed to convey through the door—including the word "motley," excellently pronounced, with no stutter.

"And where is the captain now?" Sarah asked.

"With the Pit Man," he replied, "who needs help to free his fa-family. The cap'n wanted to charge the door and free you first. But he had not sword and pistols, and there were the two men outside and I told him of the two within. But I will go fetch him back now since they have all g-gone."

"Yes!" Her second cry came as he was moving away. "No!" He only just heard it because the church bell had resumed nearby. "Dickon?" she called. "Still there?"

"S-still here." He pressed one ear to the door jamb again, shoving a finger into the other so he could hear her against the peals. Which he did, clearly and the first time, even though she asked him to repeat what she had said. He knew her words by heart, but if it made her feel better . . .

He repeated her entire message faithfully: "'To not come here straight. There is something more urgent. It is not Rochester but Lord Garnthorpe who has held me prisoner here. He has gone to Whitehall Palace about some b-business tonight. It is to do with some important p-personage. A friend joins him in his evil. You must stop them.'" Then he asked, "Is that all?"

She spoke again after a pause. "Only this. Tell him he goes with my love."

Dickon smiled as he ran. He'd repeat everything, of course. But the cap'n would know that last anyway. Any idiot could see that they loved each other.

30

REUNIONS AND FAREWELLS

Through the slats of the boarded-up and abandoned tavern, Pitman gazed at the windows on the first floor of the house opposite. His house. The first evening candles were just being lit behind them. Perhaps Bettina was about to read scripture to the children. What would the lesson be today? He hoped it was not something too strict. New Testament rather than Old, Christ's loving words over a prophet's ranting.

"'Blessed are the poor in spirit: for theirs is the kingdom of heaven,'" he murmured.

Once more, a vision of the room appeared and he had to look away, breathe deep, else he would have been across the street, hammering upon the door, crying out to those above. For he did not know who lived, who sat cross-legged upon the floor, who they hearkened to. Two he knew were dead. Was Josiah recovered? Anything could have happened in a week. The plague could have taken them all in one day. Or the pale horse could have departed,

Death upon him, and all recovered.

None of it could he know crouching there. Yet crouch he must and wait for the captain's return, though the agony of that was a physical pain in his guts worse than his wounded shoulder in its sling. For Coke was not known to the constables opposite, who kept the red-daubed house shut up. Pitman was, for he'd been one of their number, though he'd probably already been reported dead. He did not blame Coke for tending to his own affairs first, for rushing to Mrs. Chalker's lodgings. They'd both assumed that the ironmonger's shop that backed onto Pitman's house would still be abandoned and so its attic free to call Bettina up and hear all the news. But a family had moved in, refugees from France, and they had not even opened the door to him, despite his pleas.

Would he himself have opened to a coughing, wasted, scraggly-haired giant dressed in a strange assortment of clothes? He looked like too many other lost inhabitants of the sick metropolis. No, he did not blame the family. He just did the only thing he could—found a different abandoned vantage and tried not to run mad.

Thunder rumbled—in the distance, yet closer than it had been. London felt as if a heavy, hot hand was pressing down upon it, upon him. Bring the rain, he thought, looking away from the house. Wash me clean.

Soon, voices. He peered between the slats—and saw the captain, standing before his house, in conversation with the constables. As he watched, one of the men took off his hat, scratched his head, then walked away. The other spat and then raised his hands to heaven in a gesture of prayer.

Something flew up from directly below his window. He could not see what it was, until a similar thing flew up, caught on some breeze; it now lodged in the slat right before him. He stared at it: the husk of a sunflower seed. "Dickon," he whispered, "Dickon!"

The hair was visible first, thrust up straight and of the same hue as wheat sheaves in a field. The boy's eyes, wide in that wide face, followed. "Hallo, Pit Man," he said.

"Shh! Tell your captain I am here. Softly now!"

The boy nodded, ran across, tugged at Coke, who listened, nodded but continued talking with the constable. At last he sauntered across, Dickon following, offering seeds, which Coke took. "Easy," Coke whispered into the slats.

"Easy? Tell me!"

"Your family are—well enough," Coke said, adding hastily, "no one else has been carried out since I was last here. The constable thought one might still ail, but he is not sure. It might be in one of the other families within. But there is other news. It is what I was talking about, why one of your fellow watchmen left to speak to an alderman."

"What news?"

"Three parishes in the City have this very day ceased the shutting up of houses." Coke peered through the slats. "It is cruel and has cost each council money they scarce have, money for watchmen, for bread. They say—Wait! Someone comes!" He turned away. "Sir!" he called loudly. "What's the news?"

The man who'd departed was now back with another: James Morrow, headborough of the parish, in charge of all its constables. "Sir," he said, approaching Coke, taking off his hat, giving a bow, which the captain returned. Morrow went on, loud enough for Pitman to hear, "I understand you have an interest in the people within this house."

"I do. Friends. I would aid them if I could."

"And you may. The parish of St. Leonard's will follow the example set by our neighbours in St. Vedast and St. John Zachary and end the shutting up. I regret we cannot help you, but my colleague and I must go to the other houses. You will find crowbars and other tools at the door." He replaced his hat, tapped its crown. "Good evening!"

Pitman managed to wait for the men to turn the corner; and then he was out and across the street. "Bettina!" he called up. "Bettina! Dearest chuck! Look down."

He saw the candle flames flicker in movement. A face appeared. Pitman flushed hot, for it was Josiah.

"Ma! It's not a ghost. It's Father. Father stands below!"

"Pitman?"

Her face was then at the window, her beauty clear even through thick glass. She held a baby in her arms, and at her hip two more faces pushed in. "Pitman!" she cried again, then all disappeared.

"Here. Help me, Captain. Help me!"

With his one good arm he'd seized an iron bar, began smashing at the sawn planks that blocked the entranceway. Coke and Dickon also took up crowbars and used them more effectively to pry the nailed boards out. In a bare minute the door was flung open.

"Pitman! Father! Pa!"

He was engulfed under a surge of limbs. He roared in pain, in laughter, in delight.

"You were dead, Pitman," said Bettina, pulling back from her kisses to speak. "They sent the word from Newgate. I'd have given up that moment if not for my chicks."

"Hush, sweetheart. I am here. Still alive. Still alive." Pitman touched the heads of the three children who pressed him, the babe in her arms. "But not all our chicks live."

"They live with Jesus now," she replied. "A happier place, sure, though I miss them terrible." She wiped her eyes. "But whatever are you dressed like, man? You'll be carted off as a lunatic if any sees you. Aye me! From Newgate to Bedlam. What has befallen our family?"

All Pitmans laughed loud. The rumpus was drawing people from their houses. The two other families within had also emerged blinking into the street. Though he was home, he knew he was not safe. "Hush, dears. Let us go inside."

As the family crossed the threshold, Coke called. "There's other news."

"Can it not wait till the morning?"

"I fear not. Mrs. Chalker sends word of the one we seek. She says he . . . he hunts tonight. Says also that he does not hunt alone."

"I will return," said Pitman, then he vanished.

Coke sat before the house where Pitman had hidden. He and Dickon had their backs to it, to compete in the spitting of sunflower husks and wait.

The bell in St. Leonard's had just tolled again, when a familiar tall figure came through the doorway opposite, though dressed now in his own sober clothes. Pitman crossed the street, slid down beside them. Even in the twilight, Coke could see the red-rimmed eyes. "All well?" he asked.

"Not all," said Pitman, and rubbed his eyes. "Tell me."

"I'll let Dickon."

The boy spoke the message again, proudly, word for word as Sarah had said it, and when he was done, Coke asked, "You told me at the theatre you knew this lord from before. So was it this Garnthorpe who struck you in the church?"

"I cannot say." Pitman scratched the stubble on his head. "Faces are still jumbled. It could have been. What I remember most is the bloodied apron—and why would a lord be wearing that? Yet he is known for a Fifth Monarchist man, and for his cruelty, so . . ." He shrugged. "No, Captain. It appears the only answer to this riddle lies in Whitehall Palace." Pitman stood, just as another roll of thunder came. He offered his good hand, pulled Coke to his feet. "The boy should stay here with mine."

"I have already asked and been denied. He will not leave me again. Besides, Thief-taker, what you never realized was that in taking me you only gained half a highwayman. For Dickon is at least half your Monstrous Cock." He rubbed the boy's neck. "So let us to it—a winged giant, a simple lad and a thief who vomits at the sight of gore." He spread his arms wide. "What murderer could stop us?"

From the other side of the blanket, the girl's voice rose higher:

I leaned my back up against a young oak,
Thinking he were a trusty tree,
But first he bended and then he broke,
Thus did my love prove false to me.
O love is handsome and love is fine,
Bright as a jewel when first it's new,
But love grows old and waxes cold,
And fades away like the morning dew.

The song ended, the girl's voice wobbling over the sustained last note. Beyond it, he could hear the thunder, drawing nearer.

"That enough, Mr. Strong?" she asked.

Silence.

The blanket that divided the room shook under her little hand. "Are you there, Mr. Strong?"

He looked down at his hands. They seemed too pale. Not white— they would never be that; they'd had too much blood on them over the years. But they were clean, which seemed wrong. Unless he was on his way to his work. Yes. He'd come here to change clothes as he always did. His others lay scattered around. He could not go about his work in those. Neither about his—nor God's.

He ran his hands up and down his leather apron. It crackled under his touch, stiffened by lack of use. Well, that would change. Soon it would be supple again.

"Mr. Strong?"

The voice again. "Yes, Little Dot," he said, "I am 'ere."

He drew back the blanket. The child stared up. She smiled. "Goin' to work, Mr. Strong? Does that mean there'll be somethin' for us later?" She twirled before him in her smock. "I done what you asked. Took off the lace. Scrubbed me face some more. All the paint's gone now, see?"

She tilted her chin so he could observe. When he'd walked into Carrier Court earlier, he'd seen Little Dot, scarce ten, flounces on her low-cut dress, ribbon in her hair, paint on her face. A harlot like her mother—her dead mother, he had reminded himself so he did not strike her. He had told her to strip it all off which she did not understand at first, reaching fingers to his waist. Then he had seized her by the ear, dragged her to the well, scrubbed her clean. "I 'aven't eaten 'ardly nothin' all week," she'd howled as he did so. And he forgave her, as the girl emerged again from the gaudiness.

"You'll eat today and well," he said now, patting her head. "And I'll give you bits to sell. You'll come with me."

They left the room, and she capered across the yard behind him, followed him down narrow alleys till they arrived at the Hog Lane shambles. Other butchers greeted him. "Where you been, Abel?" "Got a lady friend, Strong?" they called. He ignored them all, went to his favoured bench. A pig carcass, gutted and scalded, swung on a rail nearby, one of a dozen. He hoisted it down, flung it onto the wood, picked up a cleaver, hefting its weight, gauging its balance. A finger pressed conjured a line of blood on his thumb. Blood, he thought, tasting. That's right.

He was always one of the fastest, and today he was inspired. Others yelled in admiration as he severed the pig in half, from snout to tale, in a dozen strokes. Then he set to on just one half, using saw and blade, separating it into cuts, joints. He stopped to clear sweat and gore from his forehead, glanced across at the girl perched on a blood barrel. "You use every part of the pig exceptin' the squeal, Little Dot," he said. "Remember that."

A dozen cuts more and it was done. He wiped his hands on his apron, supple again, then beckoned the girl over, handed her a shoulder joint. "Wrap that in your skirt. Don't let anyone see it. Take it to your room and put it into your ma's cauldron. Here's a coin for some turnip, some carrot. Cook that for a day and sell the stew for a sixpence a cup, a florin a pot. And tell any what tries to cheat ya—" he bent, then lifted the uncut half of the pig onto his shoulder "—that Abel Strong will be visiting soon."

When Strong reached Whitehall, he paused. He had choices to make now. He knew from other deliveries that the palace was not one single entity but a vast, sprawling jumble, straddling roads, containing parks, added to over the centuries. At the end of the roadway, on the north side and beyond the Holbein Gate, were the newer, smaller, less drafty apartments the royals favoured when in residence. To the south was the old palace proper, the parade grounds, the grand dining halls, the offices of state business. On a normal summer night these would be abuzz, with soldiers, courtiers, especially with secretaries and their minions, running the business of the realm. But London was a plague city and only a few people now moved through the large spaces he glimpsed through the gates.

He moved to one of these. He had delivered to all the kitchens of the palace before. The closest one was here. God blesses my enterprise, sure, he thought as he drew nearer, for I know that corporal.

"Abel Strong," said the man, eyeing the carcass, "you bring a feast."

"But for who?" The butcher shrugged. "Bastard master just told me to drop it at Whitehall. Dunno where."

"I can tell you that. There's rumour of a special guest. Blood royal." The man winked. "He comes but briefly, though, so they'll not open the king's apartments." He nodded to the north. "Poor fellow will have to make do with the small Great Hall, and the lesser food and wine pantries. That kitchen is fired up and the cook roaring already. So on your way."

He stepped aside, gesturing away his two shadowing pike men. But the butcher had only taken three steps when he was stopped. "Wait!" The corporal came up. "That special guest. Everyone gets searched."

One of the pike men handed his pole to his fellow, then checked inside the butcher's boots, felt up the back of each leg, reached inside his apron. High. Low. Lower. "Much more of that," Strong said, "and you'll 'ave to marry me."

The corporal laughed, slapped him on his back. "You'd best hurry." He nodded to the sky. "Storm's coming."

In the distance, across the river, lightning stabbed down, thunder rolling hard upon it. He felt the first fat drop of rain strike his forehead as he crossed Scotland Yard, entered another large parade ground . The back entrance to the kitchen was on the far side of it. The cook, a large man named Turvey, bellowed when Strong walked in, "Well, fuck the pope and thanks to Christ," he said, "for he has answered my prayers. I thought I was going to serve three poxy pigeons to the Duke of York and make out they was pheasants." He gestured. "Right here, my friend, on this table."

Once Strong had dropped the carcass, all there scurried to the cook, who started shouting orders. All except the butcher, who backed away, picked up a long-bladed boning knife and a cleaver, tucked both inside his apron. No one noticed, neither that nor the fact that Abel Strong left the kitchen the opposite way he'd entered it, as the sky flashed white and a great boom sounded just above him.

The door gave directly onto the Court and he crossed the edge of it, with no one paying him mind, because everyone was too busy hunching against the downpour, which had already created large puddles on the red clay of the path. He ran along the path, paused while the servants he'd followed wiped their feet before entering the Great Hall, then slipped into it behind them. Some men sat at a long table, papers spread among the candlesticks, bottles, the trays of nuts and fruit. Other men with halberds, the royal guardsmen, stood by.

He did not see the one he sought. Then suddenly he did, for the man entered not five paces from him, causing Strong to press his back against the door, ready to run if noticed. But the man paid him no mind for he was fiddling at his crotch.

"Damn me!" said the Duke of York, doing up buttons. "I don't know about this damnable plague. But I have been in London scarce six hours and I have already contracted watery bowels." He waved down the men who'd risen when he approached the table. "Sit, gentlemen, and stay seated, pray. If you rise each time I make for the little apartment, you'll weary your legs."

The men laughed. Strong was smiling too as he slipped the few paces down the wall, into the privy closet there. A candle burned on a shelf near the front, throwing the rear of the small space behind the commode into complete darkness. God indeed blesses my enterprise, he thought, settling on the seat still warm from the royal arse and holding the cleaver and knife on his thighs. For the one business when even a prince of the realm is truly unguarded is when he is about the business of his bowels.

31

THE PALE HORSE RIDES

From the shelter of a portico, Pitman and Coke could scarcely see the Banqueting House through the walls of rain. "Any other thoughts?" asked Coke. He got no reply. "Should we go around to the riverside and learn if Dickon has found a less-guarded entry?" He patted the space at his hip, the straps where his sword should be. "At your advice I handed my sword into the boy's care, in case we could bluff our way in and I'd have to give it up. But I sense that bluff will not work here and I'd like it back."

"Maybe the riverside will be our only way in. Unless . . . Ah!"

As Coke looked out again, the lightning moved north; the thunder followed it and the torrent ceased as swiftly as it had arrived. Immediately people who'd taken shelter like them in portico and alcove ran again to the gate of the Banqueting House.

Even in the small time they'd stood before the palace, trying to figure a way in, a crowd had formed. Londoners drawn by sudden rumour; sick Londoners in the main, men and women with grossly distended necks. "Of course!" he said, clasping Pitman's arm, who yelped in pain. "My apologies. But come. These people may force the gate. They must have heard that the king is here. They have gathered for him to heal them."

"Can he do anything for my shoulder?" Pitman moaned, and followed.

They joined the rear of a mob that had swelled to at least fifty. A youthful officer stood before the gates, arms raised, palms out, at his back four nervous pike men. "I tell you His Majesty is not here," the young man was saying. "You must disperse. You all know the dangers of gathering at this time. It is prohibited."

"He is here!" a man, his face a mass of boils, shouted. "Else why the royal guards? I know your coats!"

Others in the crowd began to shout too, pressing forward. "He's here! Charles is here! There's only a few of us. Let us in. Let him touch us! Heal us!"

"It is just the Duke of York!" the young officer blurted out. "He does not have the healing touch."

"Blood royal, ain't 'e?" the man with the boils yelled. "Touch me! Heal me!"

The mob pressed closer. The officer drew his sword. "More guards!" he screeched, while his soldiers put their pikes at port and attempted to shove back the crowd.

"Look." Pitman pointed toward the royal apartments to the north. The four sentries were running from there to their fellows' aid. "Holbein Gate's unguarded."

Waiting only for the reinforcements to rush past, Coke and Pitman ran the other way. The abandoned gates were still closed, but were no taller than the captain, and he was up and over fast. He turned straight, shot the bolts. Pitman was through and the gates reclosed and rebolted again in moments.

"Now where?" asked Coke.

"Everything to the south appears to be most guarded. So thither we go."

They splashed through puddles, gardens to their right, lawns and parterres stretching into the dark. A statue gleamed in the moon- light. Ahead, a brick passageway brought a waft of river to their nostrils. To their left, a passage opened onto a larger space beyond. Along it, light spilled from glass onto cobbles. "There, think you?" asked Coke, leaning on his knees.

A distinct pop came abruptly from where they looked. "Gunshot!" gasped Pitman.

"Champagne," said Coke. "I suspect there's only one who would be drinking that this night." Pitman made to go, but Coke took his arm. "Wait."

There appeared another glow ahead, a trace of smoke, rising into the lantern spill. "Guards, smoking their pipes," whispered Coke, pulling the larger man back into the shadows. "If we both charge forward here, we both could be taken. And our quarry may have preceded us. Or may still be approaching. Do you take this passage and come up from the river. I'll go in the front."

"Nay," said Pitman, restraining in his turn. "There might be more gates to climb down there and I cannot do it with this." He lifted the arm in the sling. "So leave me the front."

"Fair enough. But be wary, Pitman. According to Mrs. Chalker there may be two of them, and one at least the real Monstrous Cock. So I'll only say this: if you get the chance, kill both the bastards straight."

"And you the same, Captain," replied Pitman. "Go with God."

As Coke ran off down the passage, Pitman watched from the

shadows. Then, at the first screech of the fiddle, the guards tapped out their pipes upon their boot heels, and stepped inside. They stayed close to the door, so when Pitman came up to it, he was able to see, through the expensive glass and between their shoulders, near everyone in the room.

He shut his eyes, drew a deep breath, looked again. The room no longer appeared to him as a muddle of people, but of individuals. He could tell by the cut of their clothes who were the secretaries, who the noble advisers. Watch the servants enter from the opposite side of the hall pause and wipe their feet before crossing to the table to lay down jugs and platters. Note the fiddle player who'd begun to play, even see the annoyance of the other fiddler with his ear to his strings, still trying to tune. Finally see the one man moving away from the table toward a small door near the hall's main one, as he turned to call something back.

Recognize him. Not because he'd ever seen him before. But because he'd watched Charles I, the father of this man—now stepping through the door, now closing it behind him—have his head chopped off before the Banqueting House not two hundred paces from where he now stood.

The Duke of York, with his father's gait, his hair, his eyes, had just left the room—though not by the door. Pitman would have given short odds that he'd gone, in fact, into a privy closet.

With the duke safe, Pitman scanned again the others in the hall, the servants especially. If you were going to assassinate a royal, surely posing as a scullion would be the best way to achieve it.

He'd missed something. He looked back to the privy. Lamplight from above its door glimmered on some wetness on the floor before it. It was a boot print. Its toe pointed toward the door.

As he burst into the hall, Pitman was quite sure that the boot print would be red with the clay of the path outside, and that it had been left by a man too hurried to wipe his feet.

For a long moment, save for the fiddler still plying his horse-hair, he was the only one moving. Indeed the first shout did not come until Pitman was halfway across the hall.

"Stop there!" a guard screamed.

But he couldn't, and the one thing that slowed him was his need to use his injured arm to jerk open the privy door.

"What this?" snarled the duke, his hands at his hips, pushing down his breeches.

Candlelight reflected on rising steel just behind the duke's head. "Aside!" Pitman shouted as he threw his cudgel.

It missed the royal scalp by one of its hairs, striking the man behind, not on his head but on the hand that grasped a cleaver. Howling, he dropped it, raised a knife. Pitman, seizing the duke by his shoulder, hurled him from the privy. There he impeded, for just a moment, the guards for whom he was now screaming.

Pitman lunged, grabbed the man's wrist, twisted the knife down. The movement brought them close, their faces near touching. In that moment the cloud that had held him was swept away and he recognized the man who'd hit him in All Hallows.

Then all was a jumble of limbs, and yells, and blows, as the guards fell on Pitman and dragged him from the closet. The wrenching pulled away Pitman's hand; he saw the blade raised once more. "Protect the duke!" he cried, reaching again to block the strike down with his forearm. Then a blow struck hard across his head. He fell. Yet even as he did, and just before all went as dark as Limbo, he glimpsed the killer leap the struggling mass of bodies and run from the hall.

—

Coke was glad that Pitman had not come along the river path. The wounded bird would not have been able to handle the gates and walls Coke had been obliged to scramble over. He was less glad that he had, for he was filthy now, his hands scraped and bleeding. He had found the river and been forced east along it. Now he'd come to what he assumed were the palace water stairs, with several skiffs and one larger, finer wherry tied up at them. It had all taken too much time. But at least he'd found a passage heading back to the hall. Shouts had come faintly over the walls as Coke approached its entrance, and the music of fiddles had suddenly ceased.

"Now, then," he said, and had taken a step along the path, when a noise behind him had him wheeling, knife in hand. "Who's there?" he demanded.

"M-me, Cap'n," said Dickon, rising from the water like a wraith. Or so it seemed to Coke at first, till he drew closer and saw the boy was standing in a skiff.

"Jesu mercy, boy, but you frighted me. How come you there?"

Dickon put one foot on the dock. His master's sword was in his hand, still sheathed. "You told me to find an entrance from the r-riverbank, so I did."

"Good. Stay here. I go in search of Pitman."

"I go too."

"I need you here. This boat is our escape, you see?" The boy looked at him suspiciously, so Coke added, "It is like when we are about our business. I hold the gun—you keep the horses, yes?"

"Awright, Cap'n," he said. He loosed the rope. "I keep the horses."

"Good lad." Coke turned, then remembered and turned back. "Dickon, if I do not return by the next bell—" He broke off, as Dickon started. Both had heard the same noise: someone was approaching fast toward them along the walled passage from the palace. "Be still," the captain hissed, and placed himself on guard, dagger out before him.

The man who burst out of the passage's entrance didn't look like a lord. He had no wig but a stubble of greying hair ; no fine clothes but a stained butcher's apron. Garnthorpe's accomplice, then; the second man Mrs. Chalker had talked of.

"Hold there!" Coke cried. "Stand and deliver yourself to me."

The man stopped, blinked. Then with a roar ran at Coke.

The captain wished he had his sword, still in Dickon's hand in the boat. But he had his dagger, and God forgive him, he'd killed with it before. He saw a dagger also in the other's hand, his left, and in an overhand grip. So as the man came, his blade striking down, Coke stepped hard in, throwing up his own left arm, catching the blow forearm to forearm before it could descend, twisting his fingers to clamp around the wrist, pulling the body down, then punching with his dagger at the man's exposed side.

But his attacker had followed the pull, so the blade, instead of driving full into him, slipped along his leather apron. Continuing his half fall, the man used his weight to jerk himself free.

Coke kicked, missing the groin, the toe of his boot driving instead into the thigh. The man howled, slashed his knife before him, near enough to force Coke to leap back. Immediately the captain lunged again. His opponent brought his dagger hard across to parry the thrust, steel ringing.

Now, thought Coke, withdrawing his feint, dropping lower, thrusting for the gap between the front of the apron and its back. The blade entered his opponent's side . . . but only a half finger deep, for the captain's rear foot had slipped on the dock's rain-slick wood, shortening his lunge. Still, the man cried out, and staggered toward the water.

Lights glimmered along the path, voices there calling the hunt. "No!" the man roared, and ran down the jetty to where Dickon in the skiff now raised, too late, the sword he'd partly unsheathed. Coke, following fast, was not there in time to prevent the man snatching the weapon, stepping behind the boy into the boat, pressing the half-drawn blade to his throat.

"No closer," he called, "or he dies."

Dickon dropped the rope. They started drifting into the current. The skiff was yet a short leap away that Coke could have made and almost did—but for the line of blood that now appeared at his ward's throat. Then the moment was gone, the boat too far, and the man hurled both sword and Dickon into the water. Coke threw his knife; it missed, though not by much. But skiff and man were gone, taken by the swift current, blended into darkness.

Dickon clung to another boat. Untying it, Coke pushed it out as he leaped in, and managed to haul up the boy without capsizing them. Grabbing the oars, he pulled hard, just as the royal guards ran shouting from the passage.

The dizziness had increased from the time he landed at Essex House Stairs to his dropping off at Billingsgate. A fast tide had taken him and for most of the way he only had to steer, which was as well, with one hand broken. But he'd been clearer in his mind when he was alone so it was only after he'd persuaded the wherry-man—with a gold guinea, twenty times the usual fare—to shoot the race under London Bridge by moonlight and he had leaned back into the prow of the vessel that his mind clouded, and he'd dozed. The wherryman had woken him when they ground against the fish market's dock. He limped along Thames Street, up Idle Lane, into St. Dunstan's Churchyard. He could see the house. Yet here, so close to his desire, he lurched off the path. He needed to gather himself before he saw her, before his dreams were realized.

Amid the muddle of gravestones, there was one by the path he would come to sometimes, to think, to remember, to be inspired. He found it now, sank before it. Flowers lay strewn upon it, recent but past their prime. Though the moon was bright, he still had to blink several times before he could read the inscription. He knew it by heart, of course. He said it now, for it always renewed him:

Here lies Abel Strong. Butcher of this parish. From his comrades in the regiment and his brother Saints in Christ. "For the trumpet shall sound and the dead shall be raised incorruptible, and we shall be changed."

He touched the stone. Moss had grown in the letters. Damn Maggs, he thought. Did I not order him to clean this?

Garnthorpe rose as the church bells tolled. Renewed. Changed. He saw the house ahead. Within it, his bride awaited him.

Sarah sat in the chair of the bedchamber, gazing at the swaddled bundle in her arms. He had slept well, John Edward Rombaud Absolute, as his mother had named him just before she died. For the boy's father and grandfather, Lucy had whispered, and for another ancestor too. Now he stirred, his dark eyes blinking; perhaps the bells of St. Dunstan's tolling midnight had awoken him. Soon he would soon be hungry. Then what would she do?

She tried a lullaby: "'Lavender's blue, dilly, dilly, lavender's green . . .'"

Her song stilled the earl's son for a while but did not hold him long past its ending. When he cried, she rose and set him upon the bed. He protested, but she only left him long enough to lower her blouse and take him to her breast.

"There, there," she said, sitting again. Her tears flowed then, even if her milk could not.

Then she heard it—knocking on the front door, muffled shouting; finally, the turning of a lock.

She had so given up the hope of it that her tiredness almost made her forget what she'd prepared. She rose, removing the boy from her breast, lifting him to her shoulder, patting his back until he belched. Then she went to the privy closet, a door behind and to the side of the bed. The breast, even without milk, had lulled him. His eyes fluttered and closed as she laid him in a basin she had lined with ripped blankets and a pillow.

"Sleep, child," she whispered. "Sleep awhile."

As she tucked herself into her blouse, she heard the front door open.

Garnthorpe put a hand to the sticky wetness at his side and then wiped his fingers on the door before knocking loud. But Maggs did not respond to that, nor to his shouts. Fortunately he had a key, though at first it did not want to fit. When at last it did, he pushed open the door. "Maggs!" he called, but received no reply.

The door to the parlour was ajar, a lantern burning within. "Sarah," he said, moving toward the room, "where are my servants? Have they negl—"

He stopped on the threshold. At first he thought no one was in the room, for the two chairs were empty. Until he glanced down and saw the bare feet on a mattress on the floor. There was something about the colour of them that he did not like.

"Sarah?"

He entered the room, bent to the mattress. Yet it was not Mrs. Chalker upon it but Mrs. Absolute, the harlot he'd lured back from the country to influence her friend. He could tell that she would influence no more, for clearly she was dead. A closer glance told him what had killed her.

His eyes filmed as he moved back to lean against the wall. Someone else was meant to die this day. Someone who was meant to hold a jewel in their mouth.

"The first foundation was jasper; the second, sapphire; the third, a chalcedony; the fourth, an emerald."

He had an emerald in his pocket. He pulled it out. Candle flame moved in its facets, making him dizzy again.

Was it for *her* mouth? This earl's whore?

Death stank. He shut the door on it. "Sarah?" he cried.

Her voice came softly from above. "Up here."

Garnthorpe placed a foot upon the stair.

Sarah heard each footfall. She'd moved the chair to face the door, four steps away. She sat in it now.

She was surprised at him, his coarse clothes, the stained apron. No plain wig on his head, just grey stubble. "You bleed, Roland," she said.

Garnthorpe paused in the doorway. He touched his hand to his side, brought it away. "I am sorry for the state of my clothes, Sarah. Sorry too that I have not had the opportunity to have the banns read a second time. But as you said, love does not need to wait. And if I could not bring you a ring as my pledge, still I have brought you . . . this."

He held out his swollen right hand. The fingers would not open.

"Come closer," she said. "I also have something for you."

What gift could she give him? Only her love, promised in that first time they'd looked into each other's eyes, in her arms lifting to him now. He took a step into the room.

She was so tired. So she used both hands to raise the pistol Maggs had forgotten when he fled.

The explosion was loud and her first thought, as the man was lifted from his feet and thrown out of the room to crash against the banister, was that the noise would wake John Edward. But the babe did not cry out, not yet anyway.

Garnthorpe had his legs before him, his back against the railing, his eyes open. As she drew nearer, he gazed up at her over the ruin of his chest. She had loaded with two balls, as her husband had once taught her to do, since she knew she would not need much range.

His eyes were as startled as a baby's. He was trying to speak. "What is it?" she said. "What?"

He stretched out an arm. His swollen fingers unfurled. On the palm of his hand was an emerald.

She knelt, took it. "I thank you, my lord. But I told you once before, I cannot accept jewels from you. So you keep it. Keep it for John Chalker." She pushed the stone into his mouth. "Choke on that."

He was blown; he had to admit it. This night's hot actions at Whitehall had taken what remained of his jail-diminished strength. If not for Dickon urging him on, he might have curled up on some comfortable cobbles and given up.

Yet even as he thought it, Coke knew it to be untrue. There could be no rest until Mrs. Chalker was free. Afterwards . . . Well, he suspected that was still a dream: the real murderer remained at large, a price still lay on the Monstrous Cock's head and God only knew what had happened to Pitman.

Their quarry had escaped them. Coke had followed him close, but the man had hired a wherryman at Essex House Stairs and soon put distance between them. The captain knew he was not oarsman enough to shoot the race under London Bridge even when rested. They'd docked, headed to the streets. A hackney carriage heading to his home stable near the Dyers Hall had taken them most of the way for the last shilling he possessed but would take them no farther without more coin. Hence this stumbling run along Thames Street. He could only thank providence for Dickon's watch this past week. The boy knew exactly where he was going and only paused to let his captain catch up at every corner.

Finally they were in St. Dunstan's Churchyard, slipping on cobbles made slick by sudden summer rain. "Close, lad?" inquired Coke, pausing to lean on a gravestone, flowers scattered before it.

"C-close," replied the boy, gesturing him impatiently on.

When they were before the house, tiredness loosed its hold. The front door was open, and through it came a long, shrill wail. Drawing his sword, the captain ran in, Dickon a step behind. Off the hall all the doors were shut. The strange cry came again, from up the stairs. He climbed them two at a time, Dickon at his heels.

A man was sitting on the landing, his back against the railing. Coke thrust his sword before him—but he had no need of it. For the man he'd stabbed and then pursued on the Thames was dead. The glaze of his open eyes, the hole torn in his chest, showed that.

The cry that had drawn him had ceased as he'd mounted the stairs. He listened for it and heard instead a gurgling. It came from the room the dead man faced. The door was half closed. Bidding

Dickon to silence with a gesture, he used his sword to push open the door, and peered in.

He knew that when exhausted on battlefields, sea voyages, in siege works, he was prone to see things, strange things, things that were not necessarily there. So it took a moment to believe the sight before him: Mrs. Chalker, asleep on the end of a ravaged bed, a baby near a single exposed breast. And it was the baby who looked at Coke now, at Dickon behind him, then let out another cry.

Coke was so shocked that he did not move.

Sarah awoke, saw them. She made no sound, just rose, gracefully tucked away her breast, picked up the child, handed him to Dickon and then moved into Coke's arms.

"How?" he asked. "Who?"

"No words, Captain. Not yet, I beg you."

There were few orders in his life he'd obeyed so happily. He held her for the longest time, while the baby quieted with the faces Dickon was pulling at him. Only when the shuddering at his chest eased did Coke lean back, lift her teary face and, just before he kissed her, say, "And I beg you, madam. Call me William."

EPILOGUE

Seven months later—March 22, 1666

"Off out, Pitman?"

"Off out, my love. But not quite yet. I must wait."

"For what?"

"For you, dearest chuck, to accompany me. Wear your best—the new dress we just bought."

"I told you before. It is too fancy, especially for chapel. Whatever were you thinking of, you great lummox? I'm taking it back in the morning. I'll have a new sideboard for the price."

"I was thinking, love, how the green so suited your eyes."

"Go on with you. I've a mind to—Pitman! What is it that *you* are wearing?"

"My new coat. Do you like it?"

"Sure that's the table right there to go with my new sideboard! The duke has been generous, but his purse is not bottomless. And you said you would soon be giving up his allowance."

"I feel it wrong to keep accepting his money, since I am quite recovered."

"All the more reason to return this finery. We must cut our cloth, Pitman. We must cut our cloth!"

"And will, my sweet. Tomorrow. Tonight you will accompany me."

"Well, I have to say, you do look 'andsome. Where are we going?"

"You'll see."

"Truly, Mr. Etherege, Mr. Dryden, one of you must set it down," said King Charles. "'Twould be the making of either of you."

The two playwrights looked at each other dubiously. Etherege coughed. "It does not sound like a comedy, Sire."

"A comedy? No, indeed. A great drama, like the one we are in the middle of tonight. An epic tale, full of all ranks from lords to butchers. Yet now I bethink me—" the king held out his glass, which was swiftly refilled "—it does have its comic moments. A prince of the blood royal surprised in the privy with his breeches around his knees. Ain't that so, Jamie?"

"Sir, please," replied the Duke of York. "I do not find any humour in the memory. I doubt you would if it had been you with an assassin's blade so near your throat."

"Pshaw! I am still certain that whatever the state of my dress I would have come up with a better line than 'Guards! Guards!' That was his line, wasn't it, Mr. Pitman?"

"Begging Your Majesty's favour, that's Pitman, plain Pitman, Sire, no 'Mr.' As to His Royal Highness's words or clothing, I recall nothing but nobility from him in either."

The king threw back his head and roared. "You could teach my courtiers something in manners, Pitman, and in tact. Though you are something of my brother's man these days, are you not? Quite right too. The beating his guards inflicted upon you before he persuaded them you were his saviour deserves much recompense. Are you near recovered?"

"Quite near, Sire."

"And is this your wife?"

"It is, Sire."

"May I call her *Mrs.* Pitman, at least? Madam, may I say the simple beauty of both you and your dress show the grand ladies who hover about me to be the painted harlots they are." Fans fluttered nearby at that, and even more so when the king raised a curtsying Bettina and kissed her hand. "Do you enjoy the theatre, madam?"

"It is my first time, Sire, and faith, I am surprised, but I do."

"Do you, indeed? It's amusing enough, I suppose. A distraction. Though I would the matter of this play had more import. More currency." He turned back to the playwrights. "After these times we have lived through, do we not require something with more heart?" He swigged. "Sirrahs, truly, the tale these people could tell you. Of murders, of madness, of threats against the state by a nobleman who was also a damned Fifth Monarchist."

"The fanatics have already been explored upon the stage, Sire," said Etherege. "Cowley did it in his *Cutter of Coleman Street*."

"Another damnable comedy!" exclaimed the king. "I assure you, this is serious. These Saints, for all we may laugh and think them Bedlamites, *are* serious. They believe the end of the world is here. Perhaps they are right. They certainly strive to bring it on." He looked back at his courtiers and his eyes narrowed. "I know. The Earl of Rochester should take them on."

"I?" John Wilmot shrugged, his lower lip drooping. "What have I to do with such matters?"

"Oh, stop sulking, Johnnie. Three months in the Tower and three exiled to the country have made you a better man. You should be grateful to me. The time away removed your mind from drinking, your fingers from whores, and put them to poetry, while giving you matter to be poetic about. Is that not your true calling?"

"My true calling, sir, is life." The earl gave a thin smile. "As you shall see."

"Well, I consider myself forewarned." Charles turned back. "Pitman, what say you? How dangerous are these fanatics? These self-proclaimed Saints?"

Into Pitman's mind, memories came: a lady with a single stab wound in the heart; guts on a pulpit; a jewel gleaming in a tongueless mouth. "I say they are very dangerous, Sire."

"I agree. And I would talk more on that later, if you will."

"Please, to your seats. Lords, ladies, honours all." Thomas Betterton stood upon the stairs that led to the stage, looking down into the common area. "I beg you, Sire. No one will sit until you do. The play begins again."

"It does indeed," said the king, still eyeing Pitman. Then he set down his glass. "So let us to it."

Court and courtiers, orange girls, vizards and actors all made for their places. Only Pitman did not move, despite Bettina's eager tugging, for he was looking at the couple only now coming forward from the shadowed corner of the room. "Mrs. Chalker. Captain. The king will be sorry to have missed you."

"And not I him," replied Coke. "Whenever he sees me, he gives me coins. To recompense me, he says, for that one bottle of Rhenish I shared with him on the eve of Worcester. Christ's bones, I feel like one of his footmen."

"But you accept the money nonetheless," Sarah said.

347

"Oh, I accept it. A man must live, since the king's pardon for past crimes—conditional on those crimes never being repeated—has taken away me livelihood." He sighed. "Yet, hang me for a slave, I'd feel better taking his money with a gun at his belly."

"He recompenses you for more than Rhenish—you know that," Sarah said. "And he has offered to recompense you still more. With employment. You must tell Pitman." She squeezed his arm, then turned to Mrs. Pitman. "My dear, where did you get that lovely dress?"

She reached for Bettina's hand, and the two women went off a little ways. The men watched them. "So Mrs. Chalker does not play?" asked Pitman.

"No. She returned from Cornwall only yesterday, and since the ban on gatherings and the playhouse was lifted just two days before, Betterton had already assigned all roles in this new piece." He glanced to the floor above, through which the musicians' tuning could be heard. "I do not think she minds sitting out. Cornwall, parting with John Edward, was hard."

"Did she not think to keep him?"

"She did. But growing up with an actress in the Town, opposed to the boy's own family in the country? And since yond puppy Rochester still refuses to acknowledge the boy . . ." He frowned. "So it was best for the lad, and perhaps Sarah too. She would not let me escort her when she gave him up, requested to be alone."

A few paces away, Bettina was making her eyes big at Pitman, gesturing to the stage above. "I am summoned, man. So tell me quick—what is this employment the king has offered you?"

"Groom of the Bedchamber. A sinecure. I don't think I actually have to lay down in the same room with him." He laughed. "Od's life, with Old Rowley 'twixt the sheets, a man wouldn't get a wink for all the damned *cries d'amour!*"

Pitman didn't laugh. "A job for life, though—his life, anyway. You would be wise to take it."

"I would." Coke ran his fingers over his moustache. "Yet when has wisdom been one of my qualities? I'd be interminably bored. Besides, I have been offered other employment. Less wise. More interesting."

"I know. I offered it to you. Are you accepting?"

"I think I am." Coke grinned. "You said it once: thief and thief-taker—what a pair we will make!"

He held out his hand. Pitman clasped it, burying it in his massive ones. "We will, Captain. There'll be takes aplenty too, for this late plague has thrown many out of work and made them desperate. Thieves abound in London."

"And not only native ones. Did you hear that dastard Maclean escaped Newgate last Tuesday just before the courts sat again?"

"Aye, and Wednesday robbed Lord Butler on Turnham Green. Maclean's price has gone up to twenty guineas."

"Good. Though I'd pay twenty to hear him play 'Whisky in the Jar' on his damn fiddle while kicking his heels on Tyburn gallows."

"Save the king's money and your own," Pitman said, releasing the captain's hand and nodding at the approaching women, "for you'll be needing it."

"Eh?" Coke said, but was unable to question further as Bettina swooped in and dragged her husband toward the stairs, beyond which the orchestra was now in full melody.

"I like that Mrs. Chalker," Bettina said as they climbed. "She may be an actress and so hell-bound for being cousin to a whore, but she's still one of us."

"When the time comes, my dear, I hope your liking will extend to helping her with her child. In about six months, I should say."

"What? Did the captain tell you she's with child?"

"Nay. Indeed I do not think he knows."

"Then how do you?"

"'Tis my genius for observation, love. And experience." He stopped them and laid his hand briefly on his wife's belly. She won't be able to wear her new dress much longer either, he thought, but said, "Let's to the play!"

Just as Sarah and William passed the front of the theatre, the second act began. The doors were open to late trade and they could hear Betterton's rich voice: "'Sblood! She could not have picked out any devil upon the earth so proper to torment her.'"

"Are you certain you do not wish to watch the second act?" William asked.

"I will be in the playhouse soon enough again. I would rather enjoy my freedom." She sniffed the air. "It smells like spring today, does it not?"

"It does." As they crossed Lincoln's Inn Fields, he marvelled at the warmth and, even more, the normality. People strolling and enjoying the sunshine; oyster sellers selling oysters, maids their ribbons or combs.

"It is as if the plague never was. Yet I hear some still die of it."

"I have heard so as well. In the poorer parts of the city. The monster never entirely quits the labyrinth." He squeezed her hand. "But the king would not have returned nor the gathering places been reopened if there was a general danger still."

"I am not concerned for my life. Yet I am sad about those who lost theirs."

"As am I." They gazed at the ground for a moment, neither with the other, both with Lucy. He was always a little surprised how readily the tears still came. He looked up, saw a match in her eyes. "Come, love," he said. "How would you spend this free day of yours? Shall we walk? Or shall we retire to your apartments?"

There was a change in his voice, light now in his eyes. "Truly, was last night not enough for you, sir?"

"You were gone to Cornwall a long while. A month. And you only admitted me to your bed and your heart a short month before that."

"Two months. How swiftly a man forgets!" She laughed and kissed him. "Why not your apartments?"

"Dickon's there. The place is a shambles of lurid pamphlets and nut shells."

"Mine, then," she said. "But first, William—" she resisted his immediate pull toward Sheere Lane "—let us go and see the puppets."

He knew when he was beaten. "Your servant ever, madam."

As they crossed the Fields, walked down to Fleet Street and then along the Strand toward Charing Cross, she wondered if tonight would be the night to tell him. It would change what was between them, and she was not sure she wanted that, this time of happiness to end. Yet she knew there could be happiness after too. Coke was not a man like Rochester. He would not disclaim his paternity. Indeed, she felt the captain would attempt to rush her to an altar—and she was not sure how she felt about that. She'd been a widow for ten months. Should she not last at least the year?

She glanced at him. He looked content. There would always be that darkness in his eyes, which she had noticed the very first time she met him. He had seen too much in his life. As had she. Indeed, they made quite the pair. Nay, I'll leave him in this content for one more night, she thought.

The puppet theatre was as crowded as the playhouse, both newly reopened and drawing their partisans. A silver crown secured them a place on the front bench, as well as two oranges, two tumblers of ale and two bags of peanuts, one of which Coke pocketed to save for his ward.

The play had already begun, but the plots were never hard to grasp. Nor the characters: a scold, a cuckold and a curmudgeonly master who gossiped, setting the scene. Then on came Punchinello, leading with his vast belly, matched by his hunched back. "Eh! Eh! Eh!" he called, "'As anyone seen my wife, eh? Eh?"

The audience roared. The puppet turned to acknowledge them. This slow-moving marionette, with his small dark eyes peering past his huge hooked nose, always disturbed Sarah near as much as he amused. Especially now, when Punchinello appeared to stare right at her. She shivered.

"Here, my love." William unclasped his cloak, swept it off his shoulders and over hers. He tucked her tight, and she leaned her head against his chest. Must keep her warm, he thought. Especially now. Her and the new life inside her.

The audience laughed and Captain Coke did too. Only he was not laughing at the puppets.

Author's Note

I n some ways, I have been researching this book all my life.
Growing up in London helped. I believe that an event as trau-
matic as the Great Plague leaves a terrible scar on a city's psyche,
and its inhabitants can't help but sense the impact somewhere
deep within. I remember having plague pits pointed out to me as a
child, and staring fascinated at grassed mounds of earth. I was told
there was one under St. George and the Dragon at St. John's Wood
Roundabout, near Lord's Cricket Ground. Certainly the skeletons
of victims are still being excavated as the Crossrail project is dug
through the city. We walk on plague corpses every day.

As a teenager, madly in love with history, I joined the Sealed
Knot—an English Civil Wars reenactment group. I fought in a
number of battles (including Lansdown, where Quentin Absolute
fell) and rose to the rank of sergeant in the same regiment I have
placed Captain Coke, Sir Bevil Grenville's Regiment of Foote—
whose colonel, in a marvellous literary link, was Count Nikolai
Tolstoy, grandson of the novelist.

I also admit that I once went to a cockfight. I was travelling
around Peru in 1988, staying near the famous Nazca Lines, and
felt I should attend in the spirit of research—at least, that was my
excuse! It was as brutal as you can imagine. The images lodged in
my head, and are now out upon my pages.

Yet nothing could truly prepare me for the other horrors I was
to read about and ultimately set down. The period was not one I'd

studied much, except in that basic schoolboy way. The first shock was in reading about the English Civil Wars—the British, really, as they ravaged all the isles. I think I'd retained my Sealed Knot view of something rather chivalrous and romantic. They were nothing of the kind. The images we see each day from various parts of the world remind us that civil war is the most brutal of all. Close to a staggering 10 percent of the population died, many in battle, most of the starvation, sickness and violence that occurred away from the battlefield. I realized quite quickly that most of the former soldiers I turned into characters in this book would have been suffering the seventeenth-century equivalent of post-traumatic stress disorder. It does not excuse but may go a little way to explaining some of their actions.

There were happier areas of research—studying the English theatre, which I love and have been a part of; and studying that formative time when actresses were first allowed to grace the stage. (What would my life have been without actresses?) And the Twitter and email feeds of *The Diary of Samuel Pepys* I signed up for have been a daily joy, as well as vitally informative about customs, food, manners, songs . . . and pubs! Sam sure liked his bevy, from morning drafts for breakfast to Rhenish in the evening and many ales in between.

I was also fascinated by the turbulent religious times. The wars, fought at least partly about God and how you saw him, unleashed a massive diversity of belief—from the extremely puritanical to its opposite, as exemplified by the Ranters, who worshipped the Almighty by living in communes where they ripped off their clothes, swore, drank, smoked and practised free love. As Lawrence Clarkson, aka Captain of the Rant, wrote: "Devil is God, hell is heaven, sin holiness, damnation salvation: this and only this is the first resurrection."

Such was the combustible mix at the heart of London. There were so many stunning books I read about the times, and the pestilence in particular, and I list them separately. One, Defoe's *Journal of the Plague Year*, was wonderfully evocative and expounded superbly in the notes in the Oxford Classics Edition. He coined the fabulous term for the plague: "The Monster in the Labyrinth." It was, and London was, and it is with fascinated horror that I have wandered my native streets again, literally and on the page.

I hope I have come close to an accurate portrait of time and place. I am sure there are things I've got wrong. But before I receive letters, I need to confess something: I have changed a few dates. The Earl of Rochester attempted to abduct the heiress Elizabeth Mallet on May 26, 1665. The theatres were closed for the plague on June 5, 1665. For dramatic purposes, I have amalgamated the two events. I also reopened the theatres somewhat early. Also the earl may have only spent three weeks at his majesty's displeasure, rather than the three months I have here.

There are so many people I need to thank for the creation of this novel that I have done so in the Acknowledgements. Here, I just need to thank, well, London. Since I no longer live there, I find I cannot stop writing about it. Each time I go back, I learn something new. And each time I also thank providence that I get to write about these extraordinary periods in history and do not have to live through them.

Scarify the buboes, indeed!

C. C. Humphreys
Salt Spring Island, B.C., Canada
July 2014

Acknowledgements

People often think that a novel is the work of only one person: its author. This is absolutely not the case, and I am blessed in my life with highly skilled professionals who stimulate my writing and manage my career. Without them, I'd be scribbling in my garret for the amusement of my cat.

To begin at the beginning of *Plague*, the novel arose from a series of conversations with my brilliant agent, Simon Trewin, at William Morris Endeavor. It was he who talked of the plague first and got this ball rolling, sending me off to take dictation from various characters who walked into my writing hut and demanded roles in the novel. It was he who placed the novel with my new publishers, Penguin Random House. In the UK, that means the wonderful Selina Walker at Century, who had given me a ride from a festival a year before and got us productively stuck on the M1. Her notes, and her enthusiasm for the subject matter and style ever since, have been, dare I say, infectious.

In Canada, I am looked after by an extraordinary team who make me feel completely supported. These range from Brad Martin, the perspicacious CEO at Penguin Random House, through my dynamic publisher at Doubleday, Kristin Cochrane, to my superb publicist, Nicola Makoway.

My most direct contact is with my editor. Nita Pronovost is not only super smart and very funny, she also knows the genre and what people want from it. She is rigorous but never rigid, always forcing me to reach further for my best. Any failings in the book are mine and probably due to the very, very rare times I have ignored her advice.

Amazing support comes from my family—my wife, Aletha, and my son, Reith, who tolerate my writerly vagueness and stimulate me with their wit and love.

Finally, Dickon. My cat has donated his name to a character and follows me daily to my hut to help me write. (I haven't told him about the catskins.)

To all, much thanks.

Further Reading

ON LONDON:

Ackroyd, Peter. *London: The Biography*. New York: Nan A. Talese, 2001.

Hyde, Ralph, editor. *The A to Z of Restoration London*. London: London Topographical Society, 1992.

Picard, Liza. *Restoration London: Everyday Life in London 1660–1670*. London: Weidenfeld & Nicolson, 2003.

Porter, Stephen. *Pepys's London: Everyday Life in London 1650–1703*. Gloucestershire: Amberley Publishing, 2011.

ON THE TIME PERIOD:

Capp, B.S. *The Fifth Monarchy Men: A Study in Seventeenth-Century English Millenarianism*. London: Faber & Faber, 1972.

Friedman, Jerome. *Blasphemy, Immorality and Anarchy: The Ranters and the English Revolution*. Ohio: Ohio University Press, 1987.

Gyford, Phil, editor. *The Diary of Samuel Pepys*. Daily email and Twitter feed. http://www.gyford.com/.

Hill, Christopher. *The World Turned Upside Down: Radical Ideas During the English Revolution*. London: Penguin Books, 1972.

Miller, John. *The English Civil Wars: Roundheads, Cavaliers and the Execution of a King*. London: Constable & Robinson, 2009.

Palmer, Tony. *Charles II: Portrait of an Age*. United Kingdom: Littlehampton Book Services, 1979.

Pennington, Donald and Keith, Thomas. *Puritans and Revolutionaries: Essays in Seventeenth-Century History Presented to Christopher Hill*. Oxford: Oxford University Press, 1978.

Purkiss, Diane. *The English Civil War: A People's History*. London: HarperPress, 2006.

ON THE PLAGUE:

Defoe, Daniel. *A Journal of the Plague Year*. Notes by Louis Landa and introduction by David Roberts. New York: Oxford University Press, 2010.

Porter, Stephen. *The Great Plague*. Gloucestershire: Amberley Publishing, 2009.

ON THE THEATRE:

Etherege, George. *The Man of Mode*. Translated by John Barnard. London: Bloomsbury Methuen Drama, 2007.

Fisk, Deborah Payne, editor. *The Cambridge Companion to English Restoration Theatre*. Cambridge: Cambridge University Press, 2009.

Speaight, George. *Punch and Judy: A History*. West Sussex: Littlehampton Book Services Ltd., 1970.

THE BIBLE:

Daniel and *The Revelation of St. John the Divine*. King James Bible. Nashville: Holman Bible, 1973.

Photo by Ron Gilbert

CHRIS (C.C.) HUMPHREYS was born in Toronto and grew up in the United Kingdom. He has acted all over the world and appeared on stages ranging from London's West End to Hollywood's Twentieth Century Fox.

Humphreys began his writing career as a playwright. His first play, *A Cage Without Bars*, won the inaugural 24-Hour Playwriting Competition in Vancouver, and was then produced at Performance Works Vancouver, and later at the London fringe theatre, The Finborough. His second, *Glimpses of the Moon*, was commissioned and then produced by Lunchbox Theatre in Calgary. Humphreys recently adapted his novel *Shakespeare's Rebel* for the stage and it was produced at Vancouver's Bard on the Beach Festival in 2015.

The author of ten novels of historical fiction, Humphreys' books have garnered bestseller status and critical acclaim across North

America. *The French Executioner* was runner up for the CWA Steel Dagger for Thrillers in 2002 and has been optioned for the screen. Humphreys' books featuring the character Jack Absolute—the James Bond of the 1770s—are entitled *Jack Absolute*, *The Blooding of Jack Absolute* and *Absolute Honour*, the last of which was shortlisted for the 2007 Evergreen Award by the Ontario Library Association. His novel, *Vlad, The Last Confession* about the real Dracula was an international bestseller. As well as his adult fiction, Humphreys is also the author of several works for young adults: the trilogy of *The Runestone Saga*, and *The Hunt of the Unicorn*. In fall 2016, *The Hunt of the Dragon* will be published. His books have been translated into more than thirteen languages.

Fire, Humphreys' novel about the Great Fire of London, was released by Doubleday Canada in 2016.

Humphreys lives on Salt Spring Island, B.C., with his wife and young son. You can connect with him at **www.cchumphreys.com**.